THE DISAPPEARANCE OF ANNA POPOV

A dark, page-turning psychological thriller

Jack Rogan Mysteries Book 2

GABRIEL FARAGO

This book is brought to you by Bear & King Publishing.

Publishing & Marketing Consultant: Lama Jabr
Website: https://xanapublishingandmarketing.com
Sydney, Australia

Second edition 2024© Gabriel Farago

ISBN: 978-0994576316

Also by Gabriel Farago

The Jack Rogan Mysteries Series:

Novels

The Empress Holds the Key (Book 1)
The Hidden Genes of Professor K (Book 3)
Professor K: The Final Quest (Book 4)
The Curious Case of the Missing Head (Book 5)
The Lost Symphony (Book 6)
The Death Mask Murders (Book 7)
The Stolen Altarpiece (Book 8)

Novellas

The Kimberley Secret (Novella 1)
The Forgotten Painting (Novella 2)
The Postmaster of Treblinka (Novella 3)
Murder on the Ghan (Novella 4)
The Bone Scraper Legacy (Novella 5)

The lips of wisdom are closed
Except to those ears that can hear.

The Cabbala

DEDICATION

For Joan, my guiding hand.
Always steady;
Always strong;
Always there.

Contents

Acknowledgments

Preparing a book for publication requires many skills, especially today. It is a team effort. I've been very fortunate to have a group of talented and dedicated specialists help me deal with the many challenges of a rapidly changing literary landscape. Without their professional support and advice, this book would not have seen the light of day. There are too many to mention, but a few definitely stand out.

A special thank you must go to James O'Toole for designing a wonderful website which has become my online centrepiece and window into the cyber world. And then there is Gaynor Parke of the 'Social Media Business Academy', who became my guide and mentor, inducted me into the exciting world of social media and helped me discover and harness its awesome power.

Writing *The Disappearance of Anna Popov* was an ambitious project and would not have been possible without an experienced and competent editor looking over my shoulder. It began with Desney King who cast her critical eye over my work at the very beginning. I benefited greatly from her intuitive insights, sensible critique and constructive suggestions. A little later, Shelley Kenigsberg, a senior lecturer in editing, stepped in. Shelley's vast experience and guiding hand became invaluable in bringing this project to fruition.

Who says we don't judge a book by its cover? In a way we all do, especially when surfing the net for inspiration of what to read. A special thank you must therefore go to Vivien Valk for designing an imaginative cover that is true to the storyline, and captures the spirit of the book.

In this complex new world of ebooks and global print-on-demand, every author needs the assistance and logistical support of competent 'facilitators'. Jenny and Ally Mosher of MoshPit Publishing and Lama Jabr of Xana Marketing have become mine. It is because of them that I have time to write at all!

And finally, it would be remiss of me not to mention my wife, Joan, literary critic, researcher, patient sounding-board and cheerful travel companion – we visit all of the places mentioned in my books. Thank you for believing in me and what I'm trying to achieve with my writing.

Thank you all!

Gabriel Farago
Leura, Blue Mountains, Australia

The world hangs by a thread
And that is the psyche of man

Carl Gustav Jung

AUTHOR'S NOTE

I first came across the story of Jandamarra and the Bunuba Resistance in the remote Kimberley in Western Australia. Leaning against a 700 year old boab tree with my Aboriginal guide – a Bunuba elder – I was looking up at the tall cliffs guarding the entrance to Windjana Gorge; his country. We had just visited some stunning Aboriginal rock art – haunting paintings thought to be more than twenty thousand years old. Rising like a fortress out of the glare, the tall cliffs – remnants of an ancient Devonian reef – formed a forbidding barrier between his world and mine.

'This is where it all happened,' the old man said, pointing into the deep gorge cut through the rock by the Lennard River. 'And it wasn't that long ago. Jandamarra's cave is just up there.'

Jandamarra was an Aboriginal freedom fighter in the 1890s who refused to surrender his country and his freedom to the white settlers pushing relentlessly north.

As the shadows lengthened, I listened to the remarkable story of first contact between the Bunuba and the early Australian pastoralists. It was a stirring tale of heroism and despair, unspeakable brutality and acts of great courage. It was the final chapter in the long history of a proud people. With the story ending in tragedy, the painful words turned into a whisper of defeat, falling from the lips of one of its last true elders. Caught between two worlds, Jandamarra had tried to find a way of embracing the new, but the old was in his blood and could not be denied.

This conflict is by no means over. It exists today. Colliding cultures send ripples of discord far into the future and affect generations. It is as relevant today as it was in Jandamarra's time. The stage is the same, so is the plot. Only the actors are different.

As the embers of our campfire turned slowly to ash, I began to wonder ... *What if Jandamarra had lived today? What if ...*

Gabriel Farago
Leura, Blue Mountains, Australia

THE DISAPPEARANCE OF ANNA POPOV

Prologue
Alice Springs, January 2005

Anna was dancing in The Shed the night she disappeared. The Shed was a notorious watering hole frequented mainly by thirsty truckies. It called itself a bush pub, but that was an exaggeration. It was more like a long wooden bar with a corrugated iron roof held up by gnarled fence posts and barbed wire. There were no walls. The floor, hard as rock, was red desert earth compacted by thousands of feet shuffling to the bar for a drink. Because the beer was always cold and the steaks huge and cheap, the place was always packed. More recently, however, there was one more added attraction: backpackers, mainly girls, touring the Outback. Looking for cheap grog and adventure, the young nomads had made The Shed their own. Located three kilometres out of Alice, it was within easy walking distance of the youth hostels and budget motels popular with tourists.

A local bush band was playing country and western music and the mouth-watering aroma of frying onions and sizzling sausages drifted across from the barbecue. It was very hot and very late.

'Beer, mate?' asked the barmaid, sizing up the tall dark stranger.

The handsome Aboriginal took off his broad-rimmed drover's hat, wiped his forehead with a red handkerchief and nodded. 'One for your friend as well?' she asked, pointing to the huge snake wound around his neck and shoulders.

'No thanks, she's driving,' he said, affectionately stroking the exquisite python.

Standing at the other end of the bar, a group of truckies were eyeing off the girls on the improvised dance floor. 'Look, the sheilas have to dance with each other 'cause there're no blokes here having a go,' said one, downing another beer.

'I bet you can't get them to dance with you, mate; not even one,' said another, patting his friend on the hairy beer gut bulging over his shorts. 'Just look at you, you slob.'

7

'Sure can.'

'Oh yeah? You're all talk. What's it worth?'

'Ten rounds.'

The others laughed. 'You're on.'

The man slammed down his glass, wiped his mouth with the back of his hand and belched loudly. Pulling down his singlet to cover part of his protruding gut, he slipped his thongs back on and shuffled unsteadily towards the dance floor.

Barefoot and wearing the briefest of shorts and a tight-fitting pink tee-shirt accentuating her firm breasts, Anna, silky blonde hair swishing against the tips of her tanned shoulder blades, was dancing with her friend Julia. Anna was looking for freedom, Julia for the adventure which the novelty of travel to remote places invariably offered. The Shed had it all. Excitement, danger, and the lure of the unknown far away from the watchful eyes of fretting parents and curious friends. Enjoying her favourite Dixie Chicks song, Anna swayed from side to side with her eyes closed, letting the familiar beat of the music carry her away. When it stopped and she opened her eyes, she almost bumped into the grotesque, fat man towering over her.

'How about a dance, luv?' said the fat man, his bald head glistening with sweat.

'No thanks,' she snapped, turning away. 'He's gross,' she whispered to Julia. 'Let's take a break.'

As his mates at the bar roared laughing, a flash of anger raced across the face of the fat truckie.

'Come on, sweetie, just one. Be a good sport,' he persisted, putting a heavy, sweaty hand on Anna's shoulder.

'Get off me!' shouted Anna, pushing the fleshy hand away in disgust.

His mates at the bar began to whistle and hoot. Instead of walking away, the fat man grabbed Anna from behind, spun her around and lifted her up like a rag doll. Pressing her against his huge chest, he lumbered awkwardly around the dance floor like a dancing bear, performing his tricks at the fair. Anna, the man's hot beer breath in her face, began to retch.

The man with the snake sipped his beer and watched the odd couple stagger across the dance floor. Slowly, he unwound the python, lifted it over his head and gently put it down on the bar.

'Look after her for me, luv,' he said to the barmaid, 'she's harmless. I'll be right back.' He walked slowly over to the dance floor.

'That's enough, mate. Put her down,' he said, patting the fat man on the back.

The truckie turned his head and glared, his bloodshot eyes slightly unfocused.

'Fuck off, darkie. This is none of your business,' he hissed angrily.

The snake man's right hand shot up in silent reply and grabbed the fat man's ear. 'I don't think you heard me,' he said, twisting the ear. 'Let her go.'

The fat man let go of Anna, clenched his fists and spun around.

The tall man let go of the ear and stepped back.

The fat man charged – 120 kilos of rage.

Like most professional fighters, the tall man had the waist of a ballerina and the shoulders of a weightlifter. Rocking back and forth on the balls of his feet, he stood poised like a cat watching its prey. He sidestepped the charge easily, letting the fat man crash into the bar.

'Fight, you fucking coward!' bellowed the fat man, picking himself up.

'Okay.'

The tall man exploded into action. The first punch, delivered by his left fist, landed on his opponent's beer gut and went deep. The second, delivered by his right, caught the fat man on the left cheek and broke a bone. The fight was over in an instant. Two more massive blows, one to the chin and one to the nose, finished the truckie off.

'Anyone else?' the tall man asked, squaring his shoulders. No one stepped forward. 'He had it coming. It's over. Get back to your beers.'

The tall man walked to the far end of the bar, uncoiled the snake which had wound itself around a post, and slung it over his shoulders.

'Thanks for looking after her, luv,' he said to the barmaid. 'One more for the road, please.' Gulping down his beer, he reached for his hat, threw a few coins on the bar and walked out into the darkness.

Julia put her arm around her friend. 'Are you alright?' she asked, a worried look on her face. Anna nodded. 'Come on, let's get out of here before they all have a go at each other and we're caught in the middle.' The two girls left the dance floor and hurried outside.

'Shouldn't we wait for the others?' asked Anna. 'One of the guys from the hostel had a car.'

'No. They're out the back, eating. We can walk. It isn't far.'

The road leading into Alice was deserted. The girls took off their shoes and walked along the warm asphalt.

'Did you see that guy with the snake? What a hunk! And I couldn't even thank him. Pity.'

The powerful V8 of the ute purred into life after the girls had walked past. Inching slowly forward without lights, it left the car park behind The Shed and headed slowly for town. Startled by the engine noise coming towards them out of the dark, the girls turned around. The headlights came on suddenly, momentarily blinding them.

'Get off the road!' shouted Anna, pushing her friend into the bushes.

The ute accelerated and screeched to a halt next to them. 'Walking along the road after midnight isn't such a great idea. Especially 'round here,' said a voice through the open driver's window.

'Look who it is,' whispered Julia excitedly.

'Hop in. I'll give youse a lift back to town.'

'Come on,' said Julia, pulling Anna out of the bushes. 'Julia, don't!' cried Anna. 'No hitchhiking, remember?'

'It's all right ... he's your hero.' Julia walked over to the car and opened the passenger door. 'You scared us,' she said, climbing in.

The snake man smiled at her, revving the engine. Reluctantly, Anna climbed in after her friend and closed the door.

PART I.
THE WIZARD

1

Sydney Harbour, New Year's Eve 2009

The old year was dying. 'Five, four, three, two, one ...' counted the cheering crowd as the final seconds of 2009 tumbled through the hourglass. Suddenly, the massive steel arch of the Sydney Harbour Bridge erupted, forming a dazzling tiara of sparks. As they raced along the girders from both sides towards the centre like fire-breathing dragons, the fireworks spectacular lit up the night sky. Meeting in the middle between the main deck and the top of the arch, light and colour engaged in a breathtaking duel, heralding a turbulent year to come.

'Happy New Year, Jack!' shouted the stunning young woman standing next to Jack Rogan on the crowded yacht. Rebecca Armstrong reached up, threw her slender arms around his neck and kissed him passionately on the mouth. It was the first time she had kissed her famous client.

'Wow! I thought a kiss like this was strictly the province of the writer's imagination,' said Jack, coming up for air. 'Happy New Year, Becky!'

Rebecca flicked her glossy dark hair from her flushed face – as women who know they have beautiful hair often do – and took him by the hand. 'Don't get used to it. Tonight's an exception. Come on. I have a surprise for you,' she said.

'I like surprises.'

Heads turned as Rebecca pushed through the crowd with Jack by her side. Radiating sophistication and style in her New York designer clothes, she made straight for the stern of the yacht.

As the captain navigated the pitching vessel through the tightly packed spectator fleet under the Harbour Bridge, the yacht almost collided with an ostentatious motor cruiser. Sounding like a warning, the deep, throaty foghorn of a large ocean liner tied up at Circular Quay added to the crazy cacophony welcoming the new year. An acrid, phosphorous, eye-watering gunpowder smell of spent fireworks cartridges filled the balmy air as a smoke haze drifted past the Opera House.

'Who are all these people?' asked Jack, waving a hand at the crowd on the deck.

'The Sydney literary set. Don't you recognise anyone?' asked Rebecca, frowning.

'I'm new to all this, remember?'

'They all seem to know you ...'

'Am I paying for it?' Jack asked anxiously.

'No, Jack. Your publisher is. Relax. Look who's over there.' She pointed to a tall, sandy-haired man in a crumpled checked shirt leaning casually against the mast with a bottle of beer in his hand.

'China!' yelled Jack, walking over to his friend. 'What are you doing here?'

'Spinner! Your girlfriend invited me. Cheers!' They touched glasses. 'And a few of your other neglected mates as well.' The sandy-haired man pointed to the bow of the crowded vessel.

'She isn't my ...' said Jack, lowering his voice.

'China?' asked Rebecca. 'He told me his name was Will.'

'It is,' replied Jack, laughing. 'China's his nickname.'

'*China?* How come?'

'My little mate, rhymes with china plate; china. Simple – see?'

'You Aussies are something else,' said Rebecca, shaking her head. 'I can see I've a lot to learn.'

'Thanks Becky,' said Jack, giving her a hug, 'very thoughtful of you.' Her firm, toned body sent a ripple of excitement racing up his spine.

During his whirlwind book-signing tour across the US, Jack had repeatedly complained that he missed Sydney and his Aussie friends.

The surprise New Year's Eve party on Sydney Harbour was his publisher's response.

'You've got to watch Will, he's quite a lad,' warned Jack, a sparkle in his eyes.

'Don't listen to Spinner,' said Will.

'*Spinner?* Not another nickname!' said Rebecca.

'Sure is,' replied Will. 'He's always spinning yarns – right?'

The two men could have been mistaken for brothers, not only because of their rugged good looks, but also because of their good-natured banter suggesting a deep friendship forged by years spent together. Both were clearly outdoor types. Will's tanned face – lined by laughter and a little too much sun – hinted at laid-back good humour, whilst Jack's piercing green eyes and athletic physique were a magnet for women of all ages.

'You're a lucky bastard, mate,' said Will.

'How come?'

'She's not bad,' said Will pointing with his glass to Rebecca. 'Girlfriend?'

'No, mate.'

'Sure ... Don't tell me you haven't ...?'

'No, seriously. My publishers told me I needed help with PR, book signings, publicity, stuff like that. You know what I'm like. So, they appointed her to look after all that crap for me. You should see her office in New York. She's very good,' said Jack. 'Strictly business.'

Will wasn't convinced. 'I've heard that one before,' he said. 'You and women ... Lucky bastard.'

'Perhaps I am.'

'Perhaps? Jet-setting author with yachts and champagne and classy chicks like this one to look after you? You've come a long way, Spinner.'

'It all happened very fast.'

'I can see that, but you hardly have time for your old drinking buddies anymore,' lamented Will.

'I haven't got time to scratch myself.'

'Just look around, mate. This crowd isn't you.'

As a freelance journalist, Jack Rogan depended on his eclectic network of contacts and friends for leads and inspiration. It was Will who had given Jack the lead to a great story two years before – the trial of a Nazi war criminal that exposed a secret hoard of Nazi gold in the vaults of Swiss banks.

When Jack published *Dental Gold and Other Horrors* it was an international success. The Swiss, embarrassed by the outcries about 'abandoned' bank accounts of thousands of Holocaust victims, finally agreed to open their ledgers. This was seen by many as the first serious step towards compensation. Overnight, Jack had become a celebrated *Time* magazine front page hero, and his book a sensation.

'Come on, Will, it's not that bad,' retorted Jack, handing his friend a glass of champagne. 'Here, drink up!'

The famous Sydney New Year's Eve fireworks were reaching their climax with a multicoloured waterfall of sparks cascading from the deck of the bridge into the ink-blue waters of the harbour below.

'So – what next, mate?' asked Will, draining his glass.

'I'm taking a couple weeks off. First break in two years.'

'Then why don't you come with me?'

'What do you mean?'

'I'm taking some time off too ... Going bush, out west ...'

'Fossicking for bric-a-brac and old furniture?'

'Exactly. And I still have the old van.'

'I don't believe it! Just like the good old days, eh?'

'Some things never change, mate. Do you reckon they might have some more beer around here? I'm sick of this foreign crap,' said Will.

Jack pointed an accusing finger at his friend. 'This is Bollinger, you peasant,' he said. 'The best.'

'I don't give a stuff. It's crap.'

'I'll see what I can do. When are you leaving?'

'As soon as I sober up.'

'I tell you what. You clear it with Becky, and I'm in.'

'Well, well! I never thought I'd see the day. Jack Rogan actually in awe of a woman. Asking for permission?' said Will, shaking his head.

'You don't know these Yankee broads, mate. Tough as old boot leather. And besides,' continued Jack lowering his voice, 'they hold the purse strings.'

'You go and find me a beer, Spinner, and leave her to me.'

'Good luck.' *Poor bastard*, thought Jack. *She'll eat him alive!*

2

Somewhere in the bush near Bathurst, 1 January, 2010

The old van lurched alarmingly to one side – tortured gears crunching loudly – and began the steep descent down into the valley. Jack woke with a start. Rubbing his aching shoulder – a constant reminder of the sniper's bullet that ended his stint as a war correspondent in Afghanistan – he turned to Will.

'Where are we?' he asked, reaching for his sunglasses.

'Goldmining country. We just passed Bathurst. Good sleep? A little too much Bollinger, perhaps?' suggested Will good-naturedly. 'You should have stuck to the beer, mate.'

'What did you tell her?' Jack asked. Leaving the party at dawn with Will to go back home and pack was still a blur.

'I suggested she let you go for a month, and after a bit of argy bargy, we settled for a week. Done and dusted. She's taking a few days off as well. Barrier Reef. That helped. But you're right, she's one tough cookie. She even challenged me to a drinking contest – vodka shots – before she agreed. We must have downed a dozen, I reckon.'

'Who won?'

'You're here, aren't you? The things I do for a chum.'

'Where are we staying?'

'Camping, Jack. Just like we used to. I know a good spot up in the hills by the creek. This area used to be Dad's favourite, remember? The gear's in the back,' Will said, 'including the old tent.'

'It leaked like a sieve,' said Jack. He was beginning to have second thoughts. Maybe New Year's Eve nostalgia and a little too much champagne had got the better of him.

As young men, he and Will had been inseparable. Will's family had taken in the fresh-faced Queensland country boy as one of their own.

The two lads had accompanied Will's father on many a buying trip, going from farm to farm in remote rural areas and offering to buy old stuff nobody needed. Buy cheaply, take the goods back to Sydney, do them up a bit in the workshop behind the house and then sell them for a handsome profit in the shop at the front.

'Presentation is everything,' Will's dad used to say. 'Remember boys, the wrapping can be more important than the present.' He had made a good living out of this for over fifty years. After he passed away, Will continued the tradition once a year or so, for old times' sake. Jack had many fond memories of those trips: delicious roast dinners with a farmer and his family in the cosy kitchen; sitting on the veranda of a remote homestead with a cold beer at the end of a long hot day; and many a romp in the hay with a farmer's daughter. Even, sometimes, his wife. Or both.

Most of the furniture in Jack's house came from these excursions. It was surprising what curios had found their way to Australia and were waiting in disused sheds or in the back of barns to be discovered by someone with imagination and an eye for value. Jack and Will used to joke about it often. The father's buying trips had turned into a nostalgic treasure hunt for the son and his friend.

After putting up the old tent by the creek, Will made a fire and cooked some sausages. 'What's she really like?' he asked, stoking the fire.

'Becky?'

'Yeah.'

'To tell you the truth, I don't know her that well.'

'How come?'

'We've been flat out these last couple of months travelling together, on and off. All business.'

'She's a good looker, that's for sure. Very sexy; great body. She must be pushing 40, surely?'

'She's a bit of a health buff.'

'What? All carrot juice and push-ups?'

'No. Yoga and karate. She'd deck us both in three seconds flat. I've seen her do it. Very fit.'

'Bodyguard as well. Impressive.'

'She's also very smart, sophisticated and incredibly well connected. She knows all the right people.'

'Single?'

'Yes.'

'Boyfriend?'

'Not as far as I know. Career type; too busy.'

'Well, then?'

'What?'

'Come on, mate, it's me you're talking to. She'd be great in the sack.'

'I don't look at her that way. She's a professional. She takes care of my business interests. The royalties; the financial side of things.'

'Don't give me that crap.'

'No, I'm serious. Never put your dick in the cash register, as my first editor used to say.'

'You must have at least thought about it.'

'Hmm ... There's something about her ... I can't put my finger on it, but ...'

'She sure likes you ...' interrupted Will.

'You can tell, can you?'

'She and I are drinking buddies – remember?'

'Well, that explains it ...'

'We'll see. Here; done.' Will took the pan off the fire and put the sausages on a plate. Accidentally touching the hot pan, he burnt his fingers and almost dropped it. 'Shit! Throw us another tinnie, mate, and let's get stuck into it.'

They were both asleep just after sundown.

'There's enough grog in here to get an entire football team pissed several times over, but no food at all,' complained Jack next morning, searching in vain for some eggs and bacon for breakfast.

'I'm the alcohol technician, you're the cook, remember?' replied Will, tinkering with his fishing gear. 'I fixed dinner last night, mate. Breakfast is your job.'

'Sausages. Big deal.'

'If you don't like the tucker, get some fresh stuff. The village is just down the road.'

'Okay.'

The only thing open in the tiny hamlet was the corner store which also served as the post office and petrol station. The man behind the counter turned out to be the local real estate agent minding the store for a mate who'd gone to visit family. Inquisitive by nature, the agent was intrigued by the old van with 'Arthur Hamilton & Son – second-hand furniture bought and sold' prominently painted on its sides. The business logo – a laughing kookaburra perched on the arm of a rocking chair – reminded him of a biscuit tin popular in the 1950s. After half an hour of small talk, Jack had managed to buy some meagre provisions. He had also managed to arrange their first assignment.

By the time he manoeuvred the van back into camp, it was already lunchtime and very hot. Holding a fishing rod with one hand, Will was dozing under a tree by the creek.

'Enjoying your holiday, mate?' asked Jack, unpacking the groceries. 'Here, look at this.' He handed Will a crumpled piece of paper.

'What's that?'

'A map.'

'Oh?'

'Our first assignment. You didn't think I drove this contraption all the way into the village just to buy some eggs?'

'And you didn't think I invited you along just because you're a famous author, eh?' retorted Will. 'Be a good sport and throw us a tinnie.'

They waited until late afternoon had taken the sting out of the sun before setting out to find the farm. Following a rutted track for several kilometres, they turned a sharp corner and stopped in front of a wooden gate which had all but rotted off its hinges.

'What a dump,' said Jack, pushing the gate open with his shoulder. 'The agent did warn me the place is about to be demolished. No one's lived here in years. A stockbroker from Sydney just bought it and wants to get rid of all the furniture and stuff. The agent said we should grab what we want and meet him in the village tomorrow to make an offer. This could be our lucky day.'

Will looked around the ramshackle yard. 'I doubt it,' he said and shook his head.

The abandoned homestead had definitely seen better days. Part of the wooden structure had been destroyed by fire and was open to the elements. The front door was missing and the corrugated iron roof of the veranda had collapsed. Most of the windows were broken. Coming closer, Jack noticed something shiny and tightly coiled like a sailor's rope on the deck of a yacht, glistening in the sunlight. *Shit! A red bellied black*, thought Jack, watching the deadly snake sunning itself on the warped floorboards of the porch; an ominous sentinel, guarding the entrance to a forbidden place.

'You got a bum steer, mate. The place is empty. We're wasting our time,' said Will. He turned around and began to walk back to the van. 'Let's go.'

'The agent said all the stuff's in a barn behind the house – see?' Jack kept an eye on the snake, and picked his way carefully through the tall grass. 'Here, give me a hand.' Together they pushed open the old wooden door and peered inside.

The small barn was filled with all kinds of furniture, kitchen utensils, farming implements and carpentry tools. Broken crockery, pages torn from books and magazines, crumpled old newspapers and an assortment of cutlery and pottery shards littered the floor. Everything was covered in dust.

'Well, well, what have we here then, eh?' asked Jack, squinting into the gloom.

Will picked up a candle from the floor and lit it. 'Look at this,' he said.

'What's that?'

'A harmonium.' Will pulled over a rickety stool, sat down in front of the keyboard and began to operate the bellows with the broken foot pedals. He handed the candle to Jack and started to play. At first, the air in the protesting bellows responded with a tortured, wheezing sound, but it soon turned into a melody, faint and church organ-like. The hymn sounded eerie and out of place in the barn filled with abandoned possessions of generations past.

'I didn't know you could play.'

'Sunday school. You never forget.'

They pushed the harmonium aside and began to explore the barn.

Their curiosity aroused, they opened tea chests, emptied drawers and peered into hat boxes and armoires crammed with vintage clothing. They pored over photo albums filled with sepia portraits of dapper gentlemen wearing their Sunday best and Victorian matrons staring blankly into space. Pulling funny faces, they tried on waistcoats, bonnets and bowler hats and took turns parading in front of the cracked dressing table mirror.

Outside, the afternoon had turned to night, the shrill, monotonous hum of cicadas the only intrusion on the stillness. Exhausted, they lay down on an old double bed next to the window.

'It's a strange feeling, isn't it?' said Will.

'What is?'

'Being surrounded by all this stuff that once belonged to real people. Now long gone.'

'It is a bit,' said Jack.

'It makes you feel ... vulnerable.'

'In what way?'

'Here we are, both in our prime, yet ...'

'What are you getting at?'

'The Ferryman is never that far away ...'

'That's a bit morbid,' said Jack.

'It's true, though. We don't know how much time we've got ...'

'No, we don't. And yes, one day we'll have to pay the Ferryman. But ...'

'What?' asked Will.

'Not yet. Go to sleep.'

Unable to fall asleep, Will looked through the broken window panes at the stars blazing above and listened to the regular breathing of his friend lying fast asleep next to him. Feeling suddenly quite cold, he got up and began to search for something to cover himself with.

This'll do, he thought, reaching for the old moth-eaten Army overcoat he had tried on before. *I wonder what horrors this has seen?*

When Will pulled the coat up to his chin to keep warm, a dank smell assaulted his nose, conjuring up images of trench warfare, whistling shells, mateship and blood. *Smells of death*, he thought, pushing the coat aside. *Would Jack lay down his life to save a mate?* Will asked himself, *like many of the Diggers have done? I think he would.* Will closed his eyes. *Could I do the same? I guess only the real thing can answer that*, he thought and drifted to sleep.

By the time they woke up and began to load up the van, the first rays of morning sun had kissed the tiny beads of dew glistening like tears on the broken window panes.

3

Rose Cottage, Sydney, 9 January 2010

Rebecca Armstrong got out of the taxi and looked at the small sandstone cottage. It wasn't what she had expected. *I should have worn my jeans and a tank top*, she thought, looking at her tight-fitting designer slacks, high heel shoes and crisp Chanel blouse. She adjusted her hair and, clutching her tiny two-thousand-dollar handbag, walked to the front door and rang the bell.

'So, this is where the world-famous Aussie author lives,' she said, following Jack into the cottage. 'Interesting ... Homes tell us so much, don't you think?'

'They do?'

'About the people inside. Are you ready to give up your secrets?'

'Secrets? What secrets? This is a bachelor pad. A bolthole and sanctuary wrapped in one. It's all I could afford after the divorce. Sorry – I lost track of time.' Jack took off his leather apron and laid it over the back of a chair. 'I was just polishing an old secretaire out in the courtyard.'

'You were doing – what?'

'I'm restoring an antique. My booty from the little buying trip you so kindly allowed me to go on.'

'Your friend was very persuasive.'

'I did warn you about him.'

'I'm a big girl.'

'Here, I'll show you. How did you like the Barrier Reef?'

'It took my breath away.'

The back of the cottage opened into a small courtyard garden with a fountain in the middle. The small ornate desk stood on a drop sheet next to the fountain.

'This is beautiful. What is it?'

'A cedar secretaire, circa 1870, made by one of the early cabinet-makers of Sydney. Here, look at the trade label – "W. Jones & Son of

Ross Street, Glebe". Its opening is cantilevered forward and decorated with two blind drawers,' said Jack, folding down the top of the secretaire. 'There are three more drawers under here – see – supported by two turned full columns. There should also be a secret compartment somewhere in there. I was just trying to find it when you arrived.'

Rebecca held up her hand. 'Stop it,' she said, laughing. 'You sound like one of those judges on the Antiques Road Show.'

'Sorry. That's collector's speak, I'm afraid. I don't notice it anymore.'

'You're a dark horse, Jack Rogan.'

'I like working with my hands. I collect antiques, mainly early Australian colonial furniture. When I can afford it. Ah, here it is,' said Jack, exploring the back of one of the drawers with the tips of his fingers, 'the secret compartment. There must be a brass spring somewhere in here, and a knob. Yes! You pull it out,' he said. 'Who knows what treasures are hidden within?'

'How exciting!' Rebecca reached inside and carefully pulled out the little cedar drawer. 'Empty, I'm afraid,' she said, holding up the exquisite little box.

'Not quite,' Jack said. 'There's something tucked into the corner here. Well, what do you know? Look at this.' He held up a silver bracelet and began to polish it with his handkerchief. 'Here, have a look.' He handed the bracelet to Rebecca.

'How romantic. If only it could talk,' she said, holding it up to the light.

'Perhaps it can. Look over here. There's an inscription on the inside.'

'What does it say?'

'One word – Örökke. How strange. I wonder what it means.'

'Could it be a name, you think?'

'No idea. It really doesn't matter, I suppose,' continued Jack. 'I want you to have it. Here, let me put it on.'

'I couldn't possibly, Jack. It's yours ...'

'Don't be silly.' Jack reached for her wrist. 'I insist. There, it's done. Look. A perfect fit.'

'That's very sweet of you, thank you.' She gave him a peck on the cheek.

'And thanks for the party,' said Jack. 'Come on, let me show you around.'

'You have some exquisite pieces. What's this?' asked Rebecca, running her hand over the gleaming surface of a cedar chest with brass corner plates and brass handles.

'You have a good eye. This is one of my best pieces. A campaign chest.'

'What, for going to war?'

'Not quite. Governor Fitzroy commissioned a Sydney cabinetmaker, Andrew Leneham, in about 1860 – the same year, incidentally, this cottage was built – to make specimen boxes for the presentation of gold samples to Queen Victoria. This is one of them. Gold was discovered in New South Wales in 1851.'

'How fascinating. And this?'

'This is a writing slope. A kind of portable desk, also made of cedar. It's mitre joined at the corners here, with recessed brass carrying handles. It has internal compartments for writing utensils and documents. It also has a secret compartment – here. To hide love letters and gold coins.'

'Drum roll, please. And now comes the surprise; its value? What's it worth?' teased Rebecca.

'You're making fun of me. Am I boring you?'

'Not at all,' said Rebecca, putting her hand reassuringly on Jack's arm. 'You have quite a collection.' Rebecca pointed to the painting above the chest. 'This is fabulous. What is it?'

'Brett Whiteley. Do you like it?'

'Fascinating. Antiques and modern paintings. Polished wooden floorboards and sandstone walls. Not at all what I expected.'

'What did you expect?' asked Jack, handing Rebecca a glass of wine. 'Homes tell us so much ...'

'I can't really say. But not this ...' she replied.

'You know, this is the first time we've had a conversation like this since you took me under your wing,' said Jack quietly. It had been just over three months since his New York publisher had introduced him to Rebecca Armstrong. It was an unlikely fit. The tall, lanky, suntanned Australian larrikin first-time-author with the funny accent, and the elegant, sophisticated New York PR agent representing several well established writers on the bestseller list. Faded jeans and leather jackets met Hermes and Cartier; the experienced New Yorker taking on the rookie from Down Under. Yet, somehow it worked. It worked, because Jack had written an exceptional book and genuinely needed help in dealing with his success and sudden fame. Rebecca found his inexperience endearing, and his willingness to listen to her advice strangely flattering. And there was one more thing: it was exciting to be around him.

'You know a lot about me. But I know very little about you,' Jack said. 'That's not quite fair, don't you think?'

Rebecca laughed. 'What do you want to know?'

'Surely you didn't just pop up out of nowhere one day as a successful businesswoman in New York? You must have somehow clawed your way through that treacherous jungle first.'

For a while she looked at him pensively.

'Where did you come from, I wonder?' Jack asked, reaching for her hand.

Rebecca wore large glasses, giving her an endearingly studious look which didn't quite go with the designer labels and expensive French accessories. Jack suspected this was deliberate. Somehow, the glasses always stood out. She had several pairs to suit different occasions, just like handbags and shoes. That afternoon, she wore an old-fashioned tortoiseshell pair that kept sliding down her nose. She kept pushing them back up with her index finger while pursing her lips.

'That's quite a question. Have you heard of Lancaster County?' Rebecca asked.

'Pennsylvania. Amish territory ...'

'Well informed, as usual.' She nodded appreciatively. 'My maiden name was Stolzfus. I grew up on a small farm outside Philadelphia with my three brothers. We had no electricity, no television, radio or kitchen appliances. Musical instruments were forbidden and cars not allowed.'

'Buggy?' interrupted Jack.

'Right again. We spoke Pennsylvania Dutch and our only transport was a horse-drawn buggy, which took us to the markets in Philly once a week with our produce – eggs and fresh vegetables. I tended a small stall with my mother in my long black dress, apron and starched white bonnet.'

'Very cute. I can just see you ...' Jack teased.

'My brothers were all carpenters making furniture in the barn behind our house when they didn't work in the fields,' Rebecca continued, undeterred. 'Mother and I made quilts in the evenings by candlelight. My father had a long beard but no moustache – that too was forbidden – and always wore a straw hat and baggy black trousers held up by braces.'

'And I'm supposed to be the dark horse here ...' interjected Jack, refilling Rebecca's glass.

'Fun was a barn-raising with lots of laughter, prayer and games, and enough food to feed the entire county for a year. It was a community event. You know, everyone pulling together to help a neighbour. That's where I met Amos ...' Rebecca paused and turned away, her eyes misting over. It only lasted for an instant, opening a tiny crack in her otherwise carefully controlled demeanour.

'Amos?' asked Jack.

'My first husband. We fell in love and ran away, leaving everything behind ...'

'*First* husband?'

'I haven't been lucky with men ...'

Jack sensed it was time to change the subject. 'I ran away too,' he said. 'As you know, I left a Queensland cattle station for the big smoke. I started out sweeping floors and running errands for a Brisbane newspaper.'

Appreciating his tact, Rebecca looked at Jack and smiled. *There's a lot more to this guy*, she thought, *than he lets you see*. 'And I started out as a receptionist, working for a fashion magazine in New York ...' she said.

'*The Devil Wears Prada* stuff?'

Rebecca chuckled. 'A bit like that, but without the free clothes. You saw the movie?'

'Loved it.'

'What was it like? Growing up on a cattle station?'

Jack took his time before replying and looked pensively at Rebecca. 'Lonely and harsh,' he said. 'I learnt to ride before I could walk and helped around the house as soon as I could stand. Our closest neighbour was 50 miles away, and it took three hours on a good day to reach town in the old ute. I used to ride in the back with Bonny and Clyde.'

'I thought you had no siblings,' interrupted Rebecca.

Jack began to chuckle. 'Bonny and Clyde were our cattle dogs. Sharp as tacks. They were my friends. Our enemy was the drought. It was never far away,' said Jack, turning serious, 'and when it came, it lasted for years. That's when the land became a dustbowl, the cattle began to die, and the bank manager came knocking.' Jack looked away. 'Mum hated it with a passion. She was a country girl from Wales. She married my father when she was just eighteen ...'

Realising that she had opened old wounds, Rebecca reached across and put her hand on Jack's. 'What happened to your parents?' she asked.

'Mum left. One day, she couldn't take it anymore and ran off with the publican in town. We never saw her again. And then I ran away too,' Jack said, the sadness in his voice reflecting the heartache of painful memories. 'Dad eked out a living on the cattle station with three Aboriginal stockmen until he got sick ...'

'What happened to him?'

'He lost the farm and died a broken man in a boarding house in Townsville a few years ago.'

'I'm sorry.'

'Such is life,' said Jack, reaching for his wine glass. 'We all have to follow our own path. Often barefoot, and some of it is treacherous and paved with nails.'

Rebecca squeezed Jack's hand. 'Your divorce?' she asked, changing direction.

'Messy, like all of them.'

'Girlfriends?'

Jack shrugged. 'Girlfriends? Are you kidding? With my diabolical schedule? I couldn't keep a canary in a cage ...'

'Interesting comparison ...'

'You know what they say: a rolling stone gathers no moss.'

'Poor boy ... But it wasn't always that way. What about that policewoman in your book?'

'Jana?'

Rebecca nodded, watching Jack carefully.

'She was an old flame. You can't ignite old flames; it doesn't work. The spark isn't there anymore,' Jack said pensively. 'In the end, she fell for the other guy.'

'Marcus Carrington, the lawyer ...'

The look on Jack's face told Rebecca it was time to back off. 'We're still friends,' said Jack. Rebecca wasn't convinced. 'Now, let me show you something interesting ...' Jack pointed to a curious piece consisting of three wooden steps leading nowhere.

'What on earth is that?' asked Rebecca.

'Bed steps. That's how you climbed into the feathers in the good old days. The top step here opens up – see – for your jewellery and personal stuff. But the really important part was this.' Jack opened the second step and pulled out a lidded commode seat.

'Is this what I think it is?' asked Rebecca, a sparkle in her eye.

'Sure is! The chamber pot is over there,' said Jack, pointing to the window sill. But enough of the tour. How about some dinner?'

'I was beginning to think you'd never ask.' They linked arms and strolled down the corridor towards the kitchen.

'Unlucky with men, eh?'

Rebecca nodded.

'A woman like you? You're obviously looking in the wrong places,' said Jack.

'Looking under stones would be a wrong place then?'

'Definitely.'

'Thanks, Jack. I'll keep that in mind.'

'I promised to cook for you, remember? Well, this is your lucky day.'

'I'm sure it is. You're the first man who ever offered to cook something just for me. I can't wait.'

'You may be sorry.'

'I doubt it.'

'Amish, eh? You'd be used to plain tucker then ...' teased Jack, opening the door to the kitchen.

'We may be known as the Plain People, but the food, I tell you, was never plain.'

'Neither is my cooking; follow me.'

4

At the old farm near Bathurst, 10 January

'Do you know what time it is?' asked Will. He turned to look at the clock on the bedside table and almost dropped the phone.

'It's important, mate! There's something I have to show you!' said Jack urgently.

'Can't it wait till the morning?'

'No, it can't. Please, Will ...'

Will lived in the flat above his antique shop a few hundred metres up the road from Jack's place. It was faster to walk than to try to find a parking spot in the crowded Balmain street. He arrived ten minutes later, wearing a pair of baggy shorts and a crumpled tee-shirt he had obviously slept in. Jack was waiting on the front doorstep of his cottage, a glass of wine in his hand.

'I thought you were having dinner with your posh agent last night. What happened? Did you have a blue?' said Will.

'No. She caught the last ferry back to town hours ago. Come in. I've been working on this since she left.' Jack led the way to the courtyard at the back and pointed to the secretaire by the fountain.

'You dragged me out of the sack at two in the morning to show me this? Is that it? You must be blotto.'

'Not quite. Here, have a look.' Jack wiped the desktop with his polishing cloth, switched on his torch and aimed the beam at the top right-hand corner. The desktop was badly marked with deep scratches, indentations, faded inkblots and candle wax stains. All normal wear and tear from more than a century of extensive use. *Colonial patina*, as it was affectionately called in the trade.

'What am I looking for?' asked Will, rubbing his eyes.

'There's something written here – look.' Jack pointed to some letters scratched into the wood.

'What does it say?'

'First, there's a name. Here – "Anna Popov". Can you see it?'

32

'Sure.'

'And then one more word. A little to the right – "Help".'

'Yes.'

'And then comes the really interesting bit over here in the corner. A date. Well, just the year actually – "07".'

'So? Is this some kind of joke?'

'Far from it. Does the name ring a bell?'

'Should it?'

'Come on, Will. Think back! January 2005. Alice Springs, two girls disappeared ...'

'Popov ... Popov. Oh yeah ... It was in the news for months. They vanished without a trace. Backpackers.'

'That's it. I looked it up on the internet before you came. The police operation was huge at the time with lots of overseas interest and media attention, especially from Britain. Almost as big as Azaria Chamberlain. The police even brought in Aboriginal trackers and a psychic. "Operation Dingo II", it was called. It came to nothing. The case was closed a year later. No leads, no clues. Zilch.'

'What are you getting at, Jack?' asked Will impatiently.

'Aren't you even just a little bit curious? We find this old secretaire here – purely by accident – on an abandoned farm in the middle of nowhere with "Anna Popov – Help" scratched into the desktop. Next to a date – 07. That's two years after she disappeared!' Jack said, jabbing his finger at the numbers.

'You're not seriously suggesting it was this Popov girl who wrote this desktop graffiti two years after she vanished? Are you saying she could be alive, or was at least, in 2007? Come on, mate, I can think of a hundred other explanations. I'm going back to bed.'

'I have a funny feeling about this, Will,' said Jack pensively. 'What if this is for real? What if this is a desperate plea for help and we ignore it?'

'You're a hopeless romantic, Jack, admit it. This is bullshit! Sheer speculation and you know it.'

'The place was spooky, you said so yourself,' argued Jack. 'I think we should at least go back and have another look. Make some enquiries, poke around a little. You know, find out who lived there before, what happened to the place, why it was abandoned, the fire ... The agent acted strange, admit it. He accepted the pittance we offered for the stuff without argument. He was happy – no, relieved – to be rid of it.' Will shook his head. 'Come on, Will, it's only a three-hour drive. We could do the whole thing in a day, easy. There and back.'

'I thought you had to go to London. Pressing author business.'

'I'm leaving on Monday. We could do it today.'

'You're wasting your time.'

'I'll pick you up at six.'

'We're getting too old for this, Jack!'

'Bullshit!'

'Dreamer,' said Will.

'Scared?'

'Me? What of?'

'I may be on to something ...' said Jack.

They arrived at the farm just after nine in the morning. It was already very hot and the flies were unbearable. They had to walk the last 200 metres to the gate because the track was too rutted for Jack's MG. On their first visit, they had completely ignored the house. This time, however, they decided to take a closer look at it.

The fire had obviously started in the kitchen. It was almost completely gutted.

'Here, look at this,' said Jack, picking up an urn with a rubber hose attached to one end. 'And all this junk over here.' He pointed to a rusty stove-like six burner lying on top of a heap of glass tubes, steel clamps and broken bottles.

'Looks more like stuff from a laboratory than a farmhouse kitchen,' commented Will, kicking some metal tubing aside.

The front room was empty. Fingers of sunlight reaching through gaping holes in the roof illuminated intricate cobwebs ready to ensnare the careless and the curious. There were no doors left. All the windows were broken and most of the floorboards had rotted away. Lying on its back, a fly-encrusted rat was decomposing in front of the fireplace.

'Here, have a look at this,' said Jack. He pointed to a timber wall next to the fireplace. The wall was covered in black numbers carved into the wood in neat groups of three sixes: '666'

'How weird ... Look over there; above the fireplace. What do you reckon it is? A stuffed goat's head?'

The mantelpiece with its forest of black candles reminded Jack of a strange pagan altar waiting for a sacrifice. Pools of hard candle wax coated the floorboards below the mantelpiece.

'This place gives me the creeps,' said Will.

Jack picked up an iron poker and went through the mound of ash in the fireplace. Buried under the ash, charred bones, an iron cross covered in soot and a dagger with a broken blade had escaped destruction by the flames. *Leftovers from a black mass?* thought Jack, glancing at the back of the fireplace. Then something behind the grate caught his eye. It looked like a piece of limp material – burnt around the edges – with some kind of picture in the middle. He lifted it up with the poker and dropped it on the floor in front of him.

'How weird,' he said, examining the strange thing lying on the floorboards. It turned out to be a piece of leather with a picture of a human head cut in half. The left side of the face was a grinning skull, the right, the face of a bearded man. On top of the head sat a conical black hat with strange looking symbols like silver arrows and stars.

'What do you reckon? A magician?' ventured Will, pointing to the head.

'Half dead, half alive?'

'Yeah. Something like that.'

'Black magic.'

'Scary place. Let's get out of here.'

'Why don't you track down the agent?' suggested Will on their way back to the village. 'See what you can find out about the farm. I'll try the store and the pub. Let's meet there in an hour.'

Everyone they spoke to had two things in common: suspicion and a reluctance to talk about the farm. The responses varied. Moving from polite evasion via pretended ignorance and obvious lies to rude rebuff, they covered everything but the truth.

'I could do with a cold beer,' said Jack, pulling up a stool next to Will's at the bar. Apart from the publican reading the paper behind the counter, the bar was deserted.

'Any luck?' asked Will.

'Nothing! The bastard didn't want to know me and almost threw me out.'

'Same here,' said Will, lowering his voice, 'except for the vicar. You just missed him. He was having a quiet beer at ten in the morning.'

Jack ordered two beers. 'What did you find out?' he asked.

'About a year ago, there were some rather unusual characters at the farm who caused the village here, and particularly the vicar, a lot of grief. They terrorised the locals for months and only left after the farm burnt down.'

'Not your ideal tenants,' said Jack. He took a sip of his beer and nodded appreciatively. 'Who were they?'

'At first, even the vicar was reluctant to talk. But three scotches later he opened up a little.'

'Well?'

'A bikie gang,' said Will, lowering his voice even further. 'Can you believe it? Here, in this God forsaken place?'

Jack looked up, surprised. 'Yes, I can,' he said, grinning. 'And we have the proof right here.'

'What are you talking about?'

'This.' Jack pulled the piece of leather he'd found in the fireplace out of his pocket and put it on the bar in front of him. 'Do you know what this is?'

'No idea.'

'The penny dropped as soon as you mentioned the bikies. This, my friend, is the colours of an outlaw motorcycle club.'

'You're kidding! Do you know which club?'

'Yes. The Wizards of Oz.'

Will's jaw almost dropped into his glass. 'Let me buy you another beer, mate. You deserve it,' he said.

5

On the plane to London, 11 January

'You asked me the other day how I find the material for my articles, remember?' said Jack, leaning back in his comfortable business class seat just before takeoff. He reached for his glass of champagne and turned towards Rebecca sitting next to him. 'I don't find the stories, they find me. Cheers.' They touched glasses.

'You went back to that farm with Will yesterday? Why?'

'Because I believe another story has found me.'

'Oh? And are you going to tell me about it?' asked Rebecca, looking at him mischievously, 'or is it a secret?'

'You really want to know?'

'Of course. Don't tease me.'

'It's about a girl. A backpacker, who disappeared without a trace with her girlfriend four years ago in Alice Springs.'

'Fascinating.'

'Listen to this.' Reaching for his briefcase, Jack told her about his discovery at the farm. He showed Rebecca photos of the piece of leather found in the fireplace at the abandoned homestead. He described the derelict farmhouse, what was left of the kitchen, and the room with the strange wall covered with numbers.

'It all comes back to the inscription,' said Jack. 'How do we explain it? Is it some practical joke? Hardly. Coincidence? I don't think so. Popov is an unusual name in Australia. I'm convinced that the secretaire has been at the farm for a long time. So, whoever carved "Anna Popov Help 07" into the desktop, must have been there in 2007. It's the most logical explanation, don't you agree?'

'Are you trying to convince me, or yourself?' asked Rebecca.

'I thought you were on my side! Aren't you supposed to give me encouragement?' replied Jack, pretending to be hurt.

'Minders like me have to make sure that their charges keep at least one foot on the ground, and one eye on reality.'

'Inspiration moves in mysterious ways and fact can be stranger than fiction. I've seen it many times, and so have you. Take our current book, for instance. We're travelling the world promoting it, millions are reading it, the media can't get enough of it and politicians have taken notice of it and changed laws. It's a great success, yes?'

Rebecca nodded.

'Yet, as we both know, that story began with an old photograph found by accident in the ruins of a cottage destroyed by bushfire. Look where it ended up.'

'Point taken,' said Rebecca, reaching for Jack's hand.

'And guess who found that photograph and alerted me to that story?'

'Your friend Will. I know.'

'If I have any talent at all, it's certainly not my writing. Many can do that much better than I. I'm a reporter, not a writer. It's my instinct for a good story, that's the difference,' said Jack. 'I'm a newshound with a good nose. I love to investigate, get to the bottom of things, solve the puzzle, explain the mystery and if I'm really lucky, find, no, expose the truth. I can feel it in my bones that this is one of those stories. I can't wait to get back to Sydney ...'

'To do what?'

'Talk to this man,' Jack answered quietly, handing Rebecca another photograph.

'My God! Who on earth is *that*?'

The photograph looked like a typical mugshot of a delinquent under arrest. There was even a number at the bottom. Long, shiny black hair neatly parted in the middle, fell down on broad, tattooed shoulders. The eyes – a little too far apart – were slanted, reptilian, and almost almond shaped. Prominent cheekbones, a heavy jaw and a drooping moustache gave the subject a distinctly Mongolian look. A thin scar running diagonally across the forehead, brow and cheek, pointed to a large earring in the left ear.

'Eugene Alfonso Cagliostro. Aka the Wizard. Founder and president of the Wizards of Oz motorcycle club. You've already seen the club's emblem.'

'The piece of leather from the fireplace?'

'Exactly. That was the important clue. Eugene's a notorious character and very dangerous. My sources told me that he's the only son of an Italian trapeze artist and a Gypsy fortune teller – circus performers – and has spent more than half his life behind bars,' Jack said. 'Armed robbery, extortion, numerous assaults, drug trafficking and bestiality, would you believe, are some of the more colourful entries in his charge sheets over the years. The club is quite small, but run with almost military precision, demanding monastic obedience from its members.'

'He looks evil.'

'A bit different from the Amish lads you grew up with, I suppose?'

'How did you find all this out in such a short time?'

'Friends in the police force – well-placed friends, that is – and prison wardens, can be an excellent source ... of valuable information,' said Jack, enjoying himself.

'I knew it from the start: travelling with you, Jack, could never be boring. Here's the list of your UK engagements.' Rebecca thrust a sheet of paper into Jack's hand. It was time for a reality check. 'How about another glass of champagne?'

Jack signalled to the stewardess. 'I was afraid of this. Look, book signings, talk-back radio, morning TV shows, dinner engagements with book clubs, receptions, speeches and a press conference. It's never ending. I won't have time to come up for air!!'

'You're famous, Jack. That's the price you have to pay. You entered almost unnoticed through the back door and went straight to centre stage. And all that without the usual hurdles: the knock-backs, the countless rejections, the waiting ... Many would give their proverbial right arm to be in your position,' came the gentle rebuke.

'I know ... It's just ...'

'What?'

'Not me.'

'Get used to it, buster. Think of your bank balance. It must be rising at an alarming rate,' Rebecca said.

'If you can arrange a day off for me – just to give my fingers a rest during the London book signing, you understand – I really would like to meet this man before I talk to Eugene,' said Jack, handing Rebecca another photograph. 'The one on the right, here.'

Three sophisticated-looking, middle-aged gentlemen in dinner suits were smiling at the camera.

'Who is this?'

'Professor Nikolai Popov, Anna's father. The photo was taken last year in Stockholm. He received the Nobel Prize for physics.'

'You want a *whole* day off?' asked Rebecca, shaking her head disapprovingly.

'Purely for research purposes, you understand. Please?'

'All right. I'll see what I can do,' Rebecca sighed, shrugging her shoulders in resignation. 'Authors!'

'Eugene is obviously not the only one expecting monastic obedience,' mumbled Jack.

'Did you say something?'

'No, nothing,' he murmured, and closed his eyes.

Jack adjusted his seat, stretched out his long legs and nodded off. He found himself back home in his study. The old secretaire was whispering to him: 'Help me ... help me'. Jack woke with a start. He opened his eyes and stared drowsily at Rebecca's hand on the armrest next to him. The silver bracelet he had found in the secret drawer looked lovely on her slender wrist. *I wonder,* he thought, rubbing his eyes. *A link perhaps?*

6

Vienna, 13 January

Jack hurried out of the BBC studio after his early morning TV interview. It was his only engagement that day and the hire car Rebecca had arranged to take him to the airport was already waiting outside.

Contacting Professor Popov personally had been impossible. The Nobel laureate's schedule was almost as hectic as Jack's, with speaking engagements and receptions all over Europe. All Rebecca had been able to find out was that Professor Popov would be in Vienna that day, addressing a group of prominent physicists at the university. Jack was hoping to somehow catch up with him there.

Sitting in the back of the limousine, Jack opened his briefcase and began to sort through the meagre material. He had to admit, when he looked at everything objectively, it didn't amount to very much. Most of it was a hunch, and to sell a hunch was never easy. However, he had decided to borrow the bracelet from Rebecca. What if it was in some way connected to Anna? It was the only item found in the secretaire and it was in surprisingly good condition, suggesting a fairly recent origin. He would show it to Professor Popov, just in case. But first, he had to find a way to meet him.

Trying to talk to people who don't want to know you is part of every journalist's lot. The challenge was simply to find that one window of opportunity that would invariably present itself, and climb through before it closed. That needed ingenuity and luck; especially luck. Unfortunately, that day all the windows appeared to be firmly shut with typical Austrian efficiency. Security at the university was tight and Jack couldn't get near the conference building. With Islamic terrorist paranoia sweeping across Europe and Vienna's reputation as a safe conference venue at stake, the authorities weren't taking any chances. Policemen armed with machine guns patrolled the grounds with sniffer dogs and all approaches to the building had been sealed off.

Jack didn't speak German but he had to get a message to the Professor while he was still in the building. It was his only chance – Jack had to return to London that evening. Then he remembered something he had pulled off at the United Nations building in New York in similar circumstances – with spectacular success. An old CNN fox had shown him a tried and tested journo trick: how to get a message to a delegate he had never met, without going through security.

Jack walked over to one of the benches, cleared away the snow and sat down. *Here goes*, he thought, opening his briefcase. He took an enlarged photo of the desktop showing the inscription – 'Anna Popov Help 07' – out of the case and scribbled the words: 'Please call to discuss. Urgent!' on the back. Underneath, he jotted down his name and mobile number, slipped the photo into an envelope, but didn't seal it. Then he hurried across to the young policeman standing at the barricade.

Fortunately, the man spoke a little English. Jack showed him his Australian press ID and explained that Professor Popov had dropped an envelope as he was getting into his car at the hotel. Jack knew that by passing the envelope to the young officer, he had made it his responsibility to do something about it. The important thing was to leave it there and walk away.

Jack looked at his watch. 'I have to run,' he said, turning on his heels. 'Please make sure he gets it. He's a Nobel Prize winner ...'

Well, it's on its way, he thought. *Fingers crossed I'll get a call.* All going well, the envelope would move up the ladder of command and find the Professor.

At first, the policeman had been reluctant to do anything. However, with the words 'he's a Nobel Prize winner' ringing loudly in his ears, he changed his mind and took the envelope to the officer in charge.

Professor Popov called Jack two hours later.

'If this is some kind of sick joke aimed at getting an interview, forget it!' he said curtly. 'Give me one good reason why I shouldn't just hand the photograph to the police and be done with it.'

It took all of Jack's eloquence and powers of persuasion to convince the Professor to give him five minutes of his time. The Professor agreed to meet Jack at five, and gave him the name of his hotel.

Professor Popov stepped out of the lift and looked around. Although Jack recognised him instantly from the Nobel Prize photograph, the Professor was much smaller than he had expected. The closely cropped hair, the round, steel-rimmed glasses and pointed goatee made him look like a Russian revolutionary of the 1920s. The only thing missing was the starched collar and cravat. Jack walked over and introduced himself.

They found an empty table and sat down. During the next few minutes, Jack described where and how he had acquired the secretaire. Hinting that Anna could perhaps still be alive, he began to hypothesise about the inscription. At first, Professor Popov listened politely. Soon, however, he started to fidget in his seat, took off his glasses and began to polish them meticulously with his handkerchief.

'I'm sorry to interrupt you, Mr Rogan, but isn't this pure speculation? The police investigation was extremely thorough and lasted for more than a year. In the end, the case was closed. There were no leads. No clues. Nothing. You cannot imagine what my wife and I have been through. I'm sure your intentions are good, but I cannot allow this to give us false hope only to be disappointed again. We have already endured a death of a thousand cuts. To have to face it all again would be too much to bear,' said the Professor quietly. 'Please, try to understand.' He pushed the photograph across the table towards Jack and stood up.

'Before you go, Professor, there's one more thing ...' said Jack, reaching into his pocket. 'I also found this, hidden in the secretaire.' Jack placed the silver bracelet on the table in front him.

At first, the Professor just stared. Then he sat down again, looked at the bracelet more closely without touching it, and paled. Covering his face with his hands, he sat in silence.

'Did this belong to your daughter?' asked Jack quietly after a while. The Professor didn't appear to have heard him and Jack had to repeat the question.

'You'll have to ask my wife that. My *former* wife,' the Professor corrected himself, his voice sounding hoarse. Pulling a pen out of his pocket, he reached for the envelope on the table and wrote down a number. 'Now, if you would excuse me, my driver is waiting.'

Professor Popov stood up and handed the envelope to Jack.

Confronted by something too painful to remember, but impossible to forget, the celebrated Nobel laureate looked like a broken old man.

'Thank you, Professor,' said Jack, holding out his hand. 'I will do that.'

For an instant, the Professor hesitated, then reached out and shook Jack's hand.

7

London, 14 January

Barely awake, Jack reached for the mobile ringing on his bedside table. 'What time did you get in last night?' Rebecca asked. 'I was looking for you.'

'I had to put my flight back ...'

'Any luck with Popov?'

'More than you can imagine. I'll tell you at breakfast. What time is it?'

'Time to go shopping, remember? Mayfair, here we come!'

'Oh God, I forgot! Do we have to?'

'Absolutely! Your wardrobe's appalling, Jack. You can't keep turning up in jeans and checked shirts all the time. And that infernal bomber jacket! The country-boy-from-Oz image is wearing thin, believe me.'

'It is? I hadn't noticed.'

'Remember the BBC yesterday morning? The interviewer was joking about it ...'

'The guy with the bowtie? Poncy little ... Who cares?'

'Don't sound so glum. Just bring your credit card and leave the rest to me. You missed breakfast by the way. See you downstairs in half an hour. Can you manage that?'

'Jeans and checked shirt it is. I'll be down in a flash.'

'Enjoy it while you can.'

'Is that a threat?'

'No. A promise. See you in the foyer.'

'Professor Popov was quite a bit older than I expected,' said Jack, 'and very reserved. He wasn't really that interested until I showed him the bracelet. Then everything changed. He became emotional and rather strange ...'

45

'So he recognised it, you think?' interrupted Rebecca. 'Here we are. Bond Street. Stop please, driver!'

Jack paid the cabbie and they got out. 'Not sure. It was all very odd.'

'In what way?'

'It was as if the bracelet had triggered something ... A recollection; a memory. Something disturbing ...'

'Did you ask him?'

'Sure. But he was noncommittal. He avoided the question and suggested I speak to his wife instead. His *former* wife that is. And one more thing ... He didn't touch the bracelet, which I found most unusual.'

'How weird.'

'And then he wrote down a phone number and excused himself.'

'In here, Jack,' said Rebecca, taking Jack by the hand. 'Armani. That's you.'

'I feel like a five-year-old getting his first sailor suit.'

'For goodness' sake, Jack! Just for once, do as you're told!'

Rebecca was in her element. She seemed to know the entire Armani collection. 'Stop complaining and try these on,' she ordered, handing a large pile of clothes to Jack.

She was an experienced shopper with a good eye and excellent taste. The clothes looked great on Jack and suited his athletic build to perfection.

'I don't need all this stuff.'

'Keep quiet! You're taking the lot. Clothes maketh the man, remember?'

'I thought it took a little more than that,' Jack suggested meekly.

There was no reply.

He paled when he was handed the bill by the smiling shop assistant, but wisely held his tongue.

'One good thing about all this gear, I suppose,' said Jack, pointing to the Armani bags on the footpath, 'I should fit in rather well ...'

'Fit in where?' asked Rebecca, trying in vain to flag down a cab in the crowded street.

'When we meet the countess ...'

'What on earth are you talking about?'

'Anna Popov's mother is a Russian countess,' answered Jack.

'What?'

'You heard. Not only that, she runs a boutique hotel just outside Paris. We're going to stay there on Saturday,' he added, casually.

'We can't do that!' Rebecca almost shouted. 'You have commitments!'

'Haven't you forgotten something?' replied Jack, reaching into his pocket. He pulled out a crumpled piece of paper – his list of UK engagements – and pointed to a particular entry. 'It says here – in black and white, I might add – "weekend free".'

'Yes, but ...' protested Rebecca.

Jack held up the piece of paper and shrugged.

'The weekend's on me, by the way. I booked the best suite in the chateau. It'll do you good, you'll see. Especially after all this shopping. Look, here comes an empty one,' said Jack. Stepping off the kerb, he whistled like a coachman pulling up a brewery horse. The cab stopped and Jack opened the door for Rebecca. 'Après vous, mademoiselle. Don't forget the bags.'

'You are incorrigible,' said Rebecca, clenching her fists in mock frustration. 'I don't know why I bother!'

'What's wrong? I'm just practising my French for our little weekend away.'

8

Kuragin Chateau near Paris, 16 January

By the time they crossed the moat it was already dark. Jack had insisted on renting a car at Paris airport and was driving. 'There it is,' he said excitedly, pointing to the ivy-covered tower rising out of the mist ahead. 'I told you I'd find it!'

'Taking the freeway wasn't such a great idea, admit it,' replied Rebecca. 'Driving three times around Paris before finding the right exit must be a record. We should have been here hours ago. Great weekend, Jack. We'll be lucky to get dinner.'

'Stop whingeing. You're about to meet a Russian countess.'

The rented Citroen looked diminutive and out of place next to the two Bentleys and the Mercedes Maybach, parked in front of the imposing entrance.

The liveried doorman suggested politely that they should perhaps go straight to their rooms and change, as dinner would be served in half an hour. Tactfully assisting first-timers was part of his role.

'Aren't you grateful we went shopping?' whispered Rebecca, following the porter up the marble staircase. 'You heard the man: "lounge suit". No jeans here, buster. Lucky it wasn't black tie. We better hurry.'

Their suite occupied almost the entire first floor. It had three bedrooms, each with its own bathroom, and a spacious sitting room with a marble fireplace in the middle.

'My, my, look at this,' said Rebecca. 'Big enough for the entire Von Trapp family. Which room would you like?' Rebecca was testing Jack.

She thought that taking a suite with three bedrooms had been a clever way of bringing them closer without presumption. She'd wanted him to suggest they share a bedroom. However, a familiar little voice inside her told her to be careful. *Leave it up to him*, she thought, sensing that he may not be quite ready.

48

Which room would I like? thought Jack, watching Rebecca carefully. *Is she teasing me?* Despite his confident and urbane manner, deep down Jack was rather old fashioned and quite shy. Women sensed this and it added a further layer to his appeal. *Don't rush it, mate. You're her client. Give her some space ...*

'Your choice,' he said, deflecting the question. 'You're my guest, remember? I hope they have some decent tucker 'round here, I'm starving. I don't fancy frogs' legs or snails tonight. I could kill for a steak! How about a glass of champagne first?' suggested Jack, pointing to the silver ice bucket on the sideboard.

'No time. We'd better get changed and do as we're told. Move!' Rebecca chose the bedroom with the fireplace, and Jack the smaller one next to it. A little more relaxed, they spoke to each other through open doors whilst getting changed. Jack needed some help with his attire, and Rebecca was happy to oblige. It all seemed perfectly natural and good fun. Watching Jack in the mirror, Rebecca realised she had made the right decision. *Good move*, she thought. *Intimacy without risking embarrassment.*

'Not bad for a country lad,' said Rebecca five minutes later when Jack emerged wearing his suit. 'Let me have a look at you.'

She straightened Jack's tie and adjusted his collar. Satisfied, she linked arms with him and they walked downstairs to meet the other guests. Somewhere in the background, a string quartet was playing Vivaldi.

The dining room was lit entirely by candles, making the large room appear intimate and warm. Countess Kuragin knew that the difference between a memorable entrance and a flat one was timing. Wearing a simple black evening dress, but jewellery fit for a tsarina, she swept into the room just as her guests were being seated. No one would have believed that the tall, elegant woman with the youthful face and regal bearing was in her forties.

The countess knew the names of all the guests and conversed fluently in several languages. She sat at the head of the table and Jack found himself to her right. Rebecca sat opposite, next to an elderly

Texan oil baron who ogled her with interest. The other guests turned out to be an ageing French actor between fortunes, an English lord – clearly a regular – and his bored wife. Further down the table, a bombastic German industrialist from Hanover accompanied by a striking young woman – obviously not his wife – was trying to make conversation with a pianist from Prague who had seen better days.

'A long way from home, Mr Rogan,' said the countess, reaching for her glass. 'I found your book most fascinating,' she added casually. 'Do you like the Chablis?'

It was always a fine line between welcome attention and privacy, but the countess knew exactly how far she could go without annoying or, God forbid, embarrassing her guests. Jack was rather pleased with himself for having been recognised and felt instantly at ease.

As every experienced hostess knows, bringing total strangers together at the dinner table for the first time and making them feel relaxed is quite an art. However, by sitting at the head of the table, the countess was able to involve all of her guest in conversation, not only with her, but also with each other. The copious quantities of excellent wine helped as well.

'Coffee will be served in the music room,' said the countess after the last dessert plate had been cleared away. 'Please follow me.'

Standing up, she smiled at the pianist from Prague and took him by the hand, leading him into the music room where the grand piano, a Bösendorfer with the top already opened in concert hall style, was waiting.

'Do you like Chopin?' asked the countess, joining Jack and Rebecca by the fire at the other end of the room. 'He was my mother's favourite. She used to play Chopin on that very piano. Mazurkas were her forte.'

Rebecca nodded. 'Very romantic.'

The pianist sat down, stretched his fingers and began to play the Minute Waltz with the flair of a professional. The others stood around the piano and watched him perform.

'I love your dress, Rebecca,' said the countess. Smiling, she turned to Jack. 'You have come a long way for just one night, Mr Rogan, yet there's so much to see around here, even in winter.'

'I didn't come here to see the sights, Countess,' replied Jack quietly, taking advantage of the opening. 'I came to see *you*.'

The countess looked up, surprised. 'You came to see *me*?' she asked. 'But why?'

'I have something to show you.'

'I'm intrigued.'

Realising that they were momentarily alone, Jack reached into his suit pocket, pulled out the bracelet, and placed it on the marble mantlepiece. At first, the countess stared blankly at the bracelet in front of her, then her whole body began to tremble and she had to reach for Jack's arm to steady herself.

'It can't be,' she whispered, choking with emotion. 'Where did you ... *how*?' The guests standing around the piano began to clap. 'Is something written on the back?' asked the countess, her voice barely audible.

'Yes, one word,' replied Jack, turning the bracelet over. 'Right here.' All the colour had drained from the countess's troubled face, making her appear suddenly much older.

'Örökke,' she whispered. 'Oh God. Örökke!'

'What does it mean?' asked Jack.

'"Forever". In Hungarian. Please excuse me,' whispered the countess and hurried out of the room.

Jack looked at Rebecca and raised an eyebrow. 'Well, what do you say now?' he asked.

'I'm impressed, Jack. The detour is forgiven.'

'Detour? What detour? I don't know what you're talking about.'

Twenty minutes later the countess returned looking calm and composed. Jack admired her self control.

'Breeding – see?' observed Rebecca. 'Just look at her.'

The countess mingled with her other guests at the piano – Chopin had turned into jazz – and then walked across to Jack and Rebecca who were standing away from the others by the fire.

'Would you mind coming with me?' she said, taking Rebecca by the hand. 'I have something to show you.'

At the back of the chateau was a small chapel. The countess opened the heavy wooden door studded with wrought iron nails, and ushered her guests into her private world. The first thing Rebecca noticed was the photograph on the altar, its solid silver frame reflecting the dancing flames of the candles burning next to it.

'That's Anna,' said the countess, pointing to a photograph. 'She was christened in here and so was I.'

This is a shrine, thought Jack, the distinctive smell of wilting flowers, incense and candle wax reminding him of his mother's funeral.

'I come here every day to pray,' continued the countess. 'I wonder, Mr Rogan, are you the answer to my prayers, or a harbinger of more torment? I'm not sure if I'm strong enough to bear it, should you be the latter. Please tell me, how did you come by the bracelet?' The countess placed a hand on Jack's arm and looked at him intently, her eyes reflecting the hopes and fears gripping her heart. 'And please remember,' she whispered, 'we are in God's house.'

Quietly, Jack described the circumstances of the bracelet's extraordinary discovery. Hanging on every word, the countess listened in silence. Not once did she interrupt.

'This is God's work, can't you see it?' she said after Jack had finished. 'I can feel it. He has brought you here. I believe Anna is alive. I've sensed it all these years. Do you believe in destiny, Mr Rogan? I think you do. You say so in your book.'

Looking for reassurance, she reached for Jack's hand. 'Thank you for returning the bracelet to me. It's a sign. You are now part of its history. Come, let me tell you the part you don't know.'

Jack and Rebecca followed the countess upstairs to her apartment on the top floor. Dismissing her maid, she waited until they were alone.

'It all began with an old story: two young men in love with the same girl. We all lived in Paris at the time and attended the same university. Zoltan was Hungarian. His parents left Budapest during the revolution in 1956 and opened a small nightclub in Montmartre.'

The countess lit a cigarette and inhaled deeply, her gaze fixed on the bracelet on the table in front of her.

'Nikolai came from an old Russian family. His grandparents left St Petersburg in 1916. They ran away from the Bolsheviks, just like mine. Fortunately, my family already owned this place and settled here. Zolli and Nikki were inseparable. They shared a room somewhere near the university and both of them worked in the club at night. Zolli played the piano in a jazz band and Nikki worked behind the bar. That's where I met them. I'm telling you all this,' explained the countess, 'to help you understand what was to follow. Would you mind opening the champagne, Mr Rogan?' The countess motioned towards the ice bucket the maid had left for them.

'The club was very popular with the students and I went there often with friends. Zolli and Nikki became part of our little group. We met at the club almost every night. Zolli was very popular: charming, gregarious, good looking ... Nikki, on the other hand, was the silent type – deep, brooding, poetic ... typically Russian.'

Jack opened the champagne, letting the cork pop. The familiar sound brought a smile to the countess's pale face.

'We drank a lot of this,' she said, pointing to the champagne bottle, 'buckets of it. I fell in love with Zolli. We used to sneak back to the room he shared with Nikki and make love. We missed many of our lectures. Nikki never missed his. And then I fell pregnant ... I was 19.'

The countess took a sip of champagne and kept staring at the bubbles rising in the tall crystal glass.

'It was a disaster. At first, I didn't have the courage to tell Zolli and I turned to Nikki for help. Little did I know ... I had no idea how he felt about me. For an unmarried young woman to fall pregnant at that time, especially in our circles – my parents were deeply religious – was a catastrophe. Nikki understood this and spoke to Zolli. Zolli was ecstatic and proposed at once. We would get married and live happily ever after ... That was when he ...'

The countess began to choke and couldn't complete the sentence. She reached for her purse, took out a handkerchief and wiped away the tears that were rolling down her cheeks. Jack and Rebecca looked away.

'When he gave me this,' continued the countess, regaining her composure. She reached for the bracelet and held it up with both hands. 'I found out later that he had to borrow the money from Nikki.' A small smile flashed across the countess's wan face. 'He never had any money, you see, and two days later, he was dead.' For a while the countess sat in silence, staring at something only she could see.

'What happened?' asked Rebecca, trying to break the spell.

'There was a fire at the nightclub. It started in the cloakroom and spread quickly. Six people died. Zoltan was one of them and I almost followed him. I wanted to take my own life, you see. It seemed the only way out, until Nikki saved me.'

'How?' asked Rebecca, reaching for the countess's hand.

'He offered to marry me, and I accepted.'

'That's quite a story,' said Jack.

'Yes, but is doesn't have a happy ending. You met Nikolai, you say, Mr Rogan. What did you think of him?' asked the countess.

'He struck me as a very private man. Reserved. Rather shy I thought, and sad,' replied Jack. He reached for the bottle in the ice bucket, dried it with a serviette and refilled the glasses.

'Very perceptive of you. I tried to love him. I really tried, but somehow Zoltan was always there. He may have died, but he never left us, especially after Anna was born. You cannot force love, don't you think?' asked the countess, turning towards Rebecca.

'Gratitude isn't love. You cannot ignite what isn't there. Nikolai sensed this of course and buried himself more and more in his work. He was offered a teaching position in Cambridge and we moved to England. Anna became the apple of his eye. He loved her more than life itself. It was almost as if he had somehow transferred his love for me onto the child. You see, Anna returned his love. Naturally and unconditionally.

'She adored him. She became our bond, the link between our quite separate lives. Nikolai was brilliant right from the start and rose quickly in academic circles. He travelled a lot and we sent Anna to Switzerland to finish school.'

The countess lit another cigarette and reached for the photograph showing the inscription scratched into the secretaire. 'Did Anna really write this, Mr Rogan?' she asked, holding up the photo.

'I don't know, Countess,' replied Jack. He paused, choosing his words carefully. 'But every time I look at it, I'm moved ... I'm not explaining this very well, am I?' He paused again, sensing that he had almost gone too far. 'In any event, I intend to find out. I promise you.'

The countess looked at him wistfully. 'We both agreed that we would tell Anna about her father when she turned twenty-one. It seemed the right thing to do. Zoltan deserved that, and so did Anna. Nikolai dreaded this, more than I realised at the time. He left it to me to tell her. It came as a great shock to her and I thought at first that we had made a big mistake. However, rather than turning away from him, Anna cooled a little towards me. They became even closer ...'

'How do you explain that?' asked Rebecca.

'I think she sensed that I didn't really love him; couldn't love him ... Yet he loved her, fervently, and he wasn't even her father ...'

'And the bracelet?'

'I gave it to her as a twenty-first birthday present. That, and a trip to Australia. Nikolai was against the trip, but one of her closest friends – Julia, an English girl she'd met in Switzerland – was going and she desperately wanted to go with her. The rest you know.'

'The other missing girl?' asked Jack. The countess nodded sadly. 'We spent several months in Australia after Anna disappeared. The police were wonderful. They did all they could, especially one man. For a while, the loss bound us together. But then, with all hope gone, there was nothing left, only pain. Lonely pain, the worst kind. Nikolai went back to England, a broken man, and immersed himself in his work. I came here and converted the family chateau into a hotel. A year later we divorced,' she said sadly. 'Just before he received the Nobel Prize. Personal tragedy next to professional triumph – ironic, don't you think? There's one more thing you should know: Nikolai firmly believed that Anna was dead. I didn't; I still don't.'

Just then a clock began to chime – it was 2 am. The countess glanced at the clock.

'But enough of all that. I have kept you up too long already. Look at the time. How selfish of me,' she said, turning again into the attentive hostess. 'You must be exhausted. We can talk more in the morning. I'll walk with you to your suite – come.'

9

Kuragin Chateau, 17 January, 3 a.m.

Unable to sleep, Jack stared at the ceiling. His body was exhausted but his mind refused to rest.

'I know Anna is alive,' he heard the countess whisper time and time again. 'Nikolai has given up hope, but not I. Do you believe in destiny, Mr Rogan? I know you do ... I know you do ... I know you do ...'

Jack got out of bed, put on his tracksuit and walked downstairs. It was four in the morning. The logs in the fireplace had mostly turned to ash, but embers still glowed in the dark like restless eyes of demons watching. Something drew Jack towards the chapel. Bumping into furniture, he walked along the dimly lit corridor until he found what he was looking for.

The countess was kneeling in front of the altar. The candle next to Anna's picture had gone out. Jack felt like an intruder and tried to look away but couldn't. Instead, he watched the countess – motionless as a statue – praying next to her daughter's photo. After a while, he turned around, tiptoed out of the chapel and quietly closed the door.

'My father was fascinated by Goya,' murmured the countess. Startled, Jack spun around.

'Do you like it?' Coming closer, she put her hand reassuringly on his arm and left it there. Well aware of the effect she had on men, the countess lowered her voice. 'I couldn't sleep either. I heard you come into the chapel before. I was expecting you. Strange isn't it?'

Jack liked the intimacy of her touch. 'Not everyone has a Goya in the hallway,' he replied, looking at the painting. 'We are only the custodians – usually for a very short time – of other men's genius. One cannot own it. It's timeless and belongs to everyone.'

What an extraordinary man, thought the countess, feeling something long forgotten stir inside her. 'Unfortunately, not everyone thinks that way,' she said. 'Come into the kitchen. I'll make us some tea.'

A tantalising aroma of toasted almonds and spices hung in the warm air.

'Cook never lets the fire go out in here,' said the countess. 'That's why it's the cosiest place in the house. And the most popular.'

'Isn't this beautiful?' said Jack, pointing to a large urn standing on the kitchen table.

'That's a samovar, for making tea. My grandmother brought it with her from our dacha. It has been in our family forever. A tea urn warming generations.'

Jack pulled the bench closer to the table and sat down.

'This was my grandmother's favourite place,' said the countess. 'I sat here often, listening to stories of long Russian winters and sleigh rides through magic forests frozen in time.' The childhood memories brought a fleeting smile to the countess' wan face. 'Anna is the last one. The end of the line. She's my only child.'

Jack nodded.

'The Revolution and the War have decimated our family,' continued the countess. 'My parents loved it here. Many of their friends went to the Riviera, but that was not for the Kuragins. You know what my father thought of the Riviera?'

'Tell me?'

'A sunny place for shady people, he used to call it.' The countess poured the tea and handed Jack a cup.

'You appreciate art, don't you?' she asked, putting her hand on Jack's arm.

'I do. It can tell us so much more than words alone. Just like the human touch ...'

Smiling, the countess withdrew her hand and pointed to a painting hanging on the kitchen wall. Bold brush strokes and vibrant colour captured the soul of a spring garden viewed through an open window. 'What do you think of that?' she asked.

'It's lovely,' replied Jack. 'Echoes of Renoir.'

'Anna painted that when she was fourteen. She was very talented, even as a child. We used to spend hours together in the Louvre. Italian Renaissance painters were her favourites. She adored Filippo Lippi. She was due to start art school in Paris after her return ...'

'How extraordinary.'

'May I call you Jack?'

'Sure.'

'And please ... call me Katerina,' said the countess, smiling reassuringly at Jack. 'This is an intimate place and an intimate hour.'

'It sure is.'

The countess reached across the table and put her hand again on his. 'You are right about the human touch ... What did you mean when you said earlier that you intend to find out?' she asked.

'I'm a journalist, a freelancer. Putting it bluntly, I look for interesting stories. More often than not, they find me,' Jack said, searching for the right way to continue without offending the countess. 'However, this is now more than just an interesting story. This is a mystery and a challenge. I want to know, have to know ...'

'If Anna wrote those words? If she's perhaps still ...? Is that what you mean?'

'That, and more ...'

'Are you prepared to go all the way?'

'Yes, I am.'

'Then let me help you. There was this police officer in Alice Springs – Andrew Simpson, the one I mentioned earlier – who was different from all the others.'

'In what way?'

'He never gave up. He too believed, against all odds. Just like me ...'

'That Anna was alive?'

The countess nodded. 'But the case was closed. Yet there was so much more. Much, much more. You must talk to him.'

'I will.'

Reaching for Jack's hand, the countess put the bracelet into his palm.

'Take it. It will guide you to her. I firmly believe that.'

Then slowly, she leant across and kissed him tenderly on the forehead. *He's crying*, thought the countess, noticing the tears glistening in Jack's eyes. 'What's wrong?' she asked. Overcome by the beauty and sadness of the moment, Jack tried to control his racing emotions. The fascinating woman sitting so close to him drew him irresistibly towards her. He could feel the warmth of her body and the scent of her perfume, radiating allure and excitement.

'We only met a few hours ago, yet you entrust me with something so precious,' he said, choking. 'Why?'

'Intuition. Time and trust have nothing to do with each other. The length of days doesn't shape character. I'm sure you know that.'

Realising that there was only one way to respond to this, Jack took the shy boy's leap into the unknown. 'May I kiss you?' he whispered.

Surprised, the countess looked at him. 'You are asking for permission?'

Jack nodded.

'I'm sure you know the answer to that too,' she said, closing her eyes.

A rush of excitement washed over Jack as his lips brushed against hers and then locked in a kiss.

Feeling a little dizzy, the countess realised that she had already gone further than she should. It was a fine line between magic and regret. Leaning across the table she blew out the candle and watched the little plume of smoke spiral lazily towards the ceiling. Jack understood exactly what she had done: she had extinguished the flame before it could consume them both.

After a little while the countess stood up – reluctantly, thought Jack – adjusted her silk dressing gown and looked at him.

'God be with you, Jack,' she whispered, and then hurried out of the kitchen.

Jack and Rebecca were the only guests having breakfast in the glass conservatory the next morning. It was quite early, and the others were still in their rooms.

Divided by a thin sheet of glass, two worlds were rubbing shoulders: outside, it was winter. The snow-covered garden looked bleak with the frozen ponds and leafless branches of the oak trees and maples dreaming of spring. Inside, however, is was cosy and warm. Filled with ferns, flowering cacti and exotic palms, the atmosphere in the conservatory was almost tropical, conjuring up images of golden beaches and sunshine.

Sitting back in his comfortable cane chair, Jack was enjoying his second cup of coffee when the countess sent her apologies. She was unwell, the maid explained, and wouldn't be able to see them before they left.

Rebecca noticed a subtle mood change in Jack, and decided to investigate.

'A little sleepwalking last night?' she asked, buttering her toast.

'Oh, you heard me. I couldn't sleep.'

'So you went to explore the sleeping house instead,' teased Rebecca.

'Not quite. I went back to the chapel. The countess was there; praying.'

'And?'

'We went into the kitchen and had a chat ...'

'At three in the morning?' asked Rebecca, carefully watching Jack. Noticing the melancholic look in his eyes, she sensed that there had to be more to this.

'Yes. And she gave me this.' Jack pulled the bracelet out of his pocket and put it on the table next to his cup. Rebecca looked at it, surprised.

'She gave it back to you?' she asked. 'Why?'

'Because I'm going to find out what happened to Anna.'

'You promised?'

'Something like that.'

'And when, may I ask, are you going to fit all this in?'

Jack shrugged and kept staring dreamily out the window. Rebecca decided to drop the subject for now. *If we'd shared a bedroom, none of this would have happened*, she thought, marvelling at how the right decision made the night before, could look so wrong in the morning. *The countess must have turned his head*, thought Rebecca, a stubborn little needle of jealousy pricking at her heart. *Men!*

'We have to go,' she said, standing up. 'Your London commitments are waiting.'

'Don't I know it.'

When Jack went to pay the bill, he was told there wasn't one. Instead, he was handed an envelope. Inside was Anna's photograph from the chapel. Written on the back was a date – obviously Anna's date of birth – with a dash after it, but nothing else.

10

First visit to Wolf's Lair, 21 February

'What on earth is that?' asked Rebecca, pointing to the huge motorbike parked in the driveway of Jack's house.

She paid the taxi driver and walked across to where Jack was polishing the chrome handlebars. 'Last time it was furniture, now this. I'm getting worried about you, Jack.'

'This is a chopper. Every biker's dream,' he answered, proudly patting the saddle of the gleaming machine.

'Where did you get it from?' she asked.

'It belongs to Will. He lets me use it whenever I like. Isn't she a beauty?'

'Looks powerful.'

'Sure is. You're wearing your jeans. Good girl.'

'Oh no ... we're not ...' protested Rebecca, stepping back.

'Oh yes, we are,' replied Jack, enjoying himself. 'You wanted to come along to meet the Wizard, remember?'

'Yes, but ...'

'Did you really think we would arrive by hire car at the clubhouse?' Jack began to laugh. 'No way! Here, this is for you.' Jack handed Rebecca a black helmet. 'I hope it fits.'

Rebecca looked at him dumbfounded. 'I'm not doing this.'

'Suit yourself. Black. Should go well with the designer jeans and your suede jacket. At least try it on.'

Twenty minutes later they were ready to leave. 'Are you sure you can drive this?' asked Rebecca, looking suspiciously at the bike.

'Trust me. Helmet looks great with the shades,' he teased. 'Your New York buddies would be impressed.'

He adjusted his own helmet, put on his aviator sunglasses and started up the bike. It roared into life with a deafening bang.

'Hop on,' shouted Jack, checking the traffic, 'and hold on tight, Easy Rider.'

'I must be out of my mind,' mumbled Rebecca, climbing awkwardly onto the saddle behind him.

'Did you say something?'

'No, nothing.'

'Ready?' Engaging first gear, Jack accelerated smoothly into the street.

'You and your mates ...'

'It's so nice to be hugged,' Jack said, leaning into the curve.

To her surprise, Rebecca actually enjoyed the ride. The raw power of the bike, the throb of the engine, the speed, the noise and the fun of it all were exhilarating. But most exciting of all was holding Jack around the waist, and leaning against his muscular back as he weaved through the heavy traffic. They got strange looks every time they stopped at a red light or pedestrian crossing, with the occasional compliment of 'great arse' thrown in from wolf-whistling truckies. Jack was an experienced rider but it still took them over an hour to reach the hot, western outskirts of Sydney. Jack stopped several times to ask for directions.

'What are we looking for?' shouted Rebecca.

'An old cemetery and an abandoned church. We should be just about there.'

'A graveyard? Great. Now you tell me!'

They almost missed the cemetery because the grass was so high it covered all the tombstones. A broken lichgate marked the entry. Jack pulled over.

'That must be it,' he said, pointing to a small church on the top of a hill. He gunned the engine and was about to take off through the gate when two bearded men on huge bikes roared up out of nowhere, blocking the way.

'Where do you think you're going, mate?' asked one of them, spitting into the dust.

'There's no funeral today, unless you don't turn your fancy bike around. Get my drift?' said the other. 'Be a good boy and piss off.'

'I don't think the Wizard would like that,' said Jack, glancing over his shoulder at Rebecca. 'I hear he hates to be kept waiting. Tell the Wizard that Jack Rogan tried to call in as arranged. See you later, guys.' He started pushing the heavy bike backwards, away from the gate.

'Hold it!' shouted one of the bikies. He reached into his back pocket and pulled out a walkie-talkie. After much shouting and crackling static, he pocketed the walkie-talkie.

'Follow me,' he growled, gunning his Harley and roaring up the hill ahead of them.

The gleaming choppers lined up in a row in front of the church looked like a congregation of giant insects attending a funeral. Banished by loud music – heavy metal – booming through the open windows, hymns and piety had fled long ago. Jack parked his bike at the end of the queue and looked at the burly man standing at the church door. 'The Reverend?' asked Rebecca, poking Jack in the back.

'I doubt it.'

'Over here, both of you. Shakedown time. House rules,' growled the man, pointing to the landing.

Reluctantly, Rebecca walked across. Running his sweaty hands down her tight jeans, the man was enjoying himself.

'Nothing suspicious here, luv,' he said, slapping her on the bottom. Rebecca glared at him. 'You're next,' said the bearded man, looking at Jack. Jack noticed that several security cameras were pointing at them from above.

'Great idea,' whispered Rebecca, following Jack into the church. 'I hope you know what you're doing.'

'I did warn you: being an author can be dangerous. You didn't believe me,' said Jack, taking off his dark sunglasses. It took a few moments for his eyes to adjust to the gloom.

Inside, the music was deafening. In the middle of the church where rows of pews had once faced the altar, a group of girls were dancing with each other. Wearing skin-tight leather pants and high-heeled boots – their long black hair streaked with red – they looked like witches waiting for a date with the devil. Some wore glittering dog-collars, others had multiple studs in their ears and noses. One of the girls spun around as Rebecca walked past. Staring at her with unseeing eyes, she leaned forward and stuck out her tongue like a snake searching for its prey.

Standing on a dais in front of the altar, a heavily tattooed transvestite was operating a pair of turntables, cranking out audio-poison. Perched on stools along a bar fashioned out of wooden confessionals, their backs turned indifferently to the dancing girls, a couple of middle-aged bikies were drinking beer. Pungent smoke – unmistakably marijuana – curled slowly around the coloured fingers of light reaching through the stained glass windows from above.

'Down this way,' grunted the man who had frisked Jack. He pointed to a narrow set of stairs cut into the stone floor behind the altar.

'I don't like this,' whispered Rebecca, holding onto Jack's arm.

'Too late. Come on.'

Lit entirely by candles, the vaulted crypt below the altar was surprisingly cool. Except for a large round wooden table and twelve chairs, the crypt was empty.

'Look at this,' said Jack, pointing to a row of pictures hanging on the sandstone wall. 'Exquisite.' There were twenty-four pictures in all.

'Do you know what this is?'

Rebecca shook her head.

'Come over here, I'll show you. You start with this one, the Fool, and then you go anticlockwise to the next one, the Magician. Then comes the Priestess, see?'

'You're well informed. What is it?'

'The twenty-four Major Arcana of the restored Tarot ...'

'Exactly,' said a deep, gravelly voice from behind.

Jack spun around. Slowly, a dark shape separated from one of the pillars, moved a little to one side and floated into a pool of candlelight.

The Wizard was much taller than Jack had expected. Lit up from below, his face looked quite different from the police mug shot. The

66

long hair, now streaked with grey, was pulled back and tied into a pony tail, accentuating the slanted eyes and prominent cheekbones.

'You look like you've seen a ghost, Mr Rogan,' said the Wizard, his voice echoing through the chamber. 'Perhaps you have.' He began to laugh. 'You obviously know a bit about the Tarot. That's a good start. Welcome to Wolf's Lair. This is our round table where everyone is equal, but lies and deception are costly ...' The candlelight lent the Wizard's features a sinister sheen, as he pointed to the oak table.

'I'm curious, Mr Rogan', continued the Wizard. 'Why would a famous writer like you want to meet someone like me? Please, sit down.' The Wizard gestured towards the table. 'You can have the Alchemist's chair, right here, and your friend ...' he nodded, acknowledging Rebecca for the first time, 'can have Cassandra's, over there. Cassandra's the only female on our council.'

Looking wistfully at Rebecca, he asked, 'Can you see into the future? I think not', he continued. 'Cassandra can, she has the gift ...'

The Wizard sat down opposite them and rested his huge fists on the table. Unbuttoned to the waist, his black leather vest barely covered his hairy chest. The broad shoulders and bulging biceps were the result of years of pumping iron in jail. Even in middle age, the Wizard radiated brute strength. He looked like a man who could easily crush a human skull with his bare hands.

'But back to the present for now,' he continued. 'Why did you come here, Mr Rogan? Tell me.'

His mind racing, Jack watched the Wizard watching him. He realised that his answer held the key to admission into the secret world of the Wizards of Oz.

'Your success in rehabilitating prisoners,' began Jack, 'is well known in certain circles. The Parole Board, the prison authorities, even the judges are talking about it.' He paused, letting the words find their mark. 'I thought it was about time the public knew about it as well ...'

'So that's it,' said the Wizard.

Jack decided to press on. 'Setting up a successful courier business employing only released prisoners,' continued Jack, 'has been a stroke of genius ...'

'You really think so?' asked the Wizard, enjoying himself.

'One mistake, you get a warning. One more, you're out – right?' said Jack. 'Former prisoners understand that ...'

'You're well informed. I like that,' said the Wizard.

Jack took a deep breath. Dangling recognition and fame in front of the man's ego was obviously the way to go. It was widely rumoured that the Wizards of Oz used their courier business as a front for extensive and highly lucrative drug operations. The club's cat-and-mouse games with the police were legendary and the feuds with rival gangs never-ending and bloody.

The Wizard noticed that Jack kept looking at the painting hanging on the wall behind him.

'Do you like it?' he asked.

'I had no idea it was here,' replied Jack.

'You know what it is then?'

Jack looked at the Wizard sitting below a portrait of himself dressed as a clown, wearing a harlequin suit and a conical hat. The resemblance was uncanny. The artist had captured the essence of the Wizard's face with a few bold brush strokes and vibrant colour.

'Oh yes. Pagliacci – Bald Archy. Four years ago, I think.'

'Very good.'

'This place is full of surprises ...'

'So, what did you have in mind, Mr Rogan?' asked the Wizard, rocking back in his chair.

'A series of articles based on interviews. Perhaps even a short documentary ...'

'I see ... I can't give you an answer right now. Our little organisation is run by a council.' The Wizard pointed to the round table. 'The council will decide. But before that can happen, you will have to meet Cassandra and pass scrutiny ...'

'Why?'

'Because she can recall the past and see into the future ...' Jack glanced at Rebecca and frowned.

'I can see you're sceptical, Mr Rogan.'

'I'm sorry.'

'No need to be. That's to be expected. I'm sure once you meet Cassandra you'll change your mind.'

'What kind of scrutiny?'

'She will examine your intentions. Any problems with that?'

'When?'

'Soon. You'll be contacted.' The Wizard stood up. 'Next time, Mr Rogan, please come alone.'

Turning around, the Wizard walked slowly to the back of the crypt and disappeared behind a pillar.

The Wizard had gone, but his presence lingered. Reaching for Rebecca's hand, Jack took a last look around the crypt and then turned to leave.

11

Rose Cottage, 21 February

'Pagliacci and Bald Archy? What on earth was all that about?' asked Rebecca, climbing stiffly off the chopper. She pulled off her helmet and gave it to Jack. 'Here, I won't be needing this again.'

'Just because he told me to come alone next time? You're sulking, admit it.'

'Rubbish.'

'Come inside and I'll tell you about the Bald Archy.'

Stretching her stiff back, Rebecca followed Jack into the house.

'You keep reminding me that painstaking research is the path to success,' said Jack, throwing a bundle of papers on the coffee table. 'I'm listening – see? There's a lot more to the Wizard than meets the eye.'

'Oh? What's that?'

'Newspaper clippings reporting the Pagliacci incident. It happened four years ago.'

'Sounds interesting.' Rebecca raised an eyebrow and locked eyes with Jack.

'Does Pagliacci mean anything to you?' he asked.

'Yes of course. It's an opera by Leoncavallo.'

'Exactly. And the main character is Pagliaccio, the clown. It was Caruso's signature role.'

'So?'

'You saw the portrait of the Wizard in the crypt – dressed as a clown?' Rebecca nodded. 'That picture has a title – "The Untouchable Clown" – and quite a story behind it. It won the Bald Archy.'

'You've lost me, I'm afraid,' interrupted Rebecca, shaking her head.

'Let me tell you the story,' said Jack, pointing to the newspaper clippings on the table. 'The Wizard is an opera buff with a good voice ...'

'You're having me on ...'

'I'm serious. On the night in question,' Jack nodded towards the newspaper clippings, 'the Wizard arrived at the Sydney Opera house with two bodyguards dressed in full Wizards of Oz regalia. If that wasn't enough to raise a few grey eyebrows, there was more to come. It was the opening night of Pagliacci, the Wizard's favourite opera.'

'What happened?'

'Well, during the famous laughing sob of the "Vesti la giubba" aria, the Wizard began to sing along – loudly.'

'What, sitting in the audience?'

'Yes. Pagliaccio stopped singing on stage, the orchestra stopped as well, but the intrepid Wizard continued and finished the aria, apparently rather well. Needless to say, this caused quite a stir. When the security guards approached – obviously to throw him out – the Wizard stood up and made a speech.'

'You're joking, surely,' interrupted Rebecca.

'No, it's all in here,' replied Jack, picking up one of the clippings. 'The whole of Sydney was talking about it. But wait, it gets better.'

'What did he say?'

'Addressing Pagliaccio on the stage in front of him, the Wizard apologised. He said he was so moved by the aria that he got carried away and just had to sing along. He then apologised to the audience as well and promised to leave at once if they wanted him to go, but then begged to be allowed to stay.'

'What happened?'

'The audience started to clap. Then someone shouted, "Let him stay!" and everyone joined in, even the orchestra.'

Jack held up the newspaper article and began to read: '*Meanwhile back on stage, Pagliaccio took a bow, turned to the conductor and said "Da capo, Maestro"* – from the beginning – *and repeated the aria.*'

'This is incredible.'

'Sure is, but the best is yet to come,' said Jack, reaching for another page. 'Listen to this: *Apparently while the Wizard was enjoying the limelight at the Opera House, his henchmen raided the headquarters of a rival motorcycle gang, burnt down their clubhouse and shot dead three of their members. The*

Wizards of Oz denied being involved and the Wizard himself, of course, had a perfect alibi. Clever, don't you think? And that brings me to the Bald Archy and the portrait.'

'What is this Bald Archy?' asked Rebecca, looking exasperated.

'It's an art prize. Actually, it's a parody of the Archibald Prize, a prestigious Australian portraiture prize which was first awarded in 1921. The Bald Archy began in 1994 and usually consists of cartoons or caricatures making fun of Australian celebrities. It's an Aussie spoof which – rumour has it – is judged by a cockatoo called Maude. One of the Wizards of Oz, a painter who calls himself The Joker, entered the portrait of the Wizard in the competition under the title "The Untouchable Clown". It was obviously meant as a joke, but he won first prize.'

'How weird.'

'Do you know why he called it "The Untouchable Clown"?'

'No idea.'

'The title is based on a film. Have you seen *The Untouchables?*'

Rebecca nodded.

'In the film, Robert DeNiro plays Al Capone. The notorious gangster is at the opera. Pagliacci is his favourite. Moved by Pagliaccio singing the famous aria, he starts to cry. Then comes the memorable scene: one of his men leans over and tells him that he's just killed Jim Malone, the Chicago Police officer. Al Capone stops crying and starts laughing. And we have a portrait of the Wizard dressed as a clown – laughing – while his men are burning down the clubhouse of his rivals. He's the untouchable clown – get it?'

'Ridiculing the establishment.'

'Exactly. And the establishment loved it. A fascinating character, don't you reckon? Dangerous, unpredictable and ...'

Jack's mobile rang in his pocket. It was the Wizard asking him to come to the clubhouse at midnight – alone.

'... on the phone,' whispered Jack, as he thumbed the 'end call' button.

12

Second visit to Wolf's Lair,
22 February; midnight

Inside, the church was dark and silent. Gone were the lewd dancing girls, the tattooed bikies smoking dope, and the flamboyant DJ. Instead, a nauseating smell of stale beer and cigarette smoke hovered above the deserted bar littered with empty vodka bottles and broken glass. After the obligatory frisking, Jack followed a surly bikie to the stairs leading into the crypt. He was told to go down alone.

Jack stopped at the bottom of the stairs and looked around: the large round table was covered with a green pentacle-shaped cloth. The table was empty except for one item: an intricately carved wooden box positioned at its centre. A lantern made of coloured glass was the only source of light, the candles inside sending crazy shadows flickering in all directions. A cold shiver rippled down Jack's spine as his eyes followed the shadows along the ceiling to a large hook, and then down a rusty chain to the lantern before coming to rest on the stone floor below. For a moment it looked like he was standing in a pool of blood. *Someone's dancing on my grave*, he thought.

Trying to break the spell, he walked over to the Tarot pictures that lined the walls, his footsteps the only sound, and looked closely at one of the Major Arcana images. It was The Fool, with a swag slung over his shoulder.

'Do you know what The Fool is carrying in his swag?' a voice whispered from behind. Startled, Jack turned around.

'If I remember correctly, a pentacle, a wand, a cup, and a sword,' he replied, looking at the petite woman standing under the lantern.

Leaning on a walking stick, the woman limped closer, materialising out of the gloom. Combed straight back, her short hair was blue-black and shiny, like the feathers of a raven. Her face was pale and unlined –

almost translucent – like alabaster, yet the prominent features hinted at a Polynesian origin. But most striking of all were her eyes – mesmerising and dark – like deep pools in a faun's grotto.

'And do you also know what they represent?'

'His talents, I believe ... for the journey ahead ...'

'And what are your talents, I wonder, Mr Rogan?'

'I'm sure you're about to tell me.'

A hint of a smile flashed across the woman's face, momentarily creasing the corners of her mouth.

'I'm Cassandra. May I call you Jack?'

'Of course.'

'Please sit down.'

Cassandra motioned towards the two chairs facing each other across the table; all the others had been removed.

'You must be wondering why you've been summonsed here in the middle of the night – just to meet me.'

Jack shrugged.

'Ours is a closed community, almost monastic you could say, with strict rules. Before we admit anyone into our world, we have to be sure ...'

'I understand.'

'My task is to expose that which is hidden ... Would that be of concern to you?'

When Jack looked into Cassandra's eyes, he felt a little dizzy. They seemed to draw him in, radiating both mystery and danger.

'Do you wish to proceed?'

Jack nodded.

'I should warn you: this is not a game. If at any time you want me to stop, you can walk away – no questions asked.'

'Fine.'

'Let us begin.'

Cassandra reached for the ebony box on the table and pulled it towards her. Jack noticed that two words were carved into the lid – SATOR and ROTAS.

'Two potent words,' he said, pointing to the box.

Cassandra looked up, as if prodded from behind. 'Do you know what they mean?'

'The words form an anagram. They are related to certain Tarot invocations ... To me, they mean very little, but to the Templars, they meant a lot.'

'You surprise me, Jack, that's good. Very good, in fact. But then, you are somewhat of an authority on the Templars, aren't you?'

'You think so?'

'Sure. They feature in many of your articles. You seem to be fascinated by spiritual subjects involving the warrior-monks. And then, of course, you've written about the history of the Tarot as well ...'

'You've read some of my articles? I'm impressed. The internet can be very informative, don't you agree?' Jack observed.

'I don't use the internet,' replied Cassandra, opening the lid. 'There are other ways ...'

She took a small parcel wrapped in blue silk out of the box, placed it on the table in front of her and began to unwrap it by carefully folding back the silk. Jack was admiring the beautiful Celtic cross hanging around her neck and wondered if it was made of ivory.

'It's whale bone,' said Cassandra, answering Jack's unuttered question without looking at him, 'and very old. My grandmother gave it to me.'

Shaking his head, Jack lowered his eyes. *How did she know?* he thought. Inside the parcel was a deck of eighty Tarot cards. Cassandra picked up the deck and began to shuffle the cards, her long, elegant fingers moving like the trained fingers of a pianist; fast and full of purpose. Beautiful to watch, the fluid motion was both mesmerising and relaxing.

'I would like you to formulate a question.'

'What about?'

'The real reason you've come to us. Perhaps there's something you would like to know ...' Cassandra continued to shuffle the cards without taking her eyes off Jack.

'All right. How about this? Will I be admitted into the world of the Wizards?'

'Don't you want to know if you will find what you seek?'

Trying hard not to look surprised, Jack searched for the right way to answer. Had she second-guessed his real intentions? If so, how? Walking a tightrope between deception and truth was never easy. 'Yes, that would be a better question,' he conceded.

Apparently satisfied, Cassandra nodded and placed the deck of cards face down on the table in front of Jack.

'Please shuffle the cards. Take as long as you like, but when you're finished put the cards, face down, back on the table and part the deck with one hand.'

Jack did as he was told.

Cassandra placed the small pile Jack had removed back in the box and closed it. 'We only use the bottom pile,' she said. 'Your question tells me that I should use the Celtic Cross Spread. This consists of ten cards. The first one, which is the top card here, is the entry point.'

She picked up the topmost card of the parted deck, turned it over and smiled. It was the card she had expected: the Strength card.

Placing each of the ten cards, one by one, into the positions required by the Celtic Cross Spread, she explained their meaning and relationship to each other.

As she turned over the last card, her hand started to shake and tiny beads of perspiration began to form on her brow. Jack reached into his pocket, pulled out his handkerchief and handed it to her. Cassandra wiped her burning forehead and described what she had seen. After a while she closed her eyes and sank back into her chair.

'Now, please leave. I need to be alone,' she whispered, looking frail and exhausted. Jack stood up and walked slowly out of the crypt.

The guard looked at him sleepily with bloodshot eyes as he unlocked the church door. Outside, it was still oppressively hot and humid. Eager to get away, Jack strode over to his bike. He had his thumb on the throttle when Cassandra materialised out of the shadows.

'You forgot your handkerchief,' she said, pressing it into his hand. Jack could feel something hard wrapped inside.

Cassandra looked at him intently and shook her head ever so slightly. Without saying a word, Jack slipped the handkerchief into his pocket, engaged the gear, and accelerated into the night.

13
Rose Cottage, 22 February, 3 a.m.

Jack pulled into his driveway and cut the engine, conscious of the bike's rumble echoing through the quiet streets. It was three in the morning.

Walking up the stairs to his front door, he noticed that the light in the lounge room was still on. Rebecca was asleep in a chair with a book in her lap. Jack walked over to the sideboard and poured himself a large scotch. As he turned around, Rebecca opened her eyes and looked at him sleepily.

'How did it go?' she asked, rubbing her stiff neck.

'Interesting ...'

Sipping his scotch, Jack told Rebecca about his encounter with Cassandra in the crypt. 'And then came the intriguing bit,' he said, 'the cards ...' He reached for the bottle and poured himself another scotch.

'Well?'

'It's difficult to explain. I guess I was disappointed in a way ...'

'What do you mean?'

'Her interpretations sounded glib, predictable, boring even. She spoke in generalities. The usual mumbo-jumbo.'

'Come on, Jack, what did you expect?'

'Yet, when I looked at her – especially her eyes – it was a different story ...'

'In what way?'

'It was as if she was really communicating on two different levels. Her words were telling me one thing, but the expression on her face, her voice, her body language were telling me something else ... Something ominous, disturbing. I don't think she told me what she really saw.'

'Why would she do that?'

'I don't know, but maybe I'm about to find out.'

'What do you mean?'

78

'Look.'

Jack pulled his handkerchief out of his pocket and placed it on the table in front of him.

'I see. Another mysterious object with supernatural powers? I think you should go to bed, Jack.'

'Just before I left, she walked up to me and gave me back my hanky,' continued Jack, ignoring the remark.

'How nice of her.'

'This was wrapped inside it ...'

Unfolding the handkerchief, Jack pulled out a Tarot card – the Strength card, torn in half – and gave it to Rebecca.

'What does this mean?'

'Look at the back.'

Rebecca turned the card over. Scribbled in tiny, spidery handwriting was an address and the words 'Meet me there tomorrow at 10 am'.

'Surely you're not going to go along with this cloak-and-dagger stuff? This is a game, Jack. She's toying with you.'

'I'm not so sure.'

'You can't be serious!'

'There was something about her ... a presence, an aura. I can't quite explain it ...'

'Try this: how about a carefully orchestrated theatrical performance – eh? She's a clairvoyant, for Christ's sake!'

'There's more to it.'

'So, you will go there tomorrow?'

'I've nothing to lose.'

'You find her that fascinating?'

'I do, but not for the reasons you may think.'

'And what do I think? Mind reader?'

'She's not my type to begin with.'

'Not quite like the countess – eh?' snapped Rebecca, instantly regretting the comment.

Jack looked at her, surprised. 'I don't follow.'

'Oh, I think you do,' replied Rebecca, biting her lip.

'Come on, Becky, this is ridiculous.'

'Is it?'

She's jealous! thought Jack, searching for a way to defuse the growing tension. *When all else fails, try humour.* 'Do you seriously think that a Russian countess could be interested in a knockabout country bloke from Queensland? Really!'

'Oh, I should think so.'

'You reckon? Irresistible charm and all that stuff?'

'Very effective.'

'Well, blow me down. I thought a classy broad from New York, maybe, but a Russian countess? Never!'

'You are such a rascal, Jack Rogan,' said Rebecca, laughing. 'Drink?'

'Sure. Make it a large one.'

'Coming up.'

Rebecca looked pensively at Jack. 'You seem to know a lot about these things – the Tarot, I mean. The pictures in the crypt ... How come?'

'Just a second. I'll be right back.' Jack went to his study and returned moments later carrying a slim folder. 'Here, you can read all about it,' he said, opening the folder.

'What's that?'

'An article I wrote a few years ago. One of my early forays as an investigative journalist into the realm of the supernatural.' Jack handed the folder to Rebecca.

'The Tarot – Occult or Science?' read Rebecca. 'You are full of surprises, Jack Rogan.'

She walked over to Jack and ran her fingers through his dishevelled hair.

'Just look at you ... authors,' she said.

Jack shrugged his shoulders and stared wistfully into his glass. He had become very fond of Rebecca. Her wit, her sparkling intelligence and good humour had been a breath of fresh air after two tumultuous years and several dead-end affairs. He respected her professionalism and sound advice and realised that she was exactly what he needed: a hand brake to keep him in check and pull him back from the brink.

This was something very rare and precious, and Jack was afraid of losing it. It had happened to him before. He also realised that suppressing his feelings was beginning to work against him.

'And thanks for asking me to stay in your lovely house. Much nicer than a hotel room. Very thoughtful of you.'

'It's great having someone around who keeps an eye on me ...'

'You need that, do you, Jack?'

'Yes, I do.'

'I'll keep that in mind.'

Rebecca put the Tarot card with the address on the table next to Jack's glass and walked to the door. Remembering the awkward bedroom moment at the chateau, she stopped. *He's pulling back again,* she thought. *Why?* Once again, the little voice told her to be careful.

'I better start reading this, if I want to keep up with the sorcerer's apprentice,' she said, holding up the folder. 'I'm off to bed. You better get some shuteye too, if you want to be bright-eyed and bushy-tailed for your appointment with your soothsayer in the morning. Sweet dreams.'

'Sorcerer's apprentice? I like that.' Jack was about to say something else, but thought better of it. Instead, he lifted his glass and blew Rebecca a kiss.

Being tired wasn't enough; Rebecca couldn't fall asleep. *He's invited me into his house. I'm sure he knows I want to sleep with him. What's he afraid of?* Rebecca asked herself. After tossing and turning for a while and rearranging her pillow several times, she gave up. She switched on the light beside her bed, reached for Jack's folder and began to read.

Most probably, it all began in Egypt. Conceived by priests, the Tarot entered the world as a manifestation of objective knowledge – Truth – five millennia ago. Truth IS: it doesn't change and cannot be altered. It is eternal. The Tarot is objective knowledge and has been used by mankind as a philosophical and psychological tool throughout the ages.

Preserved and guarded by the initiated, this precious knowledge has been handed down from generation to generation.

Rebecca heard footsteps outside her door and looked up. 'Jack?' she called out. He put his head through the door. 'This is amazing,' she said, suddenly wide awake. 'I can't put it down. I had no idea ...'

'Where are you up to?' he asked, sitting down in the armchair beside her bed.

'Precious knowledge guarded by the initiated and handed down from generation to generation ...'

'Yes, by special schools, or secret societies. The Essenes, Cathars, Templars, the Rosicrucians and the Freemasons were all part of it.'

'How do you know all this?'

'I did a whole series of articles on the occult – fascinating stuff. Listen to this: legend has it that the Atlanteans, knowing that their island was doomed, wanted to preserve their sacred laws for posterity. So, what did they do? They engraved them onto the surface of an ivory globe and then cut it in half. There were 144 laws in all. On one half of the globe they engraved the Arcana of the Tarot – all eighty of them. On the other, they engraved the sixty-four hexagrams of the I Ching.'

'The I Ching? What's that?'

'An ancient oracle book dating back to about 1200 BC. According to the I Ching, creation begins with a line which then divides in two, bringing duality into the universe. Space and Time appear, Good and Evil, Below and Above, Left and Right and so on. But back to Atlantis. The two halves of the globe survived the calamity. The half with the Tarot engravings found its way to Crete and then Egypt; the other surfaced in India and China where it became the I Ching.'

'Incredible!'

'Yes, I came across some amazing books written by some amazing characters. Take Gurdjieff's book, for example, *All and Everything: Beezelbub's Tales to his Grandson*, arguably one of the hundred most influential books ever written. George Ivanovich Gurdjieff was a Russian mystic and spiritual healer who had an extraordinary career and many famous students. Perhaps his best known student was

Ouspensky who, in his book *In Search of the Miraculous: Fragments of an Unknown Teaching*, defined eternity as "the endless existence of each and every moment in time". Influenced by Einstein, he came up with the concept of the eternity-line or fate-line as it is also called.'

Jack paused. 'Am I boring you?'

'Far from it; this is fascinating. I feel like I'm in a lecture theatre. Go on ...'

'A Tarot consultation is a joint experience between the diviner and the questioner; their respective fate-lines intersect. That's how it works. And then there was *Le Dogme et Rituel de la Haute Magie* written by Eliphas Levi in the 1850s. Eliphas Levi was a pseudonym for Alphonse Louis Constant, a fascinating individual who dominated the development of the occult in nineteenth century France. Pseudonyms were very popular in occult circles. Take Gerard Encausse, for instance, a French doctor with remarkable psychic powers. He was known as Dr Papus and published all of his books under that name. He became a good friend and confidant of Czar Nicholas II. It was rumoured that he predicted his own death, naming the day and the hour. During his funeral service in Notre Dame, a finger belonging to a statue – an angel – high above the altar broke off all by itself and landed on his coffin. To many this was a sign. All of these writers believed in the Tarot and were instrumental in its revival and popularity during the nineteenth century.'

'Stop! My head's spinning.'

'The Tarot didn't stand still,' Jack continued, undeterred. 'Over time, different versions emerged incorporating changes and perceived improvements, not all of which were helpful. We now have the Tarot of Marseilles, the Tarot of the Cat People, the Alchemist Tarot, the Fat Woman Tarot and many others.'

'You're a walking occult encyclopaedia, Jack,' interrupted Rebecca. 'No wonder the Wizard was impressed and asked you to come back. Alright. I can see now why you want to meet Cassandra again tomorrow.' She closed the folder.

'Cassandra believes in the Tarot. That's why she fascinates me.'

'Enough for one day. I'll read the rest in the morning. Go to bed, Jack. We both need to get some sleep.'

Rebecca put Jack's folder on her bedside table and turned off the light. *He's so passionate about the subjects that interest him*, she thought, *and so knowledgeable. Amazing guy.* Without realising it, Rebecca had just glimpsed the hidden drivers behind Jack's success: an almost childlike joy of learning and discovery, a burning curiosity, and a relentless pursuit of adventure.

Jack went to his bedroom and placed the Tarot card next to Anna's photograph. Looking at the picture next to it, he traced the words – 'Anna Popov – help' – that had been scratched into the polished wood of the secretaire, with the tips of his fingers. Then he opened the secret drawer, pulled out the bracelet and dropped it on top of the card.

'What does it all mean?' he asked himself, staring at Anna's photo.

Then a familiar feeling came over him: once again, he was being swept along by forces beyond his control. Some of his best leads had started like that. He knew then that all he had to do was follow his instincts. This time, however, he would have to be careful. Very careful ...

14

Bleak House, 23 February

Jack arrived ten minutes early. He parked his MG, pulled the Tarot card out of his pocket and checked the street address again, just to make sure. Number 13 – Bleak House – turned out to be an old Victorian mansion. Neglected and in desperate need of repair, the once stately residence had been converted into a cheap boarding house, frequented by vagrants and homeless alcoholics. Fingers of ivy yearning for light reached up to the broken gutters, the grounds were overgrown with weeds, and most of the pathways impassable. The fountain in front of the entry was dry, with Neptune and his sea creatures searching in vain for water that had stopped flowing years ago. Jack decided to wait outside.

A few minutes later, a taxi pulled up at the front gate. Cassandra got out, holding a bike helmet in one hand and her walking stick in the other. Mumbling 'Follow me' as she limped past Jack, she hurried inside. Jack followed her up the wooden stairs to the first floor.

At the top of the landing Cassandra stopped. 'Please wait here,' she said.

Jack looked around: naked light globes dangled from the ceiling, the light fittings a distant memory. Most of the ornate cornices had fallen off long ago and the wallpaper was barely recognisable under the rising damp and grime of neglect. But worst of all was the stench: a nauseating mixture of urine and cleaning fluids.

'Quick, Jack. In here,' said Cassandra, opening one of the doors.

There was only one bed inside the large room. The boy lying propped up in the bed – motionless and with his eyes closed – looked like a corpse. It was impossible to tell his age, other than to know he was still a child.

Various tubes and monitoring devices were attached to him and a complicated looking piece of machinery stood next to the bed. Jack guessed that he was on life support. A woman in a nurse's uniform stood up and left the room. Cassandra closed the door, walked over to the boy and kissed him tenderly on the forehead.

'Thank you for coming, Jack. I owe you an explanation. We must talk, but there isn't much time. My escort will arrive shortly and no one must know that we've met here. Do you understand?'

'Your what?'

'I come here once a week, but never alone. One of the Wizard's lieutenants brings me. I sabotaged his bike and jumped into a cab to come here.'

Recollections of the perplexed bikie tinkering with his engine on the footpath brought a fleeting smile to Cassandra's troubled face. 'I'm sure he'll turn up soon though – we have to be quick.'

Cassandra sat down on the edge of the bed and reached for the boy's limp hand.

'This is my son, Tristan. He's been in a coma for three years.'

'What happened?'

'I'll tell you another time – there are more urgent things we have to discuss right now.' Cassandra looked at Jack. 'As you've probably guessed, what I told you about the cards last night wasn't the truth. Our entire meeting was recorded. The Wizard was watching everything. You've seen the cameras, they're everywhere. He's obsessed with security and very suspicious. I'm not even allowed access to a phone.'

'But why?'

'Jack, I know what you seek and I can help you find it ... I know why you're *really* interested in the Wizards of Oz ...'

'Oh?'

'You made a promise to a mother ...'

Jack's mouth went dry. He bit his lip, but said nothing.

'You want to find out what happened to Anna ...'

'How do you know this?' Jack almost shouted.

'Not so loud – please! The Wizards own this place. Everyone here works for them.'

Kissing Tristan again on the forehead, Cassandra stood up and walked to the window. She parted the curtain and looked down into the street. 'I know because yesterday, you and I met in an eternity moment. Our fate-lines touched.'

Jack looked at her, nonplussed.

'He'll be here any second. This is my proposal: I will help you find her, but ...'

'Is she alive?' interrupted Jack.

Ignoring the question, Cassandra held up her hand. 'But you will have to do something for me first,' she said.

'What?'

'Here he is now.'

Cassandra dropped the curtain, turned around and looked at Jack with eyes like burning coals.

'We must hurry. He won't come up here. I'll go down in a moment and you will stay here until you see me leave with him. Understood?'

Jack nodded.

'You are a man who follows his instincts. You will have to decide right now what to do. There is a karmic window of opportunity. A small one. It will remain open for only the blink of an eye. If you accept, there's no turning back. If you can't, you walk away – clear?'

'Go on.'

'I have to warn you. There's danger – great danger.'

'Alright.'

'Okay. Listen carefully. This is what you have to do for me before I can help you ...'

'I'm listening.'

15

Rose Cottage, 23 February

'How did it go, Jack?' asked Rebecca, dropping her Gucci, Louis Vuitton and Dior bags on the sofa. 'My God, it's hot. I need a drink.'

'We have to talk,' replied Jack. 'Sit down, I'll fix you something.'

Rebecca collapsed into a chair and kicked off her shoes. 'I can't wait. A little more hocus-pocus?'

Jack went into the kitchen and returned with two glasses of iced tea. He described Bleak House and Tristan, and recounted the meeting with Cassandra.

'She knew about Anna and the promise I made to the countess. How do we explain that?'

'You must have given her a clue; said something ...'

'I didn't. No way.'

'That's what clairvoyants do, Jack, they're very perceptive. They probe, ask questions and catch you off guard when you least expect it; think!'

'No.' Jack shook his head.

'Being circumspect and subtle aren't exactly your strong points. Admit it.'

'Bullshit!'

'Typical male response.'

'Try to keep an open mind.'

'Well, it must have been in the cards, then,' Rebecca said, a raised eyebrow the only sign of her growing exasperation.

'You weren't there ...'

'She's bewitched you. Snap out of it, Jack.' He shook his head.

'Tell me then, what do you have to do for her, before she'll help you – huh?'

'I have to make a phone call.'

'That's all?'

'There's more to it than that.'

'Do tell.'

'She lives in the bikie compound behind the church. You've seen the place. Apparently, most of it is underground. She's a virtual prisoner there. She can't go out by herself. She hasn't even got access to a phone.'

'This is bizarre.'

'I know. Look, she gave me this.' Jack pulled something out of his wallet and placed it on the table in front of him.

'What's that?'

'The other half of the Tarot card she gave me yesterday – Strength. This is the bottom bit with a phone number written on it.'

'And when you make this phone call, who will you talk to and what will you say?'

'I don't know yet.'

'Come on, Jack, this is crazy.'

He looked up, annoyed. 'I'll be asked to come back for another session and she'll tell me then,' he said curtly.

'I thought the suspicious Wizard was watching everything. The cameras – remember? Why didn't she tell you today? You were alone. It would have been a lot easier, and safer – right?'

'Because she doesn't know yet. She'll tell me through the cards ... discreetly. All I have to say when I make the call is the name of one of the cards she'll show me.'

'Let me get this right: after you've met her again and she's shown you a certain card during your little session, you're to call this number and tell a stranger the name of the card. And all this, because she doesn't want the Wizard to know about it and can't make the phone call herself – is that it?'

'Yes.'

'You should listen to yourself, Jack Rogan.' Rebecca looked at him and shook her head.

He hadn't told her all the instructions regarding the strange phone call he would have to make for Cassandra. Not because he didn't trust Rebecca but because, even to him, the whole episode sounded weird.

Yet rather than walking away from it all as reason and commonsense strongly suggested, Jack found himself irresistibly drawn to Cassandra and her mysterious request.

16

Third visit to Wolf's Lair, 24 February

The next morning, Wednesday, the Wizard phoned Jack again. He asked him to come to the church in the evening for another Tarot consultation with Cassandra. Apparently, a small ambiguity in the previous reading required clarification.

Using the Bow Spread this time, Cassandra picked up the first seven cards off the bottom pile after Jack had parted the deck and placed them face down on the table. Taking her time, she turned over each card and explained its meaning and position in the Spread. Jack knew that the card he had to look out for was the one in the number 2 position, symbolising the present. The card in question was the Devil.

At the end of the brief session, Cassandra gathered up the cards, put them back in the box and stood up. 'Please wait here,' she said, reaching for her walking stick. 'The Wizard wants to talk to you.'

Jack watched her limp slowly away from the table.

'Welcome to the world of the Wizards of Oz, Jack, where a promise kept is handsomely rewarded, but a promise broken, severely punished,' she said, as she disappeared into the shadows.

A subtle reminder? thought Jack to himself., *Or a threat? Or both? I wonder ...*

Jack heard footsteps approaching from behind. Looking over his shoulder, he saw the Wizard walking towards him.

'You're in, Jack, congratulations!' the Wizard's voice boomed through the chamber.

'Thank you. So where do we start?'

'I'll get to that. But first let me tell you about the conditions ...'

'Conditions?'

'We have rules. Number one. Nothing you learn or discover about us may be discussed with outsiders without my permission.'

'Agreed.'

'Everything you produce about us – and that includes photographs – must be submitted to me for approval first, before it can be shown to outsiders or published.'

'Agreed.'

'We can both terminate our little arrangement at any time. Without explanation.'

'Understood.'

'You will observe these conditions?'

'Yes.'

'We take these things very seriously, Jack. You heard what Cassandra said about promises kept and promises broken ...'

'I did.'

'Excellent.'

'So when can I begin?' Jack asked again.

'A good starting point would be the Mardi Gras on Saturday,' said the Wizard.

'The Gay and Lesbian Mardi Gras?' Jack asked, surprised. 'How come?'

'For the first time, the Wizards of Oz will participate. We will ride in the Mardi Gras Parade. I think you will find it both interesting and enlightening. Some photographs would be useful. As you know, we want to raise our public profile ...'

'No doubt to promote your courier business,' interrupted Jack.

'That too ...'

'I will be watching the parade with interest,' said Jack, 'and with a professional photographer by my side.'

'Good. I can see we understand each other.'

'Will I have access to all the members of the council?'

'Yes. Once you're admitted, there are no restrictions apart from the rules I mentioned.'

'Okay, good.'

'What did you think of Cassandra?'

'I was impressed.'

'I thought you might be. She'll be riding with us in the parade. She's the only female member of the club.'

'Will the Wizards be wearing costumes by any chance?' asked Jack, grinning.

'Perhaps.'

'I can't wait.'

On his way back to town, Jack pulled up in front of a mobile phone store and parked his bike on the footpath. With the warning about broken promises still ringing loudly in his ears, he wanted to make sure the call could not be traced back to him. Jack took the battery out of his mobile and walked into the shop.

'I just tried to make a call and dropped the phone,' he said, smiling at the eager young shop assistant. 'I think it's broken. Could you look at it for me?' Jack put the phone and the battery on the counter.

'Of course,' said the young woman, sizing up the tall stranger in the faded bikie leathers with interest.

'Look, the call was urgent, could I ...?'

'Sure, use this. It's the same as yours.' The young woman handed Jack her mobile.

He walked across to the display cabinet, pulled the Tarot card Cassandra had given him out of his pocket and dialled the number.

In a small, remote Queensland country town 700 kilometres to the north, the tent behind the rundown pub was packed and throbbing with testosterone and beer.

'Do we have a challenger?' asked the ringmaster, wiping the sweat from his brow with the back of his hand. 'A thousand bucks is yours if you can go three rounds with Captain Thunderbolt here. What's wrong with you guys, surely one of you can do it? Is there no one with guts in this godforsaken town?'

'Jacko here will take him on,' shouted one of the stockmen.

'Yeah, he'll do it,' shouted another, slapping a giant of a man on the back.

The crowd surrounding the makeshift ring – mainly young men who had had a few too many – parted to let the man through. A little unsteady on his feet and with a foolish grin on his flushed face, the man walked up to the champ.

'I'll take you on, mate, no worries,' he drawled. The crowd cheered.

'That's the spirit,' shouted the ringmaster. 'Now, step forward, fellas, and place your bets. Put your money where your mouth is.'

Captain Thunderbolt was about to take his shirt off when the mobile in his shirt pocket rang. Annoyed, he turned away from the boxing ring and pressed the 'answer' button.

Standing in a quiet corner of the mobile phone shop, Jack let the phone ring several times. He was about to hang up when a husky male voice answered. Jack could hear the murmur of a crowd in the background. Taking a deep breath, he said, 'Sator.' Pause.

'Rotas,' replied the voice.

'The Devil,' said Jack.

'The Devil it is,' said the voice, and the line went dead.

'Look, his mum just called,' shouted a man in the front row, laughing. 'He's shitting himself – see?' taunted another.

Looking a little shaken, Captain Thunderbolt handed his shirt and his phone to the ringmaster.

'This is my last fight, boss, I'm leaving in the morning,' he said.

'Are you coming back, champ?' the ringmaster asked hopefully.

'Maybe,' replied the Captain and stepped into the ring. 'Come on, you lump of lard, let's get this over with,' he snarled to the grinning challenger.

Flexing his muscles, the Captain began to rock back and forth on the balls of his feet, the sweat on his hairy chest glistening like tears.

17

Alice Springs, Wandjina Gallery, 25 February

Unable to sleep, Jack tossed restlessly in his bed. His body was exhausted but his mind refused to relax. Every time he drifted towards sleep, a persistent little voice kept whispering into his ear: *Rotas, sator, rotas* ... like a mantra. *The devil it is, the devil it is ... the devil ...*

'What on earth does it mean?' he asked himself over and over.

Feeling hot and sweaty, he threw off the sheet and switched on the light. The clock on his bedside table told him it was 2 am.

Jack had the rest of the week off. No book signings, no interviews, no appointments. Rebecca had gone away for a couple of days to a health spa in Surfers and wasn't due back until Saturday afternoon. This gave him three free days. The Mardi Gras parade was on Saturday night.

Instead of looking forward to this unexpected break, he felt anxious and apprehensive. A sense of dread was following him everywhere like a shadow.

'It's just a bloody phone call, for Christ's sake,' Jack told himself.

He got out of bed and padded down the corridor to his study. *At least I've kept my side of the bargain*, he thought. Now it was up to Cassandra to keep hers. Jack was due to meet her again on Monday at Bleak House. Until then he just had to be patient.

Sitting down behind his desk – a large Victorian partners' desk, circa 1880, with a tooled leather top – he reached for his notebook. The name of the police officer Countess Kuragin had given him was Andrew Simpson. Jack had made some enquiries: a year after the case was closed, Andrew Simpson retired from the police force and opened a small art gallery in Alice Springs. *It's time I paid him a visit*, Jack thought. He turned on the computer and booked a flight. Feeling better, he went back to bed and fell instantly asleep.

Jack pushed past the tourists waiting for their coaches, hurried out of Alice Springs Airport, and caught a taxi to the Wandjina Gallery. Located in a modest looking cottage just outside Alice, the gallery specialised in Aboriginal art. It was already after closing time when Jack walked in. He dropped his duffel bag by the door and looked around: the paintings lining the walls were striking. Jack knew enough about Aboriginal art to realise that these works were pretty special. Stopping in front of a large bark painting, he looked up to the strange Dreamtime figure staring at him with bulging eyes.

'That's Wandjina. He created everything. The Earth, the Sea, the Sky – everything. The gallery's named after him.'

Jack turned around and looked at the wiry, lean black man leaning casually against the counter. Wearing faded jeans, riding boots, and a hat that had seen more campfires than a drover's dog, he looked more like a stockman on a cattle drive than a man selling paintings in an art gallery. But most striking of all was his face: furrowed like parched earth during a drought, with deep creases and wrinkles criss-crossing the forehead and cheeks, it was like a map of a life spent outdoors under the relentless sun of the Outback. The dark eyes – shining and alert – radiated curiosity and intelligence.

His face could hold three days' rain, thought Jack, sizing up the fascinating Aboriginal man, *and is no stranger to hardship*. 'This is really something,' he said, pointing to the painting.

'Is that what you're looking for?'

'Actually, no. I'm looking for Andrew Simpson ... I rang this morning. I was told he'd be here ...'

'You must be Mr Rogan. You called from Sydney,' replied the man, extending his hand. 'You spoke to my assistant. I'm Andrew Simpson.'

Jack smiled to hide his surprise. He had expected a retired European police officer, not an Aboriginal elder. 'Call me Jack.'

They shook hands.

'Don't worry, I get this often. I'm used to it,' said Andrew, laughing. 'What can I do for you, Jack?'

'Countess Kuragin sends her regards.'

'Oh.' The expression on Andrew's face changed abruptly. The smile disappeared and a sad, melancholy look clouded his dark eyes.

'Let's go out the back. I'll make us some tea.'

Sitting on the shady back veranda, Jack recounted his extraordinary discovery at the deserted farm. He showed Andrew a photo of the desktop inscription, but didn't mention the Wizards of Oz. Listening quietly, Andrew watched the setting sun light up the red cliffs of the Western MacDonnells that rippled like a giant caterpillar across the ancient landscape behind the cottage.

'The clincher is this here,' said Jack, pulling the silver bracelet out of his pocket. 'Countess Kuragin has identified it as belonging to her daughter. Anna had it with her when she came to Australia. I found it at the farm, hidden in the old secretaire with the inscription. It's almost as if I was meant to find it. Strange, isn't it?' Jack held up the bracelet, letting the fading light play with the links.

'Perhaps you were, Jack,' observed Andrew, looking dreamily at his visitor.

'You don't seem surprised.'

'Nothing about this case would surprise me ...'

'The countess told me you were convinced Anna was still alive,' said Jack, changing direction, 'even after the investigation was closed. How come?'

'Something about the case just wasn't right. Thirty years in the police force does teach you something. You get hunches ...'

'Was that all?'

'No. There was more.'

'Can you tell me?'

Taking his time, Andrew rolled a cigarette with nicotine-stained fingers. 'As you can imagine, we left no stone unturned,' he said. 'We followed every possible lead and threw almost unlimited resources at the investigation. Whole teams of detectives came up from Sydney and Melbourne with forensics guys, mobile labs, tracker dogs, the lot. The pressure was enormous, with the press reporting every move we made.

We interviewed just about everyone who was at The Shed that night. Everyone, except ...'

'Who?'

'The guy with the snake.'

'The bloke who decked the truckie just before the girls walked out of the bar?'

'Yes.'

'You didn't find him?'

'No. It was as if he didn't exist. A figment of the imagination, a phantom, a shadow man. We even called him that – "Shadow Man". He disappeared, just like the girls, yet he was there ...'

'And you think he had something to do with it?'

'Yes.' Andrew took off his hat and ran his fingers through his thick white hair. 'Towards the end, I brought in a psychic, a good one, and was ridiculed for it. I ended up wearing the blame. Every failure needs someone to blame – right? Well, in this case, it was me. In the beginning, I was the officer in charge. But I didn't act quickly enough, they said. I let the scent go cold and was barking up the wrong tree. Bullshit! Bringing in a psychic was seen as an act of desperation, yet I believe we were actually getting close ... very close.'

'Tell me about the psychic. What was he like?'

'Not he, she. It was a woman. She had the gift ...'

Jack sat up, a cold shiver tingling down the back of his neck. '*She* was getting close?' he asked.

'Yes. She kept seeing things. She was convinced that a bikie gang was involved ...'

'What?' Jack almost shouted. 'Did she say which one?'

Andrew shot a surprised look at Jack. 'No. But somehow, the press got wind of it and went wild. Soon after that, she refused to go on and withdrew from the case – no explanation. It was all very sudden and quite strange. We hit a wall. The investigation was closed and a year later, I retired. Well, I was told to go.'

'What was her name?' asked Jack, his mouth going dry.

'Cassandra.'

'A small woman in her thirties? Islander, walking with a limp?'

'How do you know?' demanded Andrew, almost choking on his tea. 'This isn't in the files, and the press wasn't told.'

'How did you find her?' asked Jack, ignoring the question.

'Come to think of it, I didn't find her. She contacted the police and offered to help ...'

'Interesting ...'

'Come on, Jack, how do you know all this?'

Jack held up his empty cup. 'A little more tea?' he said. 'And then I'll tell you about the Wizards of Oz.'

18

Sydney Mardi Gras Parade, 27 February

Jack checked his watch impatiently. It was exactly 6 pm. He knew they'd be cutting it fine. The Mardi Gras Parade was due to start in two hours. Rebecca's flight had been delayed – engine trouble. Instead of coming in at two in the afternoon, it had just landed.

'Sorry, Jack, there was nothing I could do,' apologised Rebecca. 'There were no other flights.' Tanned and glowing, she looked like a celebrity in her high heels and designer shorts.

'Don't worry. We'll make it, but only if we hurry. We can park at a mate's place in town. We'll walk from there.'

'Where would you be without your mates, Jack Rogan?' asked Rebecca, shaking her head. 'A mate for every occasion. Unbelievable.'

'I'm a popular guy. Is this all yours?' asked Jack, pointing to the mountain of shopping bags on the luggage trolley.

Rebecca nodded sheepishly.

'Where are we going to put all this stuff? I've only got a small sports car – remember? I should have sent a limousine ...'

'Don't fuss, Jack, and hold this.'

'What's that?'

'Your present.'

'Oh? What is it?'

'Later – it's a surprise. We both know your wardrobe desperately needs an overhaul, don't we?'

'But I've got all the new stuff from London ...'

'You can't live in a pair of shorts all summer.'

'Steady on ...'

Rebecca held up her hand. 'Being your publicist goes beyond peddling your books to the world, Jack. Image, perception, impressions ... And don't look at me like that!'

'I didn't say anything.'

'You didn't have to. I know what you're thinking. You're as transparent as a glass of water, buster.'

Jack decided to go on the attack. 'Wardrobe Nazi,' he mumbled.

'What did you say?'

'Nothing.'

'And what have you been up to while I've been away?' Rebecca asked. 'Polishing more furniture?'

'Not quite. Whilst his posh publicist was being pampered in beauty parlours and soaking up the sun on the Gold Coast, this busy little author was hard at work adding another chapter to his latest story.'

'Oh really? And how did he do that?'

'Later. It's a surprise.'

'Tease.'

'Look who's talking.'

The Wizards of Oz were assembling behind the church, the polished chrome of their huge bikes gleaming in the late afternoon sun. Wearing their distinctive club vests and black leathers, they looked like a private army: disciplined and dangerous. There were twenty-four of them plus the Sergeant-at-Arms bringing up the rear with his trademark motorcycle – a vintage bike with a sidecar. Cassandra, the only woman, would be riding in it.

'We'll form three columns of eight riders each,' announced the Wizard. 'I'll lead the middle column, Carlos here the one to my right and Sladko the one to my left. Any questions?'

There were none.

'Have you got your masks? Good. We'll meet at the assembly point in front of the obelisk in an hour. Don't be late.'

The traffic from the airport to the city was almost gridlocked. Everyone seemed to be flocking into town to watch the parade. Inching slowly forward, Jack told Rebecca about his trip to Alice Springs and the meeting with Andrew Simpson.

101

'This is unbelievable, Jack,' said Rebecca, barely able to see over the shopping bags piled on her lap. 'Are you saying that Cassandra and this psychic are one and the same person?'

'Yes.'

'And she's now a member of the Wizards of Oz? It doesn't make sense!'

'I know. It's too weird.'

'And she just walked away from it all without an explanation? Just as they were getting close?'

'Not quite.'

'Oh?'

'Apparently, while she was in Alice assisting the police, her son had an accident coming home from school. A hit and run. He's been in a coma ever since. You know the rest.'

'How sad. But why this notorious motorcycle club and this strange way of life? She's a virtual prisoner there ...'

'I don't know. But there has to be a good reason. There always is, we just can't see it. Well, perhaps I'll find out on Monday. I'm meeting her at Bleak House, remember?'

'Have you arranged a photographer for the parade?'

'Sort of ...'

'What do you mean, sort of?'

'I've asked Will. He's pretty handy with the camera. He'll meet us in town.'

'Jack ... you can afford professionals, you know.'

Jack didn't tell Rebecca the real reason he'd asked Will to take the photos: he was reluctant to involve outsiders. Something about the Mardi Gras Parade made him feel very uneasy.

No one paid any attention to the tall, broad-shouldered man in the faded black jeans and tee-shirt. Carrying a sports bag under his arm, he followed the crowd across the park. The excited spectators lining the street were jostling for the best positions to watch the parade. The man, however, was more interested in the trees behind them. Going from tree to tree, he evaluated each one and finally settled on a large Morton Bay fig with massive roots. Satisfied, he leant against the huge trunk of the tree, adjusted his baseball cap, and looked around: no one appeared to be watching. With one easy, fluid motion he lifted the sports bag high above his head and placed it on top of a branch. Looking around once more, he reached for the branch with both hands, pulled himself up like a gymnast and disappeared into the shadows.

Every year in February, thousands of visitors from around the globe flock to Sydney to see the Gay and Lesbian Mardi Gras. From its humble beginnings as a controversial call for gay rights in 1978, it quickly grew into a popular event until it became the biggest parade of its kind in the world with thousands of participants and dozens of colourful floats, many of them with a political edge.

Always on the lookout for new talent, the organisers welcomed the Wizards of Oz with open arms as a new star attraction. The Wizards were allocated a prominent marching position in the parade between the popular police float and the boys from the fire brigade.

In their three columns of eight at the assembly point, the Wizards were an impressive sight. Even while idling, noise from the Harleys all but drowned out the police band playing 'YMCA'. Each of the riders wore a spectacular mask made of papier-mâché – half bearded man, half human skull with a conical black hat on top. Representing the club emblem, all the masks were identical except for those worn by the three men leading the columns. Heading the centre column, the Wizard wore the mask of the Emperor, Carlos on his right, the mask of the Devil, and Sladko on his left, the mask of Death. Zoran, the Sergeant-At-Arms, brought up the rear with his sidecar. Usually, it would carry firearms, ammunition and a first aid kit. Sawn off shotguns were the club's weapon of choice. That night, however, the Wizards' arsenal had remained in the armoury, making room for Cassandra. The club's 'surgeon' – a struck off doctor who had been to jail for assaulting female patients – sat on the pillion seat behind the Sergeant-At-Arms.

This was the club's traditional riding formation for all its outings. The Wizard insisted on strict discipline.

'Don't you think we're a bit overdressed?' asked Carlos, pointing to the police float in front of them. Apart from wearing g-strings, leather boots and their police uniform caps, the young officers marching behind the float were completely naked. Their muscular, meticulously waxed bodies had obviously spent more time in the gym than on the beat.

'Don't worry. We'll give these wussies something to talk about. Just wait and see,' replied the Wizard, laughing.

Turning around in his saddle, he raised his right hand. 'Okay, guys,' he shouted, 'let's roll!'

'Sorry, Jack, I can't walk any faster,' apologised Rebecca, struggling in her stilettos on the uneven pavement. 'I had no idea there would be so many people. Where's Will?'

'There,' replied Jack, pointing to the obelisk at the edge of the park. 'On top of the wall.'

'About bloody time,' said Will, his voice almost drowned out by the roar of the engines. 'Up here, quick! They've started.'

With Will pulling from above, and Jack pushing from below, Rebecca managed to climb on top of the wall.

'Thanks Will. Wow!' said Rebecca, 'you can see the lot from up here; fantastic! Here they come now, look at that!'

19
Mardi Gras Parade, 27 February, 7:30 p.m.

From the ground, the man in the tree was invisible, his black jeans and tee-shirt blending perfectly into the dense foliage. His field of vision through the branches wasn't quite as good as he had hoped: the window of opportunity would be small, with little margin for error. Unzipping the sports bag that hung from a broken branch beside him, he reached inside and began to assemble the rifle, never taking his eyes off the parade. The music from the marching bands bouncing off the tall city buildings echoed eerily across the park. Mingling with the roar of a thousand cheering revellers, it rose like thunder from below every time a new float appeared.

The Aids Awareness float led the parade. Its giant condom with the caption, 'No erection without protection', was lit up in red from inside and looked like a ramrod ready to assault the enemy: apathy and complacency. It was followed by the ever popular police contingent of scantily clad, bum wiggling young bucks, and right behind them marched two tall transvestites wearing knee high boots and little else. Their banner read 'A little magic goes a long way' – the motto of the motorcycle club's courier business – and announced the arrival of the Wizards of Oz.

The sniper in the tree watched the parade through the powerful scope attached to his rifle. If he had wanted to, he could easily have counted the wrinkles on the make-up-covered faces of the men parading below. But immune to such distractions, he was only interested in one thing: the appearance of his target. He didn't have to wait too long.

'Here they are!' shouted Rebecca, pointing as the first row of bikes rumbled into view. The crowd applauded and cheered.

'What a spectacle!' said Jack. 'No wonder the Wizard wanted us to take pictures. Just look at them.' Jack turned to Will clicking away next to him. 'Go for it, mate. This is a photographer's dream. We should get some great shots out of this.'

'You bet,' said Will, reaching for his wide angle lens.

Every sniper has his own technique. The sniper in the tree began taking deep breaths to calm himself. He knew that the next few minutes demanded total concentration and steady hands. Moments later, the riders leading the three columns came into view. Adjusting his scope, the sniper moved the gun barrel slowly from one rider to the next. Death was closest to him, then the Emperor. The Devil was partially hidden on the far side.

'Damn!' mumbled the sniper. It would be a tricky shot. Suddenly, the Emperor slowed down, letting the Devil move a little ahead. The sniper smiled and was about to pull the trigger when he heard a twig snap behind him. He glanced over his shoulder. A possum was staring at him with big eyes, surprised to find an unexpected intruder in its lofty domain. The sniper lined up the rifle for another shot.

Sweating profusely behind her mask, Cassandra clutched the edge of the sidecar until her knuckles turned white and her fingers began to ache. Not knowing where or when sent icy shivers of uncertainty and doubt tingling down her stiff neck. The moment she had dreamt about for so long was coming closer. But had she read the cards correctly, or had her anguish pushed aside intuition and clouded the art of reading the signs? She knew she was about to find out, and the realisation filled her heavy heart with dread.

Another twenty metres and they'll disappear behind the wall; fuck! thought the sniper in the tree, his palms turning sweaty. Remember the rules: keep calm and wait. With the target moving, everything was constantly changing. Anything could happen. Then suddenly, the column stopped and the Devil's face came into focus. Holding his breath, the sniper took aim. The tip of his index finger had begun to press against the cool steel of the trigger when the back of another head moved into his line of sight from below. Standing on a park bench, a man had lifted his girlfriend on top of his shoulders, the young woman's head blotting out the face of the Devil. *Christ, that was close*, thought the sniper, lowering his rifle. *Five more metres and they're gone.* The window of opportunity was closing. Slowly, the column began to move forward again. The sniper took aim for the last time. He had the Emperor's head clearly in his sights, but the Devil was hiding behind it. Imminent defeat sent the sniper's pulse racing. The front wheel of the Emperor's bike had already disappeared behind the wall when the unexpected happened.

Basking in the adulation of the cheering crowd, the Emperor turned his head towards the Devil and said: 'It feels good, doesn't it Carlos?'

'What?' asked Carlos, leaning back in the saddle, 'the cheering crowd?' At that moment the angles changed, and for an instant, the sniper had a clear view of the Devil's grim mask.

'Gotcha!' mumbled the sniper and pulled the trigger. It was a perfect shot. The bullet entered the head of the Devil through the left eye and blew away the back of his skull. The bike accelerated, hit the wall and fell over, and the Devil – already dead – slid out of the saddle.

Screaming hysterically, the two transvestites dropped the banner, turned on their high heels and fled.

Resisting the urge to keep watching, the sniper lowered his weapon and began to dismantle the rifle. Starting with the silencer and the scope, he unscrewed the familiar parts, slipped them back into the bag, zipped it closed, then quickly climbed down. As every assassin knows, the getaway is more important than the hit.

No one paid any attention to the man in the black jeans with a sports bag under his arm, walking slowly across the park away from the parade.

'There, look!' shouted Jack, pointing to the commotion below. 'Something's happened.' One of the bikes at the front was lying on its side with the rider trapped underneath.

'I can see it,' replied Will, furiously taking pictures.

Within moments, the Wizard had taken control. He jumped out of the saddle and rushed over to his friend who lay motionless on the ground, blood oozing out of the mouth of the mask.

'Sergeant-at-Arms!' bellowed the Wizard. 'The sidecar! Over here – now!'

'What the fuck happened?' asked Sladko, kneeling down beside the Wizard.

'He's been shot. Look, half his head's gone,' replied the Wizard, cradling his friend's head in his lap. *We've got to get out of here*, he thought. 'Keep everyone away, guys. No one comes near him. Keep your masks on. Move!' Well trained, the bikies formed a protective ring around their fallen comrade and their leader.

One of the men ran back and shouted something at the Sergeant-at-Arms. Turning to Cassandra he said: 'Get out, now!' and pulled her up roughly by the arm. Cassandra lifted herself out of the sidecar and the Sergeant-at-Arms gunned his engine and raced to the front. Ripping off her mask, Cassandra hurried after him, her heart beating like a kettledrum. Then she heard the Wizard's voice, and knew that something was terribly wrong. *The bastard*, she thought, turning pale, *he must have sensed something*.

'What's going on? Do you need an ambulance?' asked a police officer, trying to get to the man lying on the ground.

'He's had a heart attack,' said the Wizard, stepping forward. 'We'll take him to hospital ourselves; it'll be a lot quicker that way. The ambulance won't make it through this crowd in time. If you could clear a path for us through the spectators here, we can take him in the sidecar. One of our guys is a doctor, he'll travel with him.'

'Okay, good idea,' said the policeman. 'Leave it to me.' Waving to the crowd control marshals standing at the barricades, he went to work.

Cassandra watched the Emperor and Death lift up the Devil. When they lowered him into the sidecar, the Devil's mask slid off. Cassandra gasped, her eyes open wide with disbelief and fear.

Turning his head, the Wizard stared at her: the look on Cassandra's face told him everything he needed to know.

'Not exactly what you had in mind, is it, bitch?' he snarled, pointing an accusing finger at her as she screamed and moved away.

'I'll find you, you treacherous cunt!' shouted the Wizard, adjusting the Devil mask to cover his dead comrade's bloody face. 'You can't run away from me!'

It was all over within minutes. Following the policeman through a gap in the cheering crowd, the Wizards left the parade and disappeared into the night. The only thing left behind was a small pool of blood and a torn banner reminding the crowd that 'A little magic goes a long way' – an ominous signature of violence and death in the midst of a celebration of life and hope.

20
Rose Cottage, 27 February, 11:30 p.m.

When Jack pulled into his driveway, it was almost midnight. Will was already there, waiting. Getting away from the parade after the Wizards' dramatic exit had taken ages.

'You should have a look at these,' said Will, holding up his camera.

'We can use my laptop. Come inside,' suggested Jack.

'I'm starving,' said Rebecca, kicking off her shoes. 'I'll fix us some supper, okay?'

'Be my guest,' Jack said.

'What do you think really happened here?' asked Will, loading the digital photos from his camera onto Jack's laptop.

'The cop said one of the Wizards had a heart attack and was taken to hospital.'

'Really? Well, have a look at this. I took this just before the Devil's bike hit the wall.'

'What am I looking for?'

'This here,' said Will, pointing to the left side of the Devil's face.

'Part of the mask has been ripped away – so?'

'Look closer.' Will magnified the image.

'My God, there's a hole. His eye's gone!'

'Exactly.'

'What are you suggesting?'

'I think he's been shot.'

Jack paled. 'Come on, Will ...'

'Look at the evidence.'

'An assassination?' whispered Jack, remembering the phone call. *The Devil it is* ... 'And they took him away themselves ...'

'Leaving no evidence ... Bikie gangs fight each other all the time. Gangland murders are not uncommon, Jack, you know that. These are violent people.'

'But in such a public place? In the middle of the Mardi Gras?'

'It's perfect, can't you see? Huge crowds, anonymity, confusion ... code of silence.'

'I wonder ... Who's the man behind the mask?' speculated Jack, drumming his fingers against the armrest of his chair. 'Who was the Devil tonight?'

'Haven't you had enough, you two?' asked Rebecca, walking into the room. She pushed Will's camera gear aside and placed a cheese platter on the table. 'This should keep you going for a while. I'm off to bed.'

Jack looked at the cheeses, and remembering the Devil's mutilated face, suddenly felt ill. Whether he liked it or not, he was implicated – however unwittingly – in a possible murder.

'Why don't we take another look at this tomorrow? With fresh eyes,' he said. 'And let's see what the papers have to say ...'

'Good idea. See you in the morning.' Will snatched a chunk of cheese and a couple of crackers off the platter, gathered up his camera gear and left.

Sitting alone in the cool courtyard, Jack mulled over the extraordinary events of the night. Slowly, the full implications were beginning to hit home. He knew that he had skidded into a dangerous, alien world and was being swept along by events he couldn't control. *Perhaps Will's wrong*, he thought. But the photo, the missing eye ... The phone call couldn't be traced back to him, he told himself over and over, just to feel better. The only link was Cassandra. 'She used me,' Jack muttered, clenching his fist. He was having second thoughts about his involvement with the Wizards of Oz. *Too late*, he thought.

Meeting Cassandra on Monday didn't seem like such a good idea anymore. Yet she held the key. Andrew Simpson, the ex-cop from Alice Springs, was convinced of it. And she had promised to help. Anna needed the strange woman with the gift. Anna needed Cassandra ...

Jack heard a faint scraping noise coming from the side passage beside the house. It sounded like someone was dragging a leg, or walking with a limp. *A limp?* thought Jack, his heart racing. He sat perfectly still, listening. There it was again. This time a little closer and louder.

Clearly a limp. Jack held his breath. Someone was coming. 'Jack?' whispered a voice out of the dark.

'Who's there?' asked Jack, jumping up.

'It's me,' replied Cassandra, drifting out of the shadows like a ghost.

21

Wolf's Lair, 27 February, 11:30 p.m.

The Wizards carried their dead comrade's body down into the crypt and placed him on the round table. Of the twenty-four members of the council, one lay dead on the table and one was missing. The other twenty-two stood silent.

'The Alchemist is dead,' announced the Wizard, placing his huge, blood-stained hand on his dead friend's shoulder. 'He died instead of me. The bullet was meant for me, not him. That much is clear. We exchanged masks at the last minute ... There is a traitor in our midst!' bellowed the Wizard, slamming his fist on the table. 'Not a word of this must leave these walls. Understood?' Everyone nodded gravely. 'The body must disappear before any questions can be asked. Undertaker!'

'Yes, Wizard,' replied the Undertaker.

'Have him cremated at once. Get a death certificate. You know who to call ... get it done.'

'Yes, Wizard.'

'We've been betrayed by one of us. By the one who's missing ...'

'Cassandra?' asked one of the council members.

'Sergeant-at-Arms!' shouted the Wizard.

'Yes, Wizard,' replied the Sergeant-at-Arms.

'I want her found!' roared the Wizard. 'Whatever it takes. Quickly!'

'Any idea who's behind this?' asked the Sergeant-at-Arms. 'Cassandra was in my sidecar when ...'

'I do. But before I tell you, we'll take the oath.' Everyone placed their right hand on the polished wood of the round table.

'Alchemist, you were one of us. You lived by the code and you died by the code. We will avenge your death as demanded by the code. What say you?' asked the Wizard, looking around the table like a serpent ready to strike.

'We will avenge his death as demanded by the code.'

'Our honour demands that we find the culprit – fast!' announced the Wizard ominously. 'Retribution must be quick and certain. Now listen ...'

22

Rose Cottage, 28 February, 2 a.m.

At first, Rebecca tried to ignore the persistent noise that intruded on her dreams. Half asleep, she turned over and covered her head with the sheet, hoping the noise would stop. It didn't – someone was knocking on her door. Confused and a little disorientated, she opened her eyes. Darkness. Then she heard a voice. 'Becky, it's me ...' The knocking became louder and more urgent. 'May I come in?'

Sitting up in bed, Rebecca tried to focus. 'Jack? What's up?'

As he pushed the door open, a pale cone of light crept into the room. 'I'm sorry to wake you, but something extraordinary's just happened ...'

Rebecca fumbled with the switch on her bedside lamp. 'You look like you've seen a ghost,' she said, shielding her eyes from the bright light. 'What time is it?'

'Two in the morning. Perhaps I have,' he added quietly.

'Come in. Sit here,' she said, patting the side of the bed. 'What on earth's going on?'

Looking pale and exhausted with dark shadows under his eyes, Jack sat down on the bed and reached for Rebecca's hand.

'I had a visitor ...'

'Who?' asked Rebecca.

'Cassandra.'

'What? She came here?'

'Yes. Will left soon after you went to bed. I was sitting in the courtyard when suddenly there she was, right in front of me.'

'Just like that? What did she want?'

Jack reached into his pyjama pocket, pulled out Anna's bracelet and placed it on the sheet next to Rebecca's hand.

'It's all to do with this,' he said, pointing to the bracelet. 'We've often joked about how stories seem to find me – right?'

Rebecca nodded.

'Well, let me tell you a story you'll find hard to believe.'

Wide awake, Rebecca squeezed Jack's hand. 'This better be good, Spinner,' she said, leaning forward. As she did, the sheet slipped down, exposing one of her firm, tanned breasts. 'Waking a girl in the middle of her beauty sleep is about as serious as it gets. I hope you understand that, Jack Rogan,' she said, pretending not to have noticed.

Sleeping naked, thought Jack, trying to stop his eyes from wandering. 'Sorry, but it's really important.'

Rebecca was enjoying herself. *He's actually quite shy*, she thought. 'All right, then. Tell me,' she said, making a half-hearted attempt at covering up. Recalling the missed opportunity at the chateau, she wasn't going to make the same mistake again. 'But you're not off the hook yet.'

'I suspected that.'

'Good.'

'Remember we asked ourselves how the psychic who'd pointed the finger at bikies could suddenly just withdraw from the case without an explanation and then end up joining the very gang she'd accused?'

'The policeman – what's his name – Andrew Simpson, told you her son had an accident ...'

'Yes, except it wasn't accident.'

'What do you mean?'

'Just before her son was run over, Cassandra received a warning.'

'Oh?'

'A journalist had somehow picked up a rumour that a psychic was assisting the police and had mentioned bikies. It was all over the papers. Shortly after that, she received the warning.'

'What kind of warning?' asked Rebecca.

'An anonymous caller told her to forget all about the bikies and withdraw from the case if she wanted to avoid something terrible happening to her son.'

'What did she do?'

'She ignored it. Two days later, her son was knocked down by a motorbike as he crossed the road in front of his school. Hit and run.

The culprit was never found. When she visited the boy in hospital she received another warning: her son wouldn't survive if she didn't do as she was told.'

'The Wizards?'

'Yes.'

'And she knew this at the time?'

'Absolutely.'

'In that case, why on earth did she join them? I don't understand.' Rebecca shook her head.

'Justice and retribution.'

'Come on, Jack, isn't that a bit melodramatic? You can't be serious.'

'I am. Listen to this.' Jack picked up the bracelet and held it up to the light. '"Örökke",' he said, '"forever". Some things are forever. Like a mother's love for her child.'

'What do you mean?'

'With her son in hospital in a coma, Cassandra was completely helpless and vulnerable. So she did the only thing she could do. She withdrew from the case. She gave in, but she didn't give up.'

'Explain.'

'As we know, the Wizard is very superstitious and obsessed with the occult. Cassandra was well aware of this and used it to her advantage.'

'How?'

'She went to see him and confronted him.'

'Are you serious?'

'Absolutely. Of course, he knew of her powers. He was actually afraid of her. Apparently, he admitted responsibility for the hit and run, but claimed it was an accident. All that was supposed to have happened was to frighten the boy, not run him over. Well, that was the Wizard's version. Faced with astronomical medical bills she couldn't afford and her reputation as a psychic – her very livelihood – shot to pieces, Cassandra made a deal with the Wizard.'

'You're kidding.'

'No, I'm deadly serious. She demanded compensation. The Wizards would pay for her son's medical bills and her upkeep as well.

In return, she would join the Wizards of Oz and make her powers available to them.'

'And the Wizard fell for this?'

'You've met him.'

'If someone were to send me a film script based on a story like this, I'd throw it in the bin. There has to be more to it.'

'Perhaps there is, but you know what they say – fact can be stranger ... Anyway, this isn't the end of it.'

'What, there's more?'

'Sure is. Remember – justice and retribution?'

Rebecca looked at Jack, a puzzled look on her face.

'I told you earlier that she didn't give up. She didn't withdraw from the case at all. Quite the opposite. She's worked tirelessly to solve it ever since – her way.'

'Anna?'

'Yes. Another mother's anguish. Cassandra knows what that means.'

'And retribution?'

'That too. She's determined to bring the Wizard to justice – her way. Last night she came close ...'

'Came close?'

'That wasn't a heart attack at the parade. That was an assassination. The Devil was shot. Will has the photographs to prove it.'

'You're pulling my leg!' Rebecca almost shrieked.

'No. Except it all went terribly wrong and I'm right in the middle of it. That's my problem.'

'The phone call?'

'Yes. And on top of it all, the wrong man was killed. The bullet was meant for the Wizard, but for some reason he wore a different mask last night. Someone else was shot in his place. The only good thing is, the Wizards are desperately trying to cover it up.'

'What a mess. What are you going to do? Where's Cassandra?'

'I took her across to Will's place. It wouldn't be safe for her to stay here. And besides, I didn't want her here ...' Jack ran his fingers through his hair. 'She said she had a proposal.'

'A proposal? About what?'

'Anna.'

'Do you know what it is?'

'No. She'll tell us in the morning.'

'And you are going to consider it? After everything that's happened? Jack, you must be out of your mind! You should be going to the police.'

'Come on, Rebecca, that's not fair. There's no harm in at least listening to what she has to say. We've come this far, we might as well.' Jack withdrew his hand and slipped the bracelet back into his pocket. 'Now, get some sleep. We'll talk in the morning. I suspect we'll have an eventful day.'

He was about to stand up when Rebecca put her hand on his leg and ran the tips of her fingers up his thigh.

'Is that a gun in your pocket, or are you just happy to see me?' she teased.

'Mae West, 1933, in "She Done Him Wrong".'

'Not bad ...'

'I'm always armed when I go into dangerous places.'

'I should think so. Waking a girl in the middle of the night can be very dangerous, and has consequences ...' she purred.

'Consequences?' asked Jack, pretending ignorance. He could feel the hand brake losing its grip. The cart full of desire was rolling down the hill, and was quickly passing the point of no return. The sophisticated chaperone had retreated. What was left was an incredibly desirable woman inviting him into her bed.

'Come here.' Rebecca lifted up the sheet.

'Nice tan. I thought authors and agents weren't supposed to ...' Jack said, frowning.

'There are exceptions.'

'Oh? Tell me.'

'Are you going to just sit here and talk? Or ...'

Leaning forward, Jack brushed his lips ever so gently against the side of Rebecca's neck. 'Or what?' he asked.

'Take off those dreadful pyjamas and I'll show you.'

'What's wrong with them?'

'For the last time. Shut up and get into bed!'

'I have to warn you,' whispered Jack, 'my lips have a mind of their own ...'

'Oh?'

'They go places ...'

'Promise?'

'Absolutely.'

23

Wolf's Lair, 28 February, 3 a.m.

'What's up?' asked Zoran, walking sleepily into the tiny control room behind the crypt. All the surveillance cameras in the compound were being monitored from there. It was three o'clock in the morning. Staring at a computer screen, his huge bulk occupying most of the confined space, the Wizard was reviewing CCTV footage of Jack's meeting with Cassandra.

'Look at this,' he snarled, stopping the tape.

The frozen image showed Jack sitting on his bike in front of the church. Cassandra stood next to him, holding out her right hand.

'I hadn't noticed this before,' said the Wizard, 'but there's something in her hand – look.' The Wizard leant forward, pointing to the screen. 'Now watch.'

He started the tape again, showing Cassandra handing something to Jack. 'He isn't even looking at it, whatever it is – see? Instead, he quickly slips it into his pocket and takes off. Strange, don't you think? Almost as if he was expecting it, or wants to hide the fact that he's received it,' he added. 'It may be nothing, but then again ... Rogan was the only stranger she had anything to do with and everything that happened in the crypt has been recorded. I looked at it – nothing. The only thing is this here. Unfortunately there's no sound. It all happened outside.'

'And our Jack is a journalist. All journalists are curious. They snoop around, that's what they do.'

'There's got to be more to it. Obviously, someone had to let the gunman know ...'

'Are you quite sure that black mongrel's behind the shooting?' interrupted Zoran, changing direction.

'Absolutely. There are only a couple guys I know who could pull this off, and he's one of them. Just look at the logistics: the venue, the

121

timing, the shot. Straight through the eye, for Christ's sake! You've got to have cahunas of steel to do this, and you know what he was like with a rifle.'

'I've never seen anything quite like it,' Zoran agreed.

'And the word is, the cunt's vowed to kill me ...' The Wizard began to laugh.

'Especially after the fire ...'

'Exactly. Well, a few arseholes have tried, and regretted it,' said the Wizard, rubbing his knuckles. 'Let him bring it on.'

Still smarting from the humiliating debacle at the parade, the Wizard suddenly felt better. He was about to unleash a long overdue retaliation.

'We're ready, aren't we?

'Always.'

'The three of us will deal with him. You, me and Sladko. No one else! This guy's smart. The three of us are the true Wizards – right?' The Wizard slapped Zoran on the back.

'The three of us are one.'

'Just like the old days – eh?'

'You got it. Most of the new blokes in here are fucking useless. Balls without brains.'

'You can say that again.'

'You reckon someone in here told him that you'd be riding in the parade?'

'Yes. Wearing the Devil mask,' the Wizard cut in. 'And that decision was only made on Tuesday night.'

'Correct. But Cassandra handed Rogan something on Monday, the night before. That doesn't fit, does it?'

'I thought that too. But we called him back on Wednesday – remember? By then all the arrangements were in place. The second session was Cassandra's idea. She had to clear something up ...'

'You're right, that fits. She could have told him then, but how? We recorded everything. What about the tapes?'

'Nothing.'

'This was well planned. Not much time to get the information out. Four days, that's all. Apart from the guys riding in the parade, no one knew any of this stuff,' Zoran mused, stroking his beard.

'And I would trust every one of them with my life – except that bitch,' whispered the Wizard. 'I've always been uneasy about her,' he added. 'Right from the very beginning when she first came to us with the boy. Well, now we know, don't we? But how did she do it?'

'Rogan?'

'Has to be.'

'What are you going to do about it?'

'No one fucks with me and gets away with it,' snarled the Wizard, almost crushing the remote control in his hand.

'You may never know for sure.'

'Maybe, but I intend to give it a go,' replied the Wizard, a smile spreading across his craggy face.

'What do you mean?'

'We'll pay Jacko a little visit in the morning. Want to come along?'

'Just try to keep me away.'

24

Will's antique shop, 28 February, 8.a.m.

Will's antique shop occupied the ground floor of a spacious Victorian terrace. The faded sign above the door – 'Arthur Hamilton & Son – Antiques and Curios. More posh for your dosh' – brought a smile to Jack's face. The place hadn't changed at all. The workshop and kitchen were behind the shop, the living quarters upstairs.

'We'll go around the back,' he said, turning into the narrow lane leading to the rear entry.

'You once lived here, didn't you?' asked Rebecca, following Jack into the lane.

'I did, twenty years ago. With Will and his parents. Two very happy years of my life. I moved in as a lodger and ended up being part of the family.'

Reaching for Jack's hand, Rebecca stopped. Jack stopped as well and looked at her. Then, leaning slowly towards him, she kissed him on the cheek.

'What was that for?' he asked.

'Nothing in particular. I'm just happy.'

'In that case, what about here?' said Jack, pointing to the other cheek.

Rebecca kissed him on the other cheek.

'And here?'

'Don't overdo it, buster.'

'Make hay while the sun shines, as my Auntie Mabel used to say. You were right; that was one hell of a dangerous place last night,' said Jack, trying to look serious. 'Not to mention the consequences ...'

'How did you find the consequences?'

'Challenging. I can hardly keep my eyes open.'

'Lucky you were so well prepared then ...'

'Do you think that'll be the end of it, or do I have to brace myself for more consequences?'

'Oh, there'll be more for sure,' said Rebecca, pinching Jack on the bottom. 'I hope you're up to it, buster.'

'Only if I get my beauty sleep.' They both burst out laughing.

The roller door was unlocked. Jack pulled it up and stepped inside. One half of the workshop was occupied by the old van; the other had a long wooden workbench running along the sandstone wall. The bench was littered with all kinds of carpentry tools: planes, saws, carving chisels, gouges. Jars of all shapes and sizes filled with glue and varnish were neatly arranged along the back of the bench like an army waiting to go into battle to fight the relentless wear and tear of time. Everything was covered in dust. Awaiting unlikely restoration, an assortment of chairs in various stages of disrepair was hanging from the rafters. A large cast iron slow combustion stove stood in the middle of the room, its long flue reaching up to the corrugated iron roof like an accusing finger pointing to heaven.

For Jack, the familiar smell of furniture polish, glue and diesel conjured up memories of long lazy Sunday afternoons spent sanding back old furniture with Will and his dad while listening to the ABC. The old wireless, covered in sawdust, was still tucked away in its familiar place – a little shelf above the workbench. Back then, Will's mum would be baking scones in the kitchen and bringing endless cups of tea to keep 'her boys' going.

Today, though, Will was leaning against the workbench reading the Sunday paper.

'Good morning, guys. You're up bright and early,' said Will, watching Jack and Rebecca. 'You look like two kittens who have just discovered the cream bowl,' he added, raising an eyebrow. 'There's nothing in any of the papers about a shooting,' he continued, pointing to a pile of papers on the bench. 'Apart from a short piece here about the Wizards of Oz leaving the parade early with one of their members who had fallen ill, the Wizards don't feature at all. There isn't even a photo – zilch. So far so good.'

'Coffee, boys?' asked Rebecca.

'Great idea,' said Will. 'Kitchen's just over there.'

'I'll find it,' said Rebecca, and walked to the back.

'Well?' asked Will.

'Well, what?' said Jack, pretending ignorance.

'How was it?'

'Is it that obvious?'

'What do you expect? Strolling in here, glowing like two teenagers after a romp in the hay.'

'Hmm ...'

'Well?'

'She's dynamite.'

'Strictly business – eh?' teased Will, slapping his friend on the back.

'It's not what ...' Jack stopped in mid-sentence as Rebecca walked back into the workshop, balancing a pot of steaming coffee on a tray. 'Smells good,' said Will. 'I'll get the mugs.'

'Where's Cassandra?' asked Jack, looking around.

'Still asleep, I suppose. She's in your old room, by the way,' Will said.

'She's sleeping in your old room?' asked Rebecca. 'That's a bit creepy, don't you think?'

'What do you mean?'

'She's managed to enter your life, Jack, can't you see?'

'She has something we want.'

'Yes, and she knows it. She's manipulating you. Be careful.'

Jack shrugged.

'This was the hub of the house,' Jack reminisced, running his hand along the smooth timbers of the large table at the back of the workshop. 'Isn't that right, China?' Will nodded, and disappeared into the kitchen.

'Workshop, garage, dining room and lounge all wrapped in one because the parlour and the dining room in the front had been converted into a shop.'

'We had a similar room at our farm in Pennsylvania when I was a little girl. All our family life happened in that one room,' interrupted Rebecca, noticing that none of the chairs matched.

'Because we spent so much time working, we ate here every evening and then played Monopoly and Scrabble until the small hours. Will's dad sat at the head of the table, right here on this chair. Strange how simple objects can outlive people, don't you think?'

'This place looks like something out of Dickens. The only thing that doesn't quite fit is this here,' said Rebecca, pointing to the old van.

Will returned with the coffee mugs. 'Cassandra can't stay here, Jack,' he said.

'I know that. But look, she has no money, no credit cards, no phone – no one. She has nowhere to go and the Wizard is after her. We can't just throw her out either.'

'So, what are we going to do, eh?'

'First, we listen to what she has to say. The proposal – remember? Then we decide – okay?' said Jack.

'A smart decision, gentlemen,' said a voice from behind.

Jack spun around, almost spilling his coffee. Leaning on her walking stick, Cassandra stood in the doorway.

'You won't regret it, I promise.'

Slowly, she limped closer and stopped in front of Rebecca who was sitting at the table. For a while she just looked at her. Rebecca held her gaze.

'We haven't met, but I think we know each other,' said Cassandra at last.

She pulled a small wooden box out of her pocket and placed it on the table. Jack recognised the box instantly, the words SATOR and ROTAS carved into the lid reminding him of his first encounter with Cassandra.

'You're right, I have no means and nowhere to go,' she repeated, turning towards Jack. 'But I do have something you seek. I can lead you to Anna,' she said quietly.

'She's alive?' asked Jack, unable to suppress his excitement.

'All the signs say so. But I have to warn you, the journey ahead is very dangerous. In more ways than you can possibly imagine.'

'We need to know a lot more than that,' said Will, shaking his head.

'Life is full of choices,' replied Cassandra. 'This is a fork in the road. You will have to decide which way to go. But once you make your decision, there'll be no turning back. I will tell you all you need to know to make up your mind. If you decide to follow me, the path will be arduous and difficult, but will most likely lead you to Anna ... If you decide against this, I will walk out of here now and you'll never see me again.'

She opened the wooden box, took out the deck of Tarot cards and put it on the table in front of Rebecca.

'This is my proposal. Please ... listen carefully.'

25

Rose Cottage, 28 February, 9 a.m.

'Bloody hell!' said Jack, pointing to the three Harleys blocking the narrow footpath in front of his house.

'There's someone sitting on your doorstep too,' observed Will. 'Look at his tee-shirt.'

'A little magic goes a long way,' read Jack. 'Shit! Thank Christ we left Cassandra at your place.'

Cassandra had suggested they go for a little walk. She, however, had stayed behind in Will's workshop, waiting for their decision.

'Do you think they're looking for her?' asked Rebecca. 'Must be. I wonder where the other guys are,' said Jack, as a second bikie emerged out of the side passage next to the house.

'Checking the back, I'd say,' said Will.

'Can I help you?' asked Jack, walking up to the man sitting on the step.

'Jack Rogan?' replied the bikie, scrutinising Jack through dark glasses.

'That's me.'

'Out and about early? Church?'

'I like to walk.'

'You've got a visitor, mate.'

'Oh?'

'He's waiting inside, mate,' said the bikie, indicating the open front door with his cigarette.

Jack raised an eyebrow, glanced over his shoulder at Will, and said nothing.

There are certain people whose presence can fill a whole room. Balancing Jack's computer on his lap, the Wizard, decked in his regalia, sat in the small parlour looking completely relaxed among the antiques. He looked bigger and more threatening than Jack remembered.

'Nice photos,' said the Wizard, pointing to the screen.

Jack cursed himself for having left his computer switched on and open. His instincts told him to behave as if nothing out of the ordinary had happened.

'I'm glad you've already had a look. Saves me having to show them to you later,' Jack said. 'This is Will, the guy who took them.' Jack pointed to his friend standing behind him. 'And of course you've already met Rebecca. Coffee?'

This guy is good, thought the Wizard, watching Jack out of the corner of his eye. He was used to putting people off balance by catching them unawares. Uncertainty created fear – the most powerful tool of all.

'Scotch would be better,' said the Wizard. 'I haven't slept in two days. It keeps me going.'

Jack walked over to the sideboard and poured a large whiskey into a tumbler.

'Whatever brings you here must be important,' he said, handing the glass to the Wizard. 'An early interview session perhaps? After such an eventful evening ...'

Jack noticed a flash of anger race across the Wizard's face. It only lasted for an instant, but it was a warning. He'd better tread carefully.

The Wizard gulped down his scotch and held out the empty glass.

Jack refilled it and put the bottle in front of him. 'Help yourself.'

'We have to suspend our little arrangement; temporarily,' said the Wizard. 'One of our guys had a heart attack during the parade ... You may have noticed?' Ignoring Rebecca completely, he was watching Will with half-closed eyes. Will held his gaze without flinching.

'An unfortunate incident. We don't think he's going to make it.' The Wizard put the laptop on the coffee table in front of him, turned it around so that the others could see the screen and pointed to the close-up of the Devil's face. It clearly showed a gaping hole where the left eye had been. 'With a heart attack like this, that's hardly surprising, is it?' he added quietly, changing the tone of his voice.

Jack, Will and Rebecca stared at the image on the small screen, the tension in the room rising with every heartbeat.

'We're sorry to hear that,' said Jack. 'Heart attacks can be very nasty.'

'I can see we understand each other,' said the Wizard, closing the laptop. 'Therefore, no Mardi Gras story and no photos – right?'

'It would be insensitive and disrespectful in the circumstances,' said Jack, watching the Wizard carefully as he refilled his glass and sat back.

'Well put. There's one more thing ... Don't contact any of our members for the time being, and if any of them should contact you, don't speak to them. Call me instead – okay? And keep in mind,' the Wizard continued, lowering his voice, 'that we have eyes and ears in the most unlikely places ...'

'No problem.'

'I knew I could count on you, Jack,' said the Wizard, standing up. Jack stood up as well.

'Stay with your friends, I'll see myself out. I know the way.'

Jack thought it sounded more like a command than a polite suggestion and sat down. Smiling, the Wizard walked over and put his huge hand on Jack's shoulder. Bending down until his moustache almost brushed against Jack's face, he whispered, 'And remember what we said about promises kept and promises broken.'

No one said a word until the roar of the three bikes had faded away.

'Jesus, can you believe this?' said Jack, running his fingers through his hair. 'Heart attack my arse! He knows that we know that he knows ...'

'And we just go along with his crap and do bugger all about it?' interrupted Will, shaking his head.

'What a scary guy,' said Rebecca. 'He moves people around like pieces on a chessboard and thinks nothing of it. So damn confident and afraid of nothing.' Feeling suddenly quite cold, she moved a little closer to Jack sitting on the couch next to her. 'We have to be careful,' she said, reaching for his hand.

'Arrogant bastard!' said Jack, trying to control his rising anger. The audacious home invasion had made him feel vulnerable.

131

'Some warning – eh,' said Will. 'Breaking in and then just sitting in your house like he owned it. I wonder how much he knows, and how much he suspects.'

'I'm not sure I want to find out. Okay, decision time, guys. You've heard what Cassandra had to say. What are we going to do?' asked Jack. Leaning back into the couch, he put his arm around Rebecca and looked expectantly at Will sitting opposite.

'Let's have another look at what she told us,' said Will.

'All right.' Jack pulled a small notebook out of his pocket and opened it. 'I've jotted down some of the key points. Always write things down straight away before your memory plays tricks on you, as your mum used to say – right, China? I've never forgotten that.'

'You've still got it,' said Will, pointing to the notebook, 'after all these years.' The leather cover – scratched and faded, and held together with a rubber band – was all that remained of the little notebook given to Jack by Will's mother; the pages had been replaced many times. Because Jack was always jotting down ideas on scraps of paper he used to stuff into his pockets, never to be found again, Will's mother had presented him with a lovely leather-bound notebook.

'Spinner's little book of inspiration, she used to call it – remember?' said Jack. 'One day, it'll make him famous.'

'If only she knew,' said Will, a melancholy look in his eyes.

'All right boys; don't get lost strolling down memory lane,' interrupted Rebecca. 'Anna was last seen in January 2005 in Alice Springs. The police investigation lasted about a year and Cassandra was brought in towards the end to assist the authorities.'

'Correct,' Jack agreed. 'Tristan's accident happened just before Christmas 2005. She withdrew from the case after that and the investigation was closed.'

'This is when it becomes really interesting,' interjected Will. 'As I recall it, Cassandra confronted the Wizard sometime in January 06 and then joined the club.'

'Yes. According to her, the main reason for that extraordinary step was to take care of her invalid son's needs. But she had a hidden agenda: she wanted to continue with the investigation into Anna's disappearance and bring the Wizards to justice,' said Jack. 'And the best way to do that was from the inside. First question: do we believe her?'

'I do,' replied Rebecca without hesitation.

'So do I,' concurred Will.

'That's a good start,' said Jack. 'Let me read what I've got here, if I can decipher my own shorthand: C's explanation extraordinary but plausible. Does fit facts. Is there more to it? Another angle? A different motif? Gut feeling uneasy!!'

'You're not sure then?' Rebecca said.

'Just a hunch ...' Jack said.

'It's what came after that I've got problems with,' interrupted Will. 'Have you got any notes on that?'

'I have. After joining the Wizards, C. makes enquiries. She claims to have discovered what happened to Anna and her friend, but refuses to tell us ...'

'Why?' Will cut in.

'She said we weren't ready,' Rebecca said.

'Isn't that a bit too convenient?' asked Will.

'Convenient? I don't think so,' said Jack. 'Desperate more like it. She has to get us over the line. She needs to hold something back. Desperate people do desperate things.'

Will didn't look convinced.

'That's one way to look at it, I suppose,' said Rebecca.

'Any problems so far?' asked Jack.

'It's an amazing story, but it does kind of stack up. Especially with the boy ... Well, it comes down to this: we either believe her, or we don't. What possible reason could she have to lie to us?' asked Rebecca.

'I can think of a few, but I do agree with you,' Will cut in, 'it has the ring of truth about it. As far as it goes ...'

'That brings us to what happened next,' said Jack, flicking through his notes. 'Do you remember what she said when we confronted her with the assassination?'

'Yes,' Will said. 'She was evasive. She said she could only tell us about that if we decided to go along with her proposal.'

'Correct. And this is her proposal: Cassandra believes that Anna is alive. She says she can find her, but only if we help.'

'What's in it for her?' interrupted Will.

'Look, Anna's mere existence is a major threat to the Wizards – it can bring them undone. This is Cassandra's only chance. Can't you see? She may have her own agenda, but for her it's a matter of survival. Her life and her son's future depend on finding Anna before the Wizards do,' Jack said.

'And exposing their bastardry,' interrupted Will.

'And that's where retribution comes in,' Rebecca interjected.

'Yep. Call it what you like, she's desperate. That's one hell of a motivation. Also, she's been completely frank about the dangers. The Wizard will stop at nothing to prevent all this and we already have some idea what this means – right? The stakes are high, but so are the rewards. Imagine finding Anna alive after all these years,' speculated Jack, remembering the countess kneeling in front of Anna's photo in the chapel.

'Let's not get too carried away here,' cautioned Will. 'It's all a bit of a long shot – surely?'

'Perhaps it is, and bloody dangerous,' said Jack, 'make no mistake about it. We are messing with ruthless people capable of anything, guys, let's be clear about this. Big risks here, even death ... I mean it! Have you considered this?'

'Understood,' said Will, 'but we are running out of time. What are we going to do? Do we take the gamble or walk away?'

'Becky?' asked Jack.

'We're all in this together – right?' replied Rebecca. 'So, why don't we just take a vote?'

'Fair enough,' Jack agreed.

Surprising everyone, Rebecca held up her hand. 'I say we go along with her,' she said, looking first at Jack, then at Will.

'So do I,' said Will.

'Me too,' Jack concurred. 'But what about the Canadian tour? All my engagements?'

'That can wait,' said Rebecca, casually brushing the question aside. What Jack couldn't have known was that Rebecca was ready for an adventure of her own. She was prepared to risk all to find the happiness that had eluded her during her relentless pursuit of a stellar career.

'Did you hear that, Will?' asked Jack, shaking his head in disbelief. 'I never thought she'd say that.'

'New Yorkers are unpredictable creatures, mate. You should know this by now, Spinner,' said Will, slapping Jack on the back.

'Not quite,' Rebecca cut in. 'Can you imagine the publicity we'd get should we really find Anna? The impact on Jack's career, his reputation, and on current book sales alone ... I don't think you guys quite comprehend what that would mean. It's surely worth the gamble.'

'See, we got it all wrong,' said Will, lowering his voice. 'Just when we thought she'd mellowed a little, she's been on the job all the time. Tough cookie this one, mate.'

'Tell me about it,' replied Jack with a shrug.

'Did you say something boys?' asked Rebecca.

'No,' both Jack and Will replied, grinning.

26

Rookwood Cemetery, Sydney, 28 February, 10:30 a.m.

The man in the black jeans and tee-shirt was the only visitor in the cemetery. Sunday morning was always quiet. Heavy with dew, intricate spider webs covered the rose bushes clustered around the little plaques like thorny shrouds, each one of them a solemn reminder of a dear departed. Momentarily confused, the man stopped, trying to orientate himself. All the manicured rows looked alike. It had been almost two years since his last visit. Retracing his steps, he walked back to the chapel and started again. His mother was in row twelve, he was sure of it.

All the emotions he had so carefully suppressed – the regrets, the sorrow, the horror and the pain – came flooding back with frightening clarity. Turning a corner, he found himself in familiar territory. *This is it*, he thought. A yellow rosebush greeted the morning sun next to a rock. In front of it was a small brass plaque set into the ground. 'Elvie Barton. Beloved mother ...' he read.

Choking with emotion, he fell to his knees and ran his trembling fingers along the inscription, his fingers leaving a dewy trail as he traced his mother's name.

'It's done, Mum,' he mumbled. 'The monster is no more. Now you can rest in peace. I know I've disappointed you. I've let you down, but I'll make it up to you, you'll see.'

Standing up, the man wiped the tears from his cheeks. He couldn't remember the last time he'd cried, but it felt good. *Closure at last*, he thought, trying to calm himself. The consuming rage he had felt since his mother's death was slowly ebbing away. However, instead of the peace he had so desperately longed for, all he could feel was emptiness and despair. He realised then that it wasn't finished yet. Something more had to be done. Something far more difficult.

'I know I have to set it right. The debts have to be paid. You always said it's never too late as long as you try and don't give up. I'll try, I promise,' he said.

Glancing once more at the humble little plaque, he turned around and walked away. As he reached the end of the row, he looked up and let out a mighty roar, releasing some of the pent up rage and sorrow that had been tearing his heart apart.

Then he clenched his fists as he did before every fight, and prepared himself for the long journey north. Soon he would be heading back to the land of his ancestors, his true home.

27
Wolf's Lair, 1 March, 11a.m.

The Wizard stood in the crypt – motionless and silent – and stared at his dead friend lying on the table.

'What are you thinking?' asked Zoran, walking up behind him.

'It's all coming together.'

'What do you mean?'

'I know the real reason why Rogan came to us ...'

'Oh?' Zoran put his hand on the Wizard's shoulder.

'I saw something in his bedroom.'

'What?'

'A photo of Anna Popov ...' said the Wizard.

'Are you sure?' Zoran withdrew his hand as if stung.

'Absolutely.'

'After all this time? Cassandra, you think?'

'Yes. And he knows Carlos was shot with a bullet meant for me.'

'This is serious.'

'It is.'

'What are you going to do about it?'

'We have to find Cassandra. Any news?'

'Could be. One of our contacts at the airport just rang.'

'What about?'

'Some CCTV footage from a departure gate. He's sending it over now.'

The Wizard spun around. 'Cassandra?'

Zoran replied with a shrug. 'Let's have a look.'

The faxed image – a close-up of a group of people waiting in a queue – was dark and grainy. A circle had been drawn around a petite, dark-haired woman leaning on a walking stick – with a question mark next to it. '9.15 to Alice Springs' was scribbled across the top of the fax.

'What do you think?' asked Zoran, handing the Wizard a magnifying glass.

'Not sure; can't see the face. But hey, what have we here?' exclaimed the Wizard, jabbing his finger at one of the other people in the queue behind the dark-haired woman. A hint of a smile began to spread across his face.

'What is it?'

'Here, have a look.' The Wizard pointed to another woman – her face shown clearly in profile – standing next to a tall man. The man was looking straight ahead, away from the camera.

'Rogan's girlfriend?' said Zoran excitedly.

'Yes. And I'm sure the guy next to her is our dear Jack. Now we know for sure, don't you think?' The Wizard glanced at his watch. It was 11 am.

'They're still in the air. And soon we'll be too,' he added. 'But first, let's give Zac a call.'

Zac Markovich, a publican in Alice Springs, was the Wizards' largest distributor of party drugs in the Northern Territory. He was also Zoran's older brother.

28

Alice Springs, Wandjina Gallery, 1 March, 3 p.m.

The first thing everyone seems to notice on arrival at Alice Springs is the dry heat and intense glare that make the lips crack and the eyes water. The hot air baking the red earth shimmered like liquid glass in the noonday sun when the small group walked out of the airport terminal building.

'We'll go straight to the gallery,' said Jack, helping Cassandra collect her duffel bag from the baggage trolley. 'Andrew's expecting us.' Rebecca had bought some clothes for Cassandra the day before. Dressed in jeans and tee-shirts, they looked like all the other tourists visiting Central Australia.

'I'll get a cab,' said Will, guiding Rebecca to the crowded exit. None of them noticed the young Aboriginal leaning casually against the wall next to the information counter. He was watching them carefully from behind dark glasses as they walked past, his broad-brimmed hat pulled down low to hide his face. He followed them outside and got into a dusty four-wheel drive waiting behind the taxi rank.

After accepting Cassandra's proposal, they had agreed that the best way forward would be for everyone to meet with Andrew Simpson in Alice Springs and continue where Cassandra and Andrew had left off three years before. It had quickly become obvious that Cassandra wasn't safe in Sydney and couldn't stay at Will's place for much longer. The Wizard's unexpected visit had unnerved them all.

Andrew Simpson's assistant – a young Aboriginal woman – asked them to wait. Andrew was delivering a painting to one of the hotels, she explained, and would be back shortly.

Cassandra walked over to where Jack was standing at the counter.

'May I have Anna's bracelet for a moment?' she asked. 'There's something here ...'

140

'Sure.' Jack reached into his pocket, pulled out the bracelet and handed it to her. Slowly, Cassandra began to walk from painting to painting, carefully examining each one. At the far end of the room she stopped and looked up at a large painting of Dinkarra, a great Dreamtime hero. Tracing the signature – 'Lucrezia' – in the bottom right hand corner with the tip of her finger, Cassandra placed her hand on the frame, closed her eyes and stood very still. She appeared to be listening intently. Jack watched her carefully from across the room.

'What's she doing?' asked Rebecca. 'She lives in her own world ...'

'Communicating with the spirits of the Outback perhaps?' Will cut in, unable to keep the sarcasm out of his voice.

'I hope we're not making a big mistake here,' whispered Rebecca, a worried look on her face.

'You were all in favour, remember? We have to give her a chance. She's different. Patience, please.'

'You're right.'

'Here's Andrew now. Let me introduce you.'

'Your phone call has certainly made me curious,' said Andrew, extending his hand. 'Where is she?'

Jack pointed to the far end of the room. Andrew excused himself and walked over to the petite woman standing motionless in front of the Dinkarra painting.

'What do you hear, Cassandra?' asked Andrew.

'The whisper of generations past,' she replied without opening her eyes.

'Our paths cross again,' Andrew said. Such answers were usually the province of a Kadaitcha man, a wise elder sitting by the campfire in the desert, and not of a woman standing in front of a Dreamtime painting in his art gallery.

'Can you understand what they're saying?' he asked.

'No, but I can feel what they mean. There's a connection here ...' Cassandra opened her eyes and turned towards Andrew. 'Between these paintings and Anna.'

'Do you know what it is?'

Cassandra looked wistfully at the bracelet in her hand. 'Not yet,' she replied. 'I can find out. But only if you help me.'

'What do you mean?'

'There are two different spirit worlds here. They overlap and collide. You of all people will understand. You're connected.'

Andrew looked puzzled.

'We have to confront something evil,' continued Cassandra.

'What?'

'I'll tell you. Come on, let's join the others.'

The walls of the small lounge room behind the gallery were covered with paintings. Some old ones were painted on bark, the colours smudged and fading. Others were painted on canvas or wooden boards.

'These are the paintings I can't part with,' explained Andrew. 'They're the storybooks of my people. As you can see, I'm running out of space. Please, make yourselves comfortable.'

'The energy in this room is amazing,' observed Cassandra, absorbing the fantastic shapes and colours closing in on her from all sides. They were the powerful images of a strange, distant past she couldn't quite comprehend.

'This is incredible,' said Rebecca, looking at the paintings. Andrew sat down facing Cassandra and rolled a cigarette.

'Last time we met, Andrew,' began Jack, 'you told me that you interviewed everyone who was at The Shed the night the two girls disappeared. All but one – the guy with the snake. I think you called him Shadow Man.'

'That's right,' replied Andrew, lighting up. 'We couldn't find him. It was as if he hadn't existed at all. He disappeared without a trace.'

'Not quite ...' said Jack.

'What do you mean?'

'I think you should hear this from the psychic you brought in to help you find him,' replied Jack, pointing to Cassandra.

Surprised, Andrew looked at Cassandra through the cigarette smoke. Leaning back in the chair, she closed her eyes and was taking deeper and deeper breaths, shutting out everything around her.

'Let me tell you a story,' she began, speaking quite softly. 'A middle-aged, hardened criminal who has spent more than half his life behind bars, befriends a young Aboriginal man – a first timer – in jail. The older man wields enormous power and influence among the inmates and the guards. The impressionable young man falls under his spell. For the next two years the older man runs the affairs of a notorious outlaw motorcycle club from inside prison. The young man becomes his protégé.

'After his release, the young man wants to join the club. In line with club tradition, an initiation task is set by the council in charge of recruitment. If he can pass, he becomes a member. Some members of the council oppose his candidacy. They don't want to admit an Aborigine into the club and deliberately set an extremely difficult task which they don't expect him to be able to fulfil: he has to abduct two girls and deliver them to the Wizards as part of his initiation. What's more, he has to accomplish this without being caught or in any way implicating the club or any of its members ...'

Cassandra's voice became faint and trailed off. The cigarette between Andrew's fingers had turned into a column of ash which fell unnoticed to the floor. No one moved.

'What happened?' asked Jack after a while.

'Contrary to expectation, the young man is successful. He abducts two girls right here in Alice Springs and turns up with them at the Wizards' remote farm near Bathurst in New South Wales, just as the council had directed.'

'You can't be serious, surely!' Andrew was almost shouting.

Cassandra opened her eyes and looked at him. Embarrassed, he lowered his gaze and reached for his tobacco.

'Each year, the Wizards import enough pseudoephedrine from the Netherlands to manufacture many millions of dollars worth of the drug, ice. That's their core business,' continued Cassandra, closing her eyes again.

'The courier business is an ingenious cover for the distribution of the drugs. The remote farm is being used at that time by the Wizards to manufacture and store huge quantities of ice. It is also used for their initiation ceremonies,' said Cassandra, turning pale.

'What happened to the girls?' interrupted Andrew.

'Drugged and very weak, the girls arrive at the farm.'

'How?'

'In a caravan.' Satisfied with the answer, Andrew nodded.

'The Wizard officiates during the initiation ritual,' Cassandra continued. 'The girls are subjected to the most unspeakable abuse, during which one of them dies ...'

'If any of this is true, why didn't you come forward sooner?' demanded Andrew.

'Easy. Andrew, please,' Jack stepped in, 'give her a chance. There are reasons ...'

Suddenly, Cassandra's whole body began to tremble. Beads of sweat appeared on her upper lip and forehead and her eyelids began to flutter.

'I have to lie down,' she whispered, her voice barely audible. 'He's close. Very close ... He will ...'

Rebecca rushed over to Cassandra, knelt down beside her and placed her hand on the psychic's flushed forehead.

'She's fainted!' exclaimed Rebecca, looking alarmed.

'We'll take her to the bedroom,' said Andrew, getting out of his chair. 'This way, come on. Quickly!'

29
Alice Springs, The Drover's Retreat, 1 March, 6:00 p.m.

The Drover's Retreat – a rundown pub on the outskirts of Alice – was popular with the locals but had seen better days. Sitting back in his rickety cane chair, the Wizard was surveying the veranda in front of his room. The corrugated iron roof had large holes in it, the handrail was broken in several places, and the floorboards were slowly rotting away. Casting long shadows across the dusty road below, the setting sun was about to disappear behind the ancient red hills, promising some relief from the searing heat. Somewhere a bush band was playing country and western music.

'What a dump,' said the Wizard, reaching for another beer. 'And you tell me we own half of it.'

'It's making money,' replied Zoran, spreading his fingers. 'The accommodation's crap, but the bar and the steakhouse downstairs are pure gold.'

'Thank God for that.' Tired and irritable, the Wizard was drumming his fingers against the tabletop.

'Where the fuck is he? He should have been here an hour ago.' The Wizard found waiting difficult at the best of times. Sladko was pacing up and down behind him like a caged animal ready to pounce, the floorboards creaking every time he walked past.

'Sit down, for Christ's sake, you're making me jumpy.'

The late afternoon flight from Sydney had been tiresome, uncomfortable, and full of excited tourists, making them all edgy.

Sweating and out of breath, Zac the publican arrived with a case of beer under his arm.

'What a sight. The Wizards relaxing in the Outback; who would have believed it?' he said, putting the beer on the floor. 'Here, go for it, guys. Cheers.'

'It's about bloody time. Where did they go?'

'To a house just out of town. Our guys are watching it.'

'Whose house?'

'A man called Simpson, a retired cop. He runs an art gallery out there. Abo stuff for tourists.'

'Ah. Just as I thought,' said the Wizard, a smile spreading across his face. 'I wonder ... Are they still there?'

'Here comes Banjo now,' said Zac, pointing to a young Aboriginal getting out of a ute. 'He's been following them all day. Why don't you ask him?'

'Is he okay?'

'You can trust him with your life.'

Whistling loudly, Zac walked over to the handrail. 'Up here, mate,' he shouted, waving his hat.

'They arrived together from Sydney,' reported Banjo. 'Two men and two women. One of the women is really little and limps and has a walking stick. Here are some photos.' The man handed the Wizard his digital camera.

'Have a look at these, Zoran. Recognise anyone?' The Wizard pushed the camera across the table.

'Great. Now we know for sure. But what are they doing here?'

'I've got a fair idea. Where are they now?' asked the Wizard. 'Still at the copper's place?'

Banjo nodded.

'You wanted to find the bitch,' Sladko cut in, 'now we have. Why don't we just bring her in and ask her? I'm sure we can make her squeal. What do you reckon, Zoran? And we can take care of the others at the same time – right?'

'We'll do nothing of the kind. She'll tell us all right, but not the way you think.' The Wizard turned to Zac, standing beside him. 'I need your help.'

'What's mine is yours,' replied Zac, turning serious. 'You know that.'

'We need wheels, weapons, supplies, the lot. And someone reliable who knows the country around here,' added the Wizard. 'Any problems with that?'

'You got it.'

'Are we going somewhere?' asked Sladko.

'You bet we are,' said the Wizard.

'Where?' asked Zoran, belching loudly.

'Wait and see. And don't get too pissed.' The Wizard looked at Zac. 'Have the copper's place watched round the clock,' he said, standing up. 'I'm taking a kip. If they make a move, wake me.'

30
Alice Springs, Wandjina Gallery,
1 March, 8:00 p.m.

Rebecca sat by the window in Andrew's lounge room watching the sun go down, when something caught her eye. Looking up, she saw Cassandra standing in the doorway.

'Where is everybody?' asked Cassandra quietly. 'What time is it?'

'You went out like a light. The boys have gone to dinner. Come over here and sit with me.' Rebecca motioned to the chair opposite.

Cassandra limped over and sat down. Running her fingers through her short hair, she looked up at the paintings surrounding them on all sides. The strange shapes and colours looked even more mysterious at night.

'Do you mind if I ask you something?' began Rebecca, closing the book on her lap.

'Go ahead.'

'Remember what you said to me when we first met?'

'We haven't met, but I think we know each other,' replied Cassandra without hesitation.

'What did you mean by that?'

'When I meet people for the first time, I often feel things. An aura, a life force, a presence. It's difficult to articulate, but it's real. Yours was particularly strong and familiar. It was the same with Jack. It was as if we'd met before and were destined to meet again. Here, right now in these unusual circumstances. You and I have met before ... Our fate lines have touched in an eternity moment. This happens sometimes during a reading, but without the cards, it's rare.'

Rebecca tried hard not to smile.

'It's perfectly natural for someone like you to feel this way about such things,' continued Cassandra, locking eyes with Rebecca.

Rebecca bit her lip and looked away. It's always disconcerting when someone reads your thoughts.

'But it wasn't always that way, was it?'

'What do you mean?'

'You grew up in the country, in a closed community of rather special people. Different people ...'

Rebecca sat up as if pricked by a needle.

'Theirs was a different world. They had different rules and beliefs and a very different way of life. A spiritual life, withdrawn from the wider world around them – right?'

'How do you know this?' Rebecca whispered.

Cassandra reached for Rebecca's hand and closed her eyes. Suddenly, Rebecca felt relaxed and at ease. Something warm and comforting seemed to pass to her from the woman sitting opposite.

'I know because of who I am.'

'I don't understand.'

'I have a gift, handed down to me from long ago. My mother had it too, as did her mother before her, reaching back generations. It's both a blessing and a curse. But you know exactly what I mean, don't you?' Cassandra opened her eyes and looked at Rebecca.

Cassandra's eyes had turned into dark pools – deep and mysterious gateways into a different consciousness – beckoning Rebecca to enter.

Looking into those eyes, Rebecca saw herself as a little girl back on her parents' farm in Pennsylvania. Often she would see things before they happened and hear people talking to her who weren't there. When she told her brothers they laughed, until one day she warned one of them, a carpenter, not to climb on top of a particular roof. He ignored her. She even ran to her father and pleaded with him not to let him do it. He told her not to be silly. The brother fell from the roof and broke his neck. After this her life changed. She became an outcast, someone to be avoided. Her deeply religious and superstitious family was afraid of her. Rebecca could hear Cassandra's words, 'You know exactly what I mean', ringing in her ears like a mantra. Then she saw herself standing naked in front of her mother, crying. Searching for a telltale mark, her mother had cut off her daughter's long hair and examined every inch of her shivering little body. Rebecca withdrew her hand and lowered her eyes, hoping the disturbing image would go away.

'It's never easy being different,' said Cassandra, a gentle smile spreading across her troubled face.

'No, it isn't.'

'Your relationships with men ...'

'What of it?'

'They're attracted to you, and you want to like them, but ...'

'But what?' Rebecca snapped, caught off guard.

'Hush ... You're different.'

'I am?'

'You know you are. Deep down, in your own secret little place, you are attracted not to men, but ...'

'That's nonsense!' protested Rebecca, her voice sounding shrill.'

'Is it?'

Biting her lip, Rebecca looked away.

'Your marriages failed, not because you fell in love with another man, but because you fell in love with ...'

'No!' interrupted Rebecca, tears in her eyes.

'There's no need to be afraid,' said Cassandra.

'Afraid of what?' interrupted Rebecca.

'To admit it.'

'Look ... how about we have something to eat?' Rebecca asked. Pale and shaken, she changed the subject. 'Andrew said we should just help ourselves.'

The kitchen was at the back of the cottage next to the stables which had been converted into bedrooms.

'My repertoire is somewhat limited, I'm afraid,' confessed Rebecca, peering into the fridge. 'But my omelettes aren't too bad. Okay with you?'

Cassandra nodded gratefully. 'I'll set the table.'

'Another question – do you mind?' asked Rebecca beating the eggs.

'Go ahead.'

'You said this afternoon that there was great danger and evil close by. What was that about?'

Cassandra stopped rummaging through the kitchen drawers and looked up. 'I felt something ...'

'What?'

Cassandra paled. 'A presence.'

'Oh?'

'The Wizard is close by.'

'What – here?'

Cassandra nodded.

It was obvious Rebecca didn't believe her. 'Tell me more,' she said as she served the omelette.

'Every once in a while the forces that shape our destiny throw up something really frightening, something truly evil,' said Cassandra once they were seated at the table. 'History is full of examples. The Wizard is one of those ... creatures. He's the scariest person I've ever come across. A freak.'

'In what way?'

'He has no moral constraints whatsoever. He's capable of anything. For him, the unthinkable is normal. Also, he's a man without fear. I mean no fear at all. He's only in awe of one thing – the occult. The most frightening thing, though, is his ability to manipulate others. He puts people under his spell and they do his bidding – unconditionally. I've seen it many times. It's quite amazing.'

'But he's been to jail for many years ...'

'Yes, and he's built an empire from in there. He's turned being imprisoned into a career.'

'How?'

'Virtually all the club members – certainly most of the council – were recruited in jail. New members are selected very carefully. Personality traits, strengths and weaknesses, professional experience, are all evaluated by the Wizard personally. He even has what he calls a "usefulness scale". The name says it all. Look, the Wizards have accountants, doctors, engineers, lawyers, politicians, even a former police commissioner, in their ranks. What the Wizard lacks in education and skills, he takes from others. He uses people. He has finely honed instincts and a sixth sense bordering on the uncanny. Hallmarks of a very talented, evil genius.'

'Amazing.'

'When you add a lot of money to all this, and I mean a *lot* of money – almost exclusively generated through the club's sophisticated drug trafficking operations – you have the Wizards of Oz. A criminal moneymaking machine based on a winning, virtually invincible formula.'

'What formula?'

'Complete dependence of all the members on the club and each other, and a code of conduct based on obedience and silence with one man at the helm – the Wizard. Look, these men are all outcasts. They're the lepers of society. They have nowhere to go. Yet in the Wizard's world, they can become heroes where the very deeds and character flaws that turned them into criminals are valued and rewarded, even respected and admired. Everything's upside down.'

'What about your son? Isn't he at risk after all that's just happened?'

'You mean with me on the run and the Wizard after me?'

'Yes.'

'You can't harm what appears already dead,' replied Cassandra sadly. 'Tristan is beyond reach, and the Wizard knows it.'

'I see.'

'Do you? I think not.'

'Oh? How come?'

'All is not as it seems.'

'What do you mean?'

'My son is safe where he is just now. In fact, he's in the safest place I could wish for.'

'I don't understand.'

'At the moment, I can't protect him – right? I can't even visit him anymore. The worst thing that could happen is for him to come out of his coma. If that were to occur, the Wizard would gain a foolproof way to get to me. Tristan can only wake up safely when the Wizard is no more. And that is precisely what he will do – one day.'

'How can you be so sure?'

'Because I've ... made a pledge ...'

'What pledge?'

'You'll find out ...'

'I will?'

'Because you're part of it all. Our lives are intertwined – inextricably. Yours, mine, Jack's. And now, Will and Andrew are part of it too.'

'And Anna?'

'She's the hub of the wheel; we're only the spokes. She's the one who brought us here, remember?'

'And the Wizard – where does he fit into all this?'

'He knows Anna can bring him down. She's a big threat and a huge blow to his ego. She and ...'

'And who?'

'The only man who dared to challenge his authority – and is still alive. The Wizard will do everything in his power to destroy them both. Especially after the Mardi Gras, he's even more dangerous than before. This is a fight to the end. We're all at risk. I only hope I made this clear.'

'You did.'

'I won't see Tristan wake up, but *you* will.' Cassandra pushed her plate aside and got unsteadily to her feet. 'Are you prepared to make a promise?'

'What kind of promise?'

'If I lead you to Anna, will you promise to help my son?'

'I don't understand. You speak as if you ...' Sensing where this was heading, Rebecca stopped.

'Were no longer there to help him? That's exactly what I mean. It's a big ask, I know. But there's so little time ...'

Despite the balmy evening, Rebecca felt suddenly quite cold. 'But why?' she asked, struggling to understand the implications of what she was being told.

'Confronting the Wizard has a price ...'

'Could it be that high?'

'It could.'

Rebecca paused. Her mind racing, she reached deep within herself to make sure that she could make such a promise. 'Why me?' she asked, her voice sounding hoarse.

'Because this is a promise only a woman can truly comprehend. A woman just like you.'

'I will,' whispered Rebecca at last, barely able to speak.

Awkwardly, Cassandra stood and walked around the table. Standing in front of Rebecca she steadied herself and looked into her face. This time her dark eyes did not turn into seductive pools. Instead, her eyes glistened with sadness. Placing the palm of her hand gently against Rebecca's cheek, she bent down.

'Sometimes glimpsing the future can be a great burden,' she whispered, tears rolling down her pale cheeks. 'My son, too, has the gift, only his is far stronger than mine. He can hear the whisper of angels and glimpse eternity.' Slowly, she brought her lips closer to Rebecca's.

'You will see,' she sighed, kissing Rebecca tenderly on the mouth.

PART II.
PIGEON

31

Alice Springs, The Drover's Retreat,
1 March, 8:00 p.m.

'Eugene, wake up,' said Zoran. He was about to shake his leader by the shoulder when the Wizard opened his eyes, and grabbed Zoran's wrist in a vice-like grip. In jail, being a light sleeper was a matter of survival.

'Easy, mate. It's me,' soothed Zoran.

'What's up?' demanded the Wizard, releasing his friend.

'We've got visitors.'

'Who?'

'I'll show you.'

The steakhouse on the ground floor was packed and noisy. Every table was taken and there was a queue at the door. The open kitchen at the back was in full swing. Waitresses were shouting orders at a couple of Aboriginal chefs who were cooking huge steaks on the charcoal grill.

'There, can you see them?' asked Zoran, pointing to the three men seated at a table next to the crowded bar. 'Keep your head down.'

The Wizard turned to Zoran and smiled. 'How long have they been here?' he asked.

'A few minutes.'

'Where are the women?'

'They stayed at the house.'

'I'd love to know what they're talking about,' mused the Wizard, playing with his earring.

'This is our chance, can't you see? We've got to make a move,' urged Zoran, becoming excited. 'The women are at home alone, and the men are right here in the pub – our pub. Perfect!'

'You *would* say that,' replied the Wizard. 'And miss the lot!'

157

He turned to Zac, standing next to him. 'Can you ask one of your girls to stay near them? See if she can overhear something – anything at all?'

'You got it.'

'We better stay out of sight,' said the Wizard. 'Upstairs, fellas.'

'There are two reasons I brought you here,' said Andrew, handing the menu back to the waitress. 'The guy who owns this place used to run The Shed ...'

Jack looked up, surprised.

'A bit of a shady character. After The Shed was closed down, he bought the Drovers' Retreat here and is gradually doing it up. Very popular with the locals – as you can see.'

'And the second reason?' asked Will.

'Wait till you see your steak.'

'I see what you mean,' said Will, pushing his empty plate aside. 'What a piece of beef!'

'What do you make of Cassandra's story so far?' asked Jack. 'I think she's telling us the truth – as she sees it,' answered Andrew, watching the waitress clear the table. 'What else did she tell you about the girls?'

Jack waited until the waitress had finished. 'She was a bit tight-lipped about this at first. I think she knows a lot more, but all she told us was that there are no words to describe what was done to Anna and her friend at the farm. Black magic, torture, Satanism ... The Wizard is obsessed with sex and death.'

'Jesus!'

'Yeah. And that's when things started to go wrong,' Will cut in. 'Listen to this: Anna's friend died during some bizarre sexual ritual ... and Anna apparently snapped. She lost her mind ...'

'And this turned into a big problem for the Wizards,' continued Jack. 'Normally, the girls would have been drugged and dropped at a backpacker's hostel somewhere in Sydney after the event. Apparently, the Wizards have done this many times before. Usually, the girls would then get on the first available plane and leave the country, desperate to get back home. And that would be the end of it. But not this time. The body of the dead girl was disposed of. Acid. In a barrel ... Some club members wanted to do away with Anna then and there and make her disappear too, but the Wizard wouldn't hear of it. His ego got in the way. Anna was no threat, he argued. He turned her into his plaything, his slave, whenever he visited the farm. A human pet. She became the club's mascot. Because it would have been too risky to take her to Sydney, she was kept at the farm. Locked up most of the time.'

'That's when she could have carved her name into that secretaire – right?' interrupted Will.

'Most likely, yes,' Jack said. 'It all seems to fit, including the date.'

'What happened to the new member?' asked Andrew.

'He was admitted and put in charge of security,' Jack said.

'What do you mean?'

'The Wizards manufactured all their drugs – mainly ice – at the farm,' explained Jack, lowering his voice. 'The remote farmhouse had been converted into a sophisticated lab. The farm was like a fortress – armed guards, patrols, the lot. The Alchemist was in charge of producing the drugs, and the new boy looked after security.'

'Then he would have been responsible for keeping Anna locked up ...' Will said.

'Does this new boy have a name?' interrupted Andrew.

'This is where we hit a problem. Don't forget, all this happened before Cassandra joined the Wizards. Upon admission into the world of the Wizards of Oz, you leave your identity and your old life behind. Club rules. Surnames are dropped and no longer relevant. Instead, only first names or nicknames are used: Wizard, Alchemist, Undertaker ... Cassandra.'

'A bit like entering a monastery,' interrupted Will. 'Belonging, obedience, control. A new name, a new life. Even the Pope adopts a new name when he's elected – right? Leave all the baggage behind, obey the rules and the Wizard will look after you as long as you toe the line. How neat.'

Jack pushed his plate aside and looked at Andrew. 'Something keeps bothering me,' he said.

'What?' said Andrew.

'You told us that it was Cassandra who contacted the police with an offer to help.'

'That's right.'

'What reason did she give?'

'I can't remember, but I think she had some information ...'

'What, about a bikie gang being involved?'

'Yes, I think so. It was certainly Cassandra who first raised this question with the police. Until then, no one had considered such a possibility. There wasn't a shred of evidence ...'

'What reasons did she give?'

'Not sure, but clairvoyants rarely give reasons, do they?'

'Don't you think that's a little odd? She only joined the Wizards after she retired from the case.'

'With the benefit of hindsight, yes, it's certainly a little odd. But we were clutching at straws by then.'

'I wonder how she came by that information in the first place,' said Jack.

'Perhaps she saw it in the cards?' suggested Will, throwing a little mischief into the ring.

'I doubt it,' said Jack.

'More wine, gents?' asked the waitress, smiling at Jack. Jack nodded.

'I think she fancies you, mate,' teased Will. 'She can't take her eyes off you. She's barely left our table ...'

'City charm, mate. Outback chicks find it irresistible,' replied Jack, feeling a little chuffed.

'What did they call him?' asked Andrew, fidgeting in his seat. 'You know, after his admission?'

'He was known as Pigeon. Funny name. Cassandra never heard his real name mentioned.'

'Pigeon?' repeated Andrew, looking thoughtfully into his glass. 'How odd. And he was an Aborigine? I wonder ...'

The waitress put the bill on the table next to Jack. 'Does the name ring a bell?' asked Will.

'Pigeon ... Not sure. Perhaps ...' Andrew glanced at his watch. 'But it's worth finding out. Come on, I'll take you to Auntie. She might know something.'

'Auntie? How exciting,' said Jack. He drained his glass and stood up. 'Let's go and meet Auntie. What a crazy place. Lead on ...'

'Tell him,' said Zac, pointing to the Wizard. Looking a little alarmed, the waitress walked over to the three men sitting on the veranda.

'It was very difficult to hear anything,' she began haltingly, 'the noise ...'

'It's okay, luv – don't worry,' said the Wizard, trying to put her at ease. He pulled a fifty dollar note out of his pocket and handed it to her. 'Here, take it. Is there anything you can remember? Anything at all?'

'There was something towards the end ...'

Leaning forward, the Wizard watched her carefully.

'They were talking about a guy with a funny name ...'

'What name?' asked the Wizard quietly.

'Pigeon?'

32

Alice Springs, Todd River, 1March, 10:00 p.m.

'Where are we going?' asked Jack, following Andrew to the car.

'To the tragic side of Alice,' replied Andrew sadly.

To call the Todd a river was absurd, most of the time. The riverbed was completely dry and a favourite hangout for homeless Aboriginals at night. Every tourist visiting Alice had been told not to go there and tall wire fences protected the hotels and resorts along the banks of the river which cut right through town. When the rains did come, the river could turn into a torrent, but not that year.

'Stay close to me,' said Andrew, climbing down the sandy embankment past mountains of rubbish and broken glass. Dark shapes began to melt out of the shadows. A man holding a bottle staggered towards Andrew.

'It's okay, bro,' said Andrew, holding up his hand, 'they're with me.' Recognising Andrew, the man retreated.

'Where's Auntie?' Andrew called out after him.

'By the fire,' answered a voice out of the darkness.

A small fire had been lit in the middle of the dry riverbed. An old man sat on a rock next to it. Another man was throwing empty beer cartons into the flames. Surrounded by empty bottles and crushed beer cans, several men and women – obviously drunk – were lying on the ground.

'That's Auntie over there,' said Andrew, pointing to a white-haired Aboriginal woman kneeling next to the old man. She was bandaging his head.

'Auntie's a retired nurse. She set up a small group of volunteers who try to look after these lost souls,' explained Andrew. 'Without much success, I'm afraid. What you see around you is the result of alcohol abuse and despair – years of it. These guys here are too old to be rescued. They're too far gone. The only hope lies with the young ones. If we can get to them early enough. That's what I'm trying to do.'

'How goes it, Auntie?' asked Andrew, walking up to the woman.

'Only one tonight – so far. He fell and cut himself. Didn't you? Silly duffer.' The old man nodded.

Andrew pulled a small wad of ten dollar notes out of his pocket. 'Supplies cost money,' he said, stuffing the cash into Auntie's pocket.

'Thanks. You obviously didn't come here just to make a donation,' replied the woman. She gathered up her first aid kit and got unsteadily to her feet.

'No. We're after some information. This is Jack, and Will – friends of mine.'

The woman nodded. 'I thought so.'

They followed Auntie to another fire on the other side of the riverbank. A large cooking pot, its blackened rim scratched and dented, stood on a makeshift grate straddling the embers. Sitting in a semicircle on the ground, several old women were chopping up vegetables.

'Our field kitchen and my helpers,' said Auntie, pointing to the little group. 'A hot meal and a bandaid is all we can offer these poor bastards.'

'Oh no,' Andrew said, 'you offer much more ...'

'May I also ...?' Jack pulled out his wallet. Will did the same.

'Every dollar counts,' said Andrew. 'Go ahead.'

'So, what do you want to know?' asked Auntie, gesturing towards a large tree – its roots entangled under a rock – that had floated down the river during the last flood. 'We can sit there.'

'Does the name Pigeon ring a bell?' asked Andrew, rolling a cigarette.

'Sure. Pigeon was Jandamarra's nickname.' Auntie turned to Jack, leaning against the tree trunk next to her. 'Do you know who Jandamarra was?' she asked.

'No, I don't,' Jack said.

'Jandamarra was an Aboriginal freedom fighter during the 1890s up in the Kimberley. He fought the white pastoralists invading his homeland for years. He was the leader of the Bunuba Resistance. He's quite a legend 'round here.'

'I can remember a young Aboriginal man working on a cattle station up north a few years ago,' said Andrew, 'also called Pigeon. He used to get into fights – regularly.'

'Oh yes; Elvie's boy ... A wild kid that one. Always in trouble with the law,' Auntie added sadly. 'Like so many.'

'Do you know what happened to him?'

'No, but I know what happened to Elvie.'

'What?' asked Andrew, inhaling deeply.

'She went to live in Sydney with a bloke and died in a fire a couple of years ago.'

'What about the boy?'

'I could ask around. Elvie's rels still live here.'

'It's urgent.'

'As a matter of fact ... Stay here.'

Auntie got up and walked over to the women standing around the cooking pot.

'Jandamarra and the Bunuba Resistance?' asked Jack. 'What was all that about?'

'I'll tell you later,' said Andrew. 'Here she comes.'

'I just spoke to Elvie's cousin. That woman over there,' said Auntie, pointing over her shoulder. 'The last she heard, young Pigeon was travelling through Queensland with a boxing troupe. Apparently he's very good with his fists.'

'Sure is. That's what got him into trouble. Does this outfit have a name?' Andrew asked hopefully, rolling another cigarette.

'Yes. A crazy Irishman called O'Grady runs it. One of the last old-timers. He's been 'round for years.'

'Fisticuffs. Bingo!' said Andrew, pulling another wad of notes out of his pocket. 'This should pay for the spuds. Thanks Auntie. I owe you.'

33
Alice Springs, 2 March

Jack was an early riser. Rebecca was still asleep in her own room. To avoid complications – especially while travelling with the others – they had decided to sleep in separate rooms. The decision was paying off. It added an extra little spark. A knowing look, a quick touch was all it took to ignite the simmering passion. Rather naively they thought that the others were not aware of this.

'You're up early,' said Jack, walking into the kitchen.

Andrew was sitting at the table, a large map spread out in front of him. 'I went to see Elvie's cousin this morning ... Our pigeon has a name,' said Andrew. 'Billy Woorunmurra – an interesting character.' Andrew poured Jack a cup of black tea and pushed it across the table.

'You have been a busy little detective,' said Jack, sipping the hot brew.

'And the character's taking shape. He comes from Fitzroy Crossing. Apparently, his father – a Bunuba – was a Jalngangurru, just like Jandamarra.'

'A what?'

'A respected elder with magical powers. He was an activist and a spokesman for disenfranchised blackfellas, a key player in persuading the federal government to purchase several large pastoral properties on behalf of the Aboriginal communities in the Kimberley. Young Pigeon grew up on one of those – Leopold Downs, a famous property. It was later renamed Yaranggi.'

'And?'

'His mother ran off with another man and went to live in Sydney. She took Billy with her. That's when things started to go wrong.'

'In what way?'

'The usual things. Ghetto living, poverty, alcohol abuse, domestic violence, bad company. The boy was always in trouble. I already checked his record. He did two years in Long Bay for assault.'

'When was that?'

'About 2002, I think.'

'That's when he met the Wizard,' said Cassandra, limping into the room. 'They both got out in late 2004.'

'And Anna disappeared in January 2005. This could be our Shadow Man,' observed Jack.

'Maybe – but we'll only know for sure when Cassandra sees him.'

'Yes, but how ...?'

'He'll be right here tonight,' said Andrew, tapping the map with his finger.

'How do you know?' asked Jack.

'I also spoke to a few old copper mates this morning. Apparently, O'Grady's outfit left Kununurra – there – yesterday and is travelling to Fitzroy Crossing – down here. The word is, there's a big fight on tonight ...'

'Pigeon?'

'Could be, if he's still with O'Grady. We'll find out when we get there, won't we?'

'But that's a thousand kilometres away,' said Jack, studying the map.

'Relax, Jack,' said Andrew, 'this is the Outback. One of my mates will lend us his plane and I've got a pilot's licence. We'll get there in plenty of time.'

'Well? What are they up to?' asked the Wizard.

'The ex-copper just filed a flight plan to Fitzroy Crossing,' reported Zac, trying to catch his breath. 'They're about to take off.'

'What?' bellowed the Wizard, slamming his fist on the table.

'Don't worry; we've got a plane too – a faster one. We might even get there before them,' said Zac, looking pleased with himself. 'Everything's arranged – come on.'

Halfway around the world, a maid put down the phone and hurried back to the chapel. Reaching the door, she hesitated. The chapel was strictly off limits to all staff. However, the countess's instructions were explicit: if a phone call came in from Australia – day or night – she was to be informed immediately. The maid pushed open the heavy wooden door and went inside.

'A phone call for you, Madame,' she said softly, walking towards the dark figure kneeling in front of the altar. The countess didn't move. 'From Australia,' added the maid, raising her voice a little. Slowly, the countess turned her head.

'What did you say?' she whispered, looking at the maid with teary eyes.

'A phone call from Australia,' repeated the maid. 'A Mr Rogan ...

The countess drew in her breath, stood up and hurried out of the chapel.

'Jack?' asked the countess, barely able to speak.

'Yes ... can you hear me?' The voice sounded distant and distorted. 'The reception out here isn't the best I'm afraid, and it's a bit noisy. I've been trying to reach you all morning.'

'Where are you?'

'Alice Springs. At the airport with Andrew Simpson. We're about to take off.' The countess felt suddenly dizzy, the mention of Alice Springs conjuring up memories too painful to bear. 'I wanted to give you an update.'

'Oh God. Is there any news ...?'

'Not sure yet, but we have a lead ...'

'What lead?'

'We may have found the Shadow Man.'

'After all these years?'

'Yes.' Jack's voice trailed off as the engine noise in the background grew louder. 'We'll know more tonight. I've got to go. Call you later.'

The countess returned to the chapel and knelt down in front of the altar. Closing her eyes she began to pray, but the prayer sounded hollow.

Instead, pictures of Anna floated into her mind's eye. Anna as a little girl running through the gardens, her long blonde hair reflecting the sunlight; Anna sitting on her grandfather's lap, her little hand stroking his beard; Anna standing next to her in the chapel, her eyes wide with wonder. Then the pictures changed. Anna as a young woman – tanned, her hair cut short – pointing to a strange painting on a rock ledge.

'This is the Rainbow Serpent, Mummy,' the countess heard her say. 'I have to save it ... You do understand, don't you?'

Opening her eyes, the countess expected to see Anna. Instead, all she could see was the candles flickering in the silver candelabra on the altar in front of her.

34
Fitzroy Crossing: O'Grady's boxing tent, 2 March, 4:30 p.m.

'I'll be sorry to see you go, Captain,' said Jim O'Grady, handing a tent post to Pigeon. 'You've been one of my best lads. Hold this.'

Now in his seventies, but still as strong as a Brahman bull, Jim 'Fisticuffs' O'Grady wasn't known for his compliments. A notorious bare-knuckle boxing champion during the 1950s, he now ran one of the last tent boxing troupes touring outback Australia.

'It'll finish where it all began,' replied Pigeon, lifting up the post. 'Right here in Fitzroy Crossing. Remember Jock MacDonald, the mad Scotsman?'

'Braveheart with the handlebar moustache? Wearing a kilt in the ring and nothing else? Hard to forget that fight. Two hours and you beat the crap out of him.'

'Yea. And Haggis Jock almost killed me. But you patched me up and offered me a job.'

'Why the sudden departure?'

'Two years is enough. Anyway, I've got some unfinished business ...'

O'Grady nodded. Outback boxing was a fickle game at the best of times. 'I've always wanted to ask you this: where did a kid like you learn to box like that – eh?'

'In jail ... Now, let's lift it up. One, two, three ...'

'It'll be a big night. Everyone wants to see the local boy with the big reputation ...'

'Beaten by a new kid on the block, I bet? Well, let them try,' replied Pigeon, laughing. 'Don't worry, Jim, we'll make a bundle tonight, you'll see. Farewell present.'

'Midget! Where the fuck are ya?' shouted O'Grady, straining under the weight of the tent post. 'We can't hold this forever!'

Midget, all of 1.25 metres, came running with the toolbox. 'Sorry, boss. Everyone wants to know when we're starting.'

'Tell 'em the first fight's at six. Now, fix the pegs, for Christ's sake. Get a move on!'

By the time the Cessna touched down, it was almost five in the afternoon.

'Welcome to Fitzroy Crossing,' announced Andrew, adjusting the throttle.

'We came all that way in this tiny jalopy for this?' said Rebecca, climbing stiffly out of her seat, her ears buzzing from hours of monotonous engine noise. 'I don't believe it.'

'Thirty years in the air and still going strong,' replied Andrew, patting the wing of the small plane. 'She's a trusty old girl.'

'What next?' asked Jack, helping Cassandra out of the plane.

'One of my mates left his Land Cruiser here at the airport for us to use. We'll go straight to the pub, I suppose. O'Grady always uses the same spot: the beer garden at the back. Tradition,' Andrew said.

'You're just like Jack,' Rebecca cut in, shaking her head, 'a mate for everything.'

'Don't knock it. We got here, didn't we?' said Jack.

'We did. Eight hours flying across the desert in a hot sardine can.'

'Think of it as an adventure,' said Will breezily.

'Sure. Tagging along with you guys is one big party. I just hope I can survive all the fun, that's all.'

The converted old Leyland bus, decommissioned from public transport in Sydney thirty years earlier, was O'Grady's trademark. Impossible to miss with its distinctive signage – 'O'Grady's Boxing Troupe' – painted along its green sides, it served as office, change room and home. The number 3 on the indicator panel at the front and back of the bus stood for the three rounds a challenger had to last, and the destination above the windscreen said 'Never-Never'. An old caravan and two Land Rovers with boxing gloves painted on the bonnets completed the troupe's transportation. The famous candy-striped marquee with the boxing ring in the centre could be erected within minutes. A portable diesel generator supplied power to the coloured lights outside, and to the spotlights trained on the ring inside. Boxing tents were only legal in the Northern Territory. However, O'Grady regularly crossed the border into WA or Queensland for an illicit bout or two. The authorities would normally turn a blind eye as long as the situation didn't get out of hand. Legends deserved concessions.

'Okay Midget, off you go,' said O'Grady, opening the door of the bus. 'We're starting in ten minutes.'

Donning a bowler hat and dressed in black pants and a red frilly shirt with a polka dot bowtie, Midget went out to drum up business – literally. Beating the drum that hung around his neck, he walked through the crowded beer garden, hyping up the raucous patrons.

'Look at that crowd,' said Will, following Andrew to the back of the pub past dozens of excited young men drinking beer.

'Where are all the women?' asked Rebecca, trying to keep up.

'This is for blokes,' explained Andrew. 'You'll see why.'

'Are you all right?' asked Jack, guiding Cassandra through the crowd. Looking pale and exhausted, she was limping more than usual.

'Jack, he's here,' she said, squeezing his arm.

'Pigeon?'

'No, the Wizard.'

'Don't be silly.'

'I'm not sure if we should go inside,' she said, pointing with her stick to the tent.

'Come on ... we have to. If Pigeon's really here ...'

'I know,' whispered Cassandra, trying to ignore the signals assaulting her intuition from all sides.

'Did you find them?' asked the Wizard, leaning out of the car window.

'They're all in the tent,' replied Banjo, grinning. 'The first fight's almost over.'

'Good. Now listen carefully, this is what we'll do: Banjo, you stay with the cars. Zoran, you take my Barretta. Sladko, you've got yours?'

Sladko nodded, patting the bulge under his shirt.

'You're not going to be armed?' asked Zoran.

'I'll be armed all right,' replied the Wizard, clenching his fists. 'With these. Better than a gun.'

'You've got something up your sleeve, haven't you?' asked Sladko, shaking his head. 'I know you! Do you want to tell us about it?'

'Wait and see. And remember, Pigeon and Cassandra. We deal with the others later. Let's go!'

35

O'Grady's boxing tent, 7:00 p.m.

O'Grady rang the ringside bell, announcing the third and final round of the fight. The crowd cheered – the challenger was doing well. O'Grady knew how to play the crowd. The first couple of bouts usually went the challenger's way, allowing the local lad to win. By putting a few pennies into the eager punters' pockets, it loosened their purse strings for later. The real betting only started when the champ came on.

'This is gross,' said Rebecca, 'all that blood.'

The challenger, a tall Aboriginal station-hand, was hammering his opponent. Bleeding from a cut above his eye which had almost closed, the unfortunate loser was trying to stop the barrage by protecting his face with his hands. At last the bell went again, signalling the end of the fight. The excited spectators roared and helped themselves to more beer. Midget, who had exchanged his drum for a leather bag full of cash, was doing the rounds, paying up.

'Two minutes,' shouted O'Grady, banging his fist against the door of the bus. 'Ladieeeees and gentlemen, the moment you've all been waiting for! Your very own champion from right here in Fitzroy Crossing ...'

The crowd cheered.

'He rolls like thunder and moves like lightning, the one and only ... Captain Thunderbolt!'

The bus door opened and the Captain stepped out into the glare. Lowering his head, he looked down at the long shadows reaching across the floor of the open tent like accusing fingers pointing to the ring in the centre.

'Are you all right?' asked Jack, turning to Cassandra. 'Here he comes.'

Wearing a long terry towel robe with a hood, the Captain walked slowly through the parting crowd. Before climbing into the ring, he folded back his hood and took off the robe, exposing a chest rippling with tight muscles.

'There, now. Look carefully! Is it him?'

'It is,' whispered Cassandra.

Jack glanced at Andrew and nodded.

'Do we have a challenger?' asked O'Grady. 'This is your chance, fellas. Fame and wads of cash await anyone who can go three rounds with the champ. Who will it be? Who has the balls and the skill? Is there anyone?'

Three eager young men in the front held up their hands.

'You first,' said O'Grady, pointing to a stocky, broad-shouldered lad being pushed forward by his mates. 'Place your bets, fellas. Midget here will give you good odds.'

The fight was over within seconds. Knocked unconscious by a devastating uppercut, the broad-shouldered lad was lying on the mat.

'For Christ's sake, Pigeon, what are you *doing*?' hissed O'Grady, glaring at the champ. According to their usual tactics, the bout should have lasted much longer. The challenger should have been encouraged a little, at least for a round or two, before being flattened. To knock him out like that was bad for business; very bad. It scared away other challengers.

'I don't give a fuck. I'll knock the shit out of everyone who wants to have a go tonight,' replied the champ. 'This is my home turf!'

Ignoring O'Grady, Pigeon turned away and began to shadow box in the ring.

'Do we have another challenger?' asked O'Grady lamely. No one came forward. The two eager young men from before had disappeared into the crowd.

'What's wrong with you fellas? Is everyone shitting himself around here? What kind of a town is this?' taunted O'Grady, trying in vain to whip up the crowd.

'Here, I'll give you five to one,' he shouted, holding up a bundle of hundred dollar notes. 'You'll never get odds like that again.'

'Okay Zoran, this is it. You know what to do,' said the Wizard, standing behind the crowd just outside the tent. 'Do it now!'

'I'll have a go,' bellowed the Wizard, reaching into his pocket. He pulled out a wad of cash and held up the money. 'Ten grand says your champ's a gutless wonder.'

The crowd fell silent. From all sides, curious heads turned in the Wizard's direction, eager to see where the outrageous challenge had come from.

'He must be pissed,' shouted someone in the back.

'Hey, it's gramps,' shouted another, laughing. 'He's got a grey ponytail – look.'

'Let him through,' shouted O'Grady, his heart skipping a beat. A ten thousand dollar bet had never been placed before. The evening was full of surprises.

The champion in the ring stopped moving and squinted through the open flaps of the tent, the rays of the setting sun momentarily blinding him. Shielding his eyes with his hand, he stared at the dark shape pushing slowly towards the ring through the crowd. *The voice ...* he thought, *I know that voice.* Lit up from behind, the shape looked ominous and threatening, like an apparition ... The way it moved, the bulk and the outline of the head were all strangely familiar.

'Hello Pigeon,' said the shape, coming closer. 'Ready to fight the living dead?' asked the Wizard.

Feeling dizzy, the Captain reached for the ropes to steady himself. 'It can't be,' he mumbled, staring at the Wizard in disbelief.

'Look, he's shaking,' shouted someone in the front, pointing to the champ. 'He's afraid of grandpa.'

O'Grady turned to the Wizard. 'Are you sure you want to do this, mate?' he asked, his conscience momentarily getting the better of him. The Wizard thrust the bundle of notes into his hands.

'Ten grand – here. A bet's a bet – right?' said the Wizard, slapping O'Grady on the back.

Parting the ropes, the Wizard stepped into the ring. The crowd roared.

'Oh, my God – look,' said Cassandra, squeezing Jack's arm so hard, he almost cried out. 'The Wizard!'

'Can't be' said Jack, looking across.

'Oh, but it is,' whispered a voice from behind. Jack could feel something hard pressing into his back. 'Don't turn around,' said Zoran, 'or I'll blow your fucking head off.'

'Nice evening, Cassandra?' asked Sladko from the other side, pressing the tip of his gun into Andrew's ribs. 'Don't go anywhere, guys. Let's enjoy the show, shall we?'

'Don't do anything stupid,' whispered Zoran, turning to Will standing next to Jack, 'or your mate here cops it – understood?'

No one moved.

'I hope you haven't forgotten anything I taught you,' whispered the Wizard, taking off his shirt.

The crowd gasped. The Wizard had the torso of a wrestler: massive shoulders, arms like tree trunks and neck muscles like the anchor chains of a windjammer. But most striking of all was the tattoo on his hairy back – King Solomon's seal, the macroprosopus and the microprosopus. A pentacle with an old, bearded man on the top, looking at his own reflection mirrored below. God of light and God of reflection, the white Jehovah and the black Jehovah. The compassionate and the avenger.

'Is this guy for real?' shouted someone in the front.

'Jesus, I'd hate to fight him,' said another. 'Just look at him, he's fucking huge!'

'Ladies and gentlemen, we have a challenger,' O'Grady's voice boomed through the megaphone. 'Place your bets ... Five to one, you'll never get odds like this again.'

'What's your name?' he asked, turning to the Wizard in the ring.

'Lazarus,' replied the Wizard, flexing his muscles.

'Lazarus?'

The Wizard nodded.

'Lazarus here is betting ten grand. He's putting his money where his mouth is,' shouted the ringmaster.

'What, straight back from the dead?' shouted someone in the front. The crowd roared with laughter.

His mind racing, Pigeon tried to come to terms with what his eyes and ears were telling him: the Wizard was alive, standing in the ring next to him, ready to fight. One thing Pigeon knew for sure: this would be a fight to the end.

'Just in case you're wondering,' hissed the Wizard, leaning across to Pigeon, 'you shot the wrong man ... The Alchemist is dead. You didn't really think you could cross me and get away with it?'

'Come on, place your bets. That's the spirit,' shouted O'Grady, encouraging the punters.

'Enough of the bullshit!' roared the Wizard, clenching his massive fists. 'Ring the fucking bell.'

36
O'Grady's boxing tent, 7:30 p.m.

Sensing a moment of confusion in his stunned opponent, the Wizard went on the attack with a favourite combination. His first punch – delivered with the left – caught the champ off guard and dug deep into the gut. Expecting his opponent to react by bending forward, the Wizard's right shot up from below, aiming for the chin

Once again, speed was Pigeon's friend. A lightning-fast reflex – a small step back – saved him from a devastating blow. Raw power met speed.

'You remembered what I've taught you,' hissed the Wizard, grinning. 'Expect the unexpected – good. But it won't be enough.'

Bouncing off the ropes, the Wizard moved forward again, using another combination. This time Pigeon was ready for him. First, he blocked the punch by lifting his fists, then his left exploded forward. Glancing off the Wizard's wrist it connected with his right ear. The crowd roared.

'Enjoying the fight, Cassandra?' asked Zoran, putting his arm around Cassandra's waist. 'You're not betting, I see. Lost faith in your little champ, have you? Can't say I blame you. He stuffed up once already, didn't he? Big time – right?' Zoran laughed.

His mind racing, Jack was considering the alternatives. With Zoran's gun digging into his back, the choices were limited. Leaning forward, Jack was trying to make eye contact with Andrew. As Andrew turned his head towards him, they briefly locked eyes. Reading the question on Jack's face, Andrew shook his head.

'Don't move,' Zoran whispered into Jack's ear. 'You should have listened to the Wizard, mate, instead of Cassandra here. Bad choice. How about a little wager – eh?'

'What's on your mind?' asked Jack.

'If the Wizard wins, Cassandra comes with us and you and your mates forget all about this and bugger off back to Sydney.'

'And if he loses?'

'We walk away and we both forget all about this.'

'And Cassandra?'

'She stays with you.'

'And Captain Thunderbolt?'

'Not your concern.'

Go along with him, whispered the little voice inside Jack's head. 'You're on,' he said.

O'Grady rang the bell. The first round was over. Nothing excites a crowd more than the sight of blood, and both fighters were bleeding profusely. Blood was oozing out of the Wizard's battered ear. Running down his chin, it trickled onto his hairy chest, turning the glistening beads of sweat crimson. The Captain was bleeding, too. A deep cut had opened above his right eye and blood smudged his cheeks. O'Grady reached for a towel and wiped the Captain's face. Turning towards the Wizard panting in the corner, he held up the towel for him to use. The Wizard glared and shook his head.

'Get on with the next round,' he snarled. 'Now!'

Pigeon knew he was in trouble the moment the Wizard's massive fist connected with his forehead. The cut above the eyebrow would need stitches and the swelling was closing his right eye. With his vision impaired, he had to win the fight during this round. Time was running out – fast. O'Grady, too, realised what was happening. So did the Wizard. The bout wasn't going quite as expected.

'You've got to knock him out quick,' hissed O'Grady, anxious to protect his pocket. 'He put up ten grand, for Christ's sake. This could wipe us out. Work on his ear. That should do it. Ready?'

Pigeon nodded.

'Stop fucking around,' bellowed the Wizard, 'and ring the fucking bell!'

The crowd cheered. It had a new champ.

The Wizard pushed O'Grady aside without waiting for the bell and closed in on Pigeon. It was obvious that O'Grady no longer controlled the fight. Pigeon saw the Wizard coming and sidestepped the charge, speed once again giving him the edge. Before the Wizard could turn, Pigeon landed a massive punch on his bleeding ear from behind. Crazed by pain, and with sirens shrieking in his ear, the Wizard stopped in his tracks and slowly turned around.

'How about we throw away the fucking rule book – eh Pigeon?' he asked, wiping the blood from his cheek. 'This is between us.'

'Fine by me,' replied Pigeon, rocking back and forth on the balls of his feet.

'You can't do that!' interjected O'Grady, stepping between the two opponents, 'you'll kill each other.'

'No one asked you,' bellowed the Wizard, lifting O'Grady up by the collar until the old man's feet were dangling centimetres off the ground. The crowd whistled and cheered. 'We don't need a referee.'

'Stop the fight! I won't allow it! Put me down!' croaked O'Grady.

'As you wish,' replied the Wizard.

He carried O'Grady across to the corner like a rag doll, lifted him over the ropes, and dropped him on the ground outside the ring. Dazed and humiliated, O'Grady tried to get up but couldn't. Midget came running with a bucket of water which, to the great amusement of the crowd, he emptied over O'Grady's head.

'That's the way, matey,' said one of the spectators – a burly tobacco-chewing drover standing in the front. 'If that doesn't wake him, nothing will.'

Taking off his bowler hat, Midget took a bow. The spectators roared with laughter.

Pigeon had dabbled in a little kickboxing. With his left eye almost closed, he knew he had to attack. Catching the Wizard by surprise, he delivered a perfect kick into his groin. A second kick landed on the Wizard's left knee, causing serious damage. The Wizard lost his balance and went down on the other knee. Pigeon saw his chance: if he could land a kick on the Wizard's injured ear while he was down, the fight would be over. Darting forward, he took aim with his right foot and was about to deliver the fatal blow, when the unexpected happened. Out of the corner of his eye, the Wizard saw his opponent's foot flash towards him. Ignoring the excruciating pain in his groin and his crippled knee, he rolled with amazing speed to one side, at the same time reaching for the attacking foot.

Seizing Pigeon's foot with both hands, the Wizard began to twist the ankle. Pigeon lost his balance and fell, landing on his back. In an instant, his advantage of speed and surprise had evaporated – the tables had turned. The Wizard saw his chance. Letting go of the ankle, he hurled his enormous body on top of his opponent's. Before Pigeon could react, he found himself pinned to the mat.

'Got you,' snarled the Wizard, his swollen lips almost touching Pigeon's face. 'You should have taken up wrestling, mate, just like I told you to. A fighter like you lying on the mat is useless – see.'

The Wizard delivered a mighty head-butt straight at Pigeon's bleeding brow.

Revived by the water, O'Grady staggered unsteadily to his feet. 'That's enough! Stop it!' he shouted, trying to climb into the ring. 'You'll kill him.'

The Wizard kept head-butting his helpless opponent until he felt Pigeon's body go limp under him, then got slowly to his feet. The crowd cheered wildly, and the Wizard punched the air with his right fist, letting out a mighty roar as he climbed out of the ring.

'You're crazy!' said O'Grady crawling across the mat to Pigeon who was lying in a pool of blood. 'He needs help. We gotta do something!'

'I'll take care of him,' said the Wizard, looking like a wild beast after a kill, 'and you can keep the ten grand – but on one condition.'

'What do you mean?' asked O'Grady, watching the Wizard.

'You pack up and leave town – tonight.'

'What about him?' O'Grady pointed to Pigeon.

'Leave him to me. I'll make sure he gets to a quack.'

'Why are you doing this?' asked O'Grady.

'He and I go back a long way ... The best thing you can do is to stay out of this – understood? Do we have a deal?'

O'Grady nodded, relieved to find that his money was safe. Loyalty can have a short memory.

37

O'Grady's boxing tent, 8 p.m.

'I reckon we can declare the Wizard the winner, what do you think?' said Zoran to Jack, pointing to the victor carrying Pigeon out of the tent. 'Now, as for our little bet ...'

Zoran was interrupted by loud shouting coming from outside.

Tipped off by a concerned publican, two uniformed policemen burst into the tent.

'No one leaves!' shouted one of the officers, a young constable, trying to block the Wizard's path.

'This guy needs help,' panted the Wizard, pointing over his shoulder with his bloody chin. 'I'll get him to a doctor.'

'You're not going anywhere,' replied the young constable. Bare-chested, his bulging muscles dripping with sweat, the Wizard towered above him.

'Zoran,' bellowed the Wizard, his bloodshot eyes darting around the crowded tent like the eyes of an angry cobra, 'over here – now!'

'Stay where you are, mate, and don't try anything foolish, or Sladko here will ... you know,' warned Zoran, patting Jack on the shoulder. Slipping the gun into his pocket, he turned around and pushed through the crowd towards the Wizard still arguing with the policeman at the exit.

Spooked by the unexpected arrival of the law, the excited punters had only one thing on their minds: getting out fast. No one fancied being questioned, or spending a night in the lockup, or worse. Fuelled by alcohol and panic, the men in front, who were being pushed from behind, fell over the ropes holding up the tent. Others cut through the canvas with broken bottles and left through the back. Within moments the tent was in tatters.

O'Grady spotted Midget hiding under the ring. 'Get the cash!' he shouted. 'We're outta here.'

Andrew made eye contact with Jack and motioned with his chin towards Sladko standing next to him. With Zoran gone and confusion all around them, there was now only one gun they had to deal with.

Sensing that without Zoran he couldn't effectively control all the others, Sladko put his arm around Cassandra and kept pressing his gun into her back. 'Stay close to me, sweetheart,' he whispered into her ear. 'Safer that way, trust me.'

'We make a move?' asked Will, leaning across to Jack being pushed towards the exit by the crowd.

'We stay together. Keep an eye on Andrew; he's closest to the gun. I'll take care of Rebecca. Here, Rebecca, give me your hand.'

'Don't lose me, Jack,' said Rebecca, picking her way through the broken glass littering the dirt floor, the nauseating smell of unwashed bodies, alcohol and fear assaulting her powdered nose.'

'I won't. Hold on.'

With the supporting ropes no longer holding, the large post in the centre of the tent teetered, then crashed onto the ring. The roof collapsed onto the screaming crowd like a heavy shroud. Amid the chaos and confusion that followed, Andrew saw his chance. He could just make out Sladko's hand holding the gun in front of him. For an instant the gun was pointing to the floor instead of Cassandra's back. Years of dealing with delinquents had taught Andrew to seize the moment. Using both hands he grabbed Sladko's wrist from behind and twisted his arm with all the strength he could muster. But instead of loosening his grip, Slakdo pulled the trigger, shooting himself in the thigh. With a howl of pain, he dropped the weapon as the panicking crowd stampeded.

'I've got the gun!' shouted Andrew, turning to Jack. 'Take Cassandra – here. Will, you take Rebecca – run!'

'What about you?' shouted Jack.

'I'll take care of this prick. He isn't going anywhere. Wait at the car. Go!'

38

Fitzroy Crossing, 2 March, 10 p.m.

Standing next to Andrew's car behind the pub, Jack watched the angry crowd. Jumping into their dusty four wheel drives and utes – many with snarling cattle dogs guarding slabs of beer in the back – the punters were leaving. Pigeon's fight with the tattooed stranger had already become Outback legend. Rebecca and Will were looking after Cassandra who hadn't spoken a word since leaving the tent. The heat, even after sunset, was unbearable.

'I hope we aren't turning into sitting ducks here,' said Rebecca, scanning the busy street for signs of the Wizard and his cohorts.

'We've got to wait for Andrew,' replied Jack. 'But you're right. We should lie low.'

'The danger's passed,' said Cassandra, breaking her silence. 'For now.'

'The Wizard?' asked Rebecca.

'He's gone. And so's Pigeon.'

'Here he comes now,' said Jack, pointing to Andrew hurrying towards them.

'Get in,' he said and unlocked the car.

'Well?' asked Jack. 'What happened?'

'Sladko was arrested and taken to hospital under guard. The bullet went straight through his thigh.'

'And the Wizard?' interrupted Will.

'He and Zoran got away.'

'How?' asked Jack.

'You saw the confusion. The Wizard was carrying some injured guy. They let him go to get help.'

'You're kidding,' said Will.

'Look, those two constables were rookies. There was no way they could control that crowd.'

'What about their plane?' asked Jack.

'Don't worry. The plane's under guard too. I told the police the Wizard and his mates are suspected drug dealers. They're looking for them as we speak. At least the Wizard can't fly away.'

'We have to find them before they kill Pigeon,' said Cassandra quietly, 'or we'll never find Anna.'

'Can you tell us more?' asked Rebecca.

'They'll torture him until he tells them what they need to know. He won't be able to resist. The Wizard's a genius when it comes to inflicting pain ... he makes the Inquisition look like fumbling amateurs.'

'We've got a description of their car,' said Andrew. 'A black Land Rover.'

'That's supposed to help?' asked Jack. 'We're in the Kimberley. This is wilderness the size of Germany in one of the remotest corners of Australia. And we have no idea where they're heading. They could be anywhere by now.'

'It's a start.' Andrew shrugged.

'Do you think the Wizard's looking for us?' asked Rebecca.

'You mean looking for me, don't you?' said Cassandra.

Rebecca nodded.

'I don't think so. Getting to me ... well, that's only retribution. Finding Anna is a matter of survival.'

'And to do that, he needs Pigeon,' interrupted Will. 'He's the only one who can lead the Wizard to her. If she's still alive.'

'The bastard's holding all the cards: he got away, he's got Pigeon – and we have no idea where he is. It's not looking good,' said Jack.

'Not quite,' said Cassandra quietly. 'There is one more thing ...'

'What do you mean?' asked Rebecca.

'I think I can take you to Pigeon ...'

'Come on ...' said Andrew, shaking his head.

'Have you forgotten why you engaged me in the first place?'

'Of course not, but ...'

'I'm the same person, Andrew. Trust me. My powers are the same too. Perhaps even stronger ...'

'What are you suggesting?'

'I'll tell you. But first, let's get away from here.'

185

39

Approaching Bunuba country, 3 March

Sitting in the front seat of the Land Rover as it crawled through the night, the Wizard was deciding what to do next. Sladko's arrest and hospitalisation were an unexpected blow, Cassandra slipping through his fingers an embarrassment, and Jack Rogan snooping around with his mates was a nuisance. But, he reminded himself, the most important objective had been achieved. He turned around and looked at the man slumped in the backseat.

The man who had taunted him for years and had tried to kill him was, at long last, within his power.

Hovering between life and death – his bruised and blood-smeared face merely an echo of its former, handsome self – Pigeon looked defeated. But his spark of courage and defiance was very much alive.

Simmering under the battered flesh, it was the real danger the Wizard couldn't see. Broken bones are rarely a threat. What holds them together often is.

Having subdued one foe, the Wizard's thoughts turned to the one that got away. He reached for his satellite phone and called the Undertaker. When the Wizard hung up, a smile spread across his sweating face.

'What was all that about?' asked Zoran.

'Cassandra. We'll fix that bitch, you'll see.'

'I hope so.'

The rough dirt track, rutted and littered with football-sized rocks, was almost impassable in the dark. And the old black Land Rover had seen better days. With the engine labouring, it lurched and skidded as it crossed a dry river bed, almost rolling as it climbed the steep, sandy embankment on the other side.

'How much further?' snapped the Wizard, turning to Banjo. 'We've been going for hours!'

'You wanted a safe spot,' replied Banjo curtly. 'I'm taking you to one. This is an old stock route. The cops'll be looking for us by now, that's for sure. You saw that copper waiting for us at the plane, didn't you? But don't worry, those cops are lazy bastards. They won't try too hard and they'll never think of looking for us here. This land belongs to the blackfellas. This is Jandamarra country. We're almost there.'

Like Pigeon, Banjo had grown up on one of the large cattle stations near Fitzroy Crossing and knew the Kimberley well. He was used to living in the bush; finding his way in the dark.

As the hazy veil of unconsciousness began to lift, Pigeon heard voices, distant at first, and incomprehensible. Then came the pain. It crept through every fibre of his body before coming to rest in his brain. Pounding against his temples like persistent tidal waves gnawing at defiant cliffs on a rugged coast, the pain grew stronger and almost unbearable. His hands were tied behind his back and a sigh escaped his parched lips as the rope cut deep into his wrists. When he tried to move his feet, the rope cut into his bruised ankles. One eye did not want to open, its socket had closed completely. The other stared into darkness.

'I think he's coming round,' said Zoran, sitting next to Pigeon in the back.

'Make sure he's properly tied up,' growled the Wizard.

'He is, trust me.'

'Hello, Pigeon, welcome back,' said the Wizard cheerfully. 'Very soon you and I will have a little chat. Long overdue, wouldn't you say?'

Trying to focus, Pigeon closed his good eye and said nothing. Every time the car hit a bump his body screamed with pain; save for his feet, he thought gratefully, now completely numb.

'I can think of a few questions we have to ask him. What do you reckon, Zoran?'

'So can I.'

'Like, what happened to Anna?'

'That would be an excellent start,' Zoran said.

'Well, the good news is,' continued the Wizard, enjoying himself, 'that Pigeon here will give us all the answers. You can count on it.'

Pigeon heard him – loud and clear. If he wanted to stay alive, he would have to beat the Wizard at his own game. And there was only one way to do that: he had to use the occult. He had to turn fear against the Wizard.

'You want to know what happened to Anna?' croaked Pigeon, barely able to speak.

'Did you hear?' said the Wizard, turning to Sladko. 'The man can talk. That's good ...'

'Anna's alive.' Pigeon paused, letting this sink in. 'And when the time's right, she'll destroy you,' he added quietly. 'She's safe from you. You'll never find her.'

'And what makes you so sure?'

'Cassandra saw it all ...'

'Did she now?' replied the Wizard, his voice sounding hollow as a flash of uncertainty raced across his face. 'And she's right all the time? Just like she was right about the Devil riding in the parade?'

'You've been spared, Eugene, because to shoot you like a dog would have been too easy an end for a wretched creature like you. Destiny has something far more interesting in store ...'

Zoran raised his fist and was about to smash it into Pigeon's face, when the Wizard held up his hand.

'Don't bother. We'll do a lot better later. Now, let me tell you something,' he said quietly. 'You already know I'm going to kill you. But before ... well, before I'm finished, you'll tell me everything. I'll kill you so slowly you'll be begging me to do it faster. Trust me. I'll start with your feet ... we're going to burn them away in the fire until they turn into sizzling stumps. I'll peel the skin off your back and let the sun bake your flesh. I'll cut you open like a pig hanging on a butcher's hook and you'll see your guts spill into the sand. Oh yes, you'll tell me what I want to know. Of that, you can be sure.'

'And you're right all the time?' said Pigeon. 'Just like you were right when you told us that Anna wasn't a threat?'

'She wasn't a threat – you were,' came the angry retort, 'but, my friend, you are a threat no more.'

'We'll see. You can't cheat destiny, Eugene, you know that. Cassandra saw your destiny ... and so did I.'

The Wizard tried to control a rising fury. He wasn't used to defiance like this. *But*, he thought, with an icy arrow of fear piercing his chest, *what if he does know something?* Cassandra again. Damn her! *Be careful, Eugene, there could be danger here.*

40

Fitzroy Crossing, 3 March

Cassandra opened her eyes and watched the first light of the new day creep through the open window of the drab motel room. Andrew had insisted they stay the night in Fitzroy Crossing before venturing north into the bush.

She saw the five cards of the Question Spread on the table in front of her, exactly as she had left them. They reminded her of her question during the divination the night before. Cassandra closed her eyes. What had woken her?

At first, there was only a feeling. Then, an awareness of great suffering and pain. Then suddenly, a picture, hazy at first, of a naked man, his back covered in blood, hanging from the branch of a strange looking tree floated into her mind's eye. Cassandra wasn't sure if he was still alive. Then slowly, the man lifted his head a little, opened one eye and looked at her.

'Pigeon,' she moaned.

'Anna is alive.' His voice was barely audible. 'But there isn't much time. Hurry!'

'I spoke to the guys at the police station already,' said Andrew. He opened the car door and took a map out of the glove box. 'No luck, I'm afraid. They seem to have disappeared without a trace.'

'How could they? Jack said.

Andrew shrugged. 'All the roads have been checked, on the ground, and from the air. There are only a couple of them in this part of the world. They must have gone bush.'

'What are the tracks like up here this time of the year?' Will asked.

'With a sturdy four-wheel drive and someone who knows the country, they're not too bad. You get swallowed up by the land here ... you can just disappear.'

'Not quite,' interrupted Cassandra. 'They're near a river with tall red cliffs and strange trees that look like bottles.' She limped over to the car. The three men looked up, surprised.

'You saw something?' asked Andrew.

Cassandra nodded. 'Pigeon's barely alive. They've strung him up ... hanging from a tree,' she said.

'Tortured?' asked Jack. 'Just as we feared.'

'Who's been tortured?' asked Rebecca. Jack thought how beautiful she looked; but so smartly dressed, for this rugged place, in her designer shorts and Chanel tee-shirt.

'Anna's alive,' said Cassandra, closing her eyes. 'If we don't find Pigeon before they kill him, we'll never find her.'

'How big is that river you saw?' asked Andrew, poring over the map. 'And the cliffs, what do they look like? Can you describe them? Anything else about the location?'

Trying to focus on the strange landscape she'd seen, Cassandra began to take deep breaths. Rebecca walked over and put her arm around the psychic's shoulders.

'The river is quite wide,' whispered Cassandra, 'bluish-green and calm. I can see a couple of huge crocodiles on the banks and ... flocks of white birds flying around.'

'What about the cliffs?' interrupted Andrew.

'They're like massive walls on both sides of that river; they're very close to the water's edge ...'

'Windjana Gorge,' said Andrew, stabbing his finger at the map, 'that's where they are. Right there.'

'But that's more than a hundred kilometres from here,' said Jack, looking over Andrew's shoulder. 'Are you sure?'

'From what Cassandra just told us, yes. There's no other place around here that fits the description.'

'Are you going to tell the police?'

'What? That a clairvoyant saw a man hanging from a tree at a place that sounds like Windjana Gorge? I don't think so. They'd just laugh.' Andrew gathered up the map. 'We'll do this our way.'

'Oh?'

'Let's go there now and have a look around.'

'I thought we had to present ourselves at the police station to make our statements?' Rebecca said. 'You told us yesterday ...'

'That can wait,' interrupted Andrew.

'Go bush first, explain later?' Will said.

Andrew put on his hat and looked at him. 'Something like that,' he said. 'This is the Outback, don't forget.'

41

On the way to Windjana Gorge, 3 March

'This is Bunuba country,' said Andrew. Squinting into the glare, he slowly followed the old stock route north towards the Napier Range rising out of the haze ahead of them like the giant teeth of a creature long extinct. The stock route hadn't seen a vehicle in years and was almost impassable; each hidden bolder or gaping pothole could easily have meant their car rolling, but Andrew managed to guide the vehicle through.

'As in the Bunuba Resistance Auntie mentioned when she was talking about Pigeon?' said Jack.

'Yes, this is where it all happened. Pigeon grew up around here.'

'Bunuba Resistance?' said Rebecca. 'Wow. Tell us about it.'

Grateful for the diversion, Andrew began to relax. 'You heard Auntie talk about Jandamarra?' he said, wiping his brow with the back of his hand.

'The Aboriginal freedom fighter Pigeon's supposedly named after?' said Will.

Andrew nodded, barely missing a boulder.

'Well, way back ... one night in October 1894,' he said. 'Jandamarra had just shot Bill Richardson, a policeman, not far from here. There was a group of Bunuba prisoners chained to a tree nearby, and they were watching. With that one shot Jandamarra crossed the line: he left the world of the white man behind and sided with his people. The Bunuba now had a leader who could fight the white intruders on almost equal terms. After killing the cop, Jandamarra set the prisoners free, and the Bunuba struggle – which had already been going on for more than a decade – well, that's when it entered its deadliest phase.' Andrew changed gears, and carefully coaxed the vehicle up a steep embankment.

'Of course the Bunuba couldn't possibly win, but they put up a great fight and Jandamarra became a legend.'

'A legend?' said Cassandra. 'In what way?'

'As a youngster, Jandamarra had been dazzled by the white men the Bunuba called *Malngadu*, entering his world. He learnt the white man's language, he was an accomplished horseman, and most importantly, was taught how to use a gun. He was an extraordinary marksman; it became his trademark. He was inspiring, but later ... well, people were afraid of him, especially the white settlers. Still, while he was living with the frontier squatters he became a valued servant and scout. He also knew a lot of useful information about the Bunuba and their land on the other side of the ranges. Pretty fertile land. And those ranges guarded it like a natural fortress.'

'What happened to him?' asked Rebecca.

'Unfortunately, this story doesn't have a happy ending ...' said Andrew.

Sensing that it was time to change the subject, Jack reached for the water bottle next to him. 'Drink?' he asked. 'How much further to the river?'

'We should be there in a couple of hours,' replied Andrew. Looking dreamily towards the Napier Range – remnants of an ancient Devonian reef that had protected the land of his ancestors for thousands of years – he remembered the days he had spent there with his father. He always felt a sense of awe when he was near these places; places of great spiritual significance to the Bunuba. Windjana Gorge was one of the most sacred of them all. He thought he could even hear ceremonial chanting and the rhythmic stamping of feet dancing.

'What happened to Jandamarra?' asked Rebecca again.

'He was killed at Tunnel Creek not far from here ... he became a restless spirit.'

'A restless spirit?'

'All the land around us here is Djumbud – Jandamarra's spirit country. It's my spirit country too, and Pigeon's. It belongs to the Bunuba.'

'What's a restless spirit?' asked Will.

Andrew didn't reply. These subjects were strictly off limits.

'Please tell us,' said Rebecca, 'I think we should know.'

'Rebecca's right, Andrew, tell them,' said Cassandra.

Andrew wouldn't normally discuss any of this with a Malngadu. But he sensed that Cassandra was different. After all, she had brought them this far. *Perhaps her powers are somehow linked to the spirit world of the Bunuba?* he thought.

He decided to carry on. 'A restless spirit has unfinished business in the world of the living and cannot find peace. He can't be reunited with his ancestors until the matter is resolved, however long it takes.' Andrew looked over at Jack. 'Does this make sense to you?'

'It does,' said Jack.

'Jandamarra's spirit lives right here in this land – in the rocks, the trees and the water. He's searching for answers ... restless spirits do that. You know, he will tell his story to those who know how to listen. Many have heard it: at night around the campfire, carried by the wind, or whispered through the tall grass early in the morning.'

'Have you?' asked Cassandra.

'Yes. We're entering a different world up here – Bunuba country. This is a spiritual place. Wait and see.'

'I can feel it,' murmured Cassandra.

'I thought you might. I think Jandamarra has unfinished business in the world of the Malngadu.'

'What makes you say that?'

'Out here you have to learn how to listen. If you can do that, the spirit might tell you.'

'I'm a good listener,' said Cassandra.

'Many try to listen, but few know how to hear ...'

'I think I can do both.'

'Then try to listen to the wind.'

'I will.'

Cassandra looked out the car window and watched the tall cliffs come closer. *Many try to listen, but few know how to hear,* she thought. *I want to hear.* Closing her eyes, she let the hot breeze blowing through the open window caress her face. After a while she thought she could hear words being carried by the breeze; incomprehensible at first, but becoming clearer. Recognising the signs, Cassandra let herself drift. Hovering on the edge of sleep she connected with the voice and listened. Soon, she began to hear ...

'You are very lucky I'm talking to you as a spirit,' whispered the voice of Jandamarra. 'You want to know why?'

Cassandra nodded.

'When I was in the world of the living, I only spoke Pidgin English. Difficult to understand. This is what it was like: I Pigeon. Him bin – outlaw. Him bin kill many blackfellas an white p'liceman. You wouldn't want to listen to a lot of this – right?'

Cassandra nodded again.

'Well, you don't have to. Spirits are free. They can speak in many tongues, and I will speak to you in yours. All right? I remember 1 April 1897 very well,' continued the voice. 'It was the day I became a spirit. Lying in a pool of blood on the floor of the familiar cave, I could feel life slowly oozing out of my many wounds. Strangely, there was no pain anymore, only a sense of resignation and calm, and anticipation of meeting my ancestors. I knew that destiny was waiting outside. All that was left for me to do was to find the strength to face it.

'If you had to choose a place to die, Tunnel Creek wasn't too bad, I suppose. For years, it had given me shelter and protection from my enemies. In a way it was my true home, my sanctuary. But, nothing lasts forever. And besides, I've never run away from a fight.

'I could see my Winchester lying next to me on the ground. I had a few bullets left somewhere in my pocket, but when I tried to move my fingers, they wouldn't obey. I tried again. This time a little feeling had returned, and I was able to sit up and load the gun. Strange, how objects can give us strength. My Winchester was one of those. The familiar feel of the smooth metal brought back memories of the first time I held a gun. I was quite young then and eager to prove myself. A little wild, perhaps? Of course. And reckless? Certainly. Impressionable? Absolutely!

'The line between recklessness and courage is very blurred and never improves with hindsight – right? It was a dark moment that changed my life forever. Somehow, the gun and I were made for each other, or so it seemed at the time. I became obsessed with the white man's world and turned my back on my people. It was a huge mistake I've regretted ever since. Time became my enemy. Young warriors rarely make old bones.

'Following the morning light creeping into my dark cave, I began to crawl outside. I thought that the limestone pillar in front of the entrance would be a fitting place for a last stand. I don't know where the strength came from, but somehow I made it to the top of that pillar. The bright sunlight of the new morning was blinding up there. I had to close my eyes. When I opened them again and looked down, I couldn't see anything at first. Little white stars danced in front of my eyes. Then slowly, out of the glare, a shape materialised: a man – gun ready – stood next to a boab tree – waiting. With my eyesight fading, I took aim and began to fire. The man took cover behind the tree. As I fired my last bullet, the gun slipped out of my hands. Then, standing at the very edge of the pillar, I let my eyes soak up the beauty of the vast land spread out below. This was Djumbud, the sacred land of the Bunuba, my spirit country. Knowing that I was about to die didn't fill me with sadness or regrets. There was no panic and no fear. Instead, a feeling of great joy filled my heart. One last, exhilarating thought raced through my burning brain: Jandamarra has never been defeated. As I looked down at the boab tree, I could see the man slowly raise his gun and take aim. For an instant, our eyes locked. Moments later, I became a spirit. Bang, bang. Pigeon, him bin shot dead.'

As the voice became fainter, Cassandra drifted into a restless slumber, the hot breeze unable to warm the chill in her heart.

42

Windjana Gorge, 3 March, 9 a.m.

Barely able to stay awake, Banjo had driven through most of the night. They reached their destination – a narrow gorge cut through the Napier Range by the Lennard River – at daybreak, and set up camp. The sun was already searing; a shimmering haze hovered above the waking landscape, giving the boab trees – gnarled and bloated giants protecting the secrets of countless Bunuba generations past – a strangely lifelike appearance. Many of these trees had guarded the gorge entry for centuries.

'That's enough!' shouted the Wizard, grabbing Zoran by the wrist. 'Can't you see he's unconscious?'

He took the blood-encrusted belt out of Zoran's hand and threw it on the ground. For an instant, Zoran looked at the Wizard without recognition, his hooded eyes bloodshot and glassy. He and the Wizard had taken turns whipping Pigeon's back and now, transported by the frenzy, Zoran was in a trance.

'He's no good to us dead. Control yourself. Get some water.'

The Wizard walked slowly around Pigeon who was hanging by his wrist from the tree branch.

'I know you can hear me,' he said. 'What have you done with Anna?'

There was no reply.

'We'll give him a little time,' snapped the Wizard. 'He'll talk soon – you'll see. I'm going down to the river to wash this off,' he said to Zoran looking at his blood-splattered hands. 'Come with me.'

'Wait, I'll come too,' said Banjo. He walked over to the Land Rover, pulled two rifles out of the back and handed one to the Wizard. 'Never leave camp without your guns.'

'He isn't going anywhere,' said the Wizard, pointing to Pigeon. 'Unless those evil spirits you keep talking about cut him down.' The Wizard roared, 'Let's go!'

Pigeon's brain slowly clawed its way back to consciousness and, when the pain was bearable, Pigeon opened his good eye. The first thing he saw were his toes, dangling helplessly just above the ground. He managed to lift his chin, and looked at the tall cliffs towering above him. Then, turning his head left, he saw a massive rock pylon that had broken away from the petrified reef eons ago.

'Julla,' whispered Pigeon, remembering the creation hero guarding the entrance to Windjana Gorge.

Memories of the sacred place came back with vivid clarity. He remembered many exciting days at Windjana Gorge as a boy. This is where he'd been inducted into the secret world of the Bunuba by one of its revered elders, his father. What a joy and great privilege that had been. Years later as a young man he had honoured his father. He remembered wrapping his father's body in paperbark before laying him to rest in one of the small caves high above the Lennard River.

They brought me all the way to Windjana Gorge, thought Pigeon. *Why? This is Djumbud, my spirit country.* He didn't believe in coincidences, only destiny. Trying to make contact with the spirits of his ancestors, he began to chant.

Standing on a rock ledge overlooking the river, an old Aboriginal man was showing his grandson a gallery of rock paintings. Painted thousands of years ago by his ancestors, the striking images explained the creation of their land. The old man was preparing the boy for his initiation ceremony and used the paintings as an introduction to the sacred, invisible world of the Bunuba. By spending a few days with his grandfather in the bush, the boy was learning the old ways of the Bunuba. It was a great adventure and a wonderful excuse to stay away from school for a little while.

When the old man turned around and looked down to the river, he saw a vehicle parked in front of the sacred pylon. That was odd; no one came here much, but stranger still, was something hanging from a branch of the boab tree next to it. Shielding his eyes from the glare, he took a closer look.

'That's a man, a black man,' he mumbled to himself. Then, glancing across to a bend in the river, something else caught his eye: two men swimming. *Malngadu*, he thought, white men. He couldn't see Banjo, sitting behind a nearby rock and holding a gun as he watched the large crocodiles basking on the riverbank.

'You stay right here,' said the old man to his grandson. 'I'm going down there to see what's going on.'

Holding a spear in his right hand and darting silently from cover to cover, the old man approached the boab tree. As he came closer, he noticed the horrific wounds on the man's back and heard chanting in Bunuba – his own language. *One of us*, he thought.

Sensing a presence, Pigeon stopped chanting. As he lifted his head, he looked straight into the furrowed face of the motionless, silent old man. At first Pigeon thought he was seeing a ghost and quickly closed his remaining good eye.

'What happened to you, brother?' asked the old man in Bunuba. *This isn't a ghost*, Pigeon thought as he heard the sound of his familiar tongue. *The ancestors sent a man to help me.*

'Cut me down, brother, and I'll tell you.'

Coming closer, the old man pulled a knife out of his waistband.

'Where are the others?' asked Pigeon, looking around anxiously.

'Down by the river.'

'We have to get away! If they find you here with me, they'll kill us both.'

Ignoring the crocodiles staring malevolently at them, Zoran and the Wizard followed Banjo up the embankment.

'What's next?' asked Zoran, drying his face with his shirt. 'You said he'll be ready to talk.'

'He will – trust me. Come and watch,' replied the Wizard. 'It's time to ratchet things up. Believe me, given the choice, he'd rather be dead than face what's about to happen.'

'Sounds interesting. Did you hear that, Banjo?' asked Zoran. 'What do you think Eugene has in mind?'

'Fire,' replied Banjo without hesitation. 'Fire always wins.'

'He's right,' said the Wizard. 'No one can resist fire. The Inquisition found that out centuries ago.'

Banjo saw it first. Not quite trusting his eyes, he blinked and looked again. The unthinkable had happened – Pigeon had disappeared.

'Bloody hell! Look, there!' he yelled, pointing to the piece of rope dangling from the tree branch.

'Noooo!' roared the Wizard, his face contorted by rage.

Pushing Banjo roughly aside with the butt of his gun, he ran towards the tree. 'Fucking mongrel!'

'Look at this,' said Zoran, holding up the end of the rope. 'A clean cut.'

'There are no footprints,' observed Banjo, examining the ground under the tree. 'Swept clean with tufts of long grass, by the look of it.' He pointed to fan-shaped markings in the sand. 'Someone knows what he's doing.'

'Right,' said the Wizard, checking his gun. 'He hasn't done this by himself, that's for fucking sure. With all the blood he's lost, he can't have gone very far. We were down by the river for only half an hour or so. Let's go and find the bastard!'

Pigeon limped towards the entry to the gorge, leaning on the old man. But he was supremely fit and in high spirits, and was starting to cope with the pain. They made sure to stay on the rocks, so as not to leave any tell-tale tracks.

'You've gotta get away from here,' said Pigeon. 'If they find you, they'll kill you – you can count on it. This is my fight, brother, not yours. Have you got a car?'

'No.'

'How did you get here?'

'My grandson and I came on horseback.'

'That's good. A horse can go where a Land Rover can't. Where are the horses?'

'Just over there, behind Lillimooloora Station,' replied the old man, pointing to the stone ruins of the notorious homestead a short distance to the north. 'We camped there last night.'

Pigeon stopped, trying to catch his breath. 'Listen, I have an idea,' he said. 'We haven't got much time. Tell me if you're prepared to go along with it.'

'I'm listening, brother.'

As he crouched behind a rock high above the river, Pigeon watched his pursuers slowly working their way towards the ruins of Lillimooloora Station. The old man had gone along with his plan, which was as simple as it was ingenious. Pigeon would engage the Wizard by taunting him from the safety of the cliffs, just as Jandamarra had done with the troopers trying to hunt him down a century or so ago. This diversion would give the old man an opportunity to get away safely with the boy.

The old man, in return, had given Pigeon his knife and his spear and, best of all, one of the horses.

Pigeon knew Windjana Gorge well. Having spent time there with his father and uncle as a boy, he had explored the many caves and secret pathways leading to the burial sites and rock paintings. He had even camped in Jandamarra's cave in the gorge.

'You're looking in the wrong place, Eugene,' shouted Pigeon, his voice bouncing off the ancient walls of the coral reef.

'Can you see anything?' asked the Wizard, turning towards Zoran. It was impossible to pinpoint where the voice had come from. 'Where the fuck is he?'

'I can't see a thing,' replied Zoran. 'He could be anywhere.'

'It's a maze up there,' said Banjo. 'Full of caves and tunnels.'

'Great,' said the Wizard, unable to keep the frustration out of his voice. 'We'll just have to flush him out, won't we?'

'How?' asked Zoran.

'Ego and pride. Watch,' said the Wizard as he cupped his hands to his mouth and called out towards the ancient walls. 'You're quite good at hiding and running away, aren't you, Pigeon? You've been doing it for years and when it was finally time for a little action you stuffed up, didn't you? It was the same with your mother ...'

Carefully watching the cliff above – gun at the ready – the Wizard paused, giving the insult time to find its mark.

'In the end, cowards always lose,' continued the Wizard. 'You know why? Because they haven't got the guts to fight.'

'Good try, Eugene. We both know that's crap, don't we?' came the reply from somewhere above. 'I'll prove it to you.'

'Talk's cheap.'

'We'll see.'

When Pigeon turned his head, he saw a snake – a dangerous king brown – sunning itself on a rock ledge. *Another sign?* he thought. He'd caught many a snake as a boy with his father – it was part of living in the bush. All he needed was a forked twig and some bark. It didn't take him long to find both.

From his lofty vantage point, Pigeon could see the Land Rover parked down by the river to his left, and the Wizard – about 200 metres from the vehicle – to his right. If he moved quickly, Pigeon estimated he could reach the Land Rover within a couple of minutes. What he needed was a diversion. He picked up a stone and threw it across the cliff face. It bounced off the rocks, setting off a small landslide of gravel and sand.

'He's up there,' shouted the Wizard, aiming his gun at the cloud of dust rising above the shifting sand. 'Let's go get him.'

While the Wizard, Zoran and Banjo clambered up the cliff, Pigeon climbed down a steep rock shaft and made it unnoticed across to the car. Slowly and silently, he opened the passenger door. He could feel the aroused snake writhing inside the paperbark parcel wedged under his arm. Opening the glove box, he pushed the parcel inside and with the tip of his spear prodded the bark until it cracked and the head of the snake appeared. Then he pushed the glove box shut before the snake could make its escape.

Looking up from behind the Land Rover, Pigeon could see the Wizard and Zoran searching the cliff face where the stone had landed. *I've got to be quick*, he thought, lying down on the ground. Pulling himself forward on his belly, he crawled under the four wheel drive until he reached the front wheels. Searching a rim with his fingertips he found the air valve, and let the air out of the tyre. *Time to go*, he thought, peering anxiously up at the cliff from behind the wheel. *One flat tyre should do the trick.*

Scrambling away from the car on all fours, Pigeon reached the scrub without being spotted. Using rocks, clumps of tall grass and trees as cover, he doubled back to Lillimooloora Station where the old man was hiding in the ruins with the boy and the horses.

Banjo heard it first. The dull, rhythmic sound was unmistakable: hoofs pounding the ground.

'Look, over there,' he shouted, pointing to the ruins. 'It's him!'

A horse was galloping away from the ruins, the rider bent low in the saddle.

'How the hell?' growled Zoran, raising his gun.

'Don't bother,' said the Wizard, disgusted. 'He's too fucking far away.'

'Maybe not,' said Banjo. 'Give me the gun.' The Wizard handed him his rifle.

Closing one eye, Banjo held his breath and calmly took aim. Trying to clear a fallen tree, the horse jumped, momentarily providing a perfect target. Banjo pulled the trigger.

43

On the way to Tunnel Creek,
3 March, mid morning

'How much further?' asked Jack, fanning himself with his hat. The heat in the car made him feel dizzy and the sweat tickled the back of his neck.

'Not far now,' said Andrew.

'Look over there, to the left,' shouted Will. 'A horse!' Andrew slowed down. Riding a horse without a saddle, a tall Aboriginal man was galloping furiously towards the car. Barely able to hold on, a small boy was sitting behind him.

As the horse came closer, Andrew thought he could recognise the man – he knew most of the elders in the district.

'Lambardoo?' he shouted through the open window. 'What are you doing here?'

The old man pulled up the horse. 'Mr Simpson?' he said. 'I'm sure glad to see you. Something dreadful is going on at the gorge.'

Andrew stopped the car and got out. 'Tell me about it.'

'I think you've got him,' shouted the Wizard, slapping Banjo on the back. 'What a shot! After him, guys! Back to the car!'

Numbed by the searing pain in his shoulder where the bullet had shattered a bone, Pigeon was trying to hold onto the horse's mane.

Falling off would be fatal. *NO! I almost made it.* Looking down, he saw blood running down his chest. To have any chance at all, he would have to reach the sanctuary of Tunnel Creek some 20 kilometres away before the others caught up with him. Tunnel Creek was one of Jandamarra's favourite hiding places and, ominously, it was also the place of his last stand.

The Wizard was fuming. He knew he was paying the price for underestimating his foe. The man who a couple of hours ago had been at his mercy had turned into a resourceful adversary. The flat tyre – obviously Pigeon's work – was slowing them down at the very moment Pigeon should have been within their grasp. How he had managed to escape, obtain a horse and slip away remained a mystery to the Wizard. To Banjo, a Bunuba like Pigeon, the answer was simple: Pigeon was a *Jalngangurru* with magical powers.

'How much longer?' asked the Wizard impatiently, watching Banjo and Zoran change the tyre.

'Almost done,' replied Banjo. 'Don't worry, we'll find him. He won't get far with all those injuries and he can't hide his tracks. Not out here, not riding a horse.'

Banjo was right. The horse's tracks were easy to find. However, because of the rugged terrain, progress was slow.

'He's following the Napier Range south and staying close to the cliffs,' said Banjo. 'I think I know where he's heading.'

'You do?' asked the Wizard. 'Where?'

'Tunnel Creek – just over there.' Banjo pointed to the tall cliffs on his left.

'What's Tunnel Creek?' asked Zoran from the back.

'A long limestone tunnel cut right through the Napier Range by water.'

'Why would he go there?' asked the Wizard.

'It's the perfect hiding place. Hey, there he is!' Banjo pointed to a cloud of dust rising up near the cliffs. 'He's almost there!'

'Can't we cut him off?'

'Maybe. Get the map. Quick! In the glove box.'

The Wizard opened the glove box and reached inside. Coiled up tightly in the confined space, the aroused king brown was ready to attack. Moving forward like lightning, it struck. The Wizard saw something flash towards him and raised his arm to protect his face. The lunging snake, deflected by the Wizard's elbow, landed on Banjo's shoulder and buried its fangs deep in his throat.

Weakened by blood loss and barely able to see, Pigeon slid out of the saddle and dropped to the ground. For a while he lay there listening to the gurgling water rushing out of the cave, a raging thirst clawing at his throat. Memories of his childhood began to blur the painful present with seductive images of his father and uncle showing him how to make fire and hunt with a spear.

Tunnel Creek, a familiar place, gave him strength. Slowly, he began to crawl towards the entrance of the cave, the cool air drifting out of its mouth luring him inside. As he looked around, he remembered a shallow rock pool at the entrance and dragged himself a little further until he could touch the smooth, dish-like edge of the pool with the tips of his fingers. The crystal clear water was only a few centimetres deep. Licking his parched lips, he mustered all his remaining strength, rolled onto his side and let himself slide into the water. With his cheek resting against the wet rock, he opened his mouth and began to drink.

'What's that over there?' asked Jack, pointing to a cloud of dust rising up through the tall spinifex grass a few hundred metres up ahead.

'Here, use these,' said Andrew, handing Jack a pair of binoculars.

'It's an overturned vehicle. I think it's theirs.'

With the snake clinging to his neck, Banjo had lost control of the car. Mounting a termite mound and hitting a tree, the vehicle had rolled.

The Land Rover was lying on its roof, steam rising from the open bonnet. Andrew stopped the car and reached for his gun.

'Jack, you come with me. Bring the rifle. Everyone else stays in the car.'

Sitting on the ground under a tree, the Wizard was nursing his leg, a handgun within easy reach on a rock beside him.

'Help already. That was quick,' he said cheerfully. 'Hello Jack. Fancy meeting you out here. I've got a great story for you, mate, just look around.'

'Get his gun, Jack,' said Andrew, covering the Wizard with his rifle. Jack walked over to the rock and picked up the gun.

207

'What about him?' he asked, pointing to Banjo, still strapped into the driver's seat of the upturned vehicle.

'Don't worry about him,' replied the Wizard breezily, 'he's dead.'

'Where's Zoran?' asked Andrew.

'He went to get help.'

'Out here? Sure. Jack. Over there – the horse.'

Andrew pointed with his gun to the forbidding cliffs shimmering in the noonday sun like a mirage. A horse without a rider stood motionless under a tree.

'That's the entry to Tunnel Creek. Will, come over here,' shouted Andrew.

Will got out of the car and hurried over to him.

'Here, hold this and don't take your eyes off him,' said Andrew, handing his revolver to Will. 'Jack, we'll go and have a look. Everyone else stays here.'

Refreshed by the soothing water, Pigeon turned awkwardly onto his back, closed his eyes, and drifted into a restless slumber.

'This is where Jandamarra died,' he heard his father say. 'He was killed, but never defeated – remember that. You have Jandamarra's blood in your veins ... be proud of it. His spirit will live on in here forever.'

Woken by footsteps echoing through the cave, Pigeon opened his eye. A dark shadowy figure stood in front of him, backlit by shafts of bright light coming from outside. It was impossible to see if the figure had a face.

'Jandamarra?' whispered Pigeon.

'Sorry mate, it's me, Zoran,' replied the shadow, moving closer. 'Taking a bath? You're one cunning little bastard, I'll give you that.' Zoran cleared his throat and spat into the sand.

'Come over here where I can see you,' croaked Pigeon, trying to prop himself up on his elbows to get a better look. But the pain in his shoulder was too severe and he slumped back into the water.

'Get up, the Wizard's waiting.'

Zoran raised his sawn-off shotgun and pointed it at Pigeon. 'Or should I just blow your fucking head off and be done with it? What do you reckon? Shame we still have unfinished business to discuss, isn't it? Move, you black mongrel!'

Lying perfectly still, Pigeon reached slowly for the knife stuck in his belt. First, he concealed the long blade in the palm of his hand, then he bent his arm just a little and rested it on his chest. 'Jandamarra was killed, but never defeated,' Pigeon heard his father whisper in his ear.

'I don't think you heard me,' said Zoran angrily. 'Get up, you lazy cunt.'

Pigeon laughed. 'You should see yourself, Zoran. The Wizard's lapdog, we used to call you. The only thing missing is the tail.'

'What did you say?' roared Zoran bending forward, his barrel chest presenting the perfect target. Pigeon lifted his right arm out of the water and, with a lightning-fast flick of the wrist, threw the knife at Zoran. As the blade pierced his heart, Zoran's gun went off.

44

Tunnel Creek, 3 March, 12 noon

The sharp report of a single gunshot bounced off the limestone walls and rolled like thunder through the cave. The silence of the hot afternoon had been shattered.

'Did you hear that?' asked Andrew, breaking into a trot. 'I hope we're not too late. Stay behind me and be careful.'

Jack checked his rifle and followed Andrew to the cave's entrance.

Ignoring the direction to stay behind, Cassandra limped after them. 'I'll come with you,' Rebecca called out, hurrying after her.

Eyes wide open and unseeing, Zoran lay motionless on his back, still clutching the wooden handle of the knife with both hands.

'This one's gone,' said Andrew.

Jack hurried past him to the pool. The water in the rock pool had turned red and cloudy, but Pigeon was still breathing. Every heartbeat was pumping new blood through the massive hole in his chest, the tiny bubbles rising to the surface forming a crimson foam around the wound.

'This one isn't far behind,' said Jack, lowering his gun. 'What a mess.'

'Is he dead?' cried Cassandra, hobbling across to the pool.

Dropping her walking stick, she waded into the water and knelt down beside Pigeon.

'Can you hear me?' she whispered, placing her hand on Pigeon's burning forehead. 'It's me, Cassandra. 'Talk to me! Please.'

Pigeon could hear a familiar voice somewhere in the distance. It sounded like someone was talking to him through cottonwool.

'Stay with me, Pigeon,' the voice continued. 'Is Anna alive? Is she still alive?'

Anna, thought Pigeon, remembering the promise he had made on his mother's grave. *I must set things right!*

'Can't we do something?' cried Cassandra, looking pleadingly up at Jack watching her from the pool's edge. 'He's slipping away.'

Jack shook his head.

Then, as sometimes happens just before death, Pigeon's brain produced something extraordinary: a painless moment of clarity. Opening his eye, he looked at Cassandra. Recognition.

'Is Anna alive?' Cassandra asked again.

Pigeon nodded ever so slightly.

'Yes?' asked Cassandra, not quite trusting what she had just witnessed.

Pigeon nodded again.

'Where is she?' Cassandra was shouting now, her voice trembling with frustration and fear.

Pigeon opened his mouth just a little, his chest heaving for the last time, and slowly moved his lips.

Cassandra bent down lower still until her ear almost touched Pigeon's chin. 'Please, Pigeon, for Anna's sake ... tell me!' she cried, tears streaming down her blood-splattered face.

'Kalumburu,' Pigeon sighed, his voice barely audible.

'He's gone,' said Cassandra sadly. Rebecca waded into the pool and helped her stand up.

'What did he say?' she asked.

'Only one word; it sounded like 'Kalambaru' ... something like that ...'

'Come again?' said Andrew, an edge of excitement in his voice.

'Kalambaru.'

Jack looked at Andrew. 'Does that mean something to you?' he asked.

'Sure does,' replied Andrew, putting his hand on Cassandra's shoulder.

'What is it?' she asked.

'It's a Benedictine Mission ... it's way up north on the King Edward River,' said Andrew. 'A remote place ... and well, it's got a painful past. It's unbearably hot, there are crocodiles and in the wet season ... they have unbelievably violent storms.'

'Do you think ... it could be ...?' asked Cassandra hopefully, wiping Pigeon's blood from her cheeks with the back of her hand.

'Would a dying man lie?' he asked. 'I think not. He's certainly telling us something. We'll have to go up there and find out what it is.'

Cassandra wanted to be alone. Still haunted by Pigeon's last word – Kalumburu – she hurried out of the cave and sat down on a rock.

Turning her face towards the sun, she closed her eyes, hoping that the warm rays would banish the horror she'd just witnessed.

This is where Jandamarra died, she thought, *and now Pigeon too. There has to be a connection!* Wondering if the spirit would speak to her again, she listened to the breeze gently moving the dry blades of the tall grass surrounding her on all sides like waves of an ocean long gone.

Many try to listen, but few know how to hear, she heard Andrew tell her over and over. *I know how to hear*, she thought. *Jandamarra, speak to me!*

'It's difficult to explain to the living what it's like to turn into a spirit. To begin with ... imagine that you have no body,' whispered Jandamarra's spirit voice. 'There's no pain, no fear, no longing and no desire. There's no joy, either. No love, nor laughter. There are no feelings, only a sense of detachment and a great awareness of right and wrong. Yet there is more, a great deal more ... Everything is different, but there are rules; strict ones. The best way I can describe it, I suppose, is to tell you that it's liberating. You are no longer part of the physical and emotional world, yet you are aware of it and can enter it at will ...'

Suddenly, the breeze picked up. The voice became fainter and almost disappeared. 'Don't go,' pleaded Cassandra and opened her eyes. Changing direction, the breeze calmed down and the voice returned.

'Let me tell you what happened to my head,' the spirit voice continued. 'The man who killed me was Micki, a black trooper from the Pilbara with a fearsome reputation. He was a Jalngangurru, a medicine man specifically recruited by the Kimberley police to hunt me down. For years, I'd been a great embarrassment to the colonial authorities, especially the Kimberley police who had failed time and time again to crush the Bunuba Resistance. To them, and to the white settlers pushing north with their eye on the fertile land of my ancestors, I was the Bunuba Resistance.

'I have no specific recollection of my death. But after I was shot, I fell down from the pillar. Before I even hit the ground, I found myself outside my body, floating. I know this sounds strange, but that's exactly how it was. I could see everything, but felt nothing. Soon, two white troopers arrived on horseback: Buckland and Anderson. They examined my body and began to argue. They said that without evidence nobody would believe them that Jandamarra was dead. I was right there, you see, and overheard them. So, what did they do? They hacked off my head with a tomahawk and took it with them as proof. My head went on a long journey.

'First, it was taken to Derby where it was displayed during a drunken victory celebration for all to see. It was the ultimate proof that the elusive Jandamarra, notorious leader of the Bunuba Resistance, was no more. But this was just the beginning. My head became a celebrity, a macabre travelling trophy and a testament to the white man's victory over my people. After Derby, it was taken to Perth. There, the good citizens paid their money and queued for hours to see my skull, or so they thought. But I still had the last laugh. It wasn't really my skull at all, but that of Wisego, a black servant I had killed during an ambush. The good citizens of Perth had been deceived.

'Oh, you're smiling ... Do you want to find out what really happened?"

'Yes please,' said Cassandra.

'Well, my skull was sent to England and presented to a notorious arms manufacturer as a gift. A bit gruesome, don't you think?'

Cassandra nodded.

'But arms manufacturers obviously like things like that. After all, dealing in death is their trade. It probably ended up as a paperweight on a partner's desk somewhere, or in a display cabinet in an arms dealer's study as a curiosity. I'm not sure because I never bothered to find out.

'You want to know what happened to the rest of my body, correct?"

Cassandra nodded again.

'My relatives came looking for it. They found my headless corpse where the troopers had left it rotting in the sun. After wrapping it in paperbark, they placed it in a cave high up in the sandstone cliffs, right next to my ancestors. Peace at last, I thought. I was wrong ...'

As Jandamarra's last words were carried away by the breeze, Cassandra opened her eyes. Deeply moved by what she had just heard, she let her eyes roam over the ancient land Jandamarra had called home, the beauty of it filling her heavy heart with peace and joy she couldn't quite explain.

PART III.
CASSANDRA

45

Tunnel Creek, 3 March, 1 p.m.

Andrew called Fitzroy Crossing police station on his satellite phone and reported what had happened at Tunnel Creek. A police vehicle was patrolling the Gibb River Road close by and would reach Tunnel Creek within the hour, he was told. The desk sergeant reminded Andrew not to interfere with the crime scene and asked him to wait for the police to arrive.

'Am I under arrest, Mr Simpson?' asked the Wizard, massaging his aching leg.

'You are,' replied Andrew.

'In that case, I need urgent medical attention, water and some food.'

'Fuck off! The police will be here shortly. They'll look after you, the Outback way.'

'I'll take that as a refusal then.'

'Take it any way you like.'

'Just for the record,' continued the Wizard undeterred, 'as you can see, I had nothing to do with the killing ... I was injured in an accident.'

'Sure, you can explain all that to the magistrate.'

'Can you believe this mongrel?' asked Jack, turning to Cassandra.

Cassandra shrugged. 'Don't underestimate him,' she warned. 'He'll make a nuisance of himself just to annoy us, but what he's really doing is manoeuvring to improve his position. He's preparing his case.'

'You mean as in legal position? Evidence, stuff like that?'

'Precisely. He's cunning; he's a brilliant manipulator. Andrew should be careful.'

'I see you have a satellite phone, Mr Simpson. I'd like to call my lawyer,' said the Wizard.

'Get lost!'

'In that case, Mr Simpson,' said the Wizard, reaching into his pocket, 'would you be so kind and pass this to the police when they

217

arrive?' The Wizard opened his wallet, pulled out something and held it up.

'What's that?' asked Andrew.

'My lawyer's business card.'

'Give it to them yourself,' barked Andrew, turning away.

'As you wish. It's just that I won't be saying anything to the police until he gets here. Bearing in mind he's in Sydney, that may take some time. Well ...' he added, 'I tried.'

The Wizard dropped the business card in the sand, folded his arms across his chest like a petulant schoolboy and sat back.

Everyone moved away from the Wizard after that. Jack found some shade under a tree and handed his water bottle to Rebecca. Andrew sat down next to him and reached for his tobacco pouch.

'What now?' asked Will.

'We wait for the coppers,' said Andrew, rolling a cigarette. 'Smoko time. Relax.'

When Cassandra went back to the car to fetch her bag, she had to pass within earshot of the Wizard.

'Great news about the boy,' he called out. Cassandra hurried past him and didn't reply. 'Coming out of the coma like that ...'

Cassandra stopped in her tracks, turned around slowly, and looked at the Wizard.

'You don't know, do you?' he asked.

'What are you talking about?'

'He woke up two days ago.'

'Liar!'

'Why would I lie about something like that? All you have to do is call Bleak House. Simpson has a satellite phone. Why don't you ask him?'

Cassandra's stomach churned and a cold shiver rippled down her spine. She recognised the feeling only too well – fear. The Wizard's point was compelling. He wouldn't waste his time with a silly prank like that.

'Don't look so worried,' continued the Wizard. 'He's all right – I've made sure of that.'

'What do you mean?' croaked Cassandra.

'We've taken him back to the compound. He'll be far more comfortable there now that he's woken up, don't you think?'

The sick feeling in Cassandra's stomach began to rise. It took all her self control not to throw up.

'After you've made the call, come back here,' hissed the Wizard, lowering his voice. 'We have a few things to discuss ... And not a word of this to the others – the boy's life depends on it.'

The nurse at Bleak House sounded tense and apprehensive. She confirmed most of what the Wizard had said but sounded vague about the coma. Just before the police arrived, Cassandra went back to the Wizard, doubts niggling in the back of her mind.

'Anna's alive, isn't she?' said the Wizard, watching Cassandra carefully.

Cassandra didn't reply.

'And I think you know where she is. After all, that's why you came up here and made contact with Simpson, right?'

Cassandra tried to contradict him, but the Wizard held up his hand to stop her. He wasn't convinced.

'You will help me find her,' he stated calmly. 'If you want to see Tristan again, you'll do exactly as I tell you. Do I make myself clear?'

Cassandra nodded.

'Good. Now, listen carefully. This is what I want you to do.'

46

On the way back to Fitzroy Crossing, 3 March, 4 p.m.

Three hours later, two young constables arrived, irritable and tired. Their shift had started at five in the morning. They were used to dealing with road accidents, pub brawls and domestic violence, but were not experienced enough to investigate a complicated double murder. Andrew radioed the police station and asked for urgent backup. Anxious to return to Fitzroy Crossing before dark, he wanted to leave Tunnel Creek as soon as possible.

'Are we just going to leave these two kids alone with him?' asked Jack, taking Andrew aside.

'He can't cause too much mischief with a broken leg, and I did warn them about him. All they have to do is keep an eye on him, and wait. The others should get here within a couple of hours,' replied Andrew.

'If you really think so ...' Jack was unconvinced.

'We can't stay here overnight with Cassandra and Rebecca. Not after what happened in the cave and with a dead body in the car over there ...' Andrew pointed over his shoulder to the wreck. 'This is a matter for the police. Let them sort out the mess. We've got more important things to do. We'll call into Fitzroy Crossing police station in the morning and make our statements then.'

'You just want to get to Kalumburu, don't you?' said Jack.

'Yep. We'll fly up there tomorrow.'

'Are we getting any closer, do you think?'

'Not sure, but I want to find out, don't you?'

'Sure. Could Kalumburu really hold the key?'

'You heard what Pigeon said. It's our only lead.'

Cassandra was trying to come to terms with her son's new situation. Carefully, she went over everything the Wizard had told her, but something kept bothering her. It wasn't Tristan's time and Cassandra was certain she would have felt something ... And she knew the cards didn't lie. She was wrestling with the Wizard's instructions not to tell anyone about it. More troubling still were the things he expected her to do to keep the boy safe.

Seeing Cassandra's sudden mood change, Rebecca suggested they take a walk. At first she thought that the dramatic events of the day were finally taking their toll. But the haunted look in Cassandra's teary eyes told her there had to be more to it.

'What's wrong?' she asked, linking arms with her new friend. Slowly, as they walked, everything became clear for Cassandra: if she wanted to stay sane and protect her son, she had to break the Wizard's hold over her.

And to do that, she needed help.

For a while they walked in silence until they were well away from the others. Sitting on a smooth rock, they watched the changing light of the late afternoon mellow the harsh landscape. The striking colours, the browns, the reds and the many shades of ochre and yellow – more intense now that the glare had gone – melted into each other, forming a stunning canvas of breathtaking beauty.

Cassandra reached for Rebecca's hand and took a deep breath. 'I'm about to trust you not only with my own life, but,' she began, speaking softly, 'with my son's life as well.'

The rest of the story was easy. Cassandra held nothing back, telling Rebecca about her encounter with the Wizard that afternoon. Rebecca was a good listener and resisted the urge to interrupt.

After they left Tunnel Creek, Rebecca waited until they were well on their way before dropping the bombshell.

'Cassandra wants to tell you something,' she said quietly, reaching across to Cassandra and squeezing her hand.

'Oh? Why so formal all of a sudden?' asked Jack, turning around. 'What's up?'

'Back in Will's house we struck a bargain,' Cassandra began. 'I thought then that I could lead you to Anna, and you agreed to help me. I now believe more than ever that I can do just that.'

Cassandra paused, collecting her thoughts. 'You heard what Pigeon had to say. It's all coming together now in a strange kind of way. These are not coincidences. We're meant to find her. I believe, no I feel, that we're getting close. Very close.'

Taking a deep breath, she paused again. 'I'm trying to keep my side of the bargain, but unfortunately, there's now a serious complication ...'

'Jesus! What is it?' asked Jack.

'The Wizard has abducted Tristan,' Rebecca replied, her voice barely audible.

'What?' Andrew almost shouted. 'How do you know?'

'He told me.'

Cassandra repeated everything she'd told Rebecca earlier. Feeling better with every word, she knew she had made the right decision.

'Do you believe the Wizard's telling the truth?' asked Jack, after Cassandra had finished.

'About the abduction, yes. About Tristan coming out of the coma, no.'

'What makes you say that?' asked Will.

'All of this is classic Eugene – the master-manipulator at his best. He knows exactly how to get to people and which buttons to press. I've seen him do it countless times. He knows there's only one way he can get to me, especially after the fiasco in the boxing tent. Harming Tristan while he was in a coma, practically dead, was pointless. However, claiming that he's suddenly woken up and then taking him away – that's something quite different. This is the joy and the nightmare all wrapped in one. He knows I'd trade my own life for Tristan's. Perhaps one day,' whispered Cassandra, lowering her voice, 'I may have to do just that ...'

'Tell them what the Wizard's asked you to do,' said Rebecca.

'The Wizard is convinced that Anna is alive and that we know where she is. I'm to be his eyes and ears and report everything we're doing.'

'How?' asked Jack.

'I have to call one of his lieutenants in the compound.'

'Do you really believe he's bluffing?' asked Andrew. 'Even after speaking to the nurse at Bleak House?'

'Yes I do. She sounded vague and uncomfortable ...'

'What are you saying?'

'I think the Wizard orchestrated this.'

'Are you serious?'

'Absolutely! The Wizards own Bleak House and employ the nurse ...'

'Oh.'

'And besides, I'd know if my boy had really woken up. Tristan and I have a special bond that goes far beyond mother and son ... This isn't his time – not yet. That's why I'm telling you all this. The Wizard's lying. I know it. If he weren't, I wouldn't have said a word.'

'Are you saying you would have done his bidding?' asked Jack.

'To save Tristan, yes.'

For a while no one spoke. The implications of what Cassandra had just said began to sink in. Looking out the car window, Cassandra watched the tall cliffs fade away, blotted out by the glare of the relentless sun. Hoping that her fears for Tristan's safety would do the same, she closed her eyes.

There it is again, she thought, listening to the voice drifting through the open window. Grateful for the diversion, she began to take deep breaths to prepare herself for a brief escape into the spirit world.

'Bin talkin' lot 'bout my head ... Here I go again ...

'Meeting your ancestors is one of the spiritual highlights a true Bunuba can look forward to when he dies,' whispered the voice. 'I was taught this as a boy as part of my initiation into the secrets of my tribe. I often thought about this. Looking up at the stars after the logs in the campfire had turned to embers, I tried to imagine what it would be like when the time came. It was a scary thought for a young lad. When the time finally did come, nothing could have prepared me for what was waiting for me.

'Before a newcomer is allowed to take his rightful place next to his ancestors, his whole life is examined and debated. Great. Nobody had told me about that. Needless to say, my ancestors knew everything about me and questioned me intensely about certain events in my past life. As you can imagine, there's nowhere to hide in the spirit world. There were many things in my life I wasn't particularly proud of. Unfortunately, these were the very things held up for scrutiny. It's all to do with sex and kinship law. You want an example?'

Yes I do, thought Cassandra.

'But before I can elaborate, I have to tell you a little about myself.'

Please do.

'I don't know the exact year, but I was born in the early 1870s. This was a period of great conflict between the white pastoralists pushing relentlessly north in search of new grazing lands and my people, the Bunuba, the traditional owners. My spirit country on my father's side is called Djumbud. It covers an area rich in tradition and mythology, reaching from Tunnel Creek, where I died, to Windjana Gorge some twenty miles to the north where I fought many a battle defending my country. This is also the place where my ancestors reside and where I was hoping to find peace. However, as I was soon to find out, peace comes at a price; even in the spirit world.

'When I was about eleven, my mother moved to Lennard River station – a million acres of the best Kimberley frontier land – run by a white man, a very ambitious white man called William Lukin. I admired that man when I was a boy. You see, I was quite small compared to other Bunuba lads my age. But what I lacked in stature, I made up in other ways. I was really quick; my speed earned me a nickname – Pigeon – given to me by Lukin himself. This name stayed with me until I died and is now etched in Bunuba lore forever. It ... well, it put fear in my enemies, and my people got strength and pride from it, and it became synonymous with the Bunuba Resistance.

'During my time at Lennard River station, I won many foot-races – no one could outrun me over a hundred yards – and became an accomplished boxer, shearer and stockman. But my greatest achievement was with the gun. I could handle a rifle or a revolver like no other and quickly became quite famous for my marksmanship. I turned into Lukin's best black stock-boy and was proud of it. But unfortunately, there was a dark side to all this which my spirit-judges were quick to point out: I had allowed myself to be seduced by the ways of the white man and had turned my back on my people. True. I had offended against tradition and broken Bunuba kinship law. Also true. I had killed many – black and white – and lived a promiscuous life. I couldn't deny it. Things didn't look good.'

There was a moment of silence, then, 'Do you want to hear more?'

'Yes, please,' whispered Cassandra.

'When I first came to the spirit world, I had no voice. I was not allowed to speak in my defence. Believe me, that was very frustrating. Instead, the spirit of Ellemarra, a great man, was assigned to me by my ancestors. He would act as my guide, mentor and spokesman. This was good news: I had known Ellemarra in my youth and admired him greatly.

'In fact, he had been my role model. Be that as it may, it soon became obvious that I wouldn't make a good spirit.

'I was told that the right to speak had to be earned. I would be set a task: to right a great wrong in the world of the living for which I was somehow supposed to be responsible. As it turned out, the wrong hadn't even been committed yet at the time, and I had to wait almost a hundred years before I would discover what it was and why I was responsible for it. That's the spirit world for you. When the curtain was finally lifted, it came as a great shock. Why? You will find out – later. I had therefore plenty of time to learn the ways of the spirit world. And besides, I was very fortunate; Ellemarra was a great spirit guide.

'I was lucky in life and thought – rather naively as it turned out – that my luck would continue in the realm of the spirits ...'

As the voice trailed off, Cassandra opened her eyes. 'Bad dream?' asked Rebecca, glancing at her friend.

'No. Something far more interesting,' said Cassandra, but didn't elaborate. Instead, she looked out the car window and watched Jandamarra's spirit country slide past.

47
At the edge of Djumbud,
3 March, 2010, 5 p.m.

Andrew watched Cassandra's troubled face through the rear view mirror. *She's one hell of a brave woman,* he thought. *I wonder if the spirit has spoken to her.* For almost an hour no one said anything, the brooding silence and the heat becoming more oppressive by the minute.

'Let's have a break,' said Andrew, stopping the car next to a huge boab tree, its gnarled and twisted branches reaching out like the arms of a giant guarding the sacred land of his ancestors. Everyone climbed out of the hot car, and stretching tired limbs, settled down in the cool shade under the tree. Sitting apart from the others, Cassandra stared into the distance. She was trying to recall what the spirit had just told her.

Andrew rolled a cigarette with his nicotine-stained fingers, and walked over to her.

'Come, I want to show you something,' he said. Cassandra looked at him gratefully, reached for her walking stick, and stood up.

'This is the end of Djumbud, my spirit country,' continued Andrew.

Once they were well away from the others, he pointed to a rock ledge covered in paintings.

Looking up at the strange figures Cassandra could clearly hear the spirit's last words: 'Ellemarra turned out to be an excellent guide ... I was lucky in life and thought that my luck would continue in the realm of the spirits. I was mistaken.'

'Who was Ellemarra?' asked Cassandra, turning to Andrew.

'Jandamarra spoke to you,' said Andrew, a knowing smile spreading across his craggy face. Cassandra nodded. 'I thought he might. What did he tell you?'

'He spoke about the day he became a spirit and how his head was cut off as a trophy and displayed for all to see. He also told me how he met his ancestors ...'

'Did he talk about Ellemarra?' interrupted Andrew.

'Not really. He only said that Ellemarra became his spirit guide.'

'Then let me tell you who Ellemarra really was, and why he's so revered by the Bunuba.' Andrew pointed to a shady spot under the rock ledge. 'Let's sit down over there. It's a most fitting place to hear his story.'

Andrew sat down next to Cassandra, and for a while looked dreamily up at Djanbinmarra, the Rainmaker, staring down at them from above.

'As a tribal elder, Ellemarra was larger than life,' began Andrew, breaking the silence. 'Tall and muscular, with ceremonial scars on his chest, he had the bearing of a warrior and the presence of a natural leader. As a youngster, Jandamarra had aspired to become just like him; Ellemarra was his inspiration. He was also his uncle. In the spirit world, however, he became his guide and mentor. He was one of the true Bunuba greats of his time. This is why ...' Andrew reached for his tobacco pouch, and began to roll another cigarette.

'Ellemarra's story is linked to two very special places: Lillimooloora Station representing the new, and Windjana Gorge, the old. On the side of the future were the white settlers, occupying new pastures with total disregard for the rights of the traditional owners. On the side of the past were the Bunuba, defending their sacred land and way of life.' Inhaling deeply, Andrew relaxed.

'William Forrester, one of the early settlers who saw the West Kimberley as an area of tremendous potential, arrived in 1884. His pastoral property of one million acres right next to Lukin's Lennard Downs Station soon became a Kimberley showpiece. But the site Forrester chose for his homestead was as picturesque as it was ill-fated. Situated at Windjana Gorge, a sacred area of great spiritual importance to the Bunuba and their neighbours, the Unggumi, it occupied land which had served countless generations of Aboriginals as a revered ceremonial ground. So ... this is exactly where white cultural ignorance met black spirituality. The scene was set for a struggle of epic proportions.' Andrew paused, and looked across the shimmering plain reaching to the horizon. 'Let me tell you about Windjana Gorge.

'Guarded at the entrance by the Dreamtime hero, Julla – a unique rock formation – Windjana Gorge is a creation of the Lennard River. The river has cut a spectacular passage through the Napier Range. The narrow gorge with its tall cliffs, hidden caves and passages is a sacred place. The remains of thousands of Bunuba, including my own father, were laid to rest in the caves high above the river, wrapped in shrouds of paperbark. To this day, galleries of rock art created thousands of years ago preserve sacred creation stories for generations to come, just like this one right here.' Andrew pointed to the paintings above them.

'The white pastoralists setting up camp nearby knew nothing of this, nor did they care. A showdown was only a matter of time. It came soon enough, drawing Ellemarra into the tragic conflict which would ultimately crush him and his people.

'At first, Ellemarra became an intermediary between the Bunuba and the curious white strangers living at Lillimooloora homestead with their animals. The Bunuba were confused by the white man's obsession with livestock, and inquisitive by nature, they were fascinated by the white man's goods and simply took them whenever they could. Their idea of property and ownership was very different from that of their white neighbours. The settlers took a dim view of this and eventually decided that it was time to teach the 'black thieves' the meaning of what is yours and what is mine. In June 1885, Ellemarra was shot by one of Forrester's men during a raid. He recovered quickly, but this marked the beginning of a bitter conflict with lots of bloodshed and misery on both sides.'

'How come?' asked Cassandra.

'Ellemarra was the first Bunuba to be arrested by the white colonial authorities for stealing. He was chained and padlocked around the neck, and was taken by force from his land to Derby where the magistrate gave him a six months prison sentence. However, he managed to pull off a daring escape and returned to his people to continue the struggle. A few years later, in 1894, he and Jandamarra were destined to become brothers-in-arms and fought a great battle together – the battle of Windjana Gorge, the greatest battle of the Bunuba Resistance.

'Ellemarra was mortally wounded during the fighting and died in Jandamarra's arms. Jandamarra had lost a friend, and the Bunuba a great leader.'

'Why are you telling me all this?' asked Cassandra.

'Because you need to understand,' replied Andrew. 'And to understand, you need to know.'

'You told us that restless spirits cannot find peace because they have unfinished business in the world of the living,' Cassandra said.

'Correct. They are souls-in-waiting ...'

'And Jandamarra is one of those?'

'Yes.'

'And now Pigeon too?'

'Yes.'

'There's a connection?'

'I'm sure there is.'

'Involving Anna?'

'I believe so.'

Cassandra shook her head. 'I can't see it.'

'You will; trust me.'

48

On the way to Kalumburu, 4 March

News of the Tunnel Creek murders spread like wildfire through the Kimberley. When Andrew and his party presented themselves at Fitzroy Crossing police station the next morning, they were told that Broome detectives had taken over the investigation and were keen to speak to them. A forensics team was on its way from Perth to examine the crime scene and to interview the Wizard. The bodies would be taken to the morgue in Broome.

Good luck to them, thought Andrew, remembering the terse exchange with the Wizard. *He won't say a word without his lawyer.*

'What should we do?' asked Jack after they had left the police station. 'Just wait until the detectives get here?'

'No. We'll fly up to Kalumburu right now.' Andrew winked at Jack. 'Go bush, explain later.'

'Won't we get into trouble for this?' asked Rebecca, looking worried.

'Where's your sense of adventure?' said Jack, the journalist in him on fire. 'You don't come across a story like this too often. And we're right in the thick of it.'

'Wait until the media get wind of this,' said Andrew. 'It'll be madness up here, just like when the girls disappeared. Outback stories are a big hit in the cities, and they don't come much bigger than this. I've seen it all before.'

'Just imagine the publicity, Becky,' continued Jack. 'You're always telling me ...'

'Alright, alright,' said Rebecca, holding up her hands, 'I get the picture.'

'I'm with Jack,' said Will. 'This has great potential. How far is it to this Kalumburu Mission?'

'Fortunately, they've got an airstrip up there,' said Andrew.

'We should make it in about three hours, if we're lucky with the weather. It's always a bit tricky this time of the year.'

'Okay, guys, let's get cracking!' said Will, slapping Jack on the back.

The weather forecast wasn't good. A cyclone was forming in the Timor Sea and was slowly moving towards the coast. Dark, threatening storm clouds were building in the west, entertaining them with a spectacular lightening display.

'We have to skirt around this,' said Andrew, pointing to the storm brewing up ahead.

Unaffected by the excitement gripping the others, Cassandra stared out the window. The dark mood outside mirrored her own. Sheets of rain were slowly moving towards the plane like giant curtains trying to blot out the sun. Down below, nature was bracing itself for the summer storm. The Big Wet, as it's called in the Kimberley, brought the gift of life to a thirsty land every summer. Had she made the right decision in telling the others? She knew the Wizard would stop at nothing to get his way, and Tristan, the vulnerable pawn, was at his mercy.

Jack put his hand on Cassandra's shoulder and said, 'I've been thinking ... If we work together as a team, we can turn this to our advantage.'

'How?' asked Cassandra.

'We'll tell the Wizard what we want him to know.'

'And this is supposed to help my son?' she asked bitterly.

'We'll make sure it does. But we mustn't lose our nerve.'

'What's on your mind, Jack?' asked Will.

'If – when – we find Anna, we'll have something the Wizard wants – desperately.'

'So?'

'We'll use that to get the boy back. We'll play the Wizard's game and Cassandra is our seat at the table. The guy's so cocky and sure of himself, he won't suspect she's not telling him the whole truth.'

'Isn't this dangerous?' asked Rebecca.

'Sure, but until someone comes up with something better, it's the best we've got.'

'He's got a point,' said Will. 'What do you think, Cassandra?'

'I don't quite know what to think right now,' she replied, 'but Jack may have hit on something here ...'

'Oh? In what way?' asked Rebecca.

'I'll tell you later ...'

'Okay, guys, that's Kalumburu down there,' said Andrew, beginning his descent. A neat cluster of buildings surrounded by palm trees and lush gardens – a pious sanctuary in the middle of a harsh, flat, rocky landscape – came into view.

'The big stone building next to the church is the monastery. This place became quite famous during the war. The airfield here was taken over by the military because of its strategic position. The Japanese actually bombed Kalumburu in 1943. Here we go. And remember,' he added, 'we're here on a sightseeing trip.'

One of the Benedictine sisters, Sister Josephine, and a young Aboriginal girl met the plane and took them on a tour of the Mission.

'Abbot Fulgentius Torres arrived in 1905 in a sailing boat and chose a spot called Pago on the Drysdale River – not far from here – as the site of the new Mission,' said Sister Josephine, opening the door of the little church. 'That was our first Mission. A church, a monastery, and store houses were built, and market gardens established.'

'Oh! Isn't that beautiful,' said Rebecca, pointing to a large wall painting above the entry. The painting, a unique fusion of striking Aboriginal motifs and Christian themes – all in vivid colours – dominated the simple interior of the church.

'That's our Joblin painting,' replied Sister Josephine. 'We're very proud of it. It exemplifies what this Mission stands for and what it hopes to achieve. We've had some very talented painters here over the years. They drew their inspiration from the many wonderful rock art sites which abound in this region.'

'You mean the Bradshaw paintings and the Euruuru? And the striking Wandjina figures in the King Leopolds?' said Andrew.

Sister Josephine turned around, a little annoyed by the interruption. 'Yes – the native art treasures around here are truly amazing. You seem to know a lot about this.'

'Aboriginal heritage is very close to my heart,' Andrew replied, 'I own a small gallery in Alice ...'

'Ah,' said Sister Josephine, 'that explains it'. 'In 1931, the first Benedictine Sisters arrived, but plans to move the Mission from Pago, some thirty kilometres from here, to Kalumburu were already well advanced,' she continued, slowly walking down the aisle towards the altar. 'In 1932 the whole Mission was relocated to this far superior site – right next to a wonderful pool in the King Edward River.'

'I believe Sister Dolores still lives here,' said Andrew casually.

'You know her?' asked Sister Josephine, surprised.

'No, but I bring greetings from someone who knows her very well,' Andrew said. 'And some sad tidings,' he added quietly. 'Could we see her?'

'Of course. I'll make sure she joins you for morning tea. Our little tour includes refreshments. And you can visit our museum. It's well worthwhile.'

'You didn't tell us anything about this,' whispered Jack, following the others out of the church. 'Who's Sister Dolores?'

'Sister Dolores is Elvie's mother.'

'What?' Jack exclaimed.

Sister Josephine turned around and gave him a disapproving look. 'But that would make her Pigeon's ...' Jack said, lowering his voice.

'Grandmother – yes.'

'How on earth did you find all this out so quickly?'

'I phoned Auntie this morning and asked her about Kalumburu ... There had to be a connection,' said Andrew, reaching for his tobacco pouch. 'Sister Dolores is the connection. Shall we go and have some tea and meet her?'

49

Kalumburu, 4 March, in the morning

Leaning on Sister Josephine's arm, Sister Dolores – a tiny Aboriginal woman in her seventies – shuffled across the courtyard. Sister Josephine walked her over to Andrew and introduced them. Jack had explained to the others who Sister Dolores was, and they thought it best to let Andrew talk to her alone.

'Would you like to visit our little museum before we have morning tea?' asked Sister Josephine, turning to Rebecca.

'Oh yes, please. We'd love to.'

'I'll take you. It's just over there.'

The museum's eclectic collection was a colourful testimony to the Mission's chequered history. There wasn't a theme as such. Over the years, any object of interest, or with a story to tell, had been added.

However, wartime memorabilia had pride of place. Brass shell casings, a wooden propeller that had once belonged to a biplane, helmets with bullet holes, a massive anchor and chain, Japanese mines that looked like steel hedgehogs and an assortment of naval uniforms, pennants and flags greeted visitors at the entrance. Garish souvenirs from Lourdes and Rome, including a large portrait of Pope Pius XXII, were neatly arranged on top of a Victorian washstand. Wooden crates full of books in German, French, Russian, Portuguese and Spanish propped up a rickety trestle table covered in rusty kitchen utensils, tools, toys, straw hats, parasols and a harmonica with a mother of pearl keyboard. Turning its back on the world, a wooden rocking horse missing one ear faced the corner.

'We're in the middle of cataloguing the collection,' said Sister Josephine. 'It's a huge task, as you can imagine. We find a new little treasure in here almost every day.'

She ran her hand playfully along the badly scratched top of a mahogany sideboard covered in seashells. 'Take this, for instance.'

Opening a glass case, she took out a silver fob watch. 'This used to belong to the German aviator Kausman. Kausman and Bertram were rescued at Cape Bernier in 1932 by Aboriginals from the Mission. And over here, this piece of twisted metal was once part of the fuselage of the Shady Lady, a Liberator B24 which had crash-landed near Mary Island. Another famous rescue. Look at this, you'll find this interesting.' Sister Josephine held up a sepia photograph the size of a postcard. 'These are some of the survivors of the *Koolama*. The ship was bombed in 1943. A hundred and thirty civilian survivors were brought to Pago and were cared for by the Mission.'

'What happened to the ship?' asked Will.

'It was badly damaged in the attack, but didn't go down. It managed to stay afloat and limped on to Wyndham Harbour – nearly 480 kilometres away. Please feel free to move around. Any questions, just ask.'

As soon as Cassandra stepped into the museum she felt uneasy. Stuffed birds and fierce looking glass-eyed reptiles stared at her through dusty display cabinets. Spears, shields and war clubs spoke of tribal feuds, violence and death, the naval memorabilia of battles at sea and watery graves. The past was closing in on her from all sides.

'Is something wrong?' asked Rebecca placing her hand on Cassandra's arm.

'No, it's just this place ... I can't quite explain it ...'

'What do you make of Pigeon's grandmother living right here at the Mission? Surely that must mean something, don't you think?' speculated Rebecca.

'There's something in here,' continued Cassandra, ignoring the question.

'Relating to Anna, you mean?'

Cassandra nodded.

'Just look at this shambles. We'll never find anything in this place,' said Rebecca.

'Don't worry, that's not how it works.'

'What do you mean?'

'You don't find it, it finds you.'

Jack and Will were in their element. They were experts in sifting through bric-a-brac and spotting the items of real interest. However, the sheer volume and variety of the exhibits surprised even them.

'Can you believe all this stuff?' asked Jack, turning the pages of an old photo album. 'Here in this remote place ...'

'I wonder what's in there?' said Will, pointing to a small annex at the back of the room.

'Pictures,' replied Sister Josephine, 'still being sorted. We're going to set up a small gallery in here.'

'May we?' asked Jack.

'Go right ahead.'

The small room had only one window. The glass was cracked in several places and covered in cobwebs. A single light bulb dangled from the ceiling and a musty smell hung in the stale air. The pictures – most of them unframed – had been sorted according to size and were leaning against the wall.

'Just the place to find a lost Rembrandt, eh?' Jack said.

'You never know. Let's have a quick look.'

Jack sat down on a crate facing the window and began to examine the pictures. 'This isn't bad,' he said, holding up a pencil drawing of an Aboriginal woman carrying a small child on her back. Most of the pictures, however, were amateurish, almost childish, in their simplicity. 'Well, certainly no Rembrandt in here, I'm afraid,' he said, standing up. 'Let's go.'

As they walked towards the door, Will stubbed his toe against a picture frame resting against the wall. The picture – depicting Christ with a bleeding heart – fell over and hit the floor.

'Don't destroy the collection before they've had a chance to display it, mate,' said Jack.

As he crouched down to pick up the painting, something caught his eye. Partially hidden behind a little brown suitcase in the corner was a bark painting. The colours were vivid and eye-catching. Jack pushed the suitcase carefully aside, picked up the rectangular piece of bark and carried it across to the window. For what seemed a very long moment, he stared at it in silence, a stunned look on his face.

'Found the lost Kalumburu Rembrandt after all?' teased Will.

'No. Something much better. Come and have a look.'

50

Kalumburu, 4 March, in the afternoon

'Who's found the Kalumburu Rembrandt?' asked Rebecca, ducking through the narrow doorway. 'You look like two naughty boys caught in the act.'

'Here, tell us what you make of this,' said Jack quietly. He carried the bark painting over to the crate and placed it on top.

The painting was divided into three separate panels like a triptych, but painted on the same piece of bark. Following the irregular shape of the bark, the panels increased in size from left to right, giving the impression of distance in space and time.

'What do you see?' asked Jack, pointing to the smallest panel.

Rebecca covered her mouth with her hand and gasped. 'Oh my God! This looks like ...'

'Yes?' prompted Jack.

Cassandra had quietly entered the room and was looking over Rebecca's shoulder. Rebecca took a deep breath. 'Countess Kuragin's chateau in France,' she whispered, pointing to the painting. 'This is the moat right here, and over there is the bridge we crossed in the rain that night – remember? And this is the little chapel at the back with the funny onion-shaped Russian belltower ...'

Jack gave Will a meaningful look. 'That's exactly what I just told Will before you came in. And this is ...'

'Here you are. I've been looking for you everywhere,' said Andrew, walking into the crowded little room. What's that?' he asked, glancing at the bark painting.

'This is what we came here for,' replied Cassandra calmly. 'Jack just found it. Or more accurately, it found him.'

Leaning over the crate, Andrew examined the painting. 'What is it?' he asked.

'I would call it a storyboard,' replied Jack, pointing to the smallest panel. A little girl stood between two adults, a man and a woman. The girl had long blonde hair with ribbons in it and was wearing a blue polka dot dress and red shoes. All three had their backs turned and were looking at a large building – partially concealed behind tall trees and shrubs – in the distance. The woman held the girl's hand and the man was pointing to a dog running towards them.

'This is little Anna and her parents,' said Jack, 'and this is the Kuragin family chateau in France. Rebecca and I were there only a couple of weeks ago. It looks exactly like that.'

'Are you serious?' asked Andrew, surprised.

'Absolutely,' replied Jack.

'And this weird thing? What's this?' asked Rebecca, running her fingers over the centre panel.

'Ah,' said Will. 'This is a spider's web – see? Constructed entirely of numbers. Interlocking sixes, painted in black.' Forming a circle, the big sixes on the outside became smaller and smaller, moving towards the centre in concentric circles until they met in the middle. 'In the centre here where the spider would sit waiting for the fly,' continued Will, 'is something sinister – a head. And what does it remind you of? Half grinning skull, half bearded man with a conical hat?'

'The Wizards of Oz. That's their emblem' said Cassandra quietly.

'Exactly,' replied Will. 'Show them the photo, Jack.'

Jack pulled his digital camera out of his pocket, searched the stored photos and handed the camera to Rebecca. The picture on the display panel was a snapshot of the strange wall covered in black numbers – sixes – that Jack and Will had discovered in the derelict farmhouse abandoned by the Wizards of Oz.

'You're right,' said Rebecca.

'Yeah. But look at the third panel here,' said Jack. The third panel, the largest, cleverly used ridges and knots in the bark to form the interior of a large cave. Holding a paintbrush in her right hand, a young woman with short blonde hair was looking up at the low ceiling covered in striking paintings.

'Rock art,' said Andrew. 'Bradshaw paintings, they're called. Some of the most sophisticated rock paintings in Australia. There are thousands of them. They're named after Joseph Bradshaw who discovered them in 1891 during a Kimberley expedition not far from here. The paintings are very old, some say 50,000 years or so.'

'They look like stick figures,' Rebecca said.

'That's the distinctive Bradshaw style. Whoever painted this has done an excellent job of reproducing them right down to the colour. Shades of Mulberry red – see? These paintings are the stuff of legends among my people.'

'In what way?' asked Jack.

'According to the stories still being told around the campfires up here, the pictures were painted by birds. Apparently, the birds kept pecking the rock until their beaks bled and then used their tail feathers and their own blood to create these amazing paintings.'

'Okay guys, time for a reality check. What does all this mean? A weird bark painting turns up here in the middle of nowhere. Jack, you seem to think it gives us three snapshots of Anna's life – true?' said Will.

Jack nodded. 'First, her childhood in France – a little distant now – then a dark event right here in the middle, and finally her new life as a young adult. The black spider's web linking the two is clever, don't you think? She's caught ... between the past and the future ... We know what happened to her at the farm. It must have been a pretty profound event ... a real watershed ...'

'Somehow held together by something too terrifying to remember but impossible to forget,' interjected Cassandra quietly.

'Yes. Anna must have painted this,' said Rebecca.

'Looks like it. I mean, we know she's an accomplished painter. She was going to study art in Paris when she got back from Australia, right?'

'But this is crazy,' said Rebecca, shaking her head. 'Anna, up here? It doesn't make sense!'

'Perhaps it does,' said Andrew, looking thoughtfully at the painting. 'Here's what Sister Dolores had to say: She came here to Kalumburu as a young woman to work in the kitchen. She fell in love with an Aboriginal lad, a blacksmith. They had two children, a boy and a girl.

The kids grew up here at the Mission and were educated by the nuns. At seventeen, the girl, Elvie, ran away with a drover and went to live in Fitzroy Crossing. A year later she had a boy ...'

'Pigeon?' interjected Cassandra.

'Yes. Apparently, the young couple had a tempestuous relationship. The boy ended up here with his grandparents and spent his early childhood at the Mission.'

'And all this is going to help us understand the picture here?' asked Rebecca, pointing to the bark painting. 'Where's the connection?'

'I'm not sure yet, but we'll find it, trust me,' replied Andrew quietly. 'I have an idea ...' he mumbled to himself.

'I wonder how the painting ended up here,' said Rebecca.

Standing just outside the room, Sister Josephine overheard. 'Sister Dolores gave it to us recently,' she said, 'just after her son, Mungo, died. She disposed of everything that reminded her of him.'

'Did she say anything about the painting? How she obtained it, where it came from? Anything at all?' Jack asked.

'No. Sister Dolores has Alzheimer's – quite advanced, I'm afraid. She can remember events from thirty years ago in surprising detail, but she would by now have completely forgotten that she has just spoken with Mr Simpson.' Sister Josephine shrugged. 'The ravages of old age. I don't think she'd be able to help you. She couldn't tell us anything about the painting when she gave it to us, except that it reminded her of her son.'

It had turned ominously dark outside and the rumbling of thunder could be heard. Andrew looked out the window.

'Could we borrow the painting?' he asked, turning to Sister Josephine. 'It's very important. You have my assurance that we'll return it safely.'

'Of course, take it with you. As you can see, it's just one of many in here we have to sort through. We still have a long way to go with our little gallery.' Sister Josephine glanced anxiously at Andrew. 'Better hurry,' she said. 'I don't like this change in the weather.'

'I don't either,' said Andrew, remembering the cyclone warning. 'If we don't take off now, we could be trapped here for days.'

51

Never Never Downs, 4 March, 5 p.m.

The storm was closing in fast. For several days, large banks of clouds heavy with moisture had hovered above the Timor Sea. Looking like an army of Orcs ready to invade the parched land, it gained momentum and crossed the Kimberley coast. Nature was waiting for the signal to unleash the torrential rains as it had done for eons during the cyclone season. A small change in air temperature in the Admiralty Gulf was all that was needed. An age-old spectacle was about to begin.

Andrew tried to outflank the storm by flying east, but it was moving in too fast. 'We won't make it back to Fitzroy Crossing,' he said, tapping the fuel gauge. 'We'll have to land.'

'Where?' asked Jack.

'Right there,' replied Andrew, pointing down to a cluster of buildings barely visible through the driving rain.

'What's that?' asked Rebecca.

'A cattle station owned by a mate of mine. It has an airstrip and fuel, and we need both – urgently.'

'That's reassuring,' said Rebecca, looking pale. For the last hour she had anxiously watched the spectacular lightning show rage around them. The storm was racing in from the north, turning day into night. 'I must have been out of my mind to get into this jalopy,' she said under her breath.

'Did you say something?' asked Will.

'No, I've nothing to say, China, except to tell you that this is definitely the last time I'm traipsing along with you guys through the Outback.'

'C'mon, you're having fun, admit it – right?' said Jack.

'Fun? Did you say fun? We're trying to outrun a cyclone, we're low on fuel, the old plane is being tossed around like a ping-pong ball in a toilet bowl and we have to land somewhere in this godforsaken wilderness or perish. If that's your idea of fun, buster, you can keep it.'

'Research can be dangerous. You know that,' continued Jack undeterred, a mischievous smile creasing his face. 'We authors often put our lives on the line for our readers. Our publishers rarely appreciate that,' he added haughtily, patting Rebecca on the arm.

'Don't give me that crap! It's me you're talking to, not one of your starry-eyed fans.'

'This is better than being couped up in a Manhattan glass tower with your posh literary mates, admit it,' said Will cheerfully. 'One day you'll thank us, you'll see.'

'I doubt it. I may not live that long.' At that moment, a bolt of lightning exploded right in front of the plane, illuminating the inside of the small cabin with a ghostly light.

'Shit, that was close!' said Will, holding on to the seat in front of him, his knuckles turning white.

'Shut up, guys, and brace yourselves,' interrupted Andrew curtly, trying to line up the plane for landing. 'I'm flying by the seat of my pants here – I can't see a bloody thing!'

'That's just great,' said Rebecca, reaching for Cassandra's hand. 'At least if we're going down, we're going down together.'

'We'll be fine,' said Cassandra, 'it isn't our time.'

'I hope you're right,' said Rebecca, closing her eyes.

Flying almost blind, Andrew barely missed the tin roof of a shed before touching down in the mud and skidding to a halt in front of a tree at the end of the makeshift runway. He took a deep breath and turned off the engine.

'That was a little too close even for my liking,' he confessed quietly. 'Welcome to Never Never Downs, one of the most remote cattle stations in the country.' Andrew had to raise his voice to make himself heard. The rain drumming against the fuselage was deafening.

'Can I open my eyes now?' asked Rebecca.

'Don't bother, you can't see a thing,' replied Jack, staring out the window.

'We can't just get out of the plane and leave it here,' said Andrew. 'The wind's too strong. It would tip it over in no time. I've seen it happen before. Wings snapping off like toothpicks. We've got to get the plane under cover.'

'What's that?' asked Will, pointing into the gloom.

'A pair of headlights I'd say,' replied Jack. 'The cavalry coming to our rescue?'

Driving an old Land Rover without a roof, doors or windscreen, Hamish McGregor arrived with two Aboriginal stockmen.

'Stay in the plane,' he shouted. 'We'll tow you to the shed over there.'

The two stockmen jumped off the back of the Land Rover and secured a steel cable to the front of the plane. Slowly, the plane began to roll forward.

There was just enough space for the plane in the shed behind the two aircraft belonging to Never Never Downs.

'I watched you come in, mate,' said Hamish, slapping Andrew on the back. 'Didn't think you'd make it. This is the worst storm we've had in years. What are you doing out here? Your message was a bit cryptic.'

'It's a long story. I'll tell you later over a beer,' replied Andrew, lowering his voice. 'But first, meet my friends here.' Andrew introduced the owner of Never Never Downs. Hamish McGregor, a giant of a man in his sixties with a knuckle-crushing handshake and a smile that could light up an orphanage, shook hands with each of his new guests.

'Let's go over to the homestead,' he said. 'The Missus is waiting with tea and scones. Sorry about the weather.'

'Sounds wonderful,' said Jack, turning to Andrew. 'You certainly seem to have friends in all the right places, mate.'

Rebecca put her arm around Cassandra, and together they hurried across to the homestead through the driving rain.

'Get the painting, Jack, I want to show it to someone here,' said Andrew.

Jack reached into the back of the plane, wrapped the painting into an old blanket and ran after the others.

'You're full of surprises, Andrew Simpson. You must have been a hell of a detective, that's all I can say,' said Jack, standing dripping wet under the awning. He thanked McGregor's wife, Margaret, for handing him a towel and began to dry his wet face. 'Emergency landing – bullshit! You sent him a message, didn't you? He was expecting us. You planned to come here all the time – admit it.'

'What if I did?' replied Andrew.

'Why here? What else did Sister Dolores tell you, eh? Who do you want to show the picture to?'

'You're a perceptive bastard, aren't you, Jack? Bloody journalists! It's just a hunch.'

'You risked our lives over a hunch?' said Rebecca, who had overheard the exchange.

'I had no idea it would get this rough.'

'What hunch?' demanded Jack, following Andrew into the dining room.

'You'll find out soon enough. If my hunch is right, you won't be disappointed, trust me. Bring the painting.'

52

Never Never Downs, 4 March, 7 p.m.

The old homestead – constructed in the 1890s by Hamish McGregor's grandfather using local stone, and lovingly restored with much of the original furniture still gracing the rooms – spoke of a turbulent past. Never Never Downs was one of the few cattle stations in the region still being run by the same family since the first white settlers arrived in the Kimberley. Its isolation and remoteness, which during the early years had made life almost unbearable, had recently turned into an unexpected boon and source of considerable income: ecotourism.

Most of the cattle had been sold off long ago. They kept a few Brahmans – to give the place authenticity – and the sheds which once housed farm machinery and stables, had been turned into luxury accommodation oozing Outback character and charm. With its own airstrip and small planes to fly in the guests, discerning overseas tourists looking for a unique Australian Outback adventure could be met at the airport at Broome or Kununurra and find themselves sipping champagne in the pristine Kimberley wilderness within a few hours. In a world where time was at a premium, the well-heeled ecotourists were prepared to pay a small fortune for the experience. Hamish McGregor and his two sons had turned an outdated, languishing cattle station losing money into a great economic and ecological success and a 'must see' destination for the rich and famous.

Remote and different was definitely 'in'.

Most of the Aboriginal drovers had moved on but there were still a few 'oldies' who had lived on Never Never Downs all their lives. The women helped in the kitchen and took care of the household chores. The men maintained the buildings and acted as guides, taking the tourists to see Aboriginal rock art which was one of the main attractions of Never Never Downs. One old Aboriginal, Muddenbudden, a revered Bunuba elder who was almost blind, was the storyteller. He would join the guests by the fire after dinner and tell stories of Dream-time heroes and the plight of early settlers, and describe the drama of first contact between the white pastoralists and the Aborigines defend-ing their land and way of life.

Muddenbudden was very popular with the guests, and had featured in several travel shows and TV documentaries. It was Muddenbudden who Andrew had come to see.

Because Never Never Downs was closed during the rainy season, accommodating the new arrivals was no problem. After a hearty meal in the old homestead which was now used only as the dining room, common lounge and library for the guests, Andrew broached the subject of Anna's disappearance with their host.

A few years earlier, the McGregors had opened an art gallery on the property to support a small but influential artists' colony. Staff accommodation – obsolete since the departure of the cattle – was now used to house Aboriginal artists and their families. In a studio attached to the gallery, houseguests could watch artists at work and talk to them about their culture and their craft. The artists made all their own colours using techniques handed down from generation to generation. This made their work unique and highly sought after, not only by the tourists, but by galleries both in Australia and overseas. Several of the larger paintings had found their way into the boardrooms of multinational mining companies. A recent exhibition in New York – *Dreamtime Artists of Never Never Downs* – had received much critical acclaim.

'Andrew has something to tell us,' announced Jack, striding into the room with the bark painting under his arm. He walked across to the fireplace and placed the painting on the mantelpiece. Despite the harrowing flight and the storm raging outside, everyone began to relax. As experienced hosts, Hamish and Margaret knew how to put their guests at ease. All heads turned expectantly towards Andrew.

'I have a confession to make,' he said, standing up. 'As you've probably worked out already, coming here was no accident.' Andrew paused. Sitting by herself in the back of the room on a faded old leather lounge, Cassandra was watching him. The revelation came as no surprise to her.

'Also, I hope you don't mind, but I've told Hamish and Margaret all about Anna and what brought us to the Kimberley. As you are about to find out, their participation in our search for Anna is essential. I don't believe we can take the next step without their help. Here's why.' Andrew paused and took a sip of wine, the silence in the room deafening.

'It all has to do with this here,' continued Andrew. He walked over to the fireplace and pointed to the painting. 'There was something else Sister Dolores told me ... It didn't make any sense to me at the time, but when I saw this painting at the Mission, things began to fall into place.'

Andrew paused again, collecting his thoughts. 'Sister Dolores's son, Mungo – Pigeon's uncle – was a talented painter who made a good living out of copying the Aboriginal rock art found around here and selling the bark paintings to galleries in Broome and Darwin. Pigeon and Mungo were very close, and the boy spent many a month in the bush with his uncle, helping him find new rock paintings in this vast, remote wilderness. When I questioned Sister Dolores further about her son, she told me he'd recently joined his ancestors. We know she has Alzheimer's. Her answers to my other questions regarding her son were incoherent at best, except for this: when I asked her where her son had lived, where he'd painted and who his friends were, she told me to ask Muddenbudden.' Andrew paused again.

'Who's Muddenbudden?' Jack asked quietly.

'You're about to meet him,' replied Andrew. 'Hamish, would you please show him in?'

The years had not been kind to Muddenbudden, but he certainly had presence. Looking frightfully thin and frail, like a lonely reed waiting for winter in a frozen pond, his body was bent and his limbs twisted. His beard and sparse hair were as white as the first snow and his face creased like old boot leather. Milky-grey cataracts covered both his eyes, robbing him of most of his eyesight. As a Bunuba elder, a Jalngangurru, he was revered by the local Aboriginals as one of the last great law men of his generation. What he lacked in physical strength, he more than made up for mentally – he was as bright and alert as a man half his age. With a phenomenal memory and a surprisingly strong voice, he radiated authority and intelligence, commanding instant respect.

Andrew pulled up a chair in front of the fireplace and helped the old man sit down. 'We meet again, Muddenbudden. It's been a long time,' he said.

'You sound just like your father,' replied the old man, raising his hand. 'Going blind has helped me see. At times I can see the past and the future at the same time. You have come here to right a great wrong. I know,' continued the old man. 'I saw it in a dream. I have been expecting you.'

'What do you make of this?' whispered Rebecca, squeezing Jack's arm. Jack shook his head, but said nothing. Sitting on the edge of her seat, Cassandra watched the old man intently.

'Sister Dolores told me that you and her son, Mungo, were like brothers,' began Andrew.

'Not like brothers. More like father and son,' Muddenbudden corrected him. 'He came here often to visit me. He was a wonderful artist with a great gift. He could copy the sacred paintings created by our ancestors like no other. He understood their meaning. He could feel the past and connect with the Dreamtime ...'

'Where did he do his painting?'

'He spent months in the bush,' replied the old man, 'copying the originals. I used to guide him to the best locations.'

'What happened to his paintings?' asked Andrew.

'He sold them here in our gallery,' said Hamish. 'They were in great demand, not only by our guests but from art dealers as well. They used to come here regularly to buy his paintings.'

'What did he do with the money?' asked Jack.

'We have a small store here,' replied Hamish. 'He would buy supplies from us and disappear again for weeks at a time. We had no idea where he went. He was a loner, but quite a character – gregarious, well liked and full of charm. You never knew when he would turn up.'

'Would you recognise his paintings, Hamish?'

'Absolutely.'

'Please take a look at this,' said Andrew, pointing to the painting on the mantelpiece. 'Is this one of his?' Hamish walked over to the fireplace, put on his glasses, and examined the painting.

'Did he work alone?' asked Cassandra quietly from the back. Hamish turned around, surprised. 'Funny you should ask that,' he replied. 'There was this rumour ...'

'What rumour?' asked Andrew.

'That he had an assistant ...'

'How come?' interrupted Jack impatiently.

'Because some of the paintings were quite different and signed by someone else. Just like this one here – see?' Hamish pointed to the bottom right corner of the piece of bark. 'Look.'

Jack walked over to the painting and ran his finger along the signature in the corner. 'It looks like "Lucrezia",' he murmured. 'I didn't notice this before. How odd.'

'Paintings signed by this artist were greatly sought after by the dealers and, well, as you can expect, those ones got a much higher price than the ones painted by Mungo,' said Hamish. 'Everyone used to tease him about it.'

'Did he say who the other painter was?' asked Will.

'No. He was very secretive about that. I think it was a bit of a sore point.'

'How did he die?' asked Cassandra.

'About three months ago, he was on his way here to sell his paintings. Usually, he just turned up in his ute with paintings stacked on the back, but occasionally, he'd hitch a ride on one of the planes visiting from the other stations. Unfortunately, this time the plane he was on crashed into the Timor Sea during a storm – not far from here. We were all devastated.'

'Did anyone else die in the crash?' asked Rebecca anxiously.

'As far as I know, only the pilot,' replied Hamish. 'Not surprisingly, the small plane disappeared without a trace. The bodies weren't recovered.'

'Muddenbudden, you said earlier that you showed Mungo where to find the best rock art – right?' asked Andrew, changing the subject.

'Yes. Many of the locations are kept secret and are only known to the initiated few.'

'Would it be fair to say that you would therefore know where he used to do most of his work?'

'Yes, I think so,' replied Muddenbudden without hesitation. Jack gave Andrew a meaningful look.

'You also said that I've come here to right a great wrong. What exactly did you mean by that?' The old man closed his eyes and began to tremble. His whole body began to shake.

'Another time, Andrew. I would like to leave now, please,' said the old man, gasping for air. 'Give me your arm.'

Muddenbudden got unsteadily to his feet. 'Come to see me tomorrow, alone. And bring the painting,' he whispered in Bunuba, as he shuffled out of the room.

For a while, no one spoke, the old man's presence lingering in the room like the silence after the last curtain call. Hamish opened another bottle of wine and quietly went around filling up the glasses.

'What does all this mean?' asked Jack after a while. 'Where does it take us?'

'We know that Pigeon and Anna escaped from the Wizards' farm three years ago,' said Cassandra from the back of the room. 'We also know that Pigeon disappeared into the Outback and ended up joining O'Grady's boxing troupe.'

'Without Anna of course,' Will pointed out.

'Correct,' Jack agreed. 'He certainly couldn't take her with him, could he? So, what did he do with her? Any ideas?'

'He pointed us to Kalumburu just before he died. Assume for the moment that Pigeon brought Anna up here to the Kimberley,' speculated Andrew. 'Far away from her ordeal and a place he knew well, and left her in the care of someone he could trust – his uncle – before going off to box in O'Grady's tent. Can you think of a better place to hide her?'

'Isn't that a little far fetched?' said Rebecca, shaking her head. 'A white girl living here in this wilderness with ...' Rebecca didn't finish the sentence. 'And aren't we forgetting something here?'

'What?' asked Jack.

'It was Pigeon who abducted the girls – right? It was Pigeon who delivered them to the Wizards, and for all we know, willingly participated in his own induction ritual ... And we now have some idea what that was all about. In short, he's the cause of Anna's ordeal and the person responsible for her friend's death, albeit indirectly perhaps.'

'Correct so far,' said Andrew.

'Yet here we are, speculating about how Pigeon rescued her by bringing her up here to this remote place to keep her safe by hiding her among his people. Far away from the evil world of the Wizards which once he so desperately wanted to be part of. I just don't get it,' said Rebecca, shaking her head. 'How can the same man be both tormentor and saviour at the same time? For her to come up here with Pigeon and then live with the Aboriginals for two years would have required co-operation and trust. In short, a willingness to participate. I can't see how any of this could have happened against her will. How do we explain this?'

'Stockholm syndrome,' interrupted Jack.

Andrew nodded. 'I was just thinking the same thing,' he said.

'What's that?' asked Will.

'It's ... well, it's a psychological phenomenon; a paradox,' said Jack.

'Where the victim of a crime forms a strange bond with the perpetrator and sees him as their saviour?' said Rebecca.

'That's the one.' said Andrew. 'It all fits perfectly.'

'What, Anna forms an attachment to Pigeon, her abductor, and willingly participates in all this?' said Will, shaking his head.

'Exactly,' said Jack. 'Survival instinct and self-preservation.'

'What do you think happened to Anna?' asked Will, turning to Cassandra.

The psychic stood up and limped over to the fireplace. Then, closing her eyes, she placed her hand on the smooth bark of the painting. 'This is Anna's work,' she pronounced quietly after a while. 'I can feel the energy. She's reaching out through the painting here, communicating the only way she really can – through art. Don't forget, her mind's been damaged. She's retreated from reality and turned inwards.' For a while Cassandra stood in silence. 'I can sense loneliness,' she continued, 'longing, and pain, but I can also feel hope.'

Jack joined Cassandra by the fireplace and looked at the painting. 'With everything we've just learnt, what do we make of this?' he asked, pointing to the signature in the bottom corner. 'Lucrezia. How strange ...'

'Does that name mean anything to you?' asked Will, looking at Jack.

'To me? No. But I do know someone it may mean a great deal to,' he added quietly.

'Who?' asked Rebecca.

'You know her as well as I do.'

'The countess?'

'Precisely.'

53

Never Never Downs, 5 March, 3 a.m.

Instead of going to bed, Jack asked Hamish for permission to use the satellite phone in the homestead library. After several failed attempts, the signal finally connected with the Kuragin chateau.

'Oh Jack – at last!' said the countess, her voice barely audible. 'I've been to hell and back waiting for your call. Where are you? Any news?'

'We're on a remote cattle station in the Kimberley, in the middle of a cyclone,' answered Jack, hoping the countess could hear him. The reception was very bad and the connection cut out several times, the interference from the storm making a painful crackling noise. 'We have to make this short. We've found a painting that may have been painted by Anna ...'

'Oh my God. How? Where? How did you ...'

'It's signed "Lucrezia". Does this mean anything to you?' interrupted Jack.

'What did you say?'

'Lucrezia.' By now, Jack was almost shouting.

'Lucrezia? Oh yes, yes! I'll tell you ...'

Rebecca tiptoed into the library where Jack sat surrounded by open books, some of them lying beside him on the floor. He seemed oblivious of his surroundings. The bark painting was leaning against the bookcase in front of him.

'Do you know what time it is, Jack?' asked Rebecca, running her fingers through his hair from behind. 'What are you doing?'

'Research.'

'At three in the morning? Isn't that taking things a little too far, especially after the kind of day we've had?'

Enjoying the soft touch of Rebecca's thigh rubbing ever so gently against his back, Jack put his arm around her leg and pulled her towards him.

Rebecca bent down and kissed Jack on the cheek. 'You're an amazing man, you know. What kind of research?'

'Here, let me read something to you,' said Jack, reaching for one of the open books on the desk. 'Born in Tuscany in 1406, Fillipo Lippi, the fifteenth century Renaissance painter, had an eye for beauty, especially in women. This predisposition would have been acceptable had he been only a painter, but he was also a monk ... As a monk he should have known that there was one thing the Church wouldn't tolerate – scandal.'

'You're delving into the lives of Italian painters? At this hour? You must be going a little soft in the head, Jack,' interrupted Rebecca.

'Patience. Please, hear me out.' Jack closed the book and turned around to face her. 'It's a great story: One day, as the good maestro was working on a large painting in a convent chapel, he noticed a beautiful girl praying in front of the altar.

'The girl was living in the convent and was under the guardianship of the nuns. So smitten was he by her beauty that he decided to use her as his model for the Madonna. The nuns gave their permission – a fateful decision as you'll see – and she was allowed to sit for him in the chapel. During one of the sittings he got carried away and made passionate love to her. The girl obviously didn't mind, because they eloped the very next day. And who could have blamed her? Running away with a famous painter was obviously a lot more fun than living in the convent under the watchful eyes of the nuns. This caused an enormous scandal that not only embarrassed the Church, but rocked the whole of Tuscany. Had it not been for the intervention of the powerful Medici, who thought very highly of Filippo Lippi, the painter's illustrious career would have come to a sticky end in the arms of the beautiful ... Do you want to know her name?' asked Jack, touching Rebecca on the arm.

'Yes please, I can't wait ...'

'Lucrezia Buti. And just in case you're wondering what all this has to do with us, there is one more little snippet you need to know ...'

'Tell me.'

'Filippo Lippi was young Anna's favourite painter. She adored his work. So much so that she decided to paint under the name "Lucrezia". A teenager's romantic infatuation, no doubt. She became Filippo Lippi's mistress, in spirit that is, five hundred years after his death.'

Rebecca looked thunderstruck. 'You can't be serious ...'

'Oh yes, I am. I just spoke to the countess. This is Anna's painting, there's now absolutely no doubt about it.'

'That's truly amazing, Jack, congratulations.'

'The power of midnight oil – see?'

'Something to tell the others over breakfast, that's for sure.' Rebecca turned off the desk lamp, closed the book in Jack's lap and looked at him sternly. 'If you want to keep your eyes open in the morning, and be coherent, you better hit the sack, Sherlock,' she said, kissing him, this time squarely on the mouth.

'We could sneak back to my room ...' suggested Jack, a sparkle in his eyes.

'Like two naughty school kids?'

'What's wrong with that?'

'I don't think that's a good idea. We agreed, remember?'

'Yes, ma'am. And in case you're wondering, this isn't a gun in my pocket.'

Rebecca burst out laughing. 'You're an incorrigible rascal,' she said and bit Jack on the ear.

'If you do that again, it'll be the floor, or the couch over there.'

'Promises, promises.'

'Don't tempt me.'

What the hell, thought Rebecca, and bit Jack on the other ear.

Jack and Rebecca were not the only ones awake in the early hours of that stormy morning. Drenched in sweat and tossing restlessly from side to side, Cassandra tried to make sense of the disturbing images racing through her throbbing brain. All the images had one thing in common: Tristan, her son.

Sitting up in bed, Cassandra heard footsteps outside her door and old floorboards creaking like the spars of a wooden ship tortured by the wind. Cassandra knew that Rebecca's room was directly next to hers.

The footsteps stopped. Cassandra opened her door just a little and peered outside. Fumbling with the door handle in the dark, Rebecca stood in front of her room.

'Come in, please,' whispered Cassandra, pushing her door open.

Cassandra draped a blanket over her bare shoulders and sat down on the edge of her bed. Rebecca sat down next to her. The wind rattling the windows like bony fingers shaking the lid of a coffin was the only sound in the room.

'We're being swept along by events we no longer control,' began Cassandra, reaching for the box of matches on the bedside table. She struck a match and lit a candle, the flickering flame casting an eerie shadow across her pale face. 'It's like approaching a waterfall. Once you're in the middle of the torrent close to the edge, there's no turning back.'

Rebecca reached for Cassandra's hand, but said nothing. The hand felt clammy and cold.

'Not everyone going over the edge will survive.'

Rebecca felt an icy chill racing down her spine. 'You look tired,' she said, squeezing her friend's hand. 'You should try and get some sleep ...'

'I can't.' Cassandra turned to face Rebecca. 'My son is about to wake up,' she continued calmly. 'When he does, he will have to face his destiny, and he won't be the only one.'

'How can you be so ... ?'

'Sure? You know I can.'

'The Wizard?'

'Oh yes. He's a wounded animal – unpredictable, desperate and dangerous. An evil genius without scruples. You can't imagine what he's capable of. He'll fight to the end, and the battle will begin in earnest when we find Anna ...'

'You really believe that we'll find her? Out here? Alive?'

'I do. One mother's anguish is about to come to an end,' replied Cassandra sadly, 'and another's is just beginning.'

Rebecca put her arm around Cassandra's shoulder. Cassandra seemed to relax a little, a wry smile creasing the corners of her mouth. 'I'm trapped. Trapped between the girl I promised to find and the son I love. Their fates are intertwined like the roots of a tree: impossible to separate and impossible to tell apart.'

'Go to sleep,' said Rebecca, kissing Cassandra on the cheek. 'Things will look a lot brighter in the morning, you'll see.'

'I must make contact with the Wizards today, or it'll be too late. I must give them something. But what can I tell them without betraying either Anna or my son?'

'Hush,' said Rebecca, touching Cassandra's lips with the tip of her finger. 'You need some rest to clear your mind.'

Rebecca was about to get up, but Cassandra held her back. 'Please don't go,' she whispered, tightening her grip. 'I have something here I must give you. I've been waiting for the right moment ...'

Cassandra reached into the drawer of her bedside table and pulled out a small parcel wrapped in brown paper. 'We've spoken about trust before. The promise – remember?' Rebecca nodded. 'This is part of it, a very scary part. No one must know you have this, and please, only open it if ... when ...' Cassandra hesitated, looking pleadingly at Rebecca.

'Yes?'

'If something happens to me ...'

'What is it? Can you tell me?'

'You're holding the Wizard's fate in your hands.'

Looking confused, Rebecca almost dropped the parcel, her hand shaking as the words hit home.

'What am I to do with it?'

'You'll know when the time comes,' came the cryptic reply, 'but you must never show it to Anna or her mother. Never!'

'We both need some sleep,' said Rebecca and stood up.

'You and Jack are lovers?' said Cassandra, changing direction.

If Rebecca was in any way surprised by the question, she didn't show it. 'Occasionally,' she said.

'Why the separate rooms?'

'Well ... you know ... I ...'

'Hush ... I do know.'

'I don't understand.'

'I think you do. Stay with me, please,' whispered Cassandra, 'I need you, not sleep. Please help me fend off the demons ...'

Rebecca felt an unsettling wave of excitement wash through her.

She knew she was crossing uncharted waters with something dangerous, yet strangely alluring, waiting on the other side. Unsure whether to leave or to stay, and feeling like a moth circling the deadly flame, she stood and looked at the raven-haired woman sitting on the edge of the bed in front of her.

Cassandra lent forward and blew out the candle, the sudden darkness blotting out everything but imagination. 'You remind me of a song ...' she whispered.

'Oh?'

'You are like a caged bird, so it seems, not realising that the door is open wide ... Give me your hand. We're close to the edge, you and I. There's no turning back now. We must go over the waterfall together.'

54

Broome Jail, 5 March, 3:30 a.m.

It was three in the morning and the Wizard was pacing up and down in his tiny holding-cell considering his options. Pigeon and Zoran were both dead, and Sladko was in hospital recovering from gunshot wounds. These were serious setbacks, but he wasn't concerned about his own position. As usual, he had allowed others do his dirty work and take all the risks. The real danger was lurking somewhere else. The real threat was Anna. *What had Pigeon told Cassandra?* the Wizard asked himself over and over.

He'd used his one phone call to speak with his solicitor, yet he desperately needed to make another. He was certain Cassandra would have reported in by now, just as he had instructed her to do. With Tristan as his pawn, she would do his bidding – he was sure of it.

Finding out about Anna was far more important than getting out of jail. His solicitor had retained Cyril Archibald QC, the barrister the Wizards had used many times before. Both were on their way to Broome to meet their notorious client, but weren't due to arrive until the following day.

So far, the Wizard had refused to say anything about what really happened at Tunnel Creek, which had infuriated the police and angered the magistrate. In fact, he was playing for time, but time was running out. And besides, as an experienced serial offender, he was well aware of the golden rule: say nothing without your lawyer present. His injuries – extensive bruising and a dislocated ankle, not a broken leg – had been treated in hospital. Remanded in custody and due to appear in court in the morning for a bail application, the Wizard knew that every moment counted. Somehow, he had to get access to a phone and to do that, he had to get out of his cell.

The Wizard stopped in front of the cell door and began pounding his fist against the steel. When the sleepy guard opened the peephole a few minutes later to find out what the fracas was all about, the Wizard was lying on the floor. Pressing his hands against his stomach, he was complaining about abdominal pain and passing blood. He demanded to be taken to hospital. Remembering a recent death in custody of an Aboriginal man which had caused a huge fuss, the guard called an ambulance.

The young radiographer on duty at the hospital was impressed by the Wizard's physique. Intrigued by his tattoos, especially King Solomon's Seal covering his back, she struck up a conversation.

'Could I borrow your mobile, luv?' asked the Wizard, as soon as his guard was out of earshot. 'Just one call ...'

'I'm not really supposed to,' replied the radiographer, uncertain, but wavering.

'You could just leave it over there for a moment. Go on ...' suggested the Wizard undeterred, pointing to the X-ray machine. 'And send him outside,' he whispered conspiratorially, nodding towards the guard standing by the door. The Wizard knew that women, in particular, found it difficult to say no to him. Turning on the charm worked every time.

The disco in the church was in full swing. The transvestite operating the turntables was high, the music deafening, and the cigarette smoke as dense as the fog on a winter's morning. *Answer the bloody phone, mate*, thought the Wizard, listening to the ring tone repeating itself with annoying monotony. Despite the loud music pumping all around him, the Undertaker was soundly asleep on the lounge. The bare-breasted girl sitting next to him took the empty vodka bottle out of his hand, reached into his shirt pocket and answered the phone.

'Who the fuck are you?' hissed the Wizard, frustration getting the better of him. 'Where's the Undertaker?'

'Right here, asleep,' replied the girl, giggling. 'Pissed.'

'Listen, luv. If you want to leave in the morning with both of your tits still attached, you better wake him. Now!'

Silence.

Closing his fist, the Wizard almost crushed the mobile. Alarmed, the radiographer shot him a disapproving look.

'What's up?' grunted the Undertaker, barely able to speak. 'Pull yourself together, mate, it's me,' said the Wizard.

Silence.

Two thousand kilometres away, the Undertaker sat up with a jolt. 'Sorry. I didn't know it was you,' he said, massaging his aching neck and trying to concentrate.

'Has Cassandra called?'

'Yes.'

'What did she say?'

'She said she was getting close. That's all.'

'Now, listen carefully: I want you to contact the White Wolf, do you understand?'

'What?'

'You heard me. Agree to whatever he asks. I want him here in Broome as soon as he can make it. You got that?'

'Sure. But hasn't he retired?'

'Tell him, I'm calling in a favour ...'

'Okay.'

'I'm depending on you.'

'You can.'

I hope so, for your sake, thought the Wizard and hung up.

For special jobs, the Wizard always brought in outsiders. The White Wolf – no one knew his real name – was a contract killer of a different kind. Supremely fit, in his late sixties, with a shock of white hair and wearing gold-rimmed glasses, he looked more like a mild-mannered grandfather than the ruthless assassin he was. Secretive, and pedantically selective about the assignments he took on, he only worked for people he knew, or who were recommended by people he could trust. As a master of disguise with a sixth sense for danger, he had eluded capture for more than forty years. His unorthodox methods – acquired during his early years in the KGB – were the envy of his rivals. Using mainly exotic poisons which had pathologists scratching their heads the world over, he left nothing behind to link him to his crimes. His fee was exorbitant – only a privileged few could afford him. He liked it that way. But he owed the Wizard a big favour.

A few years beforehand, the White Wolf had completed a tricky assignment in Melbourne, when something went terribly wrong. During his getaway, he had committed the cardinal sin: he had accidentally shot a policeman. Instead of heading for the airport, he went into hiding.

Usually, he would have been out of the country before the body turned cold. Through an associate, the Wizard heard of the White Wolf's plight and decided to assist. That's how important alliances are forged. The White Wolf needed somewhere to hide, a new face and a passport to go with it. The Wizard could provide all three. He brought in a plastic surgeon from Malaysia and set up an operating theatre at the Wizards' compound. New papers were the easy bit. It was time to call in the debt.

55

Never Never Downs,
5 March, in the morning

Andrew was an early riser. He knew Muddenbudden was too, and that he would be expecting him. Unable to sleep with the storm raging outside, Andrew had gone over all the facts several times. His analytical mind, trained by years of police work, refused to accept the extraordinary conclusion emerging at the end of each exercise. However, his instincts told him that he was on the right track and that somehow, Muddenbudden was the missing link. Andrew found the bark painting in the library, wrapped it in a towel and hurried across to Muddenbudden's cabin.

Built of rough-sawn timber in the 1890s, the cabin had only two rooms: a sitting room with a stone fireplace and a small bedroom on the side. A lean-to at the back contained the old kitchen which hadn't been used in decades. Wrapped in a blanket, Muddenbudden sat with his eyes closed on a rocking chair facing the fireplace. For a while, Andrew stood in the doorway, unsure whether to stay or come back later.

'Dreams are strange creatures, Andrew,' began Muddenbudden, without opening his eyes. 'After a while, it's impossible to tell where the dream ends and reality begins. Come in and sit by me. I want to tell you about my dreams.'

The first thing Andrew noticed when he walked into the homestead kitchen some time later was the mouth-watering aroma of frying bacon and freshly baked bread. Seated around a long wooden table large enough for twenty, the four guests were enjoying their first cup of tea for the day. Two Aboriginal women, the homestead cooks, were preparing omelettes and pancakes by the stove. Set into the kitchen wall where the old fuel stove used to be, the cast iron stove radiated welcome warmth.

Margaret was pouring tea for her guests and Hamish was slicing bread on the chopping board. They all stopped talking when they saw Andrew's face.

Cassandra recognised the expression at once: a deep elation bursting to be shared with others.

Without saying a word, Andrew walked over to the table and carefully placed the painting on a chair for all to see. 'Jack, you told us yesterday that the painting was some kind of storyboard. You were right. That's exactly what it is and I can now tell you a little more of the story,' said Andrew, a smile lighting up his face. 'You interpreted the first two panels for us: the family in front of the French chateau, and the strange spider's web with the weird face in the middle.' Andrew pointed to the centre panel.

'However, the third panel here with all the rock art and the young woman with the short blonde hair holding a paintbrush is the really intriguing one – right? Well, I've just spoken to Muddenbudden ...' Andrew paused, enjoying the moment.

'Well? What did he have to say?' asked Jack.

'He spoke of a dream.'

'A dream?' said Will. 'And this is going to help us?'

Andrew held up his hand. 'To begin with, you should know that Muddenbudden is Sister Dolores's older brother, which makes him Mungo's uncle. A very important relationship in a Bunuba family, especially this one. Muddenbudden and Mungo were very close, just like Mungo and Pigeon were very close. What I'm about to tell you is all about trust and the power of dreams. Two years or so ago, Mungo asked his uncle for advice in a very delicate matter regarding his nephew, Pigeon. Normally, Muddenbudden wouldn't even have revealed that much – it would have been a breach of sacred trust. Anyway, that brings me to the dream ...' Andrew paused again, collecting his thoughts.

'Muddenbudden claims that since Mungo died, he keeps having the same dream over and over. Cassandra, you would understand the power of dreams better than most.' Cassandra nodded. 'In our culture, dreams are very important. I urge you to take what you're about to hear very seriously. Muddenbudden believes that his ancestors are communicating with him through this dream, and I believe it's all to do with Anna ...' he added, lowering his voice.

'Are you serious?' interrupted Will again. 'This is no longer rational, Andrew!'

Rebecca placed her hand on Will's arm and turned to face him. 'Please, Will, let's hear what Andrew has to say. Okay?' she said.

'She's right, mate,' said Jack, making eye contact with his friend. 'Especially in light of what the countess said last night,' he added quietly.

'You spoke to her? What did she say?' asked Andrew.

'I rang her and asked her about the signature on the painting ... Lucrezia,' said Jack.

'Well?'

'All of Anna's paintings are signed Lucrezia – an assumed name – a quirky whim of a budding young artist. Kind of a *nom de plume* of the paintbrush.'

For a while no one spoke as the implications of what Jack had just said began to sink in.

'Then – this is Anna's painting,' said Will, stating the obvious.

'Yes, and that fits perfectly with what Muddenbudden told me,' said Andrew. 'It explains how this painting ended up here. It offers a rational explanation for what otherwise would be no more than a baffling puzzle, leading to a dead end.'

'You were going to tell us about the dream,' said Cassandra quietly.

'In Muddenbudden's dream, the spirit of Jandamarra – one of his ancestors – appears. The spirit is floating through a cave, its walls and ceiling covered in spectacular rock art. The spirit is not alone. In the shadows behind him stand Mungo and Pigeon, looking pleadingly at Muddenbudden.' Andrew closed his eyes and stood perfectly still, his heaving chest the only sign of life. 'And now comes the interesting bit,' he continued after a while. 'In front of the spirit stands a young woman. Her skin is white, her short hair blonde.'

Andrew opened his eyes and looked at the bark painting on the chair in front of him. 'She holds a paintbrush in her right hand and is looking up at the ceiling which is covered in Dreamtime paintings. Just like the young woman right here in the picture.'

'It's weird, but in a strange way ...' interrupted Jack, shaking his head.

'Did the spirit speak to Muddenbudden?' asked Cassandra,

'Apparently he did, but Muddenbudden wouldn't reveal what it was about, except to say that he'd been expecting us.'

'Expecting us?' asked Rebecca. 'Amazing ...'

Suddenly, everyone was speaking at once, asking questions, speculating, making comments, the excitement in the room rising to fever pitch.

Andrew held up his hand. 'Not all at the same time, please,' he said. 'As you can imagine, I asked Muddenbudden the very same question. I even pressed him about the sensitive matter Mungo had raised with him two years ago. Unfortunately, he was very tight-lipped about it all, except for this.' By now everyone had calmed down again and was hanging on Andrew's every word. 'He told me that it all had to do with the young woman in the picture ...'

'Anna's right here, somewhere in this wilderness,' said Cassandra calmly, 'and Muddenbudden is guiding us to her.'

'Yes, I think you're right,' Andrew agreed. 'However, he also said that he was expecting one more person before he could tell us more ...'

'Did he say who that person was?' asked Jack.

'Not exactly, but he did say that we would find out – soon.'

'That's truly astonishing,' said Jack, shaking his head. 'How could he possibly know? There is someone ...'

'What do you mean?' asked Will.

'When I spoke to the countess last night about the painting and the signature, and what it meant ...'

'Yes?'

'She said she'd get on the next plane to Australia and meet us in Broome ... I couldn't talk her out of it. She's probably on her way right now.'

'But we're trapped here. Just look outside ...' said Will.

'Up here, the weather can change,' said Andrew. 'Very quickly. I've seen it happen many times. Let's keep our fingers crossed.'

56

Muddenbudden's cabin, Never Never Downs, 6 March, 7 a.m.

Sitting motionless in his chair, his eyes closed, Muddenbudden was listening to the wind howling outside. To him, it sounded like the voices of a thousand tortured souls screaming for forgiveness. Cyclone Leopold was slowly moving east. Bolts of lightning criss-crossed the sky like angry snakes attacking the first light of the morning as it tried to break through the clouds. Turning dry creek beds into treacherous rivers, and rivers into raging torrents, the fury of the storm made the ground shake and the ancient boab trees tremble. Life was hiding. Seeking shelter wherever it could – in crevasses, under rocks, or deep down in the ground – it was waiting for the tempest to pass. Staying out in the open would have been risking death.

An old man staggered towards Muddenbudden's cabin. He almost made it, but slipped and fell into the mud before he could reach the door.

Mustering the last of his remaining strength, he crawled up the porch and pushed the door open. Sensing that someone was there, Muddenbudden opened his sightless eyes and turned his head towards the door.

'Who is this?' he asked. *A spirit?* he thought, fear clawing at his stomach.

'It's me, brother, help me.'

'Wake up,' said Andrew, shaking Jack by the shoulder.

'What's going on?' asked Jack sleepily, rubbing his eyes.

'Someone just walked into Muddenbudden's cabin with an extraordinary story.'

'In this weather?'

'Yes. You've got to hear this.'

The old Aboriginal man, feeling better after a bowl of hot soup and some tea, was resting on Muddenbudden's bed. He had left the remote cave shelter near the Drysdale River the day before to get help, but had to make many detours through rugged terrain because the creeks had risen at an alarming rate, making them impossible to cross. His luck finally ran out 30 kilometres from Never Never Downs.

As he tried to ford a creek that had turned into a river, his old Toyota got bogged down in the torrent before he could make it across. A tree branch floating down the river helped him make it safely to the other side. Exhausted, and without a vehicle or provisions, he started walking towards Never Never Downs. Fortunately, he knew the country well and covered the 30 kilometres in the dark by following familiar landmarks. Only someone with intimate knowledge of the land and the experience of a lifetime spent in the bush could have accomplished such a feat.

Jack looked at the sleeping old man covered in blankets up to his chin.

'Come, sit with me,' said Muddenbudden to Jack. 'This is my half brother, Merriwarra. There's no need to wake him. The time has come for me to tell you the rest of the story of the young woman in the painting ... Events have overtaken us.'

'The person you're expecting is the young woman's mother, isn't it?' asked Andrew. 'She arrived in Darwin this morning – I just spoke to her. As soon as the weather clears we'll bring her here.'

Muddenbudden was not surprised. 'Yes, it's all coming together, just as the spirit ...' he replied, not completing the sentence.

Jack bit his lip, excitement tingling down his spine as reason and intuition fought to gain the upper hand.

'Three years ago,' continued Muddenbudden, speaking softly, 'Pigeon came to me for advice regarding a matter so serious that I had to give him my word not to tell anyone about it. The only reason I'm talking to you now is because much has changed: Pigeon is dead and so is Mungo. But much still has to be done – urgently. And then there's the dream ... I'll tell you about that later. The matter Pigeon came to see me about concerned a young woman, a Malngadu, a white woman ...'

Muddenbudden paused and closed his eyes. Jack leant forward to hear better and Andrew held his breath.

'Pigeon confided in me,' continued Muddenbudden, his voice barely audible. 'He told me that the young woman had been subjected to great suffering, for which he was somehow responsible. He also told me that she had lost her mind and needed protection. He pleaded with me to find a way to let her stay with our people. At first I was opposed to the idea. It sounded crazy. But then I met her and that changed everything ... Pigeon had brought her with him, you see.'

Muddenbudden paused again and sat in silence. In his mind's eye, he was revisiting his first encounter with the strange young white woman.

'Where was that?' asked Jack after a while, breaking the silence. 'Right here, in this room,' replied Muddenbudden without opening his eyes.

'How did that change everything?' asked Andrew.

'It's difficult to explain. There was something special about her. She was so childlike, so different, so trusting. And so vulnerable,' he added. 'However, she seemed to trust Pigeon completely. No, more than that, she depended on him. In every way – just like a child. She reminded me of someone possessed by spirits, floating through life, with one foot in this world, the other in the next. From time to time, we had people like that in our family. After meeting her, I knew I had to help.'

'What did you do?' asked Andrew.

'Some of our elders live up here in the Kimberley wilderness. They prefer the old ways. They are the custodians of our sacred rock art and keep our traditions alive by passing on the stories and the law. Mungo, my nephew – Pigeon's favourite uncle – found a way to make a living by combining the old with the new: restoring the rock paintings, and then making copies for sale. He was a talented artist. Soon, his bark paintings became sought after and sold very well. Not only was he able to support himself through this enterprise, he supported the elders as well. He became the go-between linking their world and his.'

'Where did all this happen?' interrupted Jack, trying in vain to sound calm.

'Right here at Never Never Downs.'

'What happened to the young woman?' asked Andrew.

'She went to live with Mungo and the elders ...'

'Where?' asked Jack.

'The elders move from site to site and cover vast distances. Depending on the time of the year, they change camp regularly.'

'Do you know where they are right now?' whispered Jack.

'They return to the same camp every year during the rainy season. It's a large cave about 300 kilometres from here. That's where Merriwarra came from.'

'Is the young woman there now?' asked Andrew, watching the old man intently.

'Yes, she is. But ...' Stopping in mid sentence, Muddenbudden closed his eyes again.

'But what?' asked Andrew.

'I think we better wake Merriwarra. You should hear this from him, not me.'

'Does this young woman have a name?' asked Jack, trying hard to stay calm.

'Yes. We call her Mayannie.'

'You were going to tell us about the dream,' said Andrew, anxious not to lose the thread of the story, 'and what the spirit told you. A great wrong that must be set right, you said – remember?'

Looking suddenly uncomfortable in his chair, Muddenbudden opened his sightless eyes.

'I will tell you when her mother arrives,' he stated calmly. 'Now, please let me wake my brother ...'

57

Broome airport, 6 March

Merriwarra's disturbing news turned the search for Anna into a desperate race against time. Unable to wait any longer, Andrew took advantage of a brief lull in the storm later in the morning, and took off. He thought it best that only Jack should accompany him on the hazardous flight to Broome to meet the countess. To avoid the worst of Cyclone Leopold, they made a risky detour and skirted around the tail end of the storm.

Watching the dark clouds race past the small window of the plane, Jack pondered how best to break the news to the countess. So close, he thought, and now this!

As soon as Countess Kuragin stepped out of the plane, the heat and humidity hit her like a slap in the face. Looking like a movie star on vacation in her designer suit, she thanked the stewardess for the umbrella and hurried across the wet tarmac to the airport building. Used to turning heads wherever she went, she wasn't surprised when a white-haired, elderly gentleman fell in beside her and offered to carry her hand luggage. The countess declined with a smile. At the baggage collection carousel inside the terminal, the same man struck up a conversation. Usually, she would feel flattered. Occasionally, she even flirted, especially with younger men. But today she had other things on her mind. Hidden behind a mask of perfect makeup, she was barely able to keep her emotions under control. She had called Nikolai from the airport in Paris and told him about the extraordinary developments and her impending trip to Australia. Always the jaded sceptic, he had warned her about getting too carried away. She knew that he had given up long ago and no longer dared to hope. She, on the other hand, didn't dare not to.

As she waited for her luggage, the countess made polite small talk with the white-haired man. For the White Wolf, airports were

273

dangerous places. Passengers travelling on their own stand out and are often remembered later. He didn't like being remembered. A tall, attractive woman left a lasting impression. Next to her, he was almost invisible.

Zoran's brother, Zac, knew where the CCTV cameras were located in the terminal. The Wizard's instructions were very specific: 'Make sure you stay out of CCTV range, leave the terminal quickly and take him to our pub'. Holding a piece of cardboard with the name *Collins* written across it, Zac was waiting at the exit with the tour operators and hire car drivers meeting the new arrivals. A bespectacled, white-haired man carrying a small duffel bag walked up to him.

'How's the Wizard?' he asked nonchalantly, handing Zac his bag.

'Still in custody,' replied Zac. 'Please follow me and stay close.'

Jack saw the countess first. She was slowly pushing her luggage trolley towards the exit. Approaching from behind, he put his hand on the trolley and said, 'It's an awkward contraption – let me help you. Welcome to Broome.'

The countess spun around, let go of the trolley and threw her arms around him.

'Men like you are rare, Jack,' she whispered, kissing him on the cheek. 'You keep your word. Thank you.'

'Look over there,' said Jack, pointing to Andrew waiting at the exit. 'Someone else deserves a hug more than I do.'

Sitting in the small airport lounge after most of the other passengers had left, Jack did his best to answer the countess's barrage of questions. The weather had deteriorated further, making it impossible to take off. To keep busy, Andrew had gone to check the latest weather forecast. Again.

'Jack, please answer me this,' pleaded the countess. 'Do you really believe that this Mayannie living with Aboriginals in some remote cave could possibly be our Anna? After all these years?'

'Yes, I do,' he said quietly, reaching for her hand.

'But we only have these stories to go on. Little more than rumours,' protested the countess, tears glistening in the corners of her eyes. 'I couldn't bear it if they were to turn out to be just that.'

'We do have more,' said Jack, reaching for the parcel wrapped in brown paper lying on the chair next to him. 'I've brought you something – here.'

'What is it?'

'Open it.'

The countess peeled back the paper and gasped.

'Oh my God,' she sighed, running her fingertips along the signature on the bark painting. 'Lucrezia!'

'Well, what do you think?'

The countess lifted the small gold crucifix she wore on a chain around her neck to her lips, and kissed it. 'It's definitely hers,' she said.

'Adding a little more substance to the story perhaps?'

'Oh yes. Thank you.' The countess squeezed his hand and looked at him intently.

'Why so glum?' she asked. Jack shook his head sadly. 'What's wrong, Jack?'

'This silver cloud has a dark lining, I'm afraid.'

'What do you mean?'

'I haven't told you why Merriwarra, the old Aboriginal I mentioned earlier, came to Never Never Downs in the middle of a cyclone.'

'Oh?'

'He risked his life to get help – medical help.'

Fear stabbed at the countess's heart.

'Help? Who for?' she asked, barely able to speak.

Jack decided to be brutally honest – the countess deserved that much. 'Apparently, Mayannie is very ill ...'

'Ill? What do you mean?' the countess said.

'She has a fever. The elders have tried everything, but it's not going away. In fact, it's getting worse. The traditional remedies aren't working. She needs urgent medical attention. That's why Merriwarra braved the storm to seek help.'

'Oh my God! We have to leave at once,' exclaimed the countess, standing up.

'We can't,' said Jack. 'There's no way a vehicle could get through at the moment. We have to wait for the floodwaters to subside before we can make a move.'

'But what about the plane? Can't we get in from the air?'

'No, there's nowhere to land. I don't think you appreciate just how rough this place really is. And how remote.'

'This is so cruel,' said the countess, sitting down again. 'Why am I being punished like this? Surely, there must be something we can do?'

'There is: hope and wait,' replied Jack calmly.

'And pray,' whispered the countess, touching the little crucifix with the tips of her fingers.

58

Never Never Downs, 6 March

Sitting alone in her room, Cassandra prepared to consult the cards but this time, the divination was for her alone. It was easy to make errors now, driven as she was by fear and concern for her son. The mother in her might dominate the impartial diviner she tried to be. Before opening the wooden box on the table in front of her, she meditated, something she did before every reading.

A new force had entered the search for Anna with the arrival of the countess. Cassandra knew that soon, several fate-lines were destined to touch somewhere in time-space. She also knew that the consequences would be far reaching. But nothing could have prepared her for what the cards were about to reveal.

Her hands were shaking when she opened the wooden box and took out the neat parcel wrapped in blue silk. To ease the tension before beginning, she decided to check the deck of cards for completeness and do a thorough karmic cleansing.

After she had placed all twenty-four Major Arcana cards in a neat row from left to right, she proceeded to place all sixteen Royal Arcana cards – Page to King – in a row below. Looking at the familiar cards calmed her as she ran her fingertips slowly along the rows to double-check that all were present. Satisfied, she gathered up the cards and shuffled them seven times.

Cassandra chose the Arbor Vitae, or Tree of Life, Spread. This, she told herself, was the perfect choice. Feeling better, she placed each card into its required place to resemble the ten centres of the Tree of Life, a Cabbalistic mandala.

When she reached the final four, she hesitated. These were the cards that would provide her with vital insight, letting her see herself reflected in the mirror. Taking a deep breath, she turned over the seventh card, glanced at it, and paled.

Anxious to return to Never Never Downs, Andrew checked the weather forecast every hour. By late afternoon the weather had improved sufficiently to allow clearance for the return flight.

Once they were in the air, exhaustion caught up with the countess. It had been forty-two hours since she'd left Paris. The excitement that had kept her going had given way to uncertainty and fear. *How quickly bad news can age a person*, thought Jack, watching her sleep with her head resting against his shoulder. Oblivious to the engine noise and the rough weather outside, the countess was curled up like a cat in the cramped seat next to him.

Touched by the intimacy of the moment, Jack remembered that fateful kiss sealing a promise in the chateau kitchen, and began to stroke her hair. It was a spontaneous gesture of affection directed towards an extraordinary woman who dared to hope, had endured so much, and never lost faith. Jack realised that to fail now was unthinkable because it would crush her. *You promised*, he thought. *Pray to God you can deliver.*

'Look, the river's falling,' said Andrew pointing down. 'With a bit of luck, we just might get through in the morning.'

'I hope you're right, for her sake,' replied Jack, glancing at the countess sleeping peacefully by his side.

Standing on the homestead veranda, Cassandra watched the tall, elegant woman climb out of the plane. Tossing back her hair, the countess hurried across to McGregor who was waiting by the Land Rover with Will, and shook his hand.

For reasons she couldn't quite explain, Cassandra had dreaded meeting the countess. Still shocked and confused by what the cards had told her, she tried to convince herself that her interpretations were inaccurate. The messages could easily become blurred when objectivity was compromised. What she found particularly disconcerting was the suggestion that there were five fate-lines destined to touch soon, not four. She could clearly identify four: the first two were easy. One belonged to herself, the other to her son, Tristan. The next pair of fate-lines belonged to the countess and Anna. However, there was a fifth line very close to Anna's that she couldn't explain. It had nothing to do with Rebecca, Will, Jack or Andrew, as the questions didn't relate to them.

Something was wrong. The obvious danger radiating from the Wizard was overshadowed by something new and far more potent and sinister.

Cassandra had only caught a glimpse of this new threat through the last card, but it had terrified her.

'Jack, could you take me to the Aboriginal elders, please?' pleaded the countess, following Jack into the homestead. She was anxious to hear firsthand what Muddenbudden and Merriwarra had to say. To everyone's surprise, Muddenbudden insisted on meeting the countess alone.

When the countess looked at the old man sitting by the fireplace, she became acutely aware that she had just entered a different world.

Muddenbudden turned his head in her direction, the stare of his sightless eyes adding to her sense of unease and foreboding.

'Do you believe in the power of dreams?' asked Muddenbudden.

'I believe in the power of prayer,' replied the countess without hesitation.

Muddenbudden nodded. 'Good. The important thing is to believe. Please give me your hand. I have to tell you about a dream.'

Everyone fell silent when the countess walked into the library half an hour later. Unable to speak, she covered her face with her hands and stood, shaking.

Not wanting to intrude into this private moment, Rebecca, Will and Andrew looked away. Jack walked over to the sideboard and reached for the scotch. Cassandra, however, recognised the familiar signs: here was someone who had just glimpsed something deeply disturbing. She had seen it all many times before. Cassandra stood up, limped over to the countess and put her arm protectively around her shoulders.

279

'Here, sit with me,' she whispered. The countess shook her head.

'I would like to go to my room, please,' she sobbed, her voice barely audible.

'I'll take you – come with me.' The countess looked gratefully at Cassandra and followed her out of the room.

Instead of leaving the countess alone, Cassandra sat quietly on the edge of the bed beside her.

Eventually, the countess spoke. 'Thank you for all you've done,' she said, composing herself. 'Andrew told me ...' She reached for Cassandra's hand. 'Strange, isn't it? We haven't even met before, yet here you are risking so much to help my daughter. Why is that?'

Cassandra turned to face the countess, a wry smile creasing the corners of her mouth.

'Destiny,' she replied after a while, 'is a complicated web. The pendulum swings, but we have no control over it. What appears to move away from us comes back when we least expect it.'

The countess squeezed Cassandra's hand. 'What I've prayed for all these years and now yearn for with all my heart is coming closer, yet I'm afraid. I'm afraid of what I may find ...'

'Muddenbudden?'

'He spoke of a dream and a spirit ...'

'Can you talk about it?'

'He asked me not to.'

'Why, do you think?'

'He said the time wasn't right.'

'Then let me tell you.'

Surprised, the countess turned her head to face Cassandra. 'He told you?'

'No. I've never spoken to him.'

'Then how ...?'

'I have different ways ... He spoke of another soul close to Anna – didn't he?'

The countess nodded.

'Vulnerable and fragile, with a connection reaching back generations.'

'Yes,' whispered the countess, 'the spirit ...'

'And all the threads of the past are coming together right now?'

'Yes, but there's very little time! He said we must hurry. If we don't reach Mayannie soon, the spark will be extinguished.'

'That won't happen – believe me,' Cassandra reassured the countess. 'You must rest now. Lie down and close your eyes.'

The countess did as she was told, every fibre of her exhausted body screaming for sleep.

'I'll stay with you, and together we'll see what the new morning brings. Think of Anna ...' whispered Cassandra.

Images of the Lucrezia painting Jack had shown her at Broome airport came flooding into the countess's consciousness. Suddenly, she found herself inside the painting. She looked down at the little girl in the polka dot dress standing next to her and smiled. Moments later, she fell asleep.

59

On the way to Djanbinmarra Caves, 7 March

During the night the wind changed direction and blew the last of the storm clouds out to sea. Andrew was woken by the silence just before dawn. Cyclone Leopold had spent its fury, allowing calm to settle over the drenched and battered land. Everywhere, life was coming out of hiding, seeking the warmth of the sun after the tempest.

When Andrew stepped outside at first light, he found Merriwarra sitting on the veranda steps, a worried look on his face. Andrew sat down next to him and together they watched the sun come up.

'We're running out of time, mate. Do you think we'll get through today?' asked Andrew.

Merriwarra took off his hat, scratched his head, but said nothing. 'Something's troubling you, isn't it?' continued Andrew.

'The Djanbinmarra caves are a sacred site – one of the most significant in the region. The location's been kept secret, handed down by the elders from generation to generation. The rock art in the caves is precious. It's thousands of years old. It's our heritage. It belongs to us. If the public gets wind of it, mate, we'll lose it. We've both seen it before.'

Andrew nodded in agreement.

'Muddenbudden is the present custodian. Once he's gone, it's up to me,' added Merriwarra gravely.

Andrew had been expecting something like this. He knew if the search was to continue, Merriwarra's fears had to be allayed.

'How about we ask everyone involved to make a promise?' he suggested.

'What kind of promise?'

'Not to reveal the location. From what you've told me, it's very difficult to find anyway. Would that do it?'

'I suppose it would.'

'You can rest easy, mate – these are all honourable people,' Andrew assured the old man. 'They understand respect, and trust. All they're interested in is finding the girl. You came here asking for help and they are responding – okay so far?'

Merriwarra nodded.

'And you can trust the McGregors. Remember what they've done for our folk round here.'

'That's what Muddenbudden said.'

'It's all settled then?'

'Suppose it is.'

Andrew held out his hand and Merriwarra shook it.

'We better get away early then, what do you reckon? I'll speak to the others,' said Andrew, standing up.

During breakfast, Andrew outlined Merriwarra's concerns and asked everyone to make a pledge to respect Aboriginal law and keep the cave site confidential. All agreed.

'I can now tell you a little more about where we're heading,' said Andrew.

He unfolded a large map and, smoothing out the wrinkles, placed it on the table.

'According to Merriwarra, the camp's about here,' he continued, stabbing his finger at a point on the map. 'This ancient wilderness is of great spiritual significance to the Indigenous people living up here. The only access to the cave is through a deep gorge. It's one of the remotest corners of the Kimberley – almost untouched. The terrain is very rugged at the best of times, but after the storm? Anything can happen. We have to accept the possibility that we might not get through. Fortunately for us, Merriwarra knows the way. We'll follow the Drysdale River here until we find a crossing. We have to get to the other side, otherwise ...' Andrew shrugged, and carefully folded the map along its well-worn creases.

After following the raging Drysdale River for several hours, Merriwarra found a rocky patch where the river had widened by breaking its banks.

At this point the water was fairly shallow with a riverbed of solid rock, making it possible for the vehicles to cross.

Merriwarra sat next to Andrew in the lead vehicle, while Muddenbudden and Jack sat in the rear. Merriwarra seemed to know every bend in the river and every landmark along the way. Even the trees were etched into his subconscious like a tribal memory-map acquired over generations. The land was in his blood. 'All going well, we should reach the camp before nightfall,' he announced, sounding confident for the first time since leaving Never Never Downs.

Andrew nodded.

'It could be tricky with all this water rushing into the gorge,' continued Merriwarra. 'If the women have gone into the cave to seek shelter from the storm, they could be trapped inside. It's happened before ...'

'What do you mean, trapped?' asked Andrew.

'The entry to the cave is deep down in the gorge. Below a rock shelf. Almost hidden and invisible from above. The cave itself is pretty big and has several upper levels and passages.'

'So?'

'If the water level has risen – as it often does after heavy rain – the entry could be under water.'

'That's all we need!'

'When I left, they were still in the tents. But the storm was unbelievable that night ... I told them to move into the cave if things got rough. But, don't worry,' added Muddenbudden, noticing the concern on Jack's face, 'most of the inside of the cave is well above the water level. They'd all be safe in there.'

'But trapped.'

'Yes. For a while ...'

Andrew looked over his shoulder at Jack.

'We should keep this to ourselves for the moment,' said Jack. 'No need to alarm the women. What do you think?'

Andrew nodded, grateful for the fact that the women were travelling with McGregor in the other vehicle.

'I don't like this,' he mumbled, changing gears. 'We'd better prepare for the worst.'

60

Broome Courthouse, 7 March

The arrival of the Wizard's legal team caused quite a stir at the sleepy Broome courthouse. It was Sunday, and a special sitting had been convened to deal with the sensational case. The magistrate wasn't used to senior counsel – with junior barrister and instructing solicitor in tow – flying in from faraway Sydney for a bail application. She was obviously impressed when Cyril Archibald QC swept into her court. It wasn't often that one of Australia's most eminent criminal lawyers appeared before her. The prosecutor, a young police sergeant, was no match for silver-tongued Archie, as he was known to his friends. Archie held the court's attention with an iron grip of authority beyond challenge.

Portly, with thinning white hair neatly parted on the left, Archie looked impeccable in his crisp white shirt and pin-striped suit. Only his ruddy complexion and the little beads of perspiration glistening on his forehead hinted at the fact that he was struggling with the oppressive heat.

First, he demolished the prosecutor's argument opposing bail with great eloquence and flair, and then mounted an irresistible plea in favour of bail. Forgotten were the facts – meekly presented by the prosecution – stating that the accused had been involved in an illegal bare-knuckle fight with one of the deceased at Fitzroy Crossing. Brushed aside was the fact that the accused had knocked his opponent unconscious and then carried him out of the ring the day before the hapless wretch was shot dead.

It didn't seem to matter that the man in the dock was a serial offender with a criminal record that would have made the Kelly gang look like pathetic amateurs. No weight was attached to the fact that he had spent more than half his life behind bars and was the reputed leader of a notorious outlaw bikie gang suspected of being the largest

285

suppliers of party drugs in the country. Archie's word was gospel and, half an hour later, the Wizard was free.

Politely declining the magistrate's invitation to morning tea, the eminent QC and his entourage caught a taxi back to the airport. His much relieved client, however, was quietly whisked away by one of his cohorts to meet the White Wolf.

'I must apologise for the accommodation,' said the Wizard, holding out his hand. 'I'm sure you're not used to staying in rundown country pubs.'

'It's safe and it's practical,' replied the White Wolf, shaking the Wizard's hand. 'That's all that matters.'

'Half the money has already been transferred into your account, as agreed,' continued the Wizard, coming straight to the point that mattered most – money.

'Broome – an exotic location for an assignment. Would you care to tell me who the target is?'

'It's a little unusual ...' said the Wizard cautiously. He reached for the bottle on the table in front of him and poured himself a large whiskey. He knew the White Wolf didn't drink.

'I deal with the unusual every day, Eugene.'

'I know, but you won't like this one.'

'Try me.'

'The target is a young woman ...'

'You know I don't do women,' said the White Wolf curtly.

'But you owe me. And this is really important.'

'That's why I'm here. However, wasting women is bad luck.'

'Leaving this one alive would be worse.'

'For you?'

'Yes. For me, and all the Wizards.'

'Tell me about it.'

Holding nothing back, the Wizard told the White Wolf about Anna and the huge threat she would pose if she were to turn up alive. He mentioned Cassandra's involvement and explained the way Jack had infiltrated the Wizards, and why. He also pointed out that the media interest would be frenzied, placing enormous pressure on the authorities to investigate what happened to Anna Popov.

'You can see why I can't take care of this myself. The Wizards can't risk being linked to the girl in any way. I need an outsider to do this – clean and fast, without leaving any clues. I need someone like you.'

'What about this Cassandra woman and the journalist? Aren't they a threat as well?'

'That's all under control. We'll take care of them ourselves. In fact, I have a little surprise in store for that cocky journo bastard,' said the Wizard.

The White Wolf found himself in an awkward position. He didn't like to be pressured, but the Wizard had cleverly manoeuvred him into a corner. It would be very difficult to turn him down.

'I want to think about it, Eugene,' said the White Wolf.

'Fair enough, but don't take too long. There is one more thing I forgot to mention ...' continued the Wizard, lowering his voice.

'Oh?'

'There's a success fee. If Anna isn't found, you get paid in full regardless. If she does surface and the hit is successful, I'll double your fee, and we're even.'

It was a shrewd offer. The White Wolf was finding it difficult to make ends meet in retirement. For one of the world's most wanted assassins to stay out of his enemies' reach, and under the radar of the law, was a costly business. He was always short of money. The Wizard knew a million US would go a long way, especially in Argentina.

'All right, Eugene, I'll do it, but strictly on my terms. I choose the time, the place and the method.'

'You got it.'

'Because there's no pattern, this is a difficult target. In fact, there's nothing to go by, nothing at all. We don't even know if she'll turn up. Everything will have to be improvised. Planning on the run is always risky. If, for some reason, things get too hot, I have the right to pull out and walk away. If that happens, you don't owe me anything and we go our separate ways. Clear so far?'

'Absolutely.' The Wizard knew it was highly unlikely that the White Wolf would throw in the towel. Professional pride and the prospect of a million bucks would see to that.

'I like clients like you, Eugene,' said the White Wolf. 'Ruthless, determined and flush with money. We both know exactly where we stand. It's a winning combination, isn't it?'

'It is. You know why?' said the Wizard.

'Tell me.'

'Because,' he said, 'we're very much alike.'

'Perhaps we are, Eugene. Except for the cash,' added the White Wolf, laughing.

During the night, Jack's house in Balmain was fire-bombed. Two Molotov cocktails were thrown through the windows – one from the back and one from the front. By the time the fire brigade arrived, the house had burnt to the ground.

61
Djanbinmarra Caves, 7 March, 2 p.m.

'Not far now,' said Merriwarra. He pointed to an escarpment rising out of the haze. 'Just over there.'

'Thank God for that,' said Jack, rubbing his aching neck. 'That last creek crossing was wild – I didn't think we were going to make it.'

'Stop whingeing, mate, it wasn't that bad,' said Will. 'You want scary? Remember those fires in 2001.'

'You're right,' said Jack, remembering the bush fires in the Blue Mountains they had fought as volunteers. 'If it hadn't been for that waterfall, I don't think we'd be here.'

'You're right. That was bloody terrifying.'

'We had to leave our truck and jump, remember?'

There wasn't a hint of a track left to follow, for the final stretch of their journey. They had to pick their way through rough open country. If it hadn't been for Merriwarra's extraordinary bush skills and familiarity with the terrain, they would have lost their way hours ago or, worse still, lost their vehicles.

Perched on an exposed plateau above a deep gorge, Merriwarra's camp had taken the full brunt of Cyclone Leopold's fury two days before. When he got out of the car and looked around, the first thing Jack noticed was the silence. The only evidence of human activity left behind after the destruction was a few charred logs, a couple of dented pots where the cooking fire used to burn, and a cast iron pan without a handle.

Small strips of canvas, caught in the twisted branches of a bush which had somehow escaped the wrath of the storm, moved slowly in the breeze. All the other vegetation had been levelled and shredded. Gone were the tents, the sleeping gear, and all the clothes. The large kitchen table and chairs Merriwarra had constructed out of tree branches and slabs of rough-sawn timber had disappeared. There was nothing left of the little improvised studio – a lean-to with a tarpaulin draped over it as protection from the sun – except two shattered terracotta paint pots stuck in a dry pool of ochre-yellow mess.

Jack followed Merriwarra to the edge of the gorge. 'This isn't looking good,' he said. 'Where did it all go?'

'Over the side, I reckon,' replied Merriwarra, pointing down into the narrow gorge. Like steam escaping from a devil's kitchen, plumes of spray rose slowly from the white water foaming angrily at the bottom.

'And the women?' asked Andrew.

'Down there as well, but inside the cave.' Merriwarra took off his hat and scratched his head. It was the only sign of his unease. 'Safe, I hope,' he added quietly.

Jack pointed to McGregor's Land Rover pulling up behind them. 'You better explain that to the others,' he said. 'Here they come now.'

Looking pale and gripped by confusion and fear, the countess was surveying the devastation around her. The little that remained conjured up images of nature at its most brutal: a tempest blindly destroying everything in its path. It was difficult to imagine how anyone could have survived that storm out in the open.

Cassandra reached for the countess's hand. 'She's alive – I can feel it. And close by,' she whispered, reassuringly squeezing the distressed woman's hand.

The countess didn't appear to have heard her. She kept staring vacantly at something only she could see, dark thoughts racing through her tortured mind.

'I have a bad feeling about this,' said Rebecca, taking Jack aside. 'What do you think?'

'I'll go down with Will for a rekky.'

'A what?'

'A little reconnaissance.'

'Be careful.'

Jandamarra

I had no idea that being a restless spirit could be so difficult. Straddling two worlds isn't easy, but when I had to convince those terrified women to leave their camp during a cyclone and find shelter in a cave that was so difficult to reach ... that one almost ended in failure. The women waited until it was almost too late, couldn't make up their mind. Instead of following Merriwarra's instructions, they huddled together in a corner of the tent. I could see what was about to happen so I had to intervene: moments before disaster struck, I showed myself.

Apart from dreams, there is another way a spirit can reach the living: through visual contact. With the storm raging outside and the tent about to be blown away, I materialised as a hazy, nebulous image, glowing faintly in the dark. As this was the first time I had attempted this, I was unsure of its effect. The women began to scream. I had to use all of my ingenuity to calm them. At first, I looked disapprovingly at Mayannie lying on the ground and shook my head. Then I conjured up images of the cave and, floating through the tent, pointed towards the gorge.

Directed by Merriwarra and Andrew from above, Jack and Will climbed down into the gorge to investigate. The narrow passage was flanked by soaring cliffs on each side and the noise of the wild, rushing water was deafening. The water level had fallen substantially since the storm had passed, but the entry to the cave was still under water. They could just see the mouth of the cave – dark and threatening, like the gaping jaws of a basilisk – a couple of feet below the foaming surface. With only a few hours of daylight left, time was running out. Jack stared down into the water.

'I know what you're thinking,' said Will.

'With a harness holding me against the current, I could give it a go.'

'What, diving down into the cave?'

'Yes, it's the only way in. According to Merriwarra, once you're inside, the cave opens up straight away and rises steeply at the entrance. I wouldn't be under water for more than a couple of metres before I resurface on the inside. If not, I turn around and come back.'

'I don't know, Jack ... The current's very strong,' said Will.

'I know. But with a harness ... I'm a strong swimmer.'

'It's your call. Or we could just wait until the morning and see if the water level falls further ...'

'What if it doesn't and the women are trapped in there? You heard what he said about Mayannie. She may not have time to wait.'

'Jack, think it through. What if you do get in? What then? You can't bring them out this way.'

'That's true, but at least we know where we stand, and we're doing something. We've come too far to stop now,' said Jack watching the rushing water draw him irresistibly closer.

'And don't forget the galleries Merriwarra mentioned. They could be connected to the caves somewhere higher up in the gorge. Who knows ...' continued Jack, forever the optimist.

'Another way out perhaps?'

'Could be. Never say never. Come on, let's get some rope.'

Despite Jack's infectious optimism, Will felt uneasy. As a seasoned volunteer fire fighter, he was used to taking risks and these two mates had been in tricky situations before. Yet, somehow, this was different.

Will wanted to stop his friend, but logic told him that it would be futile to even try. Though he couldn't dismiss the haunting premonition, he followed Jack reluctantly up the cliff and back to the cars.

Cassandra watched the two men climb out of the gorge. When she looked at Will, she saw something. It was an aura she had come across before. *He's in serious danger*, she thought, limping over to him. 'I don't think you should do this,' she said to Will.

Will shrugged. 'Try to tell him that,' he said, pointing to Jack.

Cassandra nodded. Certain situations had an unstoppable momentum. And Jack was determined to give it a go; nothing would stop him from trying.

She also knew that the bond of friendship between Will and Jack was unbreakable. Will would stand by his friend no matter what, even if common sense and reason strongly suggested the opposite.

Turning away from Will, Cassandra looked at Rebecca, staring down into the gorge. 'You can sense it too, can't you?' she said.

Rebecca looked up. *She's reading my thoughts again*, she marvelled. 'Yes I can,' she said. 'We have to warn them.'

Cassandra shook her head sadly. 'They won't listen,' she said.

As she stared back down into the foaming gorge, Rebecca saw herself as a little girl standing in front of her father the day her brother died, and her life changed. 'Don't let him go up on the roof, Daddy,' she heard herself say over and over.

'They didn't listen then,' said Cassandra, reaching for Rebecca's hand. 'And they won't listen now. Certain things cannot be changed.'

Rebecca realised, with a growing dread, that her friend was right.

62
Djanbinmarra Caves, 7 March, 4 p.m.

Jack adjusted the rope wound tightly around his waist and chest like a python embracing its prey, and carefully balanced on a rock just above the submerged entry to the cave. The rope was anchored around a tree stump a few yards upstream and held by Will and Andrew. It was supposed to act as a harness and stop Jack from being swept past the entry. Satisfied, Jack looked up and waved to the women watching anxiously from above. Then he turned around, gave Will a thumbs-up and jumped in.

'God be with you,' whispered the countess, her heart racing. She lifted the small crucifix hanging around her neck to her lips and began to pray.

With a few powerful strokes Jack propelled himself through the narrow tunnel under water and resurfaced on the inside. What only took seconds seemed an eternity.

The large entry chamber was empty, the rushing water thundering past on the outside the only sound. A shaft of light penetrated the darkness from above, like a finger of hope reaching down into the abyss. Jack slipped off the harness, secured it under a large stone and reached for his lifeline.

'Did you feel that?' asked Will. 'Three tugs. He's through!'

'I certainly hope so,' said Andrew. 'No one can stay under water that long.'

'What do we do now?'

'We wait.'

Mayannie was slipping away. With her emaciated body wracked by fever and bathed in sweat, she shivered like a terrified child facing punishment.

The two elderly Aboriginal women huddled around the small fire were expecting a visit from death, the ultimate master. To protect them from the storm, the friendly spirit had guided them to safety. However, they knew that friendly spirits had no power over death: the ancient rock art reminded them of the law. To cope with their fear, they reached far back into tribal memory, closed their eyes and began to chant.

It didn't take Jack long to find the women. By following the shaft of light as he climbed into the upper chambers, he avoided the many dead-ends and dangerous tunnels fanning out in all directions. Soon he could hear chanting and smell smoke, the shadows dancing along the walls showing him the way to the fire.

The old woman holding Mayannie's limp hand opened her eyes and screamed. Death wasn't supposed to look like that: a white man, stripped down to his shorts, dripping wet and speaking English.

'Don't be afraid,' said Jack, holding up his hands reassuringly. 'Merriwarra sent me. I've come to help.'

By speaking softly and repeating Merriwarra's name, he managed to calm the terrified woman.

'How is she?' asked Jack.

The old woman by the fire shook her head. Wrapped tightly in an old blanket, Mayannie looked like a corpse. Her eyes were closed and her head was resting in the old woman's lap.

'Is she alive?' he whispered, coming closer. There was no reply.

Expecting the worst, Jack crouched down and reached for Mayannie's wrist. At first, he felt nothing, the tense moment almost getting the better of him. Then he felt it: a pulse – weak – yet undeniably there.

My God, she's alive, *he thought*, but only just.

The gallery where the women were huddled around the fire had an opening to the gorge, like a large window set into the rock by giants, letting out smoke, and letting in light and air. Jack crawled to the very edge and looked up. He could just see the stump of a boab tree on top of the plateau some 20 metres above him, illuminated by the last rays of the setting sun. But the vertical rock face was so treacherous and steep that not even a lizard could have found a foothold. As an alternative entry to or exit from the cave, it appeared useless. Below him, the dark waters of the swollen creek thundered through the narrow gorge like an angry beast waiting to devour anything foolish enough to get in its way.

Jack considered his options: to take Mayannie out through the water was impossible. To wait for the waters to recede wasn't a solution either – she would be dead well before then. Remembering a similar situation in a cave in Ethiopia two years before, Jack made up his mind. *There's only one way to do this,* he thought. *Let's hope we've got enough rope.*

'He's coming back!' shouted Will, feeling the rope move in his hand. Moments later, Jack's head appeared in the foaming water above the cave entry. Pulling him carefully against the current towards them, Andrew and Will reeled him in like a prized catch.

'You found them?' asked Merriwarra, helping Jack out of the water.

'Yes. But we've got to hurry,' replied Jack, trying to catch his breath.

'Mayannie?'

'Alive, but in a bad way.' Merriwarra shook his head sadly. 'We've got to get her out now or ...'

'Any ideas?' asked Will.

Jack looked at him, the beginnings of a smile creasing the corners of his mouth. 'There's another way in, but it's a little tricky.'

'Where?'

'Let's climb up to the top and I'll show you.'

Cassandra stood on a rock ledge high above the gorge and watched Jack being dragged out of the torrent by Merriwarra. She admired Jack's courage and determination. Certain people thrive on danger and adversity – Jack was one of those. Cassandra knew he would never give up. Unlike the countess standing next to her, Cassandra felt calm. She knew that Mayannie was about to be rescued and would survive. The Tarot had told her so. The real danger, however, was lurking somewhere else.

Cassandra felt a pang of envy. For the countess, the ordeal was about to end. Cassandra's own journey, however, was uncertain, and so was her son's fate. The more she had tried to see what lay ahead, the murkier things had become. The messages were unclear and sometimes conflicting. The Tarot was never wrong. But those wishing to interpret its messages, when clouded by emotion, often fell into error.

Dripping wet and panting, but feeling elated, Jack reached the top and sat down on a rock to catch his breath. Anxious to get to him before the countess could overwhelm him with questions, Rebecca hurried over to Jack with a towel.

'Thank God you're all right,' she said, handing him the towel. 'Did you find her?'

Jack nodded.

'Are you sure it's Anna?'

'Yes.'

'Will she make it?'

'I hope so, but ...'

'You have to tell Katerina ...'

Jack walked over to the countess. Too afraid to ask the obvious question, she just looked at him, pain and anguish clouding her eyes.

'Anna's down there. She's alive,' announced Jack, 'but we must hurry.'

'Thank you, Lord,' said the countess, tears streaming down her pale face. 'She's here? How? Is she ill? Tell me ... please ...'

'There's only one way to get her out,' said Jack holding up his hand. He pointed over his shoulder towards the gorge. 'I'll climb down into the cave from here and bring her up. Now – before it gets dark.'

'And how exactly do you propose to do that?' asked Rebecca, worried.

'Will and I have done plenty of abseiling and rescues together during our bush fire days. I think I can do it.'

'But nothing quite like this,' interrupted Will, shaking his head.

'It's worth a go. Get the Land Rover. We'll attach a rope to the winch and I'll go down.'

'And then what?' asked Will.

'I'll improvise. Let's get cracking!'

Rebecca hurried over to Cassandra. 'This is crazy! We have to do something,' she said.

'There's nothing we can do,' said Cassandra. 'You know that.'

The countess – eyes closed – had fallen to her knees and was praying, her faith giving her strength to face the terrible twins: uncertainty and waiting.

'Thank Christ we've got enough rope,' said Jack, preparing himself for the descent.

'Are you sure you want to do this?' said Andrew.

'If we don't get her out now, it's all over. She'll be dead by the morning. Will, steady the rope.' Looking over his shoulder, Jack pinpointed the cave 'window' and, giving his friend the thumbs up, eased himself over the edge.

This time the two old Aboriginal women were certain that death had finally come to claim Mayannie. Terrified, they watched a dark shape materialise in the narrow opening, blotting out the fading light. Catching his breath, Jack secured the rope and crawled into the cave.

'It's me again,' he said softly, trying to calm them. 'I need your help. We have to get Mayannie into this.'

Jack pointed to the improvised rope harness strapped to his back. 'I'll take her up with me. It's her only chance. Here – help me lift her up. I'll show you what to do.'

'What about the ...?' asked one of the women, pointing to the little bundle in her arms.

'I'll come back for it later.'

The two women lifted Mayannie's limp body off the floor, and with Jack's help, strapped her tightly to his back. Jack went down on his knees and, moving slowly forward on all fours, crawled back to the edge.

Jesus, this won't be easy, he thought, looking up. *At least she doesn't know what's going on.*

'There he is,' shouted Will, pointing down into the gorge. 'Get ready, fellas!'

Jack checked the rope wound around his waist, gave it a tug, and then slowly began his ascent.

'Steady, on,' shouted Will, signalling to McGregor operating the noisy winch behind him. 'He's coming up.' In the approaching darkness, Jack looked like some giant hump-backed beetle crawling up the cliff.

Mayannie had her eyes closed, her bare feet protruding like an extra pair of skinny beetle legs trying in vain to get a foothold on the treacherous rock.

The countess, who had stopped praying, stared down into the gorge. Cassandra put her arm around her and pulled her gently away from the edge.

'Don't look down,' she said, comforting the distressed woman.

'I can't take this much longer,' sobbed the countess, covering her face with her hands.

'Keep it steady!' shouted Andrew to McGregor.

'He's almost up,' said Merriwarra, the rope cutting into the burning palms of his hands.

'Not much further, mate! Come on!' yelled Will, leaning over the edge.

Ignoring the excruciating pain in his thighs and calves, Jack focused on keeping his balance. With Mayannie's limp body strapped to his back, it wasn't easy. He knew that one wrong step could spell disaster. He also knew that the last step was always the hardest.

'Hang in there,' Will shouted, grabbing hold of Jack's harness from above to steady him. 'You're almost there.'

Jack made the mistake of looking up. He lost his footing and began to slide sideways.

'Pull him up. Now!' shouted Will, grabbing for the rope. Merriwarra held his breath and, giving it all they had, they hauled Jack over the edge.

Bruised and bleeding, Jack lay on his stomach, panting. 'Mayannie?' he whispered.

'Safe,' said Rebecca, kneeling down beside him. 'You made it, Jack. Thank God!'

Too exhausted to speak, Jack turned his head a little, looked at her and smiled. It was a smile Rebecca would never forget; a fleeting glimpse into Jack's soul. Bending down until her lips touched his face, Rebecca whispered, 'You're quite a guy, Jack Rogan,' and kissed him tenderly on the cheek.

63
Djambinmarra Caves, 7 March, 6 p.m.

Will and Andrew untied the harness strapped to Jack's back, and carefully placed Mayannie on a blanket. Her eyes were open, her stare vacant, the tiny beads of perspiration glistening on her forehead the only sign of a raging fever.

'Come,' said Cassandra, reaching for the countess' hand, 'she's waiting for you.' Walking slowly towards the dark shape lying motionless on the ground, half a lifetime flashed past in the countess' tortured mind. First, there was Zoltan – Anna's father – forever young and full of innocent excitement the day she told him that she was pregnant. Then Nikolai floated into view, reassuringly holding her hand in the Paris hospital the day Anna was born. With each step, a new precious memory – carefully tucked away for years – emerged with alarming clarity. 'Dear God, can this really be Anna?' she asked, barely able to speak. It sounded more like a prayer than a question. 'I'm so afraid; what if ...' Cassandra just squeezed her hand without saying anything and gently pushed her forward.

First, the countess just stared at the bare feet in front of her and then, lifting her gaze, looked at the hands. Then, coming slowly closer, she bent down and let her eyes wander until they came to rest on the face. The long blonde hair she remembered so well was gone. Instead, short hair, closely cropped and bleached almost white by the harsh Outback sun, framed a tanned face. The prominent features, however, were unmistakable.

'Anna?' whispered the countess, falling to her knees. She stretched out her hand to touch the face in front of her but stopped in midair, afraid it would disappear if she were to make contact. 'My child, can you hear me?' she asked in French. There was no response. The half-closed eyes kept staring straight ahead, the expression on the face unchanged.

301

The countess reached for her daughter's hand, lifted it to her lips and kissed it. The little hand felt limp and clammy.

Anna hadn't heard French spoken in years. Slowly, her eyes flickered wide open. Trying to focus on the face that hovered above her, she felt as if she was falling backwards through cottonwool, the comforting voice fading. Then suddenly, the face materialised again out of the fog.

'Mama?' she whispered, her voice barely audible.

'Oh yes, my darling,' replied the countess, taking her daughter into her arms.

'Where's Billy?' asked Anna.

'Hush, hush ... you're safe now ...'

The countess didn't understand the question, but Cassandra did.

'Jack! What on earth are you doing?' asked Rebecca.

'I'm going back down.'

'Are you out of your mind?'

'This is the second part of the rescue.'

Jack put on a backpack and wound the rope around his waist. 'Okay, guys – lower me down.'

'Will, do something! He's lost his marbles.'

'It's all right,' Will said, 'he has to go.'

'Why?'

'To bring someone else up ...'

'I thought the others were okay and could wait ... Anna needs help. Now!'

'No. This can't wait,' interrupted Cassandra.

'You're all in on this,' complained Rebecca, turning to Will.

'Don't worry. He can do it,' he said.

Rebecca spun around. 'Jack? What's going on?' she demanded, fear clawing at her throat.

But he had already disappeared over the edge.

Jack remembered the footholds and the tricky bits from his first descent and, retracing his steps, made it quickly to the bottom. By the time he crawled back into the cave it was almost dark. Strapping the tiny sleeping baby into the backpack was easy. Within minutes, Jack was ready to go back up.

'I can see him. He's coming,' said Will raising his arm. McGregor engaged the winch.

It's always easier the second time, thought Jack, feeling elated about Anna's rescue, the adrenalin pumping through his aching muscles masking exhaustion and fatigue. However, what he didn't take into account was the approaching darkness. Instead of going straight up as he had done the first time, he lost concentration and inadvertently moved a couple of metres to the left.

'What's he doing?' shouted Will, looking over the edge. 'Jack, you're going the wrong way!'

With the wild water thundering through the gorge below him, Jack couldn't hear the warning. By now it was virtually dark. Long shadows crept along the cliff face like claws of a hungry vulture searching for prey, and Jack didn't notice the overhanging rock shelf above him. As he approached the protruding rock from below, he disappeared from view.

'Jesus, I can't see him anymore!' shouted Will. 'Stop the winch!' McGregor didn't hear him and the winch kept going, pulling Jack towards the overhang. Jack lost his footing and became airborne, the sharp edge of the rock above him cutting into the taut rope. Andrew ran back to McGregor and stopped the winch, seconds before the rope would have snapped.

'What's going on?' asked Rebecca running across to Will. Leaving the countess with Anna, Cassandra limped after her.

'I don't know! I can't see him!' said Will. 'He must be stuck.'

'Where is he?'

'Just down there, below that rock.'

'Can't we just pull him up?'

'No way! Far too dangerous.'

'What now?'

'I'm going down to have a look,' said Will, reaching for another rope they had discarded before. The thin rope was too short, and Will had to extend it with another bit he got out of the Land Rover. *If this knot doesn't hold, I'm buggered*, he thought, checking the knot for the third time, just to make sure it was safe.

Peering over the edge, Cassandra recognised the signs only too well.

What she had sensed earlier was actually taking shape. The different threads of fate were coming together with frightening speed. Will would risk his life for his friend without blinking an eye. Rebecca could feel it too as she watched Will prepare the flimsy rope.

'You're going down with this?' she asked, looking alarmed.

'It's all we've got.'

'But ...'

'We must hurry; it's almost dark,' interrupted Will, looking down into the gorge melting into the twilight. 'Okay, guys, let's go.'

64

Djambinmarra Caves, 8 p.m.

Jack knew he was in serious trouble as soon as he lost his footing and looked up. Supported only by the rope tied around his waist, he was swinging slowly from side to side, unable to go up or down.

Jesus, how did I get into this? he thought, trying to stay calm. Jack had no proper climbing gear and only an improvised rope as his lifeline; there was nothing he could do but wait.

When Jack glanced over his shoulder, he could sense movement. Turning his head, he could see a dark shape coming slowly down the cliff on his right.

'Over here, mate,' shouted Jack, recognising his friend. The dark shape came closer and stopped just above him.

'I'll get you out of here, but only if you hold still,' said Will. 'Your rope won't last much longer.'

'Great.'

'That's what happens when you take the scenic route,' joked Will, lowering himself down next to Jack until he found a secure foothold in the rock. 'How're you feeling?'

'Stuffed.'

'You look it.'

'Thanks, mate.'

'This is what we'll do: There's an easy way up just above me. I think I can reach you from here and pull you over. You'll use me as a ladder and climb up. We've done this before during the Mount Victoria fires – remember? Once you stand on my shoulders you should be able to free your rope and move it across. After that, it's easy; straight up. It's only a few metres.'

'You're out of your mind,' said Jack. 'You can't support us both; not with that piddling excuse of a rope. We'll both go down.'

'No we won't. It's the only way; trust me. Are you ready? Give me your hand.'

Leaning over the edge, Andrew and Merriwarra stared down into the gloom. They could just see Will a few metres below them standing quite still. Andrew had his hands on Jack's rope, and Merriwarra was holding Will's. Both ropes were attached to the winch behind them.

'What do we do now?' asked Merriwarra.

'Nothing. We wait. It's all up to them down there,' said Andrew.

'Is there nothing we can do?' asked Rebecca, feeling sick.

Cassandra looked at her and sadly shook her head.

'Why did he have to go back down, the fool,' said Rebecca close to tears.

'Because he's the man he is,' said Cassandra, putting her arm around her friend.

'They're not going to make it, are they?' said Rebecca, fear stabbing at her heart.

'I'm not sure ...'

'But we both saw ...'

'Hush ... *Believe!*'

Will extended his arm towards Jack as far as he could without losing his footing, but still couldn't reach his friend's outstretched hand. 'Try to swing across to me,' he said, 'it's the only way I can get hold of you.'

'What about the rope?' said Jack.

'No choice.'

'Shit! Here we go.'

'Take it easy!'

First, Jack shifted his weight from left to right, until he began to swing like a pendulum, each arc bringing him closer to Will's outstretched hand.

'Come on, you're almost there,' said Will, encouraging his friend. As Jack's rope moved, the jagged edge of the rock above him cut deeper into the fraying hemp. 'Got you!' Will grabbed Jack by the wrist and pulled him across. 'Now, put your arm around me.' Jack did as he was told. 'And wrap your legs around mine.'

'Thanks mate,' said Jack, perspiration running down his burning forehead. 'What next?'

When Will looked at Jack's flushed face, he recognised the warning signs: exhaustion, shock, fear and disbelief, simultaneously assaulting a vulnerable mind. He realised that he would have to carefully talk Jack through each step of the difficult climb, right up to the very top.

'Now comes the tricky bit,' Will said, grabbing hold of Jack's rope. 'Let go of your rope and climb on top of my shoulders. Use my rope instead.'

'The moment I do that, I transfer my weight, and we both depend on your rope for support,' said Jack, uncertainty and hesitation making his voice quiver.

'I know that. Do it! Now! My foot's going numb.'

Jack took hold of Will's rope, and slowly pulled himself up until his knees came to rest on Will's shoulders, the thin rope cutting deep into his wrists.

'Stand up, and try to free your rope. Hurry!' Will had lost all feeling in his foot, and was afraid of losing his balance, the excruciating pain in his legs and thigh sending crazy little white stars dancing in front of his eyes. Using the slack of his own rope, Jack managed to pull the rope away from the overhanging rock and move it across next to Will's.

'Done.'

'Now let go of my rope and climb up using yours. Quickly! I can't hold on much longer.'

'What's happening?' asked Merriwarra. 'Can you see anything?'

'It's Jack! He's coming up! Let's give him a hand,' said Andrew, pulling Jack's rope with all the strength he could muster. Rebecca ran over to him and took hold of the rope from behind to help. Assuming that Will was coming up too, Merriwarra did the same and began to pull with all his might, adding to the strain on Will's fragile rope.

Looking up, Jack could see the cliff top a few metres above him. *Almost there*, he thought. *Thanks, mate. I owe you.*

He must be up by now, thought Will, moving his leg to ease the numbing pain. As he turned to begin his climb, he lost his footing. After that, everything happened with lightning speed.

Unable to support Will's full body weight, the knot began to part under the strain. Slowly at first, but accelerating with each fibre slipping through the loop, it quickly became weaker. Before Will could find another foothold in the smooth rock, the knot gave way.

Just before he reached the top, Jack saw Will's rope crack past him like a stockman's whip. Turning his head, he looked down, his eyes widening in disbelief and fear. 'Noooo!' he shouted, as he watched Will plunge backwards through the moonlight shadow into the rocky jaws of death waiting at the bottom.

Andrew and Rebecca pulled Jack up to the top, and dragged his limp body over the edge.

'He's in shock,' said Andrew, looking at Jack, cowering on the rock ledge in front of them.

'Look at this,' said Merriwarra, holding up the frayed end of his rope. 'This is what I got.'

'Oh my God!' said Rebecca, looking at Cassandra.

Cassandra limped over to Jack and knelt down next to Rebecca. 'It was Will who was in danger all along, not Jack,' she said softly, placing her hand on Jack's burning forehead. Jack opened his eyes and looked at Cassandra. 'Will's gone,' he said.

'I know,' replied Cassandra.

'Because of me ...' said Jack.

'No. Because of who he was. You would have done the same for him.'

Jack turned his face away. 'The baby?' he whispered, looking for justification.

'Asleep in your backpack; safe,' said Rebecca.

'One life in return for another?' asked Jack, searching for salvation.

'No, Jack, it doesn't work that way. True friendship has no measure,' said Cassandra.

Jack lifted his head and looked gratefully at her. 'Take it to its mother.'

'Sure.'

Feeling better, Jack closed his eyes. *Absolution perhaps?* he asked himself, overwhelmed by grief, but daring to hope.

Andrew slipped off Jack's backpack and handed it carefully to Cassandra.

'Precious cargo,' he said. 'Slept through the entire ordeal.'

Sitting on the ground with Anna's head in her lap, the countess was oblivious to what had just happened. Cassandra walked over to her, a small bundle in her arms.

'She keeps asking for Billy,' said the countess, wiping her teary eyes. 'She must be delirious, poor child.'

'Not exactly,' said Cassandra, folding back the towel to expose the sleeping baby's face. Turning towards Cassandra, the countess looked at the baby, a hundred questions screaming for answers. 'Why don't you give her this to hold?' said Cassandra. Kneeling down beside the countess, Cassandra handed her the tiny child. 'This is William, your grandson,' she whispered.

Jandamarra

We were right there when the brave man died. We saw his soul leave his shattered body moments before it was claimed by the torrent thundering through the gorge. Pigeon was beside himself with worry. He had just watched the son he had never met being rescued by two strangers risking their lives. Soon, however, anxiety was replaced by joy: mother and son were safely reunited at the top.

We thought that this moment marked the completion of the difficult task set for us by our ancestors. Mayannie had become Anna again and was about to re-enter the world of the Malngadu with her baby son.

Despite all odds, Pigeon and I had succeeded. The circle was complete and a great wrong had been addressed. Restless spirits no more, we were ready to take our rightful place by the campfire of our ancestors. As we were soon to find out, however, the spirit world had something quite different in mind.

65

On the way back to Never Never Downs, 8 March

Anna's life hung in the balance. Andrew decided to leave at once and take his chances in the dark. Jack refused to go. Crushed by grief and guilt, he wanted to begin searching for Will's body in the morning.

Andrew took him aside. 'I know how you feel,' he said, 'but there's virtually no chance of finding the body. No one can go down there ...'

'I've got to try. I owe him that much.'

'Merriwarra and McGregor will come back and have a look around further downstream, just in case.'

'I can't leave ...'

Andrew shrugged and called out to Cassandra, 'Try and talk some sense into him. He can't stay here, and we've got to go – now!'

Cassandra walked over to Jack. 'There is something you can do for Will,' she said.

'What?'

'Look after the living. And that includes you. Don't lose sight of why he died,' she added softly. The comment hit the mark. Reluctantly, Jack followed the others to the cars.

Merriwarra took advantage of the full moon casting its ghostly light across the sleeping landscape. With intuition and his extraordinary knowledge of the land guiding him, he was able to find a way back to Never Never Downs during the night. When the going got too rough, he walked in front of the cars to find a safe passage through the wilderness. There wasn't another man alive in the entire Kimberley who could have accomplished this.

Barely able to stay awake herself, the countess kept Anna alert throughout the journey by talking to her. Feeling Anna close to her gave her strength to cope with the rollercoaster of emotions assaulting her exhausted mind. However, elation and joy were soon overpowered by disbelief and fear for Anna's life.

Cassandra sensed the countess' dark mood and wanted to distract her. 'It's a beautiful baby,' she said, cradling the sleeping child in her arms.

The countess looked at Billy, tears in her eyes. 'He's gorgeous,' she said. *I must stay awake*, she thought, rubbing her aching temples.

Anna's condition appeared to have stabilised for the time being. Eyes closed and breathing regularly, she seemed content in her mother's arms.

'This is crazy,' said McGregor, trying to follow the bobbing tail lights of Andrew's Land Rover in front of him. He had to fight to keep his eyes open and his hands on the wheel. Slumped in the seat next to Rebecca in the back, head resting against her shoulder, Jack was confronting his demons. Every time he drifted towards the sanctuary of sleep his battered body craved so much, Will's bloodied face appeared, looking accusingly, he thought, at him.

'How is he?' asked McGregor, glancing over his shoulder.

'Shaking like a leaf.' Rebecca put her hand on Jack's burning forehead. 'And very hot.'

'Shock. And fever. Try to keep him warm.'

Jack opened his eyes and looked at Rebecca. 'I can't believe he's gone,' he said, his teeth chattering.

'Hush; you must rest,' said Rebecca.

'I can't. I hurt too much.'

'I know.'

Jack closed his eyes again. This time, Will spoke to him. 'There's something you can do for me, mate.'

'What's that?' asked Jack.

'Look after the living.'

'Look after the living,' repeated Jack, speaking slowly.

'What did he say?' asked McGregor.

'I think he's hallucinating, poor darling,' replied Rebecca, stroking Jack's sweaty hair. 'But he's just fallen asleep,' she added after a while. 'Thank God!'

Progress was arduous and slow, but they reached the homestead at first light. After a hot shower and a hearty breakfast in the warm kitchen, everyone felt better.

'You're going back?' asked Jack. McGregor nodded. 'What are the chances?'

'Of finding him?'

'Yes.'

'Not great.'

Looking dejected, Jack stared into his coffee cup.

'Wouldn't you rather he rested under the stars up here than in a tiny box with a brass plaque in some lawn cemetery no one comes to visit?' said Andrew.

Jack thought about this for a while, and then looked at Andrew. 'You're right,' he said, brightening up. 'What about the formalities?'

'We report the accident to the police.'

'That's it?'

Andrew shrugged. 'This is the Outback,' he said.

The weather at Never Never Downs was clear, allowing Andrew to take off later that morning. Radioing ahead, he made arrangements for an ambulance to meet them at the airport. He used his old contacts to ensure the patient's true identity was kept under wraps, at least for the moment. Everyone agreed that Anna's return should stay out of the limelight for as long as possible, as the media frenzy that was bound to erupt could only hinder her recovery. And who knew what fury the Wizard might unleash?

Andrew had asked the police to meet them on arrival. All he would say was that a matter of national importance was about to unfold.

Rebecca accompanied the countess and Anna with the baby to the hospital. Jack and Cassandra stayed with Andrew to talk to the police. Andrew made sure the ambulance had left the airport before he spoke to the two officers waiting for him.

'The patient in that ambulance is about to make history,' he said. 'Let's go to the station. We have work to do.'

At first, the visiting Superintendent investigating the Tunnel Creek murders didn't believe the retired Aboriginal police officer with the funny hat, and refused to call his superior in Perth. He wanted confirmation.

But when Andrew told him that there were two witnesses waiting outside – one of them a prominent international best-selling author – ready to make a statement, he began to listen.

Jack was taken into the interview room first and asked to give his account of events leading up to Anna's discovery. When Cassandra was called in and added her side of the story, the enormity of what was taking place dawned on the Superintendent. It soon became apparent that the recent riot and shooting at Fitzroy Crossing, the double murders at Tunnel Creek and the Wizard's arrest were somehow linked to the Popov case.

Cassandra paled when she heard that the Wizard was out on bail and had been allowed to return to Sydney. This was the danger she had sensed all along.

When Andrew explained that Countess Kuragin, Anna Popov's mother, had just identified her daughter and was with her at the hospital, the Superintendent went into a tailspin. He asked them to wait outside and called the Police Commissioner in Perth for instructions. The Police Commissioner contacted the Attorney General, who immediately briefed the Prime Minister. Within minutes, Anna Popov's baffling return had become the hottest topic in the country.

'Pretty good, eh?' said Andrew, looking rather pleased with himself. He knew his vindication had begun in earnest. 'We've just put a rocket up his arse. Arrogant prick.'

'You sure did that,' said Jack, trying to work out the impact of the dominoes starting to fall all around them.

Cassandra nodded absentmindedly, unable to banish the dark thoughts strangling her heavy heart. It was time for her to act because it was now only a matter of hours before news of Anna's extraordinary survival became public. Cassandra realised that to stay in the game, she had to be the one to tell the Wizard.

'Can I borrow your mobile?' she asked after a while. Uncertainty and hesitation had been replaced by steely resolve. She now knew exactly what she had to do. Andrew handed her his mobile, raised an eyebrow, but said nothing.

'I have to call the Wizard,' said Cassandra. Andrew nodded. He'd been expecting something like that.

The Wizard was addressing the council in the crypt when one of his lieutenants interrupted the meeting and handed him a mobile.

'You better take this,' said the man before the Wizard could reprimand him. 'It's her.'

'How nice to hear from you,' said the Wizard sarcastically, rocking back in his chair. 'You took your time. Have you got anything to tell me?'

'Anna's been found. She's alive,' said Cassandra calmly.

'What?' roared the Wizard, almost overbalancing in his chair.

Mesmerised, the others in the crypt looked on in silence.

'Where is she?'

'Broome hospital, recovering.'

'Has she spoken to the coppers?'

'Not so fast, Eugene. It's my turn to ask the questions.'

'What do you mean?' barked the Wizard.

'You claim that Tristan has come out of the coma. I don't believe you. There's one easy way to clear this up: let me speak to him, now. If he's conscious, I'll tell you all you want to know ...'

'You're in no position to make demands,' snapped the Wizard.

'You forget who you are talking to, Eugene,' said Cassandra. 'I know you ...'

'Now you listen to me!' roared the Wizard.

'The boy is a vegetable,' interrupted Cassandra. 'We both know it, and you can't hurt a vegetable. So what'll it be? Can I talk to him?'

'I'll rip him apart with my bare hands, you hear? Is that what you want?'

'I'll take this as a refusal, then. I'm not surprised,' replied Cassandra calmly. 'I've seen it all – the Tarot never lies. Now you listen to me, Eugene. I've consulted the cards ... you're in big trouble. Your end is near, and it's more horrible than even you could possibly imagine. You can't cheat fate – you know that. You can't hurt me anymore, but I can hurt you, and I will. You can count on that.'

The line went dead. For an instant, the Wizard stared into space, a ripple of fear teasing his neck.

'Fucking bitch!' he shouted, slamming down the phone.

'We've got a problem, guys, but I already have the answer,' he said, rubbing the angry looking scar on his face. 'Anna's back, but not for long. Her return will be short-lived.'

The Wizard picked up the phone, put it on speaker and dialled. He didn't have to wait long before his call was answered.

'Hello,' said a male voice on the other end.

'It's me,' said the Wizard. 'She's in Broome hospital ...'

'You're a lucky man, Eugene,' replied the White Wolf.

'Why's that?'

'I like hospitals. I've used them before. Bodies and hospitals are a good fit, don't you think?'

'Did you hear that, guys?' asked the Wizard, roaring with laughter. 'Hospitals and bodies are a good fit. Remember that!'

Professor Popov was asleep in his Rome hotel room when his mobile rang. It was two in the morning. Reaching for his glasses, he sat up in bed, fumbled clumsily with the phone and glanced at the screen. The name blinking at him in the dark was 'Katerina'. A call from his former wife at this time of the night was most unusual. *This must be important*, he thought, instantly awake. Popov pressed the answer button.

'Hello Katty,' he said, switching on the light. 'What ...'

'Anna is alive!' interrupted the countess, her voice sounding distant and hollow.

'What did you just say?' asked Popov after a while, not trusting his ears.

'She's alive, Nikki,' sobbed the countess. 'We found her.'

'Where?' he asked, choking with emotion.

'In the Kimberley wilderness right here in Australia. She was living with an Aboriginal tribe ...'

'Are you serious?'

'Absolutely.'

'How is she?'

'She's just come out of intensive care, but they say she'll make it.'

'Oh my God!' A thousand questions raced through Popov's mind. 'But what about ...'

'Here comes the doctor now, I've got to go,' the countess cut him short.

'Where are you?'

'Broome.'

'I'll be on the first plane ...'

'Please hurry!'

66

Broome, 8 March

What had kept the White Wolf a step ahead of the law all these years and out of his enemies' reach was the fact that he was a master tactician first, an assassin second. As usual, information and timing held the key. Within half an hour of speaking to the Wizard, the White Wolf had established that Zac knew the manager of the cleaning company retained by the hospital. In the drug business, cleaners were valuable contacts.

They were an invisible grey army with ready access to places others could only dream about. No one paid attention to cleaners – they were almost part of the furniture. They could appear suddenly in unexpected places like toilets, kitchens, boardrooms or hospital corridors without arousing suspicion, and without being questioned.

Half an hour later, the White Wolf had a uniform – compliments of the cleaning company – and was talking to a trusted employee familiar with the layout of the hospital. Encouraged by the $500 slipped into his pocket by Zac, the man checked with one of his colleagues who was still on duty at the hospital. He was able to confirm that only one young woman had been admitted into Emergency that morning and had just come out of Intensive Care. He promised to ring back shortly with a room number and a name. The White Wolf had everything he needed. He went through his mental checklist and returned to his room to prepare for the hit.

Countess Kuragin was asleep in a chair next to her daughter's hospital bed. The baby, also asleep, was in a bassinet beside her. Andrew, Rebecca and Jack had gone back to the police station. Careful not to wake the countess, Cassandra tiptoed into the darkened room and pulled up a chair well away from the bed. Anna had her eyes closed and was resting. She had lost a lot of blood giving birth in the desert,

317

and had developed an infection. However, after an urgent blood transfusion and antibiotics, her condition had stabilised. The prognosis was good.

According to the physician in charge, youth and a strong constitution would see her through.

As she listened to the rhythm of the countess' deep breathing, Cassandra reflected on her conversation with the Wizard. In the quiet of the room, nagging doubts were beginning to chip away at her resolve.

She had called the Wizard's bluff and taken a huge gamble with her son's life. Had she made the right decision? She had hoped to protect her son's life by making it appear worthless. *How will Eugene react?* she asked herself over and over. Surely he would now turn to the real threat – Anna. He would try to kill Anna, she was sure of it. But when and how? He would act quickly to silence her before she could say too much. The next twenty-four hours were critical – Anna had to be protected at all costs.

Cassandra covered her face with her hands. *I mustn't lose sight of the real reason I joined the Wizards of Oz,* she reminded herself. *He must be avenged before he can rest. I owe him that. He was my blood* ... Cassandra looked at Anna lying motionless in her bed. Anna had merely been the way in, and Tristan an unexpected casualty. *I used them both to get to the Wizard. Now I must save them both from him before it's too late.*

To calm herself, Cassandra decided to consult the cards one more time.

Jandamarra

Just when I thought that we'd finally done it, Ellemarra, my retired spirit guide, brought us a message. He told us that one last hurdle remained before we could finally join our ancestors. Despite all we had done, Anna wasn't safe after all.

There are many shades of bad when it comes to character, but true evil is rare. However, what Pigeon and I were about to encounter was not only evil, but wickedness of a special kind ...

Instead of finding comfort from delving into the familiar realm of the Tarot, Cassandra was getting more and more agitated. It seemed that each card wanted to tell her something important. The Hermit, The Emperor, The Magician, even The Fool wanted to speak to her. But she wasn't in the right frame of mind, and the messages weren't getting through. Frustrated, Cassandra pushed the cards aside. Then she remembered something else. *When the cards fail you, turn to the numbers,* she heard her mother whisper from afar. *Numbers never lie.*

The Fibonacci Sequence, of course! she thought. *Why didn't I think of this before?*

Cassandra closed her eyes and listened. She could hear her mother, a psychic like herself, and respected healer, explain the mystery of Fibonacci's numbers to her:

'Fibonacci was a genius. Let me tell you about him. He came up with a simple concept of elegant mathematical beauty; the Fibonacci Sequence. He published a book in 1202 AD under his real name – Leonardo of Pisa; it's all in there. However, the idea itself is much older. It goes back to Sanskrit writings. This is how it works:

The sequence begins with a simple addition: 0 + 1. Each following number is the sum of the previous two: 0 + 1 = 1; 1 + 1 = 2; 1 + 2 = 3; 2 + 3 = 5, and so on – see? The reason Fibonacci has become so popular today, is a surprising discovery: Nature is full of examples following his numbers. Isn't it wonderful? Don't you just love him!'

Cassandra opened her eyes. Remembering her mother's passionate explanation brought a smile to her face. She took a piece of paper and a pen out of her handbag and drew a line down the middle of the page. In the left column she wrote the numbers 1, 2, 3, 5, 8 – the first five numbers of the Fibonacci sequence. In the right column, next to the numbers, she wrote names.

1 Cassandra
2 Cassandra + Pigeon
3 Cassandra + Pigeon + Jack
5 Cassandra + Pigeon + Jack + Will + Rebecca

Cassandra paused, and then added Andrew's name. *Six isn't part of the sequence*, she thought. But when she crossed out Will's name, the number was back to five. Will's death had restored the balance. *Then the countess joined us, bringing the number back up to six*, Cassandra reminded herself. One too many! Anna and Billy didn't count. They weren't part of this equation. *Someone will be removed to restore the balance*, she thought, the realisation sending icy shivers racing down her spine. *If it can't be Anna, then who?*

Pigeon

Jandamarra made it clear that it was now up to me to protect Anna from the Wizard's fury. It could be my last chance to get even with the monster — from beyond the grave, he said. Perhaps I could still fulfil the promise I made in the cemetery and make my mother proud?

67

Broome Hospital, 8 March

'This is how we'll do it,' said the White Wolf.

Dressed in shorts, sandals and a tee-shirt, he looked like any other tourist visiting Broome. The uniform from the cleaning company was in his backpack, with the syringe and the precious poison safely tucked into a side pocket.

'Nugget here will drive me to the hospital. He'll say that he saw me collapse on the footpath just as he was driving past.' The White Wolf paused and polished his sunglasses.

'Then what?' asked Nugget, Zac's trusted foot soldier, not too pleased with his role.

'You'll tell them that you stopped to render assistance. Suspecting a heart attack, you decided to drive me straight to hospital rather than wait for an ambulance. Plausible and simple. The doctors will even commend you for this – you'll see.'

'And then?' asked Zac.

'He will leave me at casualty and wait in the carpark. The rest is up to me.'

'Is that all?' asked Nugget.

'Yes,' said the White Wolf, putting on his straw hat and sunglasses. 'Let's do it.'

It all went like clockwork. Within minutes, the White Wolf was inside the hospital. A car crash had kept Emergency quite busy that morning and after a brief initial examination which, not surprisingly, didn't reveal anything serious, he was placed under observation and told to wait. It was then that he made his move.

First, he went into the toilet and changed into the uniform. He stuffed his clothes into the backpack and left it out of sight on top of the cistern in the cubicle. The sick tourist who had gone to the toilet emerged as the cleaner doing his rounds. No one had noticed anything.

Pigeon

I was getting very worried by then. We had to do something! Jandamarra suggested that Cassandra was our best chance. Somehow, we had to warn her, but how? Once again, my spirit guide came up with a solution.

When Cassandra looked at Anna sleeping in her bed, she thought she could see something strange hovering above Anna's head. It was transparent like fog, only a little denser. Plasma? *An apparition?* she asked herself, leaning forward to see better in the half light. Slowly, a face materialised – fuzzy at first – but soon the features were taking shape. *Pigeon?* she whispered, her heart pounding. The face nodded and looked sadly at her. Then the face turned towards Anna and began to transform itself. Within seconds it had changed into a hideous looking mask. Cassandra gasped. The face staring down at Anna was the disfigured face of the Devil with a missing left eye, conjuring up images of the Mardi Gras assassination gone horribly wrong.

Cassandra tried to concentrate and closed her eyes. The message was clear: another assassination! *But how, and where?* When Cassandra opened her eyes again, the apparition was gone.

Moments later, she heard footsteps approaching in the corridor outside. The back of her neck began to tingle. Reaching for her walking stick, Cassandra stood up and stepped behind the door. From there she had a clear view of Anna's bed, but couldn't be seen from outside. She held her breath and stood motionless in the corner, listening. The footsteps became louder and suddenly stopped in front of the open door. Silence. Then footsteps again. Someone was entering the room. A white-haired, elderly man in a dark blue uniform approached the bed.

Cassandra saw some kind of logo on the back of his shirt. *He isn't a doctor*, she thought, trying to read the writing on the logo, *or a nurse*. Squinting to see better, she read the words, 'Nu Broome Cleaning Co' under the intertwined letters NBCC. *A cleaner*, she thought, relieved.

She was about to step forward and say something when the man reached into his pocket and pulled out a small container the size of a spectacle case. Carefully, he opened the container and took out a syringe. *Cleaners don't give injections*, thought Cassandra, her heart pounding. Holding the syringe in his right hand, the man walked silently past the sleeping countess and approached the bed.

Cassandra remembered the apparition and the warning. Holding her walking stick with both hands, she limped forward, ready to strike. The white-haired man, sensing movement behind him, stopped. Before he could turn to investigate, Cassandra's walking stick came down on his wrist with full force. The syringe fell out of his hand.

Swinging her walking stick again, Cassandra screamed for help. The countess woke with a start and opened her eyes.

Ignoring the pain, the White Wolf spun around and assessed the situation: deflecting the second blow was easy. Cassandra lost her grip and the walking stick went flying. Without the stick to support her, she staggered backwards and fell on top of the bed. Woken by the commotion exploding around her, Anna sat up and began to scream. The baby woke up as well and started to cry.

The White Wolf knew he had to retrieve the syringe lying on the floor – and quickly. He ignored the hysterical women screeching in front of him, and bent down.

Instinct told the countess that the man had to be stopped. She leapt out of the chair and hurled herself on top of the intruder crouching on the floor. Taken momentarily by surprise, the White Wolf picked up the syringe, twisted around, and attempted to stab his attacker with the needle.

The countess took hold of the White Wolf's right wrist with both hands and tried to bite his arm. He managed to grab her hair with his free hand and pulled her away just before she could sink her teeth into him.

'Help me!' shouted the countess, looking pleadingly at Cassandra, her eyes bulging.

Cassandra slid off the bed and kicked the White Wolf in the back of the head. Momentarily dazed by the unexpected blow, he let go of the countess' hair and tried to roll away. The countess sensed a flicker of weakness in her adversary and seized the moment. The screams of her terrified daughter gave her strength. She twisted the Whit Wolf's wrist towards his chest and pushed as hard as she could.

'I've got him!' she yelled.

'Hold on,' hissed Cassandra. As she reached across to help the countess, she lost her balance and pricked one of her fingers with the tip of the needle just before it entered the White Wolf's throat. Frothing at the mouth, the White Wolf went limp.

Andrew, Jack and Rebecca arrived with the police a few minutes later. The White Wolf was dead, Cassandra had been taken to Intensive Care, and the countess and Anna were being comforted by a nurse

'What the hell happened here?' demanded Jack. He turned to Andrew who had just finished talking to the doctor in charge.

'Apparently, a man tried to kill Anna, but Cassandra and the countess managed to stop him,' replied Andrew.

'The Wizard? He's behind all this?'

'Who else? I told them Anna was in danger, but no one listened,' complained Andrew with a shrug. 'I asked for police protection ...'

'Come quickly!' said a nurse, running down the corridor towards them. 'She's asking for you.'

'How is she?' asked Jack.

'Conscious, but fading fast ...' replied the nurse. 'There isn't much time.'

'What's wrong with her?'

'Her respiratory system is collapsing ...'

'Poison?' interrupted Andrew.

The nurse shrugged.

'Get the countess,' said Jack, turning to Rebecca. 'Hurry!'

Cassandra knew she was dying. Looking tiny and frail and with tubes and monitors connected to her face, arms and chest, she was watching the door intently. *I must speak to them*, she thought, *before it's too late*. Jack was the first to enter the room. Shocked by Cassandra's appearance, but trying hard not to look alarmed, he walked over to the bed. Andrew, Rebecca and the countess arrived moments later and stood by the door, watching.

Dear God, no, thought the countess and began to pray. Feeling dizzy and unable to hold back the tears, Rebecca reached for Andrew's arm to steady herself.

'A spot of wrestling, I'm told,' said Jack, reaching for Cassandra's limp hand. 'Never underestimate a determined woman, I say.'

'You should see the other guy,' replied Cassandra, her voice barely audible. 'Come closer.' Jack knelt down beside the bed. 'I kept my side of the bargain.'

'You certainly did.'

'We'll get that evil filth, Jack, you'll see ...' whispered Cassandra, a sparkle in her eyes. 'This is for my son ... and my ...' Cassandra stopped in mid-sentence and looked pleadingly at Jack. 'I want you to promise ...'

'I promise,' replied Jack, squeezing her hand.

'There's something else you need to know ...'

'Oh?'

'All of this goes back much further ... and deeper.'

'In what way?'

'Destiny and fate.' Jack looked at Cassandra, a puzzled look on his face. 'And retribution,' she added quietly. 'Don't worry. I haven't lost it – yet. Please just listen ... it will all make sense.'

During the next few minutes Jack listened intently to what Cassandra had to say. At one point he pulled his notebook out of his hip pocket, and furiously started to scribble.

'Will you do this for me, Jack?' asked Cassandra, her voice fading. Jack nodded, choking with emotion. 'I know it's a big ask, but one day, Tristan will reward you. I saw it in the cards ...' Cassandra turned her head and looked at Jack with cloudy eyes. 'She loves you. Love is precious; don't let it slip through your fingers. Remind Rebecca that the door is open wide ...'

Suddenly, Cassandra's eyes rolled back and her whole body began to shake.

'Fibonacci's never wrong,' she sighed. 'Life's but a game we play before we go ... Tristan ...'

Then the shaking stopped. For a few moments, Jack didn't move. Struggling with what he'd just been told, he reached across to the sweat-soaked body and closed Cassandra's eyes.

The countess went down on her knees and began to pray in Russian. It was a prayer for the dead her grandmother had taught her as a little girl. Sobbing uncontrollably, Rebecca covered her face with her hands. Andrew put his arm around her and bowed his head in silence.

PART IV.
THE BONE SCRAPER

68

Broome, 8 March

Nugget knew something had gone wrong the moment the police cars arrived at the hospital. Putting on his sunglasses, he started the engine and drove out of the carpark. It took Zac only a few minutes to find out what had happened. As the full scale of the disaster became apparent, he knew exactly what he had to do. First, he told Nugget to leave town at once and drive back to Fitzroy Crossing. Then he threw all the White Wolf's belongings into the incinerator and lit the fire. Only after he had satisfied himself that he had erased all traces of the White Wolf's presence at the pub did he call the Wizard.

The Wizard knew he was in serious trouble the moment he heard Zac's report.

'We've got a problem,' he said, handing the mobile phone back to the Undertaker.

'Oh?'

'The White Wolf and Cassandra are both dead. Anna's alive and under police guard.'

'Shit! What now?'

The Wizard slammed his huge fist on the table. 'We'll keep a step ahead of the game!'

'How?'

'Get the others and I'll tell you.'

The Wizard realised that sooner or later the police would identify the White Wolf and make the obvious connection. It was therefore only a matter of time before they came looking for him; not if, but when. The only thing unclear in all this was the state of Anna's mind and her capacity to remember the past. Ultimately it would all come down to that.

The Wizard also knew from experience that suspicion and proof were two very different concepts. He had successfully walked that precarious tightrope many times before. By the time the police paid him a visit, he would be ready to do it again. Should the matter end up in court, he would rely on a tried and tested legal principle: reasonable doubt.

Looking up at the picture of The Chariot on the wall in front of him, the Wizard smiled. The Chariot was his favourite Tarot card. To him it had only one meaning: controlling the situation. And that was precisely what he was about to do.

It took the Undertaker only a few minutes to assemble the council in the crypt. For a while the Wizard sat in silence, his tattooed hands looking like huge hammers ready to crush anything foolish enough to get in his way.

'We have an emergency,' he began calmly. 'A police raid is imminent. As you know, we are well prepared to deal with this ... OTAR starts now! You know what to do. Let's roll!'

OTAR was the Wizards' evacuation plan. Named after a potent Tarot invocation linked to The Chariot, the plan was simple: the Wizards would abandon the compound, split up, and go to their designated safe houses. By the time the police arrived with a search warrant, they would find an empty building. Anything remotely incriminating would have been removed or destroyed. The Wizard had insisted on regular drills to prepare for just such an eventuality.

'You're leaving as well?' asked the Undertaker, surprised.

'No. Jumping bail isn't my style. We'll play this by the book. You and I will stay right here to welcome our friends in blue and show them round.'

'What about the boy?'

'We'll deal with him later,' replied the Wizard, rubbing the scar on his chin.

Pigeon

Cassandra's deathbed conversation with Jack surprised us both. She had come up with an extraordinary plan to save her son and destroy the Wizard. And with her last breath she had managed to extract a promise from Jack to carry it out. Jandamarra and I decided then and there to remain restless spirits for a little longer and help Jack keep his promise.

Feeling drained and dejected, Rebecca sat next to Jack in the hospital waiting room. The countess had returned to the ward to stay with Anna and the baby and Andrew had gone back to the station to arrange police protection.

Rebecca looked teary-eyed at Jack. 'What's happening to us?' she asked. 'This is spinning out of control.'

Jack looked at the little notebook in his hand. Two items he had jotted down were underlined and stood out: a phone number, and a name – Bone Scraper. *Retribution?* thought Jack, stuffing the notebook into his pocket. *So be it!*

When Jack put his arm around Rebecca to comfort her, he noticed that she was shaking. 'I know how you feel, but we'll get through this, you'll see.'

'How can you be so sure? After all that's happened?'

'Cassandra asked me to remind you of something.'

'Oh?'

'The door is open wide ...'

'She said that?'

'Yes. Does this mean something to you?'

Rebecca buried her face under Jack's arm. 'Oh Jack,' she sobbed. 'Hold me.'

'You have something to show us – right? ' said Jack after a while, changing direction. Rebecca nodded. Jack pulled a handkerchief out of his pocket and handed it to her. Rebecca wiped her face and blew her nose. Feeling better, she reached for the duffel bag on the seat next to her.

'This is what Cassandra gave me,' she said, and unzipped the bag.

Remembering that fateful night at Never Never Downs, she reached inside and pulled out a small parcel wrapped in brown paper.

'Do you know what it is?' asked Jack.

'No. But after she gave it to me she did say that I was holding the Wizard's fate in my hands.'

'Interesting ...' said Jack.

'She also said that it was only to be opened if something happened to her, and that we must never show it to Anna or her mother.'

'Well, they're not here. Let's open it and have a look,' said Jack. 'And then I'll tell you what she told me about it.'

'I can't watch this any longer,' said Rebecca, feeling sick. The item in the parcel had turned out to be a DVD; a recording of the bizarre initiation ritual showing Anna and her friend being violently raped by a group of men wearing the distinctive Wizards of Oz masks. A cross between bondage and outright torture, it was a humiliating sexual power-play of male dominance and pain.

'Good God! How could anyone do something like that?' exclaimed Andrew, shaking his head.

'This happened at the farm where we found the secretaire,' said Jack, pointing to the computer screen. 'There, look. The wall of numbers – all sixes – I told you about. And the fireplace with the black candles and the goat's head above the mantelpiece – see? The room's exactly as Will and I found it.'

'That's enough for now,' said Andrew, switching off the computer. 'Jesus!' In all his years as a frontline police officer, he had never seen anything quite like it.

'Surely this is damming evidence,' said Jack, 'linking the Wizards to Anna and her friend. It can't get more explicit than this. It's what we've been looking for. What do you think, Andrew?'

'Looks like it, but with the masks and the poor picture quality, it will be difficult to identify anyone ...'

'What if Anna remembers?'

'Well ...'

'Is that all you can think of?' said Rebecca. 'Anna's friend died, and Anna lost her mind ...'

Jack walked over to Rebecca and put his hand on her shoulder. 'I know what you're saying, but that's exactly what we're thinking of,' he said quietly.

'Sorry. And Cassandra was aware of all this and sat on it all these years and kept quiet? A woman and a mother? I don't get it ...'

'It's not that simple. There's a lot more to all this ... Let me tell you what she said just before she died. You were there, but you couldn't have heard it all. I could hardly hear her myself.'

'You're right, we haven't,' said Andrew.

Jack pulled his little notebook out of his pocket and put it on the table in front of him. Taking a deep breath, he recounted almost everything Cassandra had told him. However, he didn't mention the Bone Scraper or the tunnel. Nor did he talk about how Anna's destiny and fate were intertwined with Cassandra's astonishing past and relentless pursuit of retribution.

It was a spontaneous decision; it had nothing to do with lack of trust. Jack just needed a little more time to come to terms with what Cassandra had asked him to do, and why. When he finished speaking, the silence in the room was deafening.

'Well – what do you think?' asked Jack after a while.

'We can't suppress evidence,' replied Andrew.

'We don't have to,' Jack said.

'We have to give the DVD to the police.'

'I understand that. But there's a way we can do what she asked without breaking the law.'

'How?' asked Andrew.

'It's all in the timing.'

'Explain.'

'This is how it would work. But first, we would all have to agree that we're in this together – right?'

During the next half hour, Jack outlined his plan. He had obviously given it a lot of thought because he appeared to have an answer to every question, and a convincing argument to meet every objection.

'That's about it, guys. Are you with me?'

'Not bad, but it's risky,' said Andrew.

'Look who's talking. And what have we done so far – eh?' replied Jack. 'And anyway, it's mainly my neck on the line ...'

'You're not just doing this because he burnt your house down?' asked Rebecca, a worried look on her face.

'That's part of it. But I made a promise and I intend to keep it. And besides, I owe it to Will,' added Jack, his voice sounding hoarse. 'We've come this far ... and also ... think of the story. The countess has given me exclusive rights to the whole shebang.'

'I'm for it,' said Andrew, raising his hand. 'We'll have to stretch a few rules, but ...' On top of everything else, he thought, to bring the Wizard to justice would be quite a coup and teach his former superiors a lesson they wouldn't forget in a hurry. Vindication was worth the risk.

'Me too, I'm in,' said Rebecca, feeling better. 'But I need my star author alive and in one piece. Is that clear?'

'Crystal.'

69

On the way back to Sydney, 8 March

The Sergeant-at-Arms hurried across to the Bone Scraper's table. The mole had just reported in: something unusual was afoot in the Wizards' camp. The Warriors had successfully infiltrated the Wizards' ranks by having one of their own admitted as a junior member. This had only happened quite recently, and was seen as a major coup. With eyes and ears close to the Wizard and his council, the Bone Scraper finally had a source of valuable intelligence – and it was about to pay off.

To interrupt the Bone Scraper while he was eating was never a good idea. Like most huge men, he loved his food.

'The Wizards are evacuating the compound,' said the Sergeant-at-Arms, coming straight to the point.

'Are you sure?' asked the Bone Scraper, wiping his mouth with the back of his hand.

'Looks like it.'

'When?'

'They're leaving right now.'

It took a lot to get the Bone Scraper excited, but this could be the opportunity he'd been waiting for. For the Wizards to pull out, they must be expecting trouble – big trouble. And trouble for the Wizards was good news for the Warriors. Maybe the time to strike had arrived.

'Send a couple of scouts over to watch the place.'

'I already have.'

Belching loudly, the Bone Scraper pushed his plate aside. 'With guys like you by my side, we'll go a long way,' he said and stood up. 'Let's get ready, just in case.'

Jack couldn't have timed his call better, but getting in touch with the Bone Scraper personally was never easy. The Bone Scraper didn't trust telephones and conducted most of his business face to face. As president of the notorious WMC – Warriors Motorcycle Club – he had several underlings to take care of his calls. The best Jack managed was to speak to the Sergeant-at-Arms. He said he had an urgent message for the Bone Scraper from Cassandra, and that he had to deliver it in person. The Sergeant-at-Arms rang back ten minutes later wanting to know what the message was about. Reluctant to give too much away, Jack mentioned only two names: the Wizard and Tiki Joe, the Bone Scraper's dead brother.

The feud between the Wizards and the Warriors was legendary. The two leaders hated each other as only men who had once been very close could hate. The Wizards had wounded Tiki Joe in a drive-by shooting, taken him back to their compound and let him die a slow and agonising death. It was rumoured that it had been a ritual killing. Tiki Joe's mutilated body was dumped in front of the Warriors' clubhouse as a warning. Then the conflict really escalated.

More recently, during the famous Pagliacci incident at the Opera House, the Wizards had burnt down the Warriors' clubhouse and driven them underground. Even so, the Warriors had staged a comeback and were making substantial inroads into the Wizards' lucrative drug business. They were growing stronger every year, and were waiting in the wings to take over.

With an exclusive membership of South Sea Islanders, the Warriors were a true brotherhood, practising discipline and brutality to match that of the Wizards. In many ways, they were superior, especially on the ground. The Wizards, on the other hand, had a 'brain edge' in that they managed to recruit members from all walks of life with qualifications few Islanders had. That was their strength. They were also better connected and had a stronger cash flow. And in the bikie business, cash was king.

Jack had chosen the right approach. By mentioning the two names, he had opened old wounds and stoked the fires of hatred and revenge. He was told to go to an address in Blacktown, one of Sydney's outer western suburbs, at ten o'clock that night. Jack knew he was cutting it fine, but with the plane leaving Broome within the hour, he should just make it.

'The more I think about this plan of yours, the crazier it gets,' said Rebecca. The familiar hum of the engines made her drowsy and for the first time in days, she felt relaxed. What she had experienced in the past week was more than most of her posh glass-tower colleagues in New York would experience in a lifetime. But now that the adrenaline rush had subsided, reason was beginning to examine harsh reality.

Against all odds, they had found Anna alive. Had it not been for Cassandra's insights, Andrew's contacts and outstanding detective work, and Jack's courage and dogged persistence, Anna would have died in the cave.

However, several people had died. First Pigeon, then Zoran and the hapless Banjo. Then Will sacrificed his life to save his friend, and Cassandra was killed protecting Anna. And to think that Anna's abductor had become her saviour and protector, and had fathered her child, was bordering on the unbelievable.

And there was more. After the initial euphoria of being reunited with her mother, it had soon become apparent that Anna had serious mental health problems. Acute memory loss, childlike confusion and lack of confidence were some of the more obvious symptoms. A slight speech defect and inability to express herself properly complicated matters further, especially for the investigating police. An accurate diagnosis of her condition still had a long way to go and would require specialists. Any road to recovery was certain to be paved with heartache and pain.

Refusing to leave her daughter's bedside, the countess had remained in Broome to watch over Anna and her newborn child. Professor Popov had left Rome and was due to arrive soon. The professor had engaged a leading psychiatrist from Philadelphia to examine Anna, and he too was on his way.

It had soon become apparent to the authorities that Andrew's extraordinary claim was based on fact. It was time to inform the public and to act. The Western Australian police were about to hold a press conference, and the police in Sydney were setting up a taskforce to investigate the Wizards.

The story was huge. The government's spin doctors were already hard at work putting their own interpretation on what had happened, to deflect any criticism or blame.

All hell was about to break loose. Anna and her family would find themselves in the centre of a media storm not seen in Australia since Azaria Chamberlain had disappeared at Uluru thirty years earlier. The agony of not knowing was about to be replaced by the agony of knowing too much and having to share it with a curious world.

Jack turned to Rebecca and reached for her hand. 'It's not quite as crazy as it sounds. It's not finished until it's over, and this is far from over. After all Cassandra has done, we can't just abandon her boy. Both of us have made a promise. We can't walk away – you and I couldn't live with that. And besides, the bastard burnt my house down. I liked that house ... and Will ...'

Rebecca leaned across to Jack and kissed him on the cheek.

'The door is open wide, what did she mean by that?' asked Jack.

Biting her lip, Rebecca turned away and looked out the window.

Illuminated by the late afternoon sun, the striking colours of Outback ochre and red were beginning to melt into the afternoon shadows ten thousand metres below.

'Cassandra thought that I was like a caged bird yearning for the blue sky, not realising that the door was open wide. Afraid ...'

'Afraid?'

'Yes.'

'Of what?'

Rebecca looked at Jack. 'Of love.'

'And?'

'Thanks to Cassandra, for the first time in my life I've spread my wings and left the cage.'

'What's it like outside?'

'A little frightening.'

'Could I help?'

'You could.'

'How?'

'A little kiss would be a good start.'

Jack brushed his lips ever so gently across Rebecca's cheek. 'Does this help?' he asked.

'A little.'

'There's more ... if you like.'

'You mean it?'

'Absolutely.'

For a while Rebecca and Jack sat in silence, trying to pierce the cruel veil hiding the future. Rebecca felt a level of happiness she had never dared to hope for, while Jack experienced a glow of intimacy he hadn't felt for a long time. The raw wound left behind by Will's tragic death was beginning to heal.

'We've both lost someone very dear to us,' said Rebecca, breaking the silence. 'It's a wakeup call, telling us what really matters. And you know what's particularly scary?'

'What?'

'The speed and finality of it all.'

'Death?'

'Yes. We think we're invincible, but ...'

'You're right.'

'Jack, be careful.'

'Always.'

'Convince me. Tell me again how this is supposed to work.'

'It's all based on sound principles. Fear, pride, hate, revenge to name but a few, are all part of the strategy.'

'Be serious.'

'I am. We've got to find out what happened to Tristan – right? And if he's still alive, we have to help him. It's that simple.'

'And how exactly are you going to do that?'

'I'll talk to the Wizard.'

'What makes you think he'll talk to you?'

'Oh, I think he will.'

'Just like that – eh?'

'Yes. That's where fear comes in – the first principle. A powerful one at that.'

'You're going to *threaten* the Wizard?'

'In a way, yes. Or more accurately, I'll show him a way out.'

'I was right; this is crazy. *How?*'

'Okay, I'll tell you. Sit back and listen.'

Sitting two rows behind them, Andrew scribbled away on a writing pad, preparing a timeline. Reluctantly, he had agreed to Jack's daring plan, but only on one condition: the original DVD had to be handed to the police immediately. It was crucial evidence that could bring the Wizards to justice. Andrew realised that the DVD in his briefcase was a ticking bomb and he was keen to be rid of it. Wasting no time, he had made arrangements to hand it over to the officer in charge of the new task force – an old friend, who would be waiting at Sydney airport.

Andrew knew exactly what would happen next. First, the DVD would be used to obtain a search warrant. After that, the police would raid the Wizards' compound. With the announcement by the Western Australian Police due within the hour, Anna's story would go public that afternoon. Under pressure from the politicians in Canberra, the police would act quickly. With the eyes of the world about to turn to Broome, some kind of positive result in the Popov case was vital – an arrest would be even better. That would give Jack about twenty-four hours, at best.

Andrew shook his head. *This is very tight*, he thought, *and damn dangerous. But he might just pull it off.*

The plan was as daring as it was ingenious, but Jack had done pretty well so far, Andrew had to admit. Andrew knew that by allowing Jack to copy the DVD he was sticking his neck out big time. But if Jack was prepared to risk that much himself, the least he could do was to help him.

And if Jack did succeed, it would all be worth it. If not, at least Tristan had been given a chance. Cassandra and Will deserved that much – and more. Andrew finished the timeline and went over the sequence of events that had to follow each other in strict order, making sure it was accurate. Satisfied, he sat back in his seat. Jack was right – it all came down to timing.

What Andrew's timeline failed to take into account was the riskiest part of the plan – the bit that Jack had kept to himself. Since he wasn't sure how it would work, he thought it best to leave that part out altogether. Jack was used to doing things on the run. To him, improvisation was the mother of all solutions. He was afraid that had Andrew been told about the Bone Scraper and the tunnel, he would have pulled the pin and walked away. And without Andrew's help, the plan could not succeed.

70
Warriors' clubhouse, 8 March, 10 p.m.

'That's one hell of a way to break with the past,' said Jack, looking at the ruins of his house. The police had cordoned off the area and erected a temporary hoarding. Apart from the stone chimney and sections of the outer sandstone walls, there was nothing left. A dank smell of burnt timber hung in the air.

'The last time I saw something like this was in the Blue Mountains a couple of years ago,' continued Jack, 'with Will. It was the beginning of an extraordinary story ...'

'I'm so sorry,' said Rebecca, putting her hand on Jack's shoulder. 'You didn't deserve this. All your beautiful things ... This is horrible.'

Jack shrugged. 'It's just stuff. All part of another story, I guess ... and we're about to witness the final chapter,' said Jack, reaching into his pocket. 'Listen.' He pulled out his mobile, put in on speaker, and dialled. 'Hello Eugene. Guess where I'm calling from.'

'Who is this?' demanded the Wizard gruffly.

'It's Jack ...'

'You've got a bloody nerve.'

'You don't want to know where I am?' continued Jack undeterred. 'I'll tell you anyway. I'm standing in front of my house. What's left of it, that is.'

'What are you talking about?'

'I think you know exactly what I'm talking about.'

'What do you want?'

'We have unfinished business. We need to talk; face to face.'

The Wizard laughed. 'You want to meet me?' he asked. 'You're out of your mind, you crazy bastard. This conversation's over.'

'Before you hang up,' said Jack calmly, 'there's something you should know ...'

Something in Jack's tone made the Wizard stay on the line.

'I have something of yours that may interest you ...' Jack paused, letting the tension grow. 'Something from the past – your past.'

'What bullshit is this?'

'You're still there? That's good – lucky for you. It's a DVD, Eugene. CCTV footage recording a particular incident that took place at a remote farm near Bathurst a few years ago ... Two girls, a group of naked men wearing masks ... Do you want me to go on?'

'I have no idea what you're talking about,' snapped the Wizard.

'Oh? Well, in that case, there's no point in meeting, is there?'

'You know where to find me,' interrupted the Wizard. 'Come, if you've got the balls,' he added, and hung up.

'Did you hear that?' asked Jack, grinning. 'We're in!'

'You've got him hooked,' said Rebecca.

'We'll stay in Will's house tonight.'

'Do you think that's a good idea?'

'I do. I've lost my home. He would want it that way. And besides, I'll have to use his bike to ...'

'Oh, no, Jack,' interrupted Rebecca, holding up her hands. 'Not the bike. I said never again – remember?'

'Don't worry. This time, I'm going alone. You have to stay in the house and keep in touch with Andrew. He'll be with the police all night and let us know what they're up to. You and Andrew are my backup. We'll do this as a team. Timing, remember? It all comes down to timing.'

Jack knew he was late. He switched off the bike and looked around. The derelict panelbeating shop appeared deserted in the dark. Most of the windows were broken and the doors were boarded up. Two rusty car bodies without wheels were blocking the driveway, their headlights staring at Jack like eyes of guard dogs watching. Jack was about to check the address again to make sure he was in the right place when he heard sounds coming from somewhere out the back – the clinking of iron against iron, and a slapping sound. *Weights and punching bags*, thought Jack. *A gym.*

As he walked past the car bodies, Jack saw something move. A dark shape materialised out of the shadows in front of him.

'Looking for something, mate?' it asked, coming closer.

'Yes – the Bone Scraper,' replied Jack.

'Wait here.'

Suddenly, floodlights came on above him, illuminating a large yard. Momentarily blinded, Jack closed his eyes. When he opened them again, he was looking at two huge men, both Maoris, standing directly in front of him.

'Turn around and hold up your hands where I can see them,' said one of the hulks. Jack felt a pair of hands running down his back and legs.

'Clean,' said the man behind him. 'Come with me.'

Jack followed the man across the yard, past rows of gleaming bikes to an open steel door. Inside, he could see several men lifting weights so heavy, they made the steel rods bend. The two fans turning lazily overhead did little to stir the stale air heavy with the acrid smell of sweat and diesel.

'That's him over there,' said the man pointing to a wrestling mat in the middle of the room. 'The one on top.'

Wearing only loincloths, the two men on the mat reminded Jack of Sumo wrestlers, only taller and more muscular. Each had his long black hair pulled back and tied into a knot. The man on top had his opponent pinned to the mat.

'Concede,' he barked.

Barely able to breathe, the man lying face down on the mat nodded. The bout was over. The winner disengaged, rolled away with surprising agility and stood up. Towering over Jack, he picked up a towel and looked at him. His massive arms, buttocks and back were heavily tattooed with Maori motifs, but most striking of all was his *Moko*. In the old days, the *Moko* – the traditional Maori facial decoration – was applied with a chisel that left grooves in the skin. In more recent times, the tattoo needle had replaced the chisel, leaving the skin smooth. Delicate scrolls, dots and fine lines – especially around the mouth and forehead – accentuated the prominent features of the Bone Scraper's face, making him look like a carving of a Maori god come to life.

'A bout like this is better than the haka,' he said, wiping his face. 'The haka only intimidates, this ends in victory or defeat. That's why I like to wrestle – it prepares you for the real thing. You're the journalist whose house burnt down?'

Jack nodded. He hadn't mentioned anything about this on the phone.

'I know how it feels.'

'Cassandra's dead,' said Jack.

'I heard. Why are you here?'

'I made a promise. On her deathbed.'

'Tell me about it.'

Jack followed the Bone Scraper around the gym and explained why he had come and what he had in mind. Listening carefully, the Bone Scraper was evaluating Jack's proposal. He was used to making quick decisions and taking risks. If there was a chance – however remote – of getting even with the Wizard, he was in. The only real question was the commitment of the man standing in front of him, and the accuracy of the intelligence he was providing. Without that, this couldn't work.

The Bone Scraper's own sources had already confirmed most of what Jack was telling him, but there was something new that could change everything: a tunnel. The Wizard was obsessed with security. The compound was built like a fortress, with sophisticated round-the-clock electronic surveillance and security systems covering every square centimetre. It was impossible to enter the place undetected, unless Cassandra was right about the tunnel. But what really tipped the scales in favour of the daring plan was the fact that the man telling him all this was taking most of the risk and had a hell of a lot to lose. This was the kind of insurance the Bone Scraper liked.

'Do you understand what you're proposing?' he asked, watching Jack carefully. 'This is war. Once you start, there's no turning back, for us or for you.'

Jack nodded.

'It's like breaking my opponent's neck here on the mat a moment ago, rather than letting him go. Are you prepared for that?'

'Yes.'

'When's all this supposed to happen?'

'Tonight. After I leave here, I'm going to see the Wizard. He's kind of expecting me. The police will raid the compound in a few hours. I'll know exactly when. That gives you a small window ...'

'Something puzzles me,' interrupted the Bone Scraper.

'What?'

'Why isn't the Wizard leaving with the others? What makes you so sure he'll be there, virtually alone? Waiting for the police, and for you?'

'That's been troubling me, too. You know the Wizard better than most. I believe the answer is right there in his character: arrogance, pride and bravado. He likes to taunt and to show off. He believes he can beat the system, and to do that, he mustn't violate his bail conditions. He has to remain at the compound and report to the police daily. He can't abscond – pride won't let him. And besides, the police will find nothing incriminating. He's already made sure of that. Bravado. That's why the compound's been evacuated. As usual, his police contacts have tipped him off, giving him plenty of time to cover his tracks. It's the same with this tunnel.'

'What do you mean?'

'His obsession with security is both a strength and a weakness. The whole place is protected like Fort Knox. But he has to have a secret escape route only he and a couple of his close cronies know about. That's why there are no alarms, no surveillance, nothing. Arrogance. He kept it all to himself.'

Impressed, the Bone Scraper nodded. 'And the boy?' he asked. 'If you're right, he won't be there. Not with the police coming.'

'No, but the Wizard will know where he is.'

'The boy may be dead.'

'I don't think so.'

'How come?'

'The moment Cassandra died, the boy became worthless. Why kill him? Why take the risk? Especially now, with the spotlight of the law on the Wizards. No, the boy's alive and I'm going to find him.'

'But you don't need me for that, do you? You have your own ways ...'

This was the one question Jack had been dreading. It was the one flaw in his argument and it hadn't taken the Bone Scraper long to find it. It was time to come clean.

'Strictly speaking, no. But there were two parts to my promise.'

'Oh?'

'The boy, and ...'

'And?'

'Retribution. Cassandra said that you of all people would understand; and act. Your own brother ...'

The Bone Scraper traced one of the tattoos on his chin with his index finger. The finger went round and round, following the intricate scrolls engraved onto his skin. He always did this when he was about to make an important decision. Suddenly, the finger stopped.

'You don't know, do you?' he said after a while. 'About Tiki Joe?'

'What about him?'

'You don't know who he was, do you?'

'I don't understand,' said Jack, looking puzzled.

'You'll find out. Another time.'

'Are you in, Parema Te Pahau?' Cassandra had briefed Jack well.

The Bone Scraper looked up, surprised. Just like the Wizard, he was very superstitious. *How come this Pakeha knows my true name?* he thought. *Is it a sign?*

The Bone Scraper claimed to be a direct descendant of Parema Te Pahau, a famous Maori chief who lived in the late 1800s and was one of the last cannibals. The Bone Scraper had used Charles Goldie's splendid portrait of the chief hanging in the Auckland Museum as inspiration for his own *Moko*.

'I'm in,' he said.

'If the Wizard lives, we're both dead,' said Jack, holding out his hand.

347

Finally convinced that Jack understood what he was in for, the Bone Scraper relaxed a little.

'You well before me, mate,' he said, and shook Jack's hand. 'Now, tell me more about this tunnel.'

71

Wolf's Lair, 8 March 11:30 p.m.

'I was wrong,' said the Wizard pointing to the CCTV screen in front of him. 'Look who's coming to visit us – alone.'

'He's got balls,' replied the Undertaker. 'Now we know.'

'Crazy bastard. Bring him down to the crypt.'

Jack turned off the engine, got stiffly off his bike and stretched his back. The place looked deserted. Gone were the bikes and the sentries. There was no thumping music, no tattooed girls, no lights, and the church door looked firmly bolted. But most unsettling of all was the silence.

Everything around him seemed to be telling him to stay away. Certain he was being watched, Jack walked slowly up the stairs. The door opened all by itself.

'Take off your clothes and put them on the floor,' said the Undertaker, pointing a gun at Jack. Jack did as he was told. The Undertaker picked up the leather jacket and the jeans and examined the pockets. 'Now turn around.'

'No wires and no guns,' said Jack.

'Just making sure,' replied the Undertaker. Satisfied that Jack was clean, the Undertaker handed him the jeans. 'Get dressed and follow me,' he said.

'Where is everybody?' asked Jack. The Undertaker didn't reply.

Jack knew he was walking a tightrope without a safety net. One slip could cost him his life. Success or failure depended on how accurately he had read the Wizard's character. And luck of course – quite a bit of it.

Heart pounding like a drum, he followed the Undertaker down the narrow stairs into the crypt. The Wizard was as unpredictable as he was dangerous. Normal rules of behaviour and morality just didn't apply to him. There were no boundaries and no lines he wouldn't cross. Not only was he capable of the unthinkable, he seemed to revel

349

in it, and find new ways to surprise and shock even the most callous. But there was one important exception: self-preservation. Powerful, instinctive, predictable. Jack's plan depended on it. The Wizard knew a police raid was imminent and was ready for it. He would have been extensively briefed by his lawyers on how to handle the situation. Jack's careful timing of his visit was paying off. The imminent raid was his safe conduct pass. Even so, Jack was realistic enough to understand that it wouldn't take much for it all to go horribly wrong. Despite all that, he felt strangely elated, the rush of excitement masking the danger signals flashing all around him.

The Wizard sat in his chair at the round table, like some evil emperor mourning an empire lost. The candles flickering in the large lantern on the table sent crazy shadows dancing along the sandstone slabs. Long fingers of light pointed to the Tarot pictures hanging on the walls, making the Pagliacci portrait behind the Wizard look strangely out of place.

'It doesn't make any sense,' said the Wizard, rocking back in his chair.

'What?' asked Jack.

'You coming here in the middle of the night. Why this particular night?' added the Wizard, stabbing his finger at Jack. 'And when something doesn't make sense, I get nervous.'

Jack walked slowly around the table, pulled up a chair, and sat down facing the Wizard.

'It's quite simple really,' he said.

'Enlighten me.'

'You have something I want, and I have something you need.'

'Is that so?' said the Wizard.

Without saying a word, Jack pulled the DVD out of his jacket pocket and pushed it across the table towards the Wizard.

'Check it out,' barked the Wizard, passing the DVD to the Undertaker.

'This is a copy. The original is in safe hands,' said Jack. 'And there are certain arrangements in place about the tape and about my coming here.'

'Arrangements?' The Wizard looked amused. 'Not much use with a bullet through your head.'

'Not much good to you either,' said Jack. 'A body with a bullet through the head would need a little explaining when the police raid this joint.' Jack looked at his watch. 'In about an hour, I'd say. But your guys would have told you that already.'

Jack noticed a flash of anger race across the Wizard's face, a sure sign that he had found the mark.

'We're wasting time ...'

'It's the real thing,' said the Undertaker, coming down the stairs.

'So, what's on your mind?' asked the Wizard, well aware of the DVD's devastating potential.

'An exchange.' Jack paused, deliberately taking his time. 'The tape for Tristan.'

The Wizard laughed until his whole body shook uncontrollably. 'Did you hear that, mate?' he asked, turning to the Undertaker. 'The DVD for the boy. The old witch is trying to manipulate us from beyond the grave. Her White Knight is offering salvation in exchange for a vegetable.'

Pigeon

Normally, restless Bunuba spirits like Jandamarra and me wouldn't leave Djumbud, their spirit country. However, these were exceptional circumstances and we decided to venture outside our comfort zone where the rules were different and we were limited in what we could do.

It was a strange feeling being back in the old place. We had entered the world of the Malngadu, the white people I had once so admired.

Floating through the empty compound with Jandamarra was bringing back memories of a part of my past life I would rather forget. I found it difficult to imagine that not so long ago I had craved to become like the Malngadu, and the man I had admired most, was also the man responsible for all the deception, misery and pain that had destroyed my life. Yet there he was right in front of me, sitting there, laughing. He seemed indestructible in his lair, even without his adoring cohorts by his side.

'Stop dreaming, Pigeon, and concentrate,' I heard Jandamarra reprimanding me.
'There, look.'

'I'm not sure that the police will find the DVD as humorous as you do,' said Jack.

The Wizard shot him an angry look.

'You'll see the humour in a moment,' snapped the Wizard.

'Do we have a deal?' asked Jack.

'We have a deal.'

'I need proof that the boy is okay.'

'That's easy. And I need the original tape and guarantees that there are no copies.'

'That's easy too. You first.'

'The boy isn't here.'

'I didn't think he would be.'

The Wizard turned to the Undertaker.

'Tell him where you took the boy this morning,' said the Wizard.

'Back to Bleak House,' replied the Undertaker. 'He's in the best of care, just like before.'

'Do you see the humour now?' asked the Wizard.

Jack looked thunderstruck. Reaching into his pocket he pulled out his mobile. 'I need confirmation,' he said, composing himself.

'Be my guest.'

Pigeon

Jandamarra noticed it first. Something strange was going on along a disused back road leading to the compound. A group of bikies had pulled up at a bridge nearby. Carrying crowbars, bolt cutters and gas cylinders, they were clambering down an embankment. Hardly something people did at one in the morning without good reason. As the Wizards' compound was the only habitation in the vicinity, it had to be something to do with that.

We decided to investigate. Floating closer I recognised who they were: a contingent of Warriors, and the huge man at the front was their leader, the Bone Scraper himself.

I remember meeting the Bone Scraper once during a pow-wow between the two rival gangs. A truce was in place and the two leaders were meeting to settle a bloody turf war that had raged for more than a year. I had never seen a man so huge. The Wizard was big, but the Bone Scraper towered over him. His facial tattoos gave him a most frightening appearance which made it impossible to guess his age. The meeting ended with more acrimony than it had started with and was followed by more killings.

The Warriors were on a warpath. Jandamarra and I decided to stay close.

72

Wolf's Lair, 9 March, 1 a.m.

Waiting for Andrew to call back was excruciating. Jack stared at his phone on the table, aware that the Wizard was watching him intently. Precious time was running through the hourglass. Resisting the temptation to glance at his watch again, Jack felt perspiration trickling down his back. He knew the Wizard was a master of reading body language. Mercifully, the phone rang.

It had taken Andrew only a few minutes to verify the Wizard's claim.

'Tristan is at Bleak House; safe,' he said. 'Well done, Jack. Get out of there, now!' Then the phone went dead.

'Satisfied?' asked the Wizard. Jack nodded. 'That's my part delivered. Now, what about yours?'

Jack knew that the next step couldn't be rehearsed. Nevertheless, he had gone over and over it in his mind a hundred times before. It had to appear spontaneous and obvious. He was about to propose something he was desperately hoping the Wizard wouldn't be able to accept. Everything depended on that, and the slightest miscalculation could be fatal.

'I can have the original brought here if you like,' Jack said casually. 'This is the only copy – I can vouch for that. I'll stay here until the original arrives. Will that do?'

Jack looked past the Wizard at the garish portrait hanging on the wall behind him. An eternity seemed to pass before the Wizard answered.

'No. That will not do!'

'Oh? What do you suggest then?'

'As of now, the DVD belongs to me, and you will take good care of it until I tell you what to do,' snapped the Wizard, his mind already on the imminent police raid.

'I don't understand ...'

'I think you do. Now go, and take the copy with you. I don't want it here ... I'm sure you know why. A word of caution,' added the Wizard, lowering his voice. 'Should the DVD fall into the wrong hands, you're a dead man. Clear so far?'

Jack nodded.

'You already know what happens when you disappoint me, Jack, don't you?'

Jack nodded again, trying hard not to show his elation. Used to getting his own way, the Wizard failed to notice that the look on Jack's face wasn't fear.

The Wizard stood up and pushed the DVD towards Jack. 'Take him outside,' he said to the Undertaker. 'Our visitor is leaving.'

When he heard the church door close behind him, Jack resisted the temptation to punch the air. Instead, he walked across to his bike and made another call on his mobile.

'He's inside with the Undertaker – no one else,' said Jack. 'The police are on their way. You've got less than an hour.'

'The boy?' asked the Bone Scraper.

'Safe.'

'And you?'

'On my bike, leaving. You found the tunnel?'

'Retribution is on its way! You can count on it,' said the Bone Scraper and hung up. Jack started the engine and accelerated into the night. Slowing down at the lichgate at the bottom of the hill, he didn't notice the Bone Scraper's scout in the bushes, waiting for him to pass.

The Warriors were slowly working their way through the stormwater drain under the bridge. They almost missed the vital turn. Difficult to see, and blocked by another rusty grate, a narrow tunnel was branching out to the left towards the compound. Using a large bolt cutter, one of the men cut through the second grate within minutes. Led by the Bone Scraper, the raiders hurried along the tunnel until they reached a steel door blocking their path. They were now directly below the crypt.

'Okay, guys,' said the Bone Scraper. 'It's time for a little diversion.' He pressed a button on his mobile. The scout in the bushes answered at once. 'Go!' said the Bone Scraper. 'Now!'

Having the best men in the business certainly helped. All of them had done time for break-ins or armed robberies of the heavy kind. There wasn't a building they couldn't get into, or an alarm system they couldn't disable. No security door was strong enough to keep them out. They were used to strict discipline and to-the-second timing. And most important of all, they worked as a team.

'This is it,' said the Bone Scraper, looking at the steel door. 'We must be somewhere right under the compound by now. Can you open this?'

'Sure, but it'll be a bit noisy,' replied one of the men standing behind him.

'What do we do now?' asked the huge man next to him.

'We wait, and we listen,' said the Bone Scraper, and sat down on the ground. 'When you hear the bang, break down the door.'

The Wizard and the Undertaker sat in the control room monitoring the CCTV screens. They were expecting the police to come charging up the driveway at any moment. The Wizard was going to let the SWAT team in personally, and couldn't wait to see the looks on their faces when they discovered that the entire compound was empty. He was also following his legal advice to the letter: cooperation without resistance, and full compliance with the bail conditions. His daily report to the police would be made by him in person when they arrived.

'Who the fuck's that?' asked the Undertaker, pointing to one of the screens. A lone biker came roaring up the hill and pulled up in front of the church. 'Looks like a Warrior.'

'That's all we need!'

His face concealed behind a scarf, the rider didn't get off his bike. Instead, he reached into the saddlebag, pulled out a brick and threw it through one of the church windows.

'Get the guns!' shouted the Wizard, seething. 'We'll teach that prick a lesson!'

Before the Wizard and the Undertaker could reach the church above the crypt, the bikie had pulled a sawn-off shotgun from the other saddlebag. Taking aim, he emptied both barrels into the church door – sending splinters flying in all directions – and then disappeared into the night.

'He's gone,' said the Undertaker, trying to catch his breath.

'What's this?' The Wizard kicked aside the shards of coloured glass that littered the floor and bent down. 'This is what came through the window,' he said and picked up the brick with a piece of paper wrapped tightly around it with string. 'Ars Moriendi' read the Wizard. He instantly recognised the message and its author. The Warriors had declared war.

Composed by a Dominican Friar in about 1415, Ars Moriendi – 'The Art of Dying' – is a Latin text offering advice on how to die well. It was widely read during the Middle Ages and very popular, especially after the ravages of the Black Death. Fascinated by death literature, the Wizard and the Bone Scraper had studied the text in gaol and had formulated their own Ars moriendi rules. They even made a pact to follow them to the letter.

'Did you hear that?' asked the Bone Scraper, jumping to his feet. It was the distraction he had been waiting for.

'Gunshots,' answered the man next to him. 'Break down the door. Now! Let's go!'

A drive-by shooting with a message from the Bone Scraper? thought the Wizard, shaking his head. Why right now? Coincidence? Hardly. What was the Bone Scraper telling him? Ars moriendi? Here? And what of this exchange? The DVD for the boy, played out by Jack the messenger? Just before the police raid? the Wizard asked himself. Something was wrong here! He had sensed it all along, but still couldn't put his finger on it. The events of the past hour swirled through his mind – but crucial pieces of the puzzle were missing.

Cassandra's death had rattled him more than he cared to admit. In awe of her powers during life, he now feared her reach from the grave. It was a new and unsettling sensation for a man who wasn't afraid of the living.

'Did you hear that?' he asked.

'What?' replied the Undertaker.

'A thump. Downstairs.'

'There's no one here.'

Without saying another word, the Wizard rushed back to the control room. All the CCTV screens looked normal. Then, suddenly, one of the screens went blank.

'There. The strongroom. It's just gone off!'

'I'll go down and have a look. Could be the damp – we've had problems there before.'

'There – another one!' said the Wizard, pointing to the screen. as a second screen went blank.

'The crypt!'

The Wizard stood up and checked his gun. 'I don't like this. We'll have a look together. Let's go!'

73

Wolf's Lair, 9 March, 2:30 a.m.

The Wizard reached the bottom of the stairs first and was about to turn right to check the strongroom under the crypt when something caught his eye.

The Bone Scraper sat in the Wizard's chair at the round table, motionless and silent like a statue. Two of his men stood under the stairs, guns drawn, and the others were lurking in the shadows behind the stone pillars. The Wizard's eyes darted around the room like the desperate eyes of a cornered animal searching for a way out.

'Hello Eugene. Got my message?' said the Bone Scraper. It was more of a statement than a question. 'Ars moriendi – remember? Can't say I didn't put you on notice.'

'How the fuck did you bastards get in?' roared the Wizard.

'What do you think? Back door of course. Great tunnel. Leaving it unprotected like that ... very careless. Not like you at all.'

'How did you know?'

'Cassandra ...'

That's it! thought the Wizard. *Jack!* Suddenly it all made sense. *A set up!* Strangely, knowing made him feel a little better.

The Bone Scraper was enjoying himself. 'Where's your little mate, the Undertaker?' he asked. 'Why don't you ask him to come down? You'll be needing his services – soon.'

Standing perfectly still in the silent church above the crypt, the Undertaker had overheard everything. Leaning forward a little at the top of the stairs, he could just see the Bone Scraper's chest through the stone balustrades. Slowly, he raised his gun and took aim.

Sensing danger, the Bone Scraper turned his head. 'Gun! Twelve o'clock!' he shouted, struggling out of his chair.

The Warrior standing by the pillar looked up and fired his shotgun.

The Undertaker's Beretta went off at the same time. It missed. The shotgun didn't. The Undertaker came tumbling down the stairs like a limp sack of potatoes.

'Now look what you've done. You should have asked him to come down,' said the Bone Scraper as if nothing had happened. 'But then, you were never one to listen, Eugene, were you? Failure to listen has a price. So does murder ...'

The Wizard stared at the Undertaker lying at his feet with a large, bleeding hole in his chest, but didn't reply.

Jack was on a high. He could hardly believe his luck. He'd done it! The plan had worked! He was about to turn into the main road at the bottom of the hill when he passed an overgrown track. Recalling the diagram he'd drawn for the Bone Scraper, he stopped the bike and turned around. *This must be it*, he thought, looking at the fresh tyre marks in the long grass. *Why not?*

At first, the sentry at the bridge didn't want to let him pass, but Jack insisted that he contact the Bone Scraper on his radio.

The Bone Scraper didn't sound too pleased. 'Leave this to me,' he said curtly. 'You've done your bit. You don't want to be mixed up in this, believe me ...'

Still pumped, Jack didn't listen. Reluctantly, the Bone Scraper relented.

'Come if you must then, but don't fuck around getting here. And don't say I didn't warn you.'

Jack left his bike under the bridge, followed the drain, and then turned into the tunnel, the small cone of light from the torch the sentry had given him snaking along the uneven ground. *It's exactly as she described it*, he thought, barely able to control his excitement.

Jack could hear the chanting well before he reached the rusty door at the end of the tunnel. Faint at first, but growing louder with every step. The door was ajar, its hinges twisted to one side. Jack squeezed through and stopped. The chanting was coming from above. 'Ka mate, ka mate! Ka ora! Ka ora ...' Walking slowly up the stairs leading from the tiny strongroom – which was once a family vault – to the crypt above, Jack tried to make sense of the strange chorus. It sounded warlike, threatening, yet strangely familiar. *The haka*, he thought, *that's it! Just like at the beginning of an All Blacks football game.*

When he reached the top of the stairs and looked into the crypt, he almost tripped over something lying on the floor. He stepped back quickly, only to find himself standing in a pool of blood next to the Undertaker's twisted body.

The chanting became louder and more urgent.

'Tenei te tangata puhuruhuru ...'

As Jack stepped over the body, he saw the backs of six huge men standing in a semicircle in the middle of the crypt. With their arms raised and stamping their feet in rhythmic unison, they chanted at something he couldn't quite make out. Jack moved a little to one side, and gasped.

The Wizard teetered on tiptoe on a skull the size of a large watermelon, blood dripping down his naked chest from a gaping wound at the throat. With his hands handcuffed behind his back and his ankles tied together with rope, it seemed an impossible balancing act. What Jack couldn't see in the gloom was the noose made of fine piano wire around the Wizard's neck, and the hook in the ceiling to which the wire was attached. The only reason the Wizard wasn't dead yet was because he was able to support his weight on the skull – just.

As his eyes became accustomed to the candlelight, Jack noticed that something was trickling out of the eye sockets and the nose of the skull. *Looks like sand*, he thought. The skull, carved out of wood, was a copy of an ingenious device invented by the Inquisition – a hanging-stool with a sinister twist. Hollow inside, it could be filled with sand from the top. Once it was full, a small round piece of wood could be placed on top like a lid. But the lid was smaller than the opening and as the sand ran out the lid would sink into the skull. The eyes and the nose were blocked by marbles which could be removed to let the sand trickle out, giving the executioner many options. The Wizard stood on a deadly hourglass, suspended between life and death.

Pigeon

I saw him move first. Despite the gaping wound in his chest, the Undertaker was still alive! Eyes wide open, he was staring at the gun – tantalisingly close – lying next to him on the floor. Slowly, his fingers began to move forward. Jack stood directly in front of him, mesmerised by the dance of death. It was obvious what was about to happen: the Undertaker was going to shoot the messenger responsible for the disaster. I began to panic ... After all he had done, Jack didn't deserve this. We had to do something! Once again, Jandamarra came up with the answer. 'Show yourself, quickly!' he urged, hovering just above the Undertaker. 'Now!' Fortunately, this time I already knew what to do. I floated down until I was almost level with the Undertaker's face and began to materialise.

With white stars beginning to dance in front of his eyes and his stiff fingers refusing to obey, the Undertaker was about to give up, when suddenly he could feel it: steel – cold and reassuring – reviving his fingertips. Because it was covered in blood, the gun was slippery and he had to try several times to get a grip on it. Barely able to breathe he closed his eyes, as the strange chanting assaulted his exhausted brain.

'Ka mate, ka mate! Ka ora ...'

You can do it, he thought, *he's right in front you.* Despite life oozing out of the mortal wound, one last bit of strength remained. The Undertaker opened his eyes and raised the gun. Squinting, he took aim ...

Pigeon

That's when I appeared. Just in time. Our faces were so close they almost merged and I saw terror in the Undertaker's eyes. 'Pigeon?' I heard him say, just before the gun went off. Too late, I thought, but fortunately I was wrong. The bullet grazed Jack's right temple and ripped apart the face of the clown in the Pagliacci portrait before coming to rest in the wall behind it. I had spoilt the Undertaker's aim!

Dazed, and with the gun shot still ringing in his ears, Jack spun around. The Bone Scraper standing directly in front of him did the same. Pulling a gun out of his belt the Bone Scraper fired two shots at the

Undertaker lying on the floor. Jack looked down and saw the Undertaker's head being blown away.

'That was close,' said the Bone Scraper, checking his gun. 'Let me have a look.'

'It's nothing, just a scratch.'

'You're a lucky guy! A little to the left, and ...' Jack pulled a handkerchief out of his pocket and pressed it against his bleeding temple.

'I did warn you,' said the Bone Scraper.

'You did. Thanks. You saved my life.'

The Bone Scraper pointed to the Wizard. 'You gave us this ...' he said.

'That's some retribution,' said Jack quietly.

'He deserves it.' The Bone Scraper looked anxious: to interrupt the haka was bad luck. 'You've seen it. Now please leave. We have unfinished business here.' Jack realised this was an order, not a request.

The Bone Scraper's radio began to crackle. One of his scouts was reporting in.

'The cops just passed the roundabout,' announced the Bone Scraper. 'We have ten minutes.' Without saying another word, he turned around and began to chant:

'Kikiki kakaka kauana!

Kei waniwania taku tara

Kei tarawahia, kei to rua i te kerokero!'

Careful not to step in the bloody mess, Jack walked around the Under-taker's body and hurried down the stairs and into the strongroom below.

'Ka mate, ka mate! Ka ora! Ka ora!' chanted the Warriors behind him.

With the adrenalin rush ebbing away, elation gave way to panic. Dashing through the tunnel, his head throbbing with pain, Jack had only one thing on his mind: to get away. As he reached the outside, he took a deep breath and wondered if the Wizard was still alive.

74

Wolf's Lair, 9 March, 3 a.m.

The Bone Scraper was the last to leave. The Sweeper had meticulously removed all traces of any evidence that might implicate the Warriors. This was standard club procedure. There were no fingerprints because everyone wore gloves. Satisfied that no clues had been left behind, the Bone Scraper went to the control room, pushed a CD into the player and turned on the speaker system. Then he hurried back to the crypt and stood in front of his old foe, his tattooed face almost touching the Wizard's chin. He noticed that the wire had cut deep into the Wizard's throat, with only the bulk of his huge neck muscles standing between the wire and decapitation.

'You can't say I'm not giving you a chance, Eugene, which is more than you did for my brother. For once in your wretched life, you'd better hope the cops get here soon. Ironic, isn't it? But even if they do, which I doubt,' taunted the Bone Scraper, 'it won't make much difference. You've lost too much blood,' he added, walking towards the stairs.

'You wanted a beautiful death – remember? Ars moriendi. This is your chance to show them how it's done. I've kept my side of the bargain. I even turned on some music for you.' The Bone Scraper took one last look at his former friend. 'See you in hell.'

Death was slowly sucking the last sparks of life out of the Wizard's tortured brain. Drifting in and out of consciousness, his breathing reduced to a wheezing gurgle, he could feel his strength ebbing away with each drop of blood that trickled down his chest. Lucid moments gave way to psychedelic hallucinations and a crazy cocktail of emotions: frustration, anger and hatred changing places with amazement, surprise and disbelief.

During a flash of clarity, the Wizard thought he could see it all. It was so simple: Cassandra was the cause of his downfall. She had succeeded where others had tried and failed. She had made allies out of his deadliest enemies – first Pigeon, then the Bone Scraper – and had skilfully used Jack as the go-between. To have been defeated by a weak cripple of a woman was not only humiliating, it was unthinkable. But the unthinkable had come to pass. She had even found a way to reach out from beyond the grave! Her precious boy was safe and the Bone Scraper was having the last laugh.

But hadn't it all started with Anna?, the Wizard reminded himself. If only he had made her disappear like everyone around him had urged him to do. Things would have been very different. What could have possessed him to ignore something so obvious? That's when superstition came to the Wizard's aid. *Perhaps it was meant to be,* he told himself, feeling better. Once again, fate was being used to excuse failure. It was a convenient deception. Seeing the irony of it all, the Wizard managed a crocked smile. It only lasted for an instant because it let the wire cut deeper into his throat.

Hovering on the edge of unconsciousness, the Wizard thought he could see the Bone Scraper's tattooed face sneering at him, and hear his gravelly voice. 'You brought yourself down, Eugene,' he heard him say. 'You are to blame, no one else. You let Cassandra in. She was the Trojan horse ...'

Then he heard laughter echoing through the empty crypt, but it wasn't the Bone Scraper laughing at him – he had already left – but Pagliaccio, the clown.

As the Warriors got on their bikes under the bridge, three black unmarked four-wheel drive vehicles pulled up in front of the church a little further down the road. Within minutes the SWAT team had broken down the door. Moving systematically from room to room, the masked commandoes began to secure the compound.

Andrew made eye contact with the team leader. 'Can you hear that? What is it?' he asked.

'Sounds like music,' replied his friend and former colleague. 'How weird. Where's it coming from?'

'Downstairs.'

'Let's have a look.'

'Jesus, what a mess,' said Andrew, almost falling over the Undertaker's bloody corpse.

'Shit! Look at that!' Andrew pointed to the Wizard. 'Someone likes him even less than we do.'

Three commandoes were already inside, searching the crypt. 'This one's still alive,' one of them said.

Andrew walked over to the Wizard.

'Hello, Eugene, remember me?' he said quietly. 'I'll tell your lawyer that you won't say anything until he gets here. Okay? Which means of course that you can't tell us who did this. Pity. We'll just wait for the legal eagles then.'

'Cut him down!' shouted the team leader. Andrew took him aside.

'I wouldn't,' he said quietly. 'He's almost gone ... If something goes wrong, you'll get the blame. This way – case solved, book closed – you'll probably get promoted. The wolves have devoured each other. That's what happened here.'

Remembering what was at stake, the team leader nodded. 'You're right,' he said.

'Inside job?' asked Andrew, changing direction.

'What else? Forensics will have an interesting day.'

'Trying to piece this together? Good luck! But Jesus – look at him! Someone went to a lot of trouble. Looks carefully orchestrated. Ritualistic.'

'Bondage with a deadly twist?'

'Something like that.'

Andrew was wondering what part Jack had played in all of this.

Considering the timing, he must have been right in the thick of it all. And he certainly couldn't have been alone. Andrew didn't believe in coincidences, but with the Wizard conveniently dead, no one would ask too many questions.

'You live with one foot in hell,' he mused, 'the devil is bound to get you.'

'He had it coming ...'

'For a long time,' said Andrew, watching the last of the sand trickle out of the skull's gaping jaw. 'Isn't that right, Eugene?' he added quietly. 'Lovely music. Nice touch.'

But the Wizard was already beyond hearing – the wire had just cut through his neck. His massive body crashed to the floor in silent reply. Andrew looked up at the grotesque head left dangling from the ceiling.

'I think the devil just got him,' he said to his friend. 'It's over.'

Pigeon

Jandamarra and I were right there when the Wizard died. It was an eerie moment, even for spirits like us. Something dark and evil swept through the crypt and claimed his soul. Anna was safe at last – our work was done. It was time to return to Djumbud, our spirit country. As we floated north across this ancient land we loved so much, a tremendous sense of peace descended on us both and everything became clear. Restless spirits no more, we were going home.

75

Bleak House, 9 March, 4:30 a.m.

Feeling nauseous and dizzy, Jack found it difficult to focus and keep the heavy bike on the road. Thankfully, there was very little traffic at four in the morning. Andrew had arranged a police car to take Rebecca to Bleak House to be with Tristan, and Jack was anxious to see the boy. He found the house almost by accident and pulled up in front of the old fountain. Looking up at what used to be Tristan's room, he could see light.

The events of the past few hours had become a blur, the pain hammering away inside his head a reminder of the horror he had witnessed in the crypt. His two phone calls had unleashed a sequence of events with a deadly momentum of their own. Jack felt like a messenger of doom who had delivered the missing script for a macabre play, only to find himself centre stage with a leading part. With the gunshot wound to his head still bleeding, he walked to the front door and pressed the bell.

Must have been more than just a scratch, he thought, running his fingers gingerly down the side of his face. When he looked at his hand, it was covered in blood.

'What happened to you?' asked the nurse, opening the front door.

'A little accident,' said Jack, giving her his best smile. 'Came off the bike.'

'You're here to see Tristan, yes?' Jack nodded.

'Let me have a look. I'll clean it up for you – come.' Jack followed her into the kitchen. 'Everyone's coming to see him. We called the specialist straight away. He's with him now,' the nurse rambled on. 'He can't believe it either. Hold still; nasty gash.'

I'm missing something here, thought Jack. 'The specialist? At this hour? Why?' he asked.

'To come out of a coma after all these years ... just like that. Well, we don't see that every day, do we? There, you're almost done.'

Walking slowly up the stairs, Jack heard muted voices. He stopped at the landing and looked down the dimly lit corridor: Rebecca was talking to a female police officer in front of Tristan's room. The door to the room was closed. Turning around, Rebecca saw Jack and hurried towards him. Silently, she put her arms around him and gave him a gentle hug.

'Are you all right?' she whispered, 'I was so scared. Look at yourself. Been in a war?'

'Worse. The edge of hell, and I looked inside ...'

'What did you see?'

'One day I may tell you.'

'That bad?'

'Yes. What's going on here?'

'Tristan woke up.'

'Cassandra was right. When?'

'About an hour ago. The doctor's with him now.'

Jack nodded.

'You don't seem surprised.'

'After what I've just seen, there are no surprises left. The Wizard's dead,' Jack said quietly. 'That's why the boy came out of the coma. Cassandra knew ...'

'What happened to your head?'

'It's nothing.'

'Sure. Are you going to tell me about it?'

Jack shook his head.

'I think you need some rest,' said Rebecca, a worried look on her face. 'Let's go home.'

'I have to see Tristan first. After all that's happened ...' said Jack just as the door to Tristan's room opened.

'You can go in now,' said the doctor. 'You're relatives?'

'Of a kind,' said Jack. 'How is he?'

'Remarkably well. I haven't seen anything quite like it. But then, the human mind is full of surprises,' replied the doctor. 'The more we learn about it, the less we seem to know. Go and talk to him a little. He's weak, but the stimulation will do him good. I'll be back in the morning to assess him further.'

Quietly, Jack opened the door and walked towards the bed by the window. Rebecca watched from the door. It was Jack's turn to meet Tristan. Without the life support apparatus and all its paraphernalia everything looked different, but the boy sitting up in bed in no way resembled the breathing corpse Jack had visited with Cassandra only a short time ago.

The first thing he noticed were the boy's eyes: dark, shiny pools radiating curiosity and intelligence. His black hair, neatly parted, framed a handsome face. *He's got his mother's eyes*, thought Jack.

'Hello, Tristan,' he said, coming closer. 'I'm Jack.'

Tristan continued to look calmly at his visitor, but didn't say anything. Jack held his gaze. *We'll have to tell him she's dead*, he thought. *That'll be tough.*

'You can tell me now,' said Tristan, his voice soft and strangely comforting.

'What?' asked Jack, taken aback.

'My mother's dead, isn't she?' said Tristan.

Jack looked away, feeling suddenly cold. *How does he know?* he asked himself, his mind racing. *What am I going to say? He deserves the truth.*

'How do you know?' asked Jack, biting his lip.

'You just told me.'

'But I didn't say anything ...'

'You didn't have to.'

'I don't understand ...'

'But she does,' said Tristan, pointing to Rebecca standing at the door. 'Thank you for being honest with me. It's a good beginning,' he added quietly after a while and closed his eyes. 'Please go now, I need to be alone.'

'What did you make of that?' asked Jack, walking down the corridor with Rebecca. 'Amazing kid.'

Remembering her conversation with Cassandra in Andrew's kitchen in Alice Springs, Rebecca stopped. 'He has the gift, just like his mother,' she said.

'You mean he's a ...' Jack said, searching for the right word.

'Seer? Yes. Do you want to know what Cassandra said about him?' Rebecca asked.

Jack nodded.

'She told me his powers are much stronger than hers. And there was something else she said. Something extraordinary. It's all coming back to me ...'

'What?' asked Jack.

'He's one of a chosen few ...'

'In what way?'

'He can hear the whisper of angels and glimpse eternity ...'

Overwhelmed by fatigue, Jack put his hand on Rebecca's shoulder and said, 'If I don't get some shuteye, I'll pass out. Let's go home.'

'I don't quite know how, but you've pulled it off,' said Rebecca, linking arms with Jack. 'It's finished.'

'Not quite. There's one more thing – remember?'

'The funeral?'

'Yes. It's part of it,' said Jack. 'Somehow, the last step is always the hardest, isn't it?'

76

Will's antique shop, 10 March

Jack slept for eighteen hours straight, the stress of the past two days finally taking its toll. Anna had been transferred by air ambulance to Sydney for admission into a private hospital.

The Australian government's spin doctors had lost no time. Andrew had become the public face of the police investigation and was hailed as a hero who had never lost faith. The authorities, they said, had kept the case alive in the background all these years. Following new leads, the police had acted quickly, a proud Police Commissioner told the media during a news conference. Raiding premises belonging to the notorious Wizards of Oz outlaw motorcycle club, they had discovered new evidence linking club members to the abduction of the two backpackers in 2005. Investigations were continuing.

A statement issued by Professor Popov on behalf of Anna and her family thanked the Australian authorities for their diligence and support and appealed for privacy. But the statement also said that Anna had suffered serious psychological trauma and had been hospitalised, which fanned the flames of curiosity and speculation of a voracious press. Only round-the-clock police protection ensured that Anna and her family weren't mobbed by the media.

Rather than waking Jack to find out what had happened, Andrew decided to let him sleep. The longer Jack could be kept out of the investigation the better.

'He's just getting up,' said Rebecca a while later, handing Andrew another mug of coffee. 'I've never seen anyone sleep this long.'

'It's the way the body deals with stress,' Andrew said. 'And from what I've seen, there would have been quite a bit of that ...'

Unshaven, head bandaged, and wearing an ill-fitting pair of pyjamas borrowed from Will's wardrobe, Jack padded into the kitchen.

'You look like I feel,' said Andrew, pushing his mug of coffee towards Jack. 'Here, drink this.' Jack drained the mug without saying a word and looked at Andrew through bleary eyes.

'I'm here as a friend and not as a police officer,' began Andrew. 'First, listen to what I've got to say. Please?'

Jack nodded.

'So far, believe it or not, your name hasn't come up in the investigation. No one knows that a copy of the DVD exists, or that you were at the compound. Let's hope it stays that way. The Wizard and the Undertaker are both dead. Therefore – no witnesses. But I'm sure you already know that.'

Jack reached for the coffee plunger on the table.

'When I last saw the Wizard, he had lost his head,' said Andrew, watching Jack carefully. 'I mean literally. He'd been decapitated. But you probably know that as well ...'

'He didn't tell us anything,' said Rebecca, beginning to understand why Jack had been so reticent with details.

'Good. Let's keep it that way,' said Andrew. 'Of course the police found the tunnel.' Andrew paused, letting his words sink in. 'The official version is that it was an inside job. Bikie gangs fight each other all the time, but the code of silence makes it very hard to prove. There's been a suggestion that the Warriors may have been involved, but of course you wouldn't know anything about that, would you, Jack?'

Jack frowned. 'Warriors?'

'I don't know how you've done it and frankly I don't care. Tristan's safe and the Wizard is no more. That's good enough for me. I guess what I'm telling you is that you've been incredibly lucky.'

'Rebecca keeps telling me I'm a lucky guy,' said Jack, a twinkle in his eyes.

'One last question, Jack,' said Andrew. 'What happened to the DVD?'

'It's right here. I can give it back to you now, if you like.'

Andrew shook his head, dismayed. 'You mean you didn't have to use it?'

'I did, in a way.'

Relieved, Andrew changed direction. 'How's your head?' he asked.

'It's all right. It stopped bleeding and doesn't hurt that much anymore.'

'You didn't go to a hospital?'

'No.'

'Good. No records. Incidentally, the forensics guys reckon that the Undertaker fired a shot just before he died. They dug the bullet out of the wall behind the Wizard's portrait. But you wouldn't know anything about that either, would you?'

'No. Should I?' Jack said, a mock frown creasing his face. 'Rebecca's right – you're one lucky guy.' Andrew stood up, walked across to Jack and held out his hand. Jack stood as well and the two men shook hands.

'It's been quite a ride, Jack,' Andrew said. 'I could make a reasonable detective out of you yet. Given a little time, that is. Interested?'

'A part-time Poirot, perhaps? I'd like that.'

'You don't speak French, and you're too skinny,' Rebecca cut in.

'I could learn ...'

'Don't you dare! You're an author not a sleuth.'

'There is one more thing,' said Jack. 'Cassandra's funeral.'

'I know. The body's been released and is on its way back to Sydney,' Andrew said.

'Good. I'll make the necessary arrangements, just as she requested.'

'It's the least we can do for her,' said Rebecca.

Andrew lit a cigarette and looked at Jack. 'What are you going to do now?' he said.

'I'll stay here for a while and sort out Will's affairs. I'm his executor. He's got no family to speak of; both his parents are dead. And then there's my own mess. Ruined house, insurance claims, exciting stuff like that.'

'And then?' asked Rebecca.

'I'll write Anna's story, I suppose. Exclusive rights – remember?'

'You *suppose*?'

Jack pulled the little notebook held together with rubber bands out of his pocket, and threw it on the kitchen bench. 'It's all in here,' he said, 'and up here,' he added, pointing to his bandaged head. 'Well, most of it is. However, there are a few gaping holes and nagging questions in the story I have to look into.'

'What are you going to do about that?' asked Rebecca.

'The only thing I can. Find the answers; my way. That's what I'm good at. All I need is a little time, and a bit of peace and quiet.'

'And what about you?' asked Andrew, turning to Rebecca.

'I've got to get back to New York in a hurry and see if I still have a job. I have to make peace with Jack's publishers. They must be tearing their hair out ... I've been too afraid to open my emails. The new book should help ...'

'Don't worry about the publishers,' interrupted Jack. 'I'll sort them out.'

'Sure ...' said Rebecca.

'Tell them life is what happens while they fret about sales.'

'That should really do it, Jack. Tactful, and businesslike.'

'Frankly, I don't give a stuff! My best friend's dead.' Rebecca reached across and squeezed Jack's hand. 'I still can't believe it,' Jack said, looking at her.

'Neither can I. You're right – there are more important things.'

'Did you hear from McGregor?' asked Jack, looking at Andrew.

'Yes. He went back with Merriwarra and got the women out.'

'And?'

'He drove downstream and had a look ...'

'Yes?'

'Nothing, I'm afraid. Sorry.'

'Perhaps it's better that way,' said Jack sadly, and began to play with the little notebook on the bench.

'What's troubling you?' said Rebecca, feeling Jack's pain.

'When it all began, it looked so exciting and so promising. A great new story, we thought, a winner with fantastic potential. *Go for it, Jack,* I told myself. Not in our wildest dreams could we have imagined that a few short weeks later, Cassandra and Will would both be dead, and Anna ...'

'We cannot change the past, Jack, only the future,' interrupted Andrew, realising where this was heading.

'You're right, and that's exactly what's worrying me.'

'In what way?' said Rebecca.

'Being a responsible writer is a delicate balancing act. I learnt that in Afghanistan. The line between decency and exposing something at all cost is a fine one, requiring both judgement and moral values. And most importantly, the courage to say no.'

'Yes, that's never easy,' Rebecca agreed, 'but what has that to do with us here?'

'Not sure ...'

'What are you saying?'

'I feel like an umpire who has to adjudicate between competing interests: between what is right, and what will sell.'

Rebecca stood up in a huff. 'I'm keeping out of this,' she said, and walked to the door.

'Well, do you have an opinion on this?' Jack called out.

'You want to know what I'm thinking?'

'Sure.'

'You're an adventure junkie, Jack, who's got cold feet. Post-excitement blues. Go back to bed and sleep it off,' Rebecca said.

Andrew waited until Rebecca had left the kitchen and he was alone with Jack. 'You've pissed her off big time, mate,' he said.

'You reckon?' Jack watched Andrew roll another cigarette. 'Adventure junkie, that's a good one.'

'What was all that about?' asked Andrew.

'I'm not sure about the book ...'

'In what way?'

'I'm too close. I'm no longer on the outside looking in. Anna may have survived, but objectivity, impartiality and sober judgement all died in the gorge. I've become part of the story. It's too personal.'

'Is that a problem?'

'Could be.'

Andrew lit his cigarette and looked pensively at Jack through the spiralling smoke. 'Will?' he asked.

'Yes; and all the others. And that includes you. We've become like ...'

'A family?'

'Something like that.'

'And that family has gone through a lot together?'

'Yes, and it doesn't stop here.'

'And you don't want to jeopardise or expose ...?'

'The problem is I know too much,' interrupted Jack, 'and a lot of what I know was given to me in confidence. No, more than that, I've lived it.'

'You have obligations?'

'Precisely; I made promises. I cannot be true to myself as a writer and ...'

'A human being?' suggested Andrew.

'Yes; you are absolutely right. That's my dilemma.'

'Ironic, don't you think?'

Jack shrugged. 'What do you reckon I should do about that?'

'You'll know when the time comes, mate.'

'I hope you're right.' Jack looked pensively into his empty coffee mug, dreading the choices he would soon have to make. 'What are you going to do now?' he asked, changing direction.

'I'm going back to Alice, the gallery, and fundraising for the kids. That'll do me.'

'You're a lucky guy, but it must feel good, though ...'

'Vindication?'

Jack nodded.

'You bet. We've taught the bastards a lesson. Even the Commissioner sent congratulations. That must have really hurt.'

'You're the man of the moment. Celebrity cop and Outback legend. I bet they'll roll out the red carpet for you in Alice.'

Andrew laughed. 'Perhaps they will,' he said.

'You deserve it, mate.'

Andrew began to laugh. '*Deserve?* Life doesn't work that way, and you know it.'

'You know me too well.'

'I tracked down the cemetery and the plot number Cassandra gave you,' Andrew said, changing the subject.

'Good. We can go right ahead then. She was quite specific. She wants to be cremated and laid to rest in that plot.'

'That's right. But there's a complication ...'

'Oh?'

'Someone claimed the body.'

'When?'

'This morning.'

'I thought she had no one. Apart from her son.'

'Not quite true.'

'Where does this leave us then, with the funeral?'

'Well ... this is where it becomes interesting ...'

'In what way?'

'The person who claimed the body wants us to go ahead with the funeral exactly as Cassandra requested.'

'Don't you think that's odd?'

'Not really. He wants to honour her wishes.'

'Who is he?'

Andrew was enjoying himself. 'You're in for a big surprise,' he said.

'Are you stringing this out for a reason? Who claimed the body, Andrew?'

'There's more.'

'For Christ's sake, just tell me!'

'Do you want to know who's buried in the plot next to hers?'

'This is relevant?' asked Jack.

'Sure is.'

'Then tell me.'

'I will, but only if you tell me about the Bone Scraper.'

Jack looked apprehensive. 'Why do you want to know?' he asked.

'You'll find out in a moment, but you have to keep all this to yourself for the time being.'

'Okay, Andrew. You first.'

77

Cassandra's funeral, 13 March

Cassandra's funeral was to be a quiet and private affair with only a handful of mourners attending. Jack and Rebecca were waiting outside the church for the hearse to arrive, and the countess and Professor Popov sat next to Andrew inside.

Tristan's sudden recovery had surprised everyone. He had insisted on coming along, and was seated next to a nurse who had accompanied him on doctor's orders. Otherwise, the church was empty.

All was quiet until the bikies turned into the street – thirty of them – riding in formation. Led by the Bone Scraper in full Warriors regalia astride a bike with sidecar, they pulled up in front of the church, the throaty burble from their bikes all but drowning out the lonely little bell tolling in the steeple above.

'Friends of yours?' asked Rebecca, taken aback by the Warriors' unexpected appearance.

Jack didn't reply. Instead, he was remembering another funeral not that long ago where a mother and daughter killed by terrorists had been laid to rest.

'Quiet funeral, you said?'

The Bone Scraper and five others – all huge Maoris with tattooed faces just like his – lined up on the footpath behind the hearse.

'We'll take it from here,' said the Bone Scraper to the undertakers, placing his huge hand on the coffin.

Confused, the men stepped aside. Lifting the coffin onto their broad shoulders, the Maori pallbearers walked slowly into the church.

'What are these guys doing here?' whispered Rebecca.

'Wait and see,' replied Jack.

'You knew, didn't you?' said Rebecca. Jack squeezed her hand in confirmation.

'You're a dark horse, Jack Rogan.'

'The best is yet to come – watch.'

379

If the celebrant waiting in front of the altar was surprised by the strange procession coming towards him, he didn't show it. Jack and Rebecca followed the coffin down the aisle and sat down next to Tristan in the front.

Jack had requested a short and simple service, and the celebrant, a friend of Will's, was about to deliver just that. Within minutes the small church was filled to capacity with unexpected mourners as the Warriors filed in and took their seats at the back.

With the short service almost at an end, the celebrant asked if anyone wanted to say a few words. Having been told earlier that there would be no eulogy, the question was merely routine.

But the Bone Scraper stood up and spoke. 'Yes, I do,' he said.

For a moment there was complete silence as all heads turned towards him. Walking slowly down the aisle until he reached the coffin, he turned and looked first at Tristan, and then at the others seated close to him.

'I owe you all an apology and an explanation,' he began, his distinctive New Zealand accent giving his deep voice a pleasant, melodious tone. 'Firstly, I want to apologise for coming here unannounced and uninvited, but there are good reasons why that had to be so. A funeral is a solemn and serious occasion which must be treated with respect. It is respect that brings me here. And a lot more ...'

He speaks with great eloquence, thought Jack, spellbound like all the others. A pin dropping on the stone floor would have sounded like thunder in the silent church as the Bone Scraper paused.

'Cassandra is an assumed name. Most of you would have at least suspected this, and some of you knew. But I'm sure none of you know her real name. Not even you, Tristan,' he said, looking at the frail boy sitting in the front row.

'Yet a name is very important. It tells us who we are and where we come from. Hers is a traditional name, an echo of our Maori past. She and I, and my late brother Joe, are branches of the same tree reaching back to Parema Te Pahau, a great warrior chief. Now I'm the last one ...'

The Bone Scraper turned towards the coffin and put his hand on the lid.

'The woman lying in this box is my sister,' he said quietly. 'That's why I'm here.' Staring at the coffin, the Bone Scraper paused again, not sure if he should go on. 'She had a twin,' he said at last, 'our brother Joe. She and Joe were one. Now they are together again.'

The Bone Scraper stood in silence for what seemed an eternity, his striking face like chiselled stone. Then softly, he began to chant in Maori. He was saying goodbye to a younger sister he had lost along the way, only to find her again when it was already too late. After a while the chanting turned to a whisper and then stopped completely. Turning around, the Bone Scraper looked straight ahead and stared at something only he could see, before walking slowly back to his pew.

'Why didn't you tell me?' whispered Rebecca, tears streaming down her pale face. Jack squeezed her hand, but didn't reply.

Choking with emotion, the countess stood.

'I, too, would like to say something,' she said, her voice quivering. Clutching a handkerchief in her right hand, she walked over to the coffin and stood where the Bone Scraper had addressed them just moments before.

'My daughter Anna is too ill to be here and speak, but I know in my heart that she would like to be. So I shall speak on her behalf. A few days ago, Cassandra saved my daughter's life. I was there and saw it all. There is no greater gift one mother can give to another, yet Cassandra did just that. Tragically, in doing so, she gave up her own life, without hesitation or complaint. It is important that you, Tristan, should know this. There are no words to describe the gratitude I feel towards this woman we came here to honour and farewell. Not only did she save Anna's life, she was instrumental in finding her and bringing her back to us. During all these lonely years Anna has been missing, presumed dead by most, I believed that she was alive. Unbeknown to me, Cassandra believed that too. My belief was based on faith, but Cassandra knew. She had a gift to see and feel what others couldn't, and her extraordinary mind was able to go where others feared to tread. I believe she was an instrument of God.'

The countess paused and looked at the Bone Scraper. 'Can you tell us her real name, Sir,' she asked, 'so that all of us here can learn who she really was and where she came from?'

How extraordinary. The Russian countess is addressing the Maori bikie in church, thought Jack.

'She's named after a famous Chieftainess of our tribe. Her name is Ina Te Papatahi,' replied the Bone Scraper, speaking slowly.

'Ina Te Papatahi,' repeated the countess, 'you will live in our hearts forever.'

'Does anyone else wish to speak?' asked the celebrant after the countess had returned to her seat. With her aching heart almost bursting in her chest, Rebecca listened to the silence around her urging her to say something. *Do it*, she told herself, *you owe her so much!*

'Yes; I do,' said Rebecca, her voice barely audible. Jack looked at her, surprised. Rebecca wiped the tears from her cheeks, stood up and turned to the Bone Scraper watching her. 'With your permission,' she said. The Bone Scraper nodded and pointed to the casket covered in flowers.

Rebecca walked slowly down the aisle until she reached the coffin. Remembering that stormy night at Never Never Downs, she stared at it for what seemed – to her – an eternity. There was so much she wanted to say, but she couldn't find the words.

'Ina Te ...,' she began haltingly at last, trying to remember the name.

'Papatahi,' whispered the Bone Scraper softly.

'Papatahi,' said Rebecca, 'you reached out in friendship, took me by the hand, and touched my soul. When you looked inside and saw that I was lost, you lit up the darkness with your wisdom and your kindness and showed me the way. When you saw that I was searching for love, you showed me where to find it.' Rebecca paused, and dug her fingernails into the palms of her hands, hoping that the pain would stop her from losing control. 'You were right,' she sobbed, 'love was right there in front of me. The door was open wide. Thanks to you, I'm in the cage no more.'

Leaning forward, Rebecca pulled a red rose out of the floral arrangement covering the lid of the coffin. As she lifted the exquisite little flower to her lips – her fingers trembling – a teardrop fell on one of the petals and slowly rolled towards the thorny stem. 'Goodbye, dear friend,' she whispered and placed the rose carefully back on the lid. 'You've joined the whisper of angels, and become part of eternity. Watch over us.'

After Rebecca had returned to her seat, the Bone Scraper stood up and started to sing. As the haunting Maori farewell to the dead rose to the rafters, the Warriors stood as one and joined in. What had started as a quiet service had turned into an unexpected celebration of an extraordinary life.

At the conclusion of the funeral, the Maori pallbearers stepped forward again and carried the coffin outside. The Bone Scraper placed it carefully on the waiting sidecar, dismissed the funeral director, and sent the hearse away. In line with club tradition, Cassandra – Ina Te Papatahi – would be taken to the crematorium in style, and laid to rest next to her twin brother. Riding slowly in groups of four, the Warriors formed a deafening guard of honour as they followed the coffin down the street.

Jack and Rebecca stood outside the church and watched the Warriors leave. Jack turned to Rebecca. 'That took some guts in there,' he said. 'Not many are brave enough to bare their soul.'

'She was an extraordinary person.'

'I didn't know you were so close.'

Rebecca looked away. 'We were,' she said, a wave of sadness washing over her.

Linking arms with Rebecca, Jack pointed to the bikies. 'I wouldn't mind a send-off like that one day ... And have the things you said about Cassandra ...'

'Yes?'

'Said about me.'

'The way you've been going lately, your send-off could be closer than you think,' said Rebecca, feeling better.

'Are you kidding? I haven't done all the things I want to do before I die.'

'Bucket list?'

'Something like that.'

'You must be getting close.'

Jack shook his head and waited until the last bikie had turned the corner before replying. 'Still a long way to go,' he said.

'I was afraid you'd say that.'

'Have you found what you were looking for?' Jack asked, a sparkle in his eyes.

'I think so, but only time will tell ...'

'Then why don't you stick around, and we can find out?'

'Together?'

'Is there another way?'

'You mean it?'

'Absolutely! And I can promise you one thing ...'

'What?'

Jack pulled Rebecca into a doorway and kissed her tenderly on the back of the neck. 'The ride of your life.'

EPILOGUE
KURAGIN CHATEAU, THREE MONTHS LATER

I

Jack put on a brave face. He found driving in France challenging at the best of times, but the traffic leaving the airport was particularly chaotic that morning. The pressure was on. Getting lost again was unthinkable. 'I hope you're impressed,' he said, furiously changing lanes.

'Why? Should I be?' asked Rebecca.

'I've taken the correct exit – there. See?'

'Good boy. I wasn't looking forward to getting lost in Paris again. As long as we get to the chateau today, I'm happy, but the countess is expecting us around lunchtime. I would keep that in mind.'

'No worries. I know the way to the Kuragin estate. We'll get there with time to spare. Trust me.'

'I'm glad you're confident. Just remember what happened last time.'

'Bloody French drivers! Did you see that?' Jack raised his fist. 'Bastard!'

'Temper, temper. If you don't keep your eyes on the road, we might not get there at all!'

'You know what?'

'Tell me?'

'It's a bit of a worry ...'

'What is?'

'I'm getting used to your nagging.'

Gritting her teeth, Rebecca looked out the window.

The meeting with Jack's New York publisher the week before had been quite a challenge. It was Jack's first visit to New York since Anna's return. Rebecca, on the other hand, had barely left the Big Apple, and had looked after Jack's interests and placated the impatient publishers demanding results. Rebecca realised that her relationship with Jack had turned into an internet arrangement suffering from all the symptoms imposed by different time zones and the tyranny of distance. Skype and Viber had become their bedfellows and Rebecca was hoping that this was about to change.

Author-publisher meetings were always a bit tricky – big egos rubbing shoulders. That's why Rebecca, as Jack's PR agent, insisted on attending all the meetings in person. Rebecca remembered the showdown with the publishers two days before. Jack had become more assertive and less reluctant to express his point of view. To her surprise, instead of being put off by this, the publishers didn't seem to mind. They began to look at the boy from Down Under in a different light.

Patronising complacency had given way to respect; the soaring book sales spoke volumes. *Well done, Jack*, thought Rebecca.

The outline of *The Disappearance of Anna Popov* had more than piqued the publishers' interest. Helped by the huge international publicity Anna's remarkable survival story had received around the globe, and Jack's exclusivity arrangements with the Popov family, the book appeared to be well on its way and had the market buzzing with anticipation. It had all the hallmarks of a blockbuster with serious movie potential.

However, before formally submitting the manuscript, Jack had insisted on first showing it to the countess and Professor Popov in person. This wasn't unusual, but when questioned further about this by Rebecca, Jack appeared evasive and a little uneasy. Rebecca sensed that there was more to all this than he was prepared to tell. All he said was that he wanted to talk to Anna and see for himself if she was able to throw further light on her story.

So far, Jack had relied entirely on others and had painstakingly pieced the facts together, from the outside. He had told the publishers that he was hoping to add at least a glimpse of what it must have been like to be on the inside. This trip to the Kuragin chateau would be his first opportunity to speak to Anna and her family since her rescue. What Rebecca didn't know was that Jack had another, hidden, agenda that would take everyone by surprise, and change everything.

After the turbulent events surrounding the Wizard's death and Cassandra's funeral, no one had been allowed near Anna. The medical advice had been both clear and adamant: the patient required rest and treatment. From the day she had been reunited with her daughter, the countess wanted to take Anna and her baby back to France and away from the glare of publicity surrounding her in Australia. Professor Popov agreed and came up with the answer: he made arrangements to have Anna admitted to a private clinic just outside Paris. One of his close friends, an eminent neuro-psychiatrist, would oversee her recovery and rehabilitation.

Anna had spent more than two months at the clinic, and had only recently been discharged. She was now living with her baby son at the Kuragin chateau.

Right from the beginning, Anna's parents had been tight-lipped about their daughter's condition and return home, and had kept her out of the limelight. The Australian authorities had welcomed this, and had assisted the family in protecting Anna's privacy. The spin doctors were happy too: the heat had been taken out of a potentially embarrassing situation.

However, fascinated by leaked snippets of Anna's remarkable survival, a news-hungry public wanted to know more. The press had a juicy tabloid bone it wouldn't relinquish without a fight.

Privately, Professor Popov and the countess had become increasingly concerned about the impact Jack's much awaited book would have on their lives in general, and Anna's recovery and future, in particular. However, due to their relationship with Jack and the understanding reached between them regarding the book, they hadn't voiced their concerns. After all that Jack had done for them, he deserved his reward.

With the Wizard and his henchmen dead, the notorious Wizards of Oz had all but disappeared. Without leadership and most of their assets confiscated under the Proceeds of Crime legislation, the once feared outlaws had become a nonentity. This was hailed a great success by the police and the Australian government.

'There, what did I tell you?' said Jack, pointing ahead to the moat. 'Just like the Kalumburu painting, don't you think?' Rebecca nodded. 'Here we are. On time and without detours. Please take note.'

'Not bad,' conceded Rebecca. 'You are getting better.'

'I do try hard, admit it.'

'You also know how to boast.'

'You call this boasting? I get us here safely, I'm driving on the other side of the road and I cannot read the bloody street signs, and you ...'

'Enough!' interrupted Rebecca. 'Watch the peacock! There – by the moat!' Jack had to swerve to miss the strutting bird and almost ran off the road. 'Leaving a dead peacock in the middle of the bridge wouldn't look too good, admit it.'

'Feathers flying on arrival? No.' They both burst out laughing.

The countess ran outside to greet them as soon as the car pulled up. She threw her arms around Jack and kissed him on the cheeks. 'I can't begin to tell you how good it is to see you both,' she said, taking Rebecca by the hand. 'Come, Anna's waiting inside. She's been excited for days.' Jack shot Rebecca a meaningful look. They had received mixed reports about Anna's recovery and state of mind.

'How is she?' asked Jack.

'Judge for yourself,' replied the countess, turning serious. 'We have good days and bad ones.'

To protect the family's privacy, the countess had temporarily closed the hotel, and had the conservatory at the back of the chateau converted into a studio for Anna. The conservatory had plenty of light and a splendid view of the garden and was the ideal setting for an artist. Anna spent most of her time there – painting.

The specialists at the clinic had discovered that Anna's mind had made a remarkable adjustment: it had retreated from reality in order to deal with the trauma and horror she had been subjected to. At first, this was viewed as a temporary defence mechanism. However, instead of returning slowly to normal with the passage of time as the specialists had expected, Anna was channelling all of her energy and emotions into her art. She was expressing herself through her paintings, and her paintbrush had become her pencil. Anna was communicating through brushstrokes and paint, but kept reality at arm's length.

The countess opened the glass door to the conservatory and stepped aside. 'There she is,' she said. 'She has something to show you ...' Dressed in jeans streaked with paint and a long white shirt, the young woman standing in front of the easel looked confident and at ease. Jack could barely recognise her as the frail creature he had rescued from the cave. Her hair had grown longer and was a shade or two darker than he remembered. Her face had filled out a little and her skin had a healthy glow. The baby was asleep in a bassinet by the window, with the countess' Labrador watching over him.

'Thanks to you, Jack, I have a family again,' whispered the countess, gently pushing Jack towards Anna.

'Brown is a difficult colour,' said Anna without turning around. 'Ochre or yellow are easy. Brown is hard, especially Outback-brown. I can't seem to get it right. Merriwarra knew how to make it by using the earth itself. Painting colour from memory is very difficult. There are so many shades of brown, don't you think?'

Jack walked across to Anna and looked over her shoulder. 'You may not remember me,' he said quietly.

'We thought you were death coming into the cave to take me away, but you turned out to be life itself,' said Anna, pointing with her paintbrush to the canvas in front of her. 'That's you, right here.' The painting captured the inside of a cave decorated with spectacular rock art in surprising detail.

Looking fearful and dejected, two Aboriginal women sat on the floor. Wrapped in a blanket, a blonde girl was lying on the ground next to them. One of the women was cradling the head of the girl – obviously Anna – in her lap. A shaft of light reached inside from an opening in the cave wall and fell on a white man dressed only in shorts.

He was kneeling in front of the women with his hands – palms up – pointing to the girl in a gesture reminiscent of prayer. The wide-eyed women, however, stared at something behind the crouching man, an expression of horror and shock on their wan faces. Jack could just make out the outline of a human skeleton painted in shades of grey, floating through the shaft of light away from the women. *An apparition?* he thought, trying to interpret the strange composition. 'That's death leaving,' said Anna, pointing to the skeleton. 'It's almost finished. I just have to get these annoying browns right.'

'You have a great gift,' said Jack. 'Will you sign it Lucrezia?'

Anna looked at him and smiled. The painting reminded Jack of a strange nativity scene. *It looks like the adoration of the Magi*, he thought, *but with only one king, bringing the gift of life after banishing death.*

'You saved Lucrezia. Thanks to you, she can paint again ...' Looking dreamily out the window, Anna paused, but said nothing further. Then, turning back to her easel, she picked up the paintbrush and continued to paint as if nothing had happened.

'We'd better go,' whispered the countess, holding the door open. 'Her concentration spans are short. But there, look who's coming. Perfect timing.' Relieved to have found a distraction, the countess pointed to the window. Taking great delight in chasing an indignant peacock along the road, a young boy was riding his bicycle across the bridge. 'He must have left school early – come.'

The boy left his bike at the bottom of the stairs and ran towards the countess waiting for him by the front door. 'They are here, aren't they?' he said, trying to catch his breath, his flushed face aglow with excitement.

Jack hadn't seen Tristan since Cassandra's funeral. After that, everything had happened very fast. Tristan had become an orphan and needed care and a home. There was no way his uncle, the Bone Scraper, could look after him. Neither were Rebecca or Jack in a position to take on such a responsibility. Always practical, and quick when it came to making important decisions, the countess came up with the obvious answer: Tristan would come and live with her in

France. After what Cassandra had done for Anna, the countess was more than willing to open her heart and her home. The boy embraced the idea, his uncle agreed, and Andrew took care of the formalities.

Remembering his injury, Jack traced the thin scar on his temple with his finger where the Undertaker's bullet had missed him by a whisker. Looking at the boy bursting through the door, Rebecca remembered the promise she had made to his mother. *She would be pleased*, she thought. *We have kept our side of the bargain too*. The complicated threads of the past few months were coming together at last.

'How's your French, mate?' asked Jack, stepping forward to greet the boy.

'Tres bien, monsieur,' replied Tristan, taking a bow. 'How's your head?'

'A little better, thanks.' *Life goes on*, thought Jack, remembering Cassandra lying on her deathbed. Turning suddenly quite sad, Tristan looked at Jack as if he, too, had just remembered his dead mother. *He's reading my thoughts again*, thought Jack. Sensing the boy's unease, the countess walked over to Tristan and tousled his hair. 'His French is quite amazing,' she said. 'He learnt the language in just a few weeks. The teachers were very impressed. Run along now, and get changed.'

'When can I read the book?' asked Tristan, walking reluctantly to the stairs.

'Later,' said the countess. 'Off you go.' Then turning to Rebecca she said, 'He hasn't stopped talking about Jack's book. I don't think we can keep it away from him.'

'Neither should we,' said Jack. 'He's part of the story. He's entitled to know what happened.'

'How's he fitting in?' asked Rebecca.

'He's become part of the family. I've acquired a son. He and Anna are particularly close. They talk without speaking. It's quite remarkable. They are communicating on a different plane.' The countess shook her head. 'You should see them together. But you must be exhausted,' she said, turning once again into the consummate hostess.

'What about the good Professor?' asked Jack.

'Nikki will join us later tonight. He had to give a talk in Berlin this morning and will try to get here as soon as he can. Let me show you to your rooms.'

II

Professor Popov arrived just after dinner. Tristan had gone to bed, and Anna was in her studio with the baby. Anxious to give Jack and Popov an opportunity to talk privately, the countess kept Rebecca busy by showing her a family photo album filled with snapshots of Anna's childhood.

'I owe you an apology,' Popov said, joining Jack on the terrace. 'I behaved rather badly. In Vienna, I mean.'

'It was a bit of an ambush on my part. At times it's the only way to open a difficult door,' Jack said, diplomatically brushing the comment aside.

'Very gracious of you, thank you. You and Katty were right, and I was wrong. About Anna. I had lost faith; Katty never did. What you have done for this family cannot be put into words. At times I still find it difficult to accept that all of this is real. I still have to come to terms with the fact that Anna has been given back to us. It's a big emotional adjustment. Especially for me.'

'Anna looks remarkably well,' said Jack, changing direction.

'Physically, she's made a full recovery. As for her state of mind ...'

'What's the prognosis?'

'Opinions vary. The only thing everyone seems to agree on is giving it time.'

'She seems very happy here.'

'Yes she is. She's surrounded by love, but she has become a different person,' said Popov, lowering his voice. 'She's not the young woman I remember. But Katty cannot see this. She's blinded by gratitude and devotion.'

'Is that such a bad thing?'

'No, it isn't. She has her life back, and a lot more.'

'The grandson?'

'Yes, and Tristan. He's incredibly bright. His insights ... miles ahead of his years. It's quite scary ...'

'He had an exceptional mother ... and ...'

'And he has acquired a new one,' interrupted Popov. 'Katty adores him. It's her way of repaying a huge debt. As you know, she's very religious. She's guided by faith.'

'Not such a bad thing either. Happy endings are rare.'

'Do you think this has a happy ending?'

'Do you?'

Taking his time, Popov considered the question. He almost raised the topic of Jack's book that had worried him so much lately, but thought better of it. 'Only time will tell,' he said instead.

The countess walked out onto the terrace and looked at the two men locked deep in conversation. She knew that it was time to intervene. The experienced hostess in her recognised the danger signals: leaving them alone for much longer, could upset the balance of the evening. 'Jack, it's time for your book, don't you think?' she said. 'The suspense is killing me. Come inside, you two.'

Jack opened his briefcase, pulled out a copy of his manuscript and put it on the coffee table in front of him. The cover, a plain white page, had only the title typed across it: *The Disappearance of Anna Popov*.

The writer in Jack knew that he had crafted a remarkable account of tragedy and love, of deep suffering and acts of selfless sacrifice. And he knew the triumph that he could write about; of faith and hope over unimaginable evil and despair. He also knew that the story had a dark side as well.

During his recent investigations, Jack had come across new material he had not included in the manuscript. With knowledge comes responsibility. What Jack had discovered had the power to ruin lives, affect generations, and send ripples of pain well into the future.

During the past three months, Jack had all but locked himself away in Will's terrace to write the book. Living like a hermit, and leaving the house only to do research and conduct interviews, he had completed the book in record time. Rebecca had returned to New York to cover for him by postponing his commitments and making excuses. She had even managed to keep his publishers happy by promising them something special.

Taking a deep breath, Jack pushed the manuscript across the table towards the countess and Popov sitting opposite.

'Thank you for letting me into your lives,' he said. This is a story that has to be told – the right way. I only hope that I'm doing it justice. However, this has now turned into much more than just a fascinating book. This is a record of life. It belongs to you.' Jack paused, searching for the right way to continue.

'Some parts have been left out – quite deliberately – but you of all people will understand exactly why. In one important respect, the book isn't finished yet.' Jack looked anxiously at Rebecca. 'Not even Rebecca knows about this. I wanted to tell you all at the same time. It's that important.'

Rebecca lowered her eyes, a surprised look on her face. Sensing her disappointment, the countess reached for Rebecca's hand, but said nothing.

'I'm sorry, Becky. I've been wrestling with this for some time ... I ...' Jack shook his head, collecting his thoughts. For a while, no one said anything, the tension in the room rising by the second.

'Are you going to tell us about it?' prompted Popov quietly.

'During my recent investigations, I've discovered something disturbing that will rock you to the core. If we are not careful, it could even destroy ... And it concerns someone right here, under this very roof,' added Jack quietly.

'Who?' asked the countess, he voice quivering with apprehension.'

'What is it?' said Rebecca.

'I thought very hard about how I should tell you this. I'm a storyteller. So, I'll tell you a story, and a good story has to start at the beginning.'

'Come on, Jack,' interrupted Rebecca, 'is all this really necessary? Why not just tell us?'

'It's not that simple; trust me. You all heard what the Bone Scraper said at the funeral about his brother Joe, and Cassandra. It was quite a revelation – right? But that was just the beginning. There's a lot more. Dark secrets and twists ... and a terrible death. So horrible that I have difficulty finding the words to describe it. But it's all part of the puzzle.' Jack paused and reached for his Cognac.

'It all began in a travelling circus owned by the Wizard's parents twenty years or so ago. Eugene was the strong man, and his friend, the Bone Scraper, was his sidekick. They were part of an acrobatic act, The Flying Kiwis, would you believe? The youngest and most exciting members of the troupe were Cassandra and her twin brother Joe. They were the star attraction. She could contort her body in ways that seemed impossible, and both of them could do somersaults that had the audience gasping. Then one day, Cassandra had a terrible accident. Joe missed his timing. His hands just weren't there when his sister came flying through the air. Cassandra broke her hip and a leg. Badly. The doctors thought that she would never walk again. But in a circus, everyone has to pull his weight. The boys found a new girl and Cassandra, by now a cripple, became a fortune-teller.

Eugene's mother, a colourful Gypsy who dabbled in the occult, introduced her to the Tarot. Soon after that, Eugene got into trouble with the law and went to jail. The Bone Scraper followed in his footsteps and the Flying Kiwis were no more. For several years, Joe stayed with the circus and looked after Cassandra, until one day, Eugene returned. Fresh out of jail and with nowhere to go, he wanted to join the circus again. By now, Cassandra, the girl, had turned into an attractive young woman with a boyfriend, a talented young juggler from Argentina called Merlin – the new star attraction. The scene was set for trouble. Big trouble.'

'Why are you telling us all this?' asked Rebecca. 'Do we really have to know?'

'Oh yes, you do. Something about Cassandra has troubled me from the very beginning,' Jack said.

'What?' asked the countess.

'The initial contact between her and the police. Andrew told us that it was Cassandra who approached the authorities during the investigation with an offer to help. The question is why. She was a psychic living in faraway Sydney, hardly the kind of assistance the police would normally take seriously, don't you think? What else did she offer? Did she have some information? Andrew couldn't quite answer this. All he said was that by then the police were desperate and ready to try anything. Yet soon after that, the possibility of a bikie gang being involved was somehow floated by Cassandra – a psychic, remember – apparently without a shred of evidence. I thought this was odd, to say the least, unless you believe in magic. I don't. There had to be more to this. And as it turned out, there was. Just how much more, I couldn't have imagined in my wildest dreams.'

Popov shook his head. 'This is incredible,' he said.

'It is, but it's just the beginning. The years spent in jail had changed Eugene. He had become violent and aggressive and prone to fits of rage. Everyone was afraid of him. He took a particular dislike to Merlin, the fiery young lover, and became infatuated with Cassandra.

'She rejected his advances. We must remember that Eugene was almost 20 years older. She had always looked up to him. The circus was her family, and for years he was the father-figure in a young, impressionable girl's life without parents. Then one day, things came to a head. There was a fight. Knives were involved and Merlin was badly wounded and later died of his injuries. Eugene pleaded self defence, but was convicted of manslaughter and sent to prison. The Bone Scraper was still inside, doing time – remember? He bribed the guards, and he and Eugene ended up sharing a cell. It became the birthplace of the Wizards of Oz.'

'Why is none of this in your book?' asked Rebecca, 'if it's as relevant as you say?'

'Because of what's still to come. Please bear with me. A few months after Merlin died, Cassandra gave birth to a boy and left the circus. Tristan was born. That was thirteen years ago. She supported herself and her child by reading Tarot cards for the superstitious and the curious at markets and country fairs. At first, she and her twin brother, Joe, remained very close. However, after their older brother, the Bone Scraper, got out of jail, Joe joined the Wizards of Oz, and things began to change.

'The boys were together again, only this time, they were running a notorious bikie gang. They got into drug trafficking and all kinds of criminal activity and were constantly in and out of prison. Then something happened between the Wizard and the Bone Scraper. They had a spectacular falling out and went their separate ways. The Bone Scraper founded the Warriors, a rival gang, and the turf-war was on in earnest.

'The long and bloody feud came to a head during the famous Pagliacci incident. The Wizards burnt down their rivals' clubhouse, and Joe was killed soon after. That happened just before the girls disappeared in Alice Springs. The rest you know. But what you don't know is that Cassandra had vowed to destroy the Wizard long before Anna and Julia were abducted, and had been plotting his downfall for years. The question is, why?

'Was it because he had killed her young lover in a fight all these years ago, or was it her twin brother's death? Or was there something else altogether? Something deeper? Joe's death was certainly the catalyst that spurred her into action, but had she contacted the authorities because she knew something? Of course she did! She knew that the Wizards were involved in the abduction and that one of the girls was already dead. How did she know this? There was an informant in the ranks of the Wizards who fed information to the Warriors. She heard it from her brother, the Bone Scraper, and together, they decided to act.

'Cassandra made her move: she went to the police. This started an extraordinary chain of events that ultimately led us to Anna and brought her back home – alive. And all of us here have played a part in that journey – right?'

'This is quite a story, but you still haven't told us what you found. What about the person who died?' Rebecca said. 'Where does all that fit into this?'

Sitting back in his chair, Jack traced the little white scar on his temple again with the tip of his finger. 'I haven't told you how I received this injury. It was a gunshot wound. I was there just before the Wizard died and almost got killed. This is what happened.'

III

Beginning with the deathbed promise he had made at the hospital, Jack repeated everything Cassandra had told him just before she died. Then, turning to the events of the night the Wizard was tortured and killed, he described his meeting with the Bone Scraper and told them how the Warriors had used the secret tunnel to break into the compound. Finally, leaving nothing to the imagination, he painted a vivid picture of what took place in the crypt. He told them in brutal detail how the wire-noose had slowly cut into the Wizard's neck, and described the strange wooden skull contraption the Wizard was standing on, and why. He explained how the Warriors had watched the Wizard die while performing the haka in front of him. Pointing to his scar, he told them how the Undertaker had tried to shoot him, but missed, and then had his head blown off. The only thing Jack didn't mention was the tape.

Looking quite pale, the countess kept staring at the manuscript on the table, afraid of the horrors lurking inside, ready to shock the unwary. Then she reached for Popov's hand. 'Tell me this is a bad dream,' she said in Russian. 'How did we get mixed up in all this, Nikki?' Popov didn't reply.

'You must have been out of your mind, Jack,' whispered Rebecca, 'to go in there alone.'

'I promised,' said Jack.

'Does Andrew know?'

'Not all of it. He tried to keep me out of the investigation – remember? He didn't want to know.'

'I'm not surprised.'

'Shocking as it is, how can this destroy the life of someone under this roof? I don't understand,' said Popov.

'What I've told you so far is only the background,' Jack said, nervously running his fingers through his hair, 'to help you understand what you are about to hear.'

'Come on, Jack, what is it?' said Rebecca, drumming her fingers against her armrest.

'It explains why the Wizard and the Bone Scraper parted company and became mortal enemies. Disturbed by all the violence and crime her two brothers had become involved in, Cassandra confided in the Bone Scraper. She wanted to warn him about the Wizard. She did this by telling him why Merlin got himself killed all those years ago.' Jack paused again, still not quite sure if he should continue. 'It was an incident that had destroyed her life, and would ultimately take it away altogether.'

'What did she tell him?' asked Rebecca quietly.

Here it comes, thought Jack, taking a deep breath. 'Infuriated by Cassandra's steadfast rejection, the Wizard finally lost control. In a fit of jealous rage, he raped her, and beat her almost to death.' Jack squirmed in his chair, a clear sign of his unease. 'When Merlin found her – bleeding and barely alive – he confronted the Wizard. They had a fight, and Merlin was killed. Remember, the Bone Scraper was still in prison at the time. Crushed by feelings of guilt and shame, Cassandra had kept this to herself during all that time. Somehow, she felt responsible for Merlin's death. Also, she was afraid of the Wizard. However, there was another, more compelling reason she didn't talk about it.'

'How did you find all this out?' interrupted the countess.

'The Bone Scraper told me. I had several meetings with him, and the reason he told me, was you.'

'Me? How come?' asked the countess, surprised.

'Because of Tristan. He's now in your care.'

'I don't understand.'

'You will in a moment,' said Jack quietly. 'When Cassandra gave birth after Merlin died, everyone naturally assumed that he was the father ...'

'Oh, no!' interrupted the countess, covering her mouth with her hand.

'As it turned out, destiny had something quite different in mind ...'

Jack paused again, giving his words time to sink in. 'Tristan has a different father ...' he said quietly.

'The Wizard?' whispered the countess, barely able to speak.

'Yes.'

'Oh my God!' exclaimed Rebecca. 'Are you sure?'

'Absolutely. And I can tell you why. Cassandra only confronted the Wizard with all this after Tristan had been run over by the bikie and fell into a coma. At first, the Wizard didn't believe her and insisted on a DNA test. The test was positive. He had almost killed his own son! That's the reason he took Cassandra in, and looked after the boy's treatment. That too, had worried me right from the beginning – remember?'

Rebecca nodded. Suddenly it all made sense.

'Now we know why Cassandra joined the Wizards, and why the Wizard admitted her – the only female – into his inner circle. I'm sure it had all to do with ego and power, nothing else. The man was incapable of feeling remorse or regret. He was blinded by arrogance and thought he was winning; the jilted lover had prevailed. However, what he didn't realise was that by bringing Cassandra back into his life, he had sealed his fate. She was out to destroy him, and that's exactly what she did. Retribution by stealth. Now we also know why, and how.'

'This has more twists and turns than a Greek tragedy,' said Popov shaking his head.

'You have an important decision to make, Katerina,' said Jack, turning to the countess. 'The Bone Scraper is leaving it up to you to decide whether or not Tristan should be told about this. That's why the book isn't complete...'

At first, Jack thought that the countess was staring at him, but he soon realised that she was staring at something *behind* him. Popov and Rebecca were looking in the same direction. Sensing a presence, Jack turned around.

Tristan stood motionless by the piano in the other room, barefoot, and dressed only in pyjamas. He was watching them through the open door. Because it was dark in the music room, it was impossible to see his face. The question on everyone's mind was obvious: how long had he been standing there, listening? Then slowly, Tristan came towards them out of the shadows.

'Don't worry, Mama, I have known for some time,' he said, speaking softly.

He called me mama, thought the countess, unable to hold back the tears.

'How did you know?' asked Jack.

'Mum told me. She spoke to me every time she visited me at the home. She used to pour her heart out, not realising that I could hear her. I heard every word, but couldn't reply. I was in a coma. It was torture and bliss, exquisitely wrapped in love. Please put it all into the book. A coat with large holes in it isn't a coat you can wear.'

Astonishing, thought Jack. *He speaks like an erudite adult, not like a 13 year old boy.*

The countess got out of her chair and rushed over to Tristan. She put her arms around him and kissed him on the forehead. 'Hush, now. That's enough,' she said, hugging him tightly. 'Love heals all.'

'I know it does, Mama.'

Jack realised it was time to diffuse the tension in the room. The right moment had arrived.

'I've made an important decision about the book that concerns us all,' he said.

'What decision?' demanded Rebecca frowning.

Popov was the only person in the room who had an inkling of what was about to happen. Leaning forward, he watched Jack intently.

'I thought very long and hard about how to tell you this. I think the best way to explain my decision, is to tell you a little about myself first. Writing a book is a lonely business. It gives you plenty of time to think and to reflect. I wrote most of it alone, in Will's house, surrounded by all the memories that place holds for me. As you know, he was my closest friend, and his family was my family.

'It would be an understatement to say that Anna's story is as extraordinary as it is unique. It is unique because it isn't fiction. It's based on real events and deals with the lives of real people. This alone would guarantee the success of the book. When we add to this the unprecedented publicity and media interest surrounding Anna's return, the sky's the limit. But at what price?' Jack paused, and then looked first at Tristan, and then at the countess and Popov.

'Often, life throws you in at the deep end and it's up to you, and you alone, to reach the safety of the shore. Some succeed, others don't. I believe, I've just made it to the shore. It wasn't easy; I almost drowned.

'This book belongs to you; to us. To Anna and her baby, to you, Tristan, to you Katerina, and you, Nicolai. It also belongs to you, Rebecca, to Will, Cassandra, to Andrew and to me. It is our story. It is part of our lives.

'It will not be published. It will not be handed to a sensation hungry world to be picked over until only the bare bones are left for all to see. I couldn't live with that.'

'But Jack, think! You can't just ...' Rebecca interrupted. Jack held up his hand, and Rebecca fell silent.

'It is a piece of history that is ours,' continued Jack. I may have lost a friend, but I believe I've found a family. I'm not going to risk losing it. I only hope that all of this makes some sense to you.'

Reaching into his briefcase, Jack pulled out the photo of Anna the countess had given him from the chapel. 'I'm returning this to you, Katerina, because I don't need it anymore,' he said as he placed the photo on top of the manuscript.

For a while no one spoke, the silence in the room deafening. Then the countess stood up and slowly walked over to Jack. Without saying a word, she put her arms around him and kissed him on both cheeks.

'Thank you, Jack,' she said. 'When I gave you Anna's photo from our chapel here, I entrusted you with a dream. You brought her back, and made that dream come true. You've earned your place in this family.'

Jack looked across to Rebecca. 'Is this the end of my career?' he asked.

Having had a little time to think, Rebecca managed a hint of a smile. 'No, Jack,' she said, 'it's just the beginning.'

'What are you going to tell my publishers?'

'Life is what happens, while they fret about sales, of course. What else? I'm proud of you, Jack.'

Then Popov, too, walked over to Jack, and without saying anything, shook his hand. It was a gesture of deep-felt gratitude from a lonely man who blamed himself for having lost faith.

The countess let go of Jack and looked anxiously at Tristan.

'I knew this would happen, Mama,' said Tristan calmly. 'If you open my diary, you'll see that I've written it down ...'

'Come, I'll take you back to bed. School tomorrow ...' said the countess, ignoring the extraordinary remark.

'Please, Mama, not yet. Anna's coming.' Before the countess could question him about this, Anna walked into the room with a painting under her arm.

'I got the browns right – look,' she said excitedly, holding up the painting. 'It's finished.' She walked over to Jack and put the painting on the table in front of him. 'This is for you.'

'It's brilliant,' said Jack, admiring the painting. He noticed that it was signed Lucrezia. 'Thank you, Anna. Now it's my turn. I have something that belongs to you.' Jack reached into his jacket and pulled the bracelet that had started it all, out of his pocket. 'Recognise this?' Jack held up the bracelet. 'May I put it on?' Anna presented her right wrist, tears welling up in her blue eyes.

The countess held her breath, her heart skipping a beat. *Oh, Zolli, if only you could see this*, she thought.

Amazing, thought Rebecca, watching the countess, *it's about to finish where it all began.*

Biting his lip, Popov looked away.

'Örökke,' said Jack, clicking the little lock into place. 'There, it's done. Some things are forever.'

For a while, Anna just stared at the bracelet on her wrist. 'Forever?' she whispered. 'Oh, yes. Lucrezia will be forever in your debt.' Then, without saying another word, she turned around and walked out of the room.

'Amazing girl,' said Jack walking up the stairs with Rebecca. The countess had taken Tristan back to his room, and Popov had excused himself. Everyone needed some space. 'The painting's surprisingly good; Anna's very talented.'

Rebecca nodded.

'She lives in her own world as artists often do.'

'And isn't Tristan something else?' she said.

'Yes, but there's something chilling about that boy. He can hear the whisper of angels, yet he's been sired by a monster.'

'The Wizard lives on, you think?' said Rebecca. 'Let's hope not, for Tristan's sake.'

'The gift and the curse?'

'Something like that. It could overwhelm him.'

'I don't think it will. He has a powerful weapon.'

'What?'

'Love.'

'I don't know about you, but my head's spinning,' said Jack, suddenly looking very tired. 'There's so much to think about ...'

'Not tonight, Jack, please.' Rebecca stopped on the landing and put a finger on his lips. 'Katerina has given us the same suite as last time: three bedrooms,' she said, opening the door. 'We have a choice.'

'Why don't we take the one with the fireplace?' said Jack.

'If you've brought those dreadful pyjamas with you, you're sleeping in your own room, buster – alone.'

'I haven't brought any.'

'Good. You're safe then.'

'I'm sorry, Becky ...' said Jack, putting his arms around her waist, 'for not telling you earlier ... I just ...'

'Hush ...' interrupted Rebecca. 'There's no need to apologise. You're not afraid of doing the right thing, Jack, regardless of the consequences. You've shown us that tonight. And you know what's right because of who you are. Never change that.'

'I'm an open book, you reckon?'

'To me, yes.'

'That's a bit of a worry.'

'Your secrets are safe with me. Shall I tell you what I really love about you?'

'What?'

'You're special, but you don't seem to know it. Look at you! You're blushing,' said Rebecca, kissing Jack on the cheek. 'Let's go inside.'

Rebecca stood in front of the dressing table and looked over Jack's shoulder. 'What's that?' she asked, taking off her ear rings.

'My Bucket List. I'm just checking the next item.'

'Oh? What does it say?'

'Living in New York with someone exciting.'

'You're moving to New York?'

'Only if I find someone exciting.'

'Still looking then, are you?'

Jack nodded, trying to appear serious.

'Any contenders?'

'Only one; so far.'

'What's the problem?'

'The excitement needs a little more work, before I can make such an important decision,' he said.

'How come?'

'Long-distance-excitement isn't much fun ...'

'Are you doing something about it?'

'I've tried, but it's difficult over the phone ...'

'I see.' Rebecca turned around and kissed Jack passionately on the mouth. 'How's this for a start?' she said.

'Wow! I thought a kiss like that was strictly the province of the writer's imagination.'

'Now, where have I heard this before, I wonder?' said Rebecca, giving Jack a gentle push. Losing his balance, he fell backwards against the edge of the huge bed and landed on the bedspread. Kicking off her shoes, Rebecca climbed on top of him and sat astride his chest. 'When are you going to decide?' she said, unbuttoning his shirt.

'Tomorrow morning.'

'Will it take that long, do you think?'

'That depends ...'

'On what?'

'The excitement, of course.'

'I hope you're up to this.'

'Try me.'

'I will, you can bet on it. I'll show you excitement you never thought possible.'

'Is that a threat or a promise?'

'Both.'

'I like living dangerously.'

'Tell me about it.'

More Books by the Author

THE EMPRESS HOLDS THE KEY

A disturbing, edge-of-your-seat
historical mystery thriller

Jack Rogan Mysteries Book 1

A journey through time, mystery and intrigue.
For Jack Rogan, an old photograph found in the ruins of a fire becomes the key to a forgotten history—and a deadly secret. In *The Empress Holds the Key*, the quest to uncover the truth sends Jack across the globe, from wartime Austria to the ancient temples of Egypt, unearthing buried secrets that powerful forces want to keep hidden.

Guided by the haunting phrase, "The Empress holds the key," Jack's search takes him deep into the hidden archives of the past. Along the way, he encounters ancient artifacts, cryptic codes, and the legendary Knights Templar—all pieces of a puzzle connecting people across time and fate. As the mystery unfolds, Jack must navigate a treacherous path where history, power, and myth collide.

Join Jack Rogan in this captivating thriller that weaves history and suspense into an unforgettable tale. Uncover the mystery today.

The Empress Holds the Key
is now available in ebook and paperback

THE HIDDEN GENES
OF PROFESSOR K

A dark, disturbing and nail-biting
medical thriller

Jack Rogan Mysteries Book 3

A medical breakthrough. A greedy pharmaceutical magnate. A brutal double-murder. One tangled web of lies.
World-renowned scientist Professor K is close to a groundbreaking discovery. He's also dying. With his last breath, he anoints Dr Alexandra Delacroix as his successor and pleads with her to carry on his work.

But powerful forces will stop at nothing to possess the research, unwittingly plunging Delacroix into a treacherous world of unbridled ambition and greed.

Desperate and alone, she turns to celebrated author and journalist Jack Rogan.

Rogan must help Delacroix, while also assisting famous rock star Isis in the seemingly unrelated investigation into the brutal murder of her parents.

With the support of Isis's resourceful PA, Lola; a former police officer; a tireless campaigner for the destitute and forgotten; and a gifted boy with psychic powers, Rogan exposes a complex web of fiercely guarded secrets and heinous crimes of the past that can ruin them all and change history.

Will the dreams of a visionary scientist with the power to change the future of medicine fall into the wrong hands, or will his genius benefit mankind and prevent untold misery and suffering for generations to come?

"Outstanding Thriller" of 2017
Independent Author Network Book of the Year Awards

The Hidden Genes of Professor K
is now available in ebook and paperback

PROFESSOR K:
THE FINAL QUEST

An action-packed historical medical mystery

Jack Rogan Mysteries Book 4

A desperate plea from the Vatican. A kidnapped chef. An ambitious mob boss. One perilous game.

When Professor Alexandra Delacroix is called in to find a cure for the dying pope, she follows clues left by her mentor and friend, the late Professor K, which lead her on a breathtaking search through historical secrets, some of them deadly.

Her old friend Jack Rogan must step in to assist while also searching for kidnapped Top Chef Europe winner Lorenza da Baggio.

He joins forces with his young friend and gifted psychic, Tristan; a dedicated Mafia-hunting prosecutor; a fearless young police officer; and an enigmatic Egyptian detective who is on a perilous hunt for a notorious IS terrorist.

Together, they stand off with the head of a powerful Mafia family in Florence and uncover a network of corruption and heinous crimes reaching to the very top.

Will Rogan and his friends succeed in finding Lorenza and curing the pope, or will the dark forces swirling around them prevail in their sinister plots?

Gold Medal Winner in the Fiction – Thriller – Medical Category
Readers' Favorite 2019 International Book Awards Contest

Professor K: The Final Quest
is now available ebook and paperback

THE CURIOUS CASE OF THE MISSING HEAD

A gripping medical thriller

Jack Rogan Mysteries Book 5

A headless body on a boat. An international conspiracy. Can a kidnapped genius survive a controversial scientific discovery?

Esteemed Australian journalist Jack Rogan is on a mission to solve the disappearance of his mother in the 70s. But when a friend needs help rescuing a kidnapped world-renowned astrophysicist, he doesn't hesitate. Struggling with more questions than answers, his investigation leads them aboard a hellish hospital ship, where instead of finding the kidnap victim, he's confronted with a decapitated corpse.

As the search intensifies, Jack bumps up against diabolical cartels with hidden agendas. And when his research reveals dubious experiments, a criminal on death row, and a shocking revelation about his mother's fate, he must uncover how it's all linked.

Can Jack unravel the twisted connections and catch the scientist's killer, or will the next obituary published be his own?

Gold Medal Winner in the Fiction – Thriller – Conspiracy Category
Readers' Favorite 2020 International Book Awards Contest

"Outstanding Thriller/Suspense" - Category Winner of 2020
Independent Author Network Book of the Year Awards

The Curious Case of the Missing Head
is now available ebook and paperback

The Lost Symphony

A historical mystery thriller

Jack Rogan Mysteries Book 6

A murdered tsarina. A lost musical masterpiece. A stolen Russian icon. Can Jack honour a promise made a long time ago, and solve an age-old mystery?

When acclaimed Australian journalist and author Jack Rogan inherits an old music box with a curious letter hidden inside, he decides to investigate. As he delves deeper into a murky past of secrets and violence, he soon discovers he's not the only one interested in solving the puzzle.

Frieda Malenkova, a ruthless art dealer; and Victor Sokolov, a Russian billionaire with a dark past, will stop at nothing to achieve their dark desires and foil Jack's valiant struggle to uncover the truth.

Joining forces with Mademoiselle Darrieux, a flamboyant Paris socialite; and Claude Dupree, a retired French police officer, Jack enters a dangerous world of unbridled ambition, murder and greed that threatens to destroy him.

On a perilous journey that takes him deep into Russia, Jack follows a tortuous path of discovery, disappointment and betrayal that brings him face to face with his destiny.

Will Jack unravel the hidden clues left behind by a desperate empress? Can he save the precious legacy of a genius before it's too late, and return a holy icon revered by generations to where it belongs?

Gold Medal Winner in the Fiction – Mystery – Historical Category
Readers' Favorite 2021 International Book Awards Contest

Award-Winning Finalist in the Fiction: Thriller/Adventure Category
The 2021 International Book Awards

"Outstanding Mystery" of 2021 - Category Winner
Independent Author Network Book of the Year Awards

The Lost Symphony
is now available in ebook and paperback

THE DEATH MASK MURDERS

A historical mystery crime thriller

Jack Rogan Mysteries Book 7

Seven brutal murders. A cursed Inca burial mask. A lost treasure. One deadly game.
When convicted killer Maurice Landru reaches out from a Paris prison and asks for help to prove his innocence, celebrated author Jack Rogan cannot resist. Drawn into a web of hidden clues pointing to an ancient mystery, Jack decides to investigate.

Joining forces with Francesca Bartolli, a glamorous criminal profiler; Mademoiselle Darrieux, an eccentric Paris socialite; and Claude Dupree, a retired French police officer, Jack enters a dangerous world of depraved cyber-gambling, where the stakes are high and the players will stop at nothing to satisfy their dark desires.

Following his 'breadcrumbs of destiny', Jack soon comes up against an evil genius who terminates his enemies without mercy and is prepared to risk all to win.

On a perilous journey littered with violence and death, Jack uncovers dark secrets of a murky past of ruthless conquistadors, bloodthirsty pirates and shipwrecked priests, all pointing to a fabulous treasure, waiting to be discovered.

Can Jack expose the mastermind behind the horrific murders and retrieve the legendary treasure before it falls into the wrong hands, or will the forces of darkness overwhelm him and destroy everything he believes in?

Gold Medal Winner in the Fiction - Mystery - Historical Category
Readers' Favorite 2022 International Book Awards Contest

"Outstanding Mystery" of 2022 - Mystery Category Winner
Independent Author Network Book of the Year Awards

The Death Mask Murders
is now available in ebook and paperback

THE STOLEN ALTARPIECE

A historical mystery crime thriller

Jack Rogan Mysteries Book 8

A long-forgotten amulet. A stolen painting. A dark threat reignited. One deadly geopolitical power-play.

Jack Rogan's discovery of a hidden letter reaching out of the past unwittingly embarks the journalist into a perilous quest to find a holy relic that has the power to fight evil.

As he follows a web of intriguing clues that take him on a dangerous journey to the Middle East, Rogan soon crosses swords with an old adversary, who is determined to destroy him and those he holds dear.

Soon, secrets buried in a famous stolen painting point to Russia and the threat of war in Ukraine. Joining forces with Tristan, a gifted psychic; Abbot Serapion, a Russian monk; and Sasha, the daughter of a Russian billionaire, Jack enters a dangerous geopolitical arena ruled by a deranged, corrupt man consumed by unbridled ambition and lust for power, who threatens to enslave a nation and destroy an entire country to satisfy his misguided vision of greatness.

Can Jack find a way to defeat the dark forces of evil and turn the tide of history before it's too late, or will the horrors of war continue, and consume a people who dared to stand against tyranny and dream of freedom?

Gold Medal Winner in the Fiction - Thriller - Political Category
Readers' Favorite 2023 International Book Awards Contest

Gold Medal Winner in Amateur Sleuth - Thriller Category
The Global Book Awards 2023

"Outstanding Mystery" of 2023 Category Winner
Independent Author Network Book of the Year Awards

ABOUT THE AUTHOR

Gabriel Farago is the *USA TODAY* best-selling and multi-award-winning Australian author of the Jack Rogan Mysteries series for the thinking reader.

As a lawyer with a passion for history and archaeology, Gabriel Farago had to wait for many years before being able to pursue another passion – writing – in earnest. However, his love of books and storytelling started long before that.

'I remember as a young boy reading biographies and history books with a torch under the bed covers,' he recalls, 'and then writing stories about archaeologists and explorers the next day, instead of doing homework. While I regularly got into trouble for this, I believe we can only do well in our endeavours if we are passionate about the things we love. For me, writing has become a passion.'

Born in Budapest, Gabriel grew up in post-war Europe and, after fleeing Hungary with his parents during the Revolution in 1956, he went to school in Austria before arriving in Australia as a teenager. This allowed him to become multi-lingual and feel 'at home' in different countries and diverse cultures.

Shaped by a long legal career and experiences spanning several decades and continents, his is a mature voice that speaks in many tongues. Gabriel holds degrees in literature and law, speaks several languages and takes research and authenticity very seriously. Inquisitive by nature, he studied Egyptology and learned to read the hieroglyphs. He travels extensively and visits all of the locations mentioned in his books.

'I try to weave fact and fiction into a seamless storyline,' he explains. 'By blurring the boundaries between the two, the reader is never quite sure where one ends, and the other begins. This is of course quite deliberate as it creates the illusion of authenticity and reality in a work that is pure fiction. A successful work of fiction is a balancing act: reality must rub shoulders with imagination in a way that is both entertaining and plausible.'

Gabriel lives just outside Sydney, Australia, in the Blue Mountains, surrounded by a World Heritage National Park. 'The beauty and solitude of this unique environment,' he points out, 'gives me the inspiration and energy to weave my thoughts and ideas into stories that in turn, I sincerely hope, will entertain and inspire my readers.'

Gabriel Farago

Author's Note

I hope you enjoyed reading this book as much as I enjoyed writing it. I'd be very grateful if you'd post a short review on Amazon. Your support really does make a difference.

www.ingramcontent.com/pod-product-compliance
Lightning Source LLC
Chambersburg PA
CBHW030547020726
47494CB00005B/1515

Connect with the Author

Amazon
https://www.amazon.com/stores/
Gabriel-Farago/author/B00GUVY2UW

Website
https://gabrielfarago.com.au/

Goodreads
https://www.goodreads.com/author/show/7435911.Gabriel_Farago

Facebook
https://www.facebook.com/GabrielFaragoAuthor

BookBub
https://www.bookbub.com/profile/gabriel-farago